Long, Long Tales from the Russian North

◆ ◆ ◆

Long, Long Tales from the RUSSIAN NORTH

◈ ◈ ◈

Translated and edited by Jack V. Haney

University Press of Mississippi / Jackson

www.upress.state.ms.us

The University Press of Mississippi is a member
of the Association of American University Presses.

Manufactured in the United States of America

First printing 2013
∞
Library of Congress Cataloging-in-Publication Data

Long, long tales from the Russian North / translated and edited by Jack V. Haney.
pages ; cm
Includes bibliographical references.
ISBN 978-1-61703-730-6 (cloth : alkaline paper) —
ISBN 978-1-61703-731-3 (ebook) 1. Tales—Russia (Federation)—Karelia—Translations into Enlgish. I. Haney, Jack V., 1940–, translator, editor.
GR203.19.K33L66 2013
398.20947—dc23 2012031548

British Library Cataloging-in-Publication Data available

For Paul Foote
1926–2011

Contents

Preface

This volume contains seventeen folk tales from the Russian North that have never before appeared in English. Unlike tales in my *The Complete Russian Folktale,* these tales were selected because they are outstanding examples of a genre—what I have elsewhere termed serial tales[1]—largely neglected in the scholarship of the Russian folktale. The tales were published in Russian in the USSR, mainly incidentally in collections of folk tales that include material collected from a particular geographic area.

The tales represent a sample of the repertoires of but five narrators of these serial stories. Two of these raconteurs were from the Pomor region of Russian Karelia: M. M. Korguev and P. Ia. Nikonov. Three were from the Pudozh region, also in Karelia: M. O. Dmitriev from the village of Avdeevo, his father, O. I. Dmitriev, from Ragnozero, and F. F. Kabrenov from the town of Pudozh.

Korguev, the undoubted master of the genre, narrated more than half of the tales. Some of his other tales appeared in my previous collections. Only a single tale by Kabrenov has previously been published in English.[2] To my knowledge, the other masters of the serial tale are represented here in English for the first time.

Work on this volume of tales (known to the narrators themselves as *dolgie skazki* or lengthy tales) has taken place over the last several years. I have been encouraged in this undertaking by colleagues, friends, and family, and I hope that with this volume the English-reading public will gain a more complete understanding of the rich narrative tradition of the Russian people. I wish to take this opportunity to thank the editor and staff of the University Press of Mississippi for their courteous and professional support throughout the long process leading to publication. I am dedicating the volume to I. P. Foote, late fellow of the Queen's College, Oxford, my tutor and friend.

---

1. Haney, *An Anthology of Russian Folktales*, p.274.
2. *Ibid.* pp. 274–84.

Technical Note

The seventeen tales presented in this volume are arranged according to the geographic locales where their narrators lived: Korguev and Nikonov were from the Pomor'e region of Russian Karelia, the Dmitrievs and Kabrenov from the Pudozh region. A brief notation at the end of each translation gives the Aarne-Thompson (A-T) number, which is the same as the Russian SUS number. The tales in this volume for the most part consist of several tale types woven together by the narrators. This points out the basic problem with the original A-T indexing system: How should the tales be catalogued? I have simply given the SUS number for each type in the order in which they appear in the tale. The commentaries to the tales, an appendix to this volume, list the source of each tale by author and its initial printed version.

The bibliography is limited to sources for the tales, standard reference works on the folktale, and relevant works from preceding publications by the editor/translator of this volume.

The transliteration system used here is the Library of Congress system, with some simplifications to enhance readability. Proper names in the texts reflect their originals: Ondrei and not Andrei, Koshchai and not Koshchei, Olena and not Elena, etc.

Each of the narrators possessed his own speech idiosyncrasies. It would be impossible to duplicate the pronunciation and grammar of the tales. Not even all the Russian editors have tried to do as much. With regard to particular words, however, I have generally tried to translate into English the characteristic vocabulary of the tellers of these tales. M. M. Korguev, for instance, peppers his tales with the Russian word "konechno" ("of course"), and I have reflected this use in my translations.

Russian has evolved an elaborate system of naming persons, using both patronymics and diminutives. In the texts included in this book it is customary for the narrator to refer to persons by their first names (Ivan, Maria); by their first name and father's first name (patronymic) (Ivan Ivanovich, Maria Ivanovna); by the first name and a father's—exclusively royal—title (Ivan Tsarevich, Maria Tsarevna). Occasionally one encounters a person named only by patronymic: Sergeich (son of Sergei), for example. This latter practice is regarded as extremely colloquial. In a few instances the patronymic may also be used to indicate the unusual or unnatural father of a future hero: Ivan Medvedevich is literally Ivan the son of a bear or Ivan Bearson, while Ivan Sosnovich is Ivan the son of a pine tree. Sometimes animals have patronymics too: Raven Ravenson, even Talon Talonson.

Diminutives are more complicated. They express emotional or kinship relationships between persons, or in these stories between characters. Ivan, the usual Christian name for the hero, may be Vania, Vaniusha, Vanechka, and so on, although formally he is Ivan plus his patronymic, less formally just Ivan. The same is true for females. Maria is Masha or Mashenka, Marusia, Mania, etc. Adults in the tales are not referred to by diminutives; such a practice would definitely not be wondertale etiquette! Note, however, that children refer to their parents as "papa" or "mama."

Glossary

Anker, ankerok	Liquid measurement equal to two–three buckets
Arshin	.711 meters
Ataman	Headman
Baba Yaga	Russian witch
Bast	Cambium layer of the lime or linden tree.
Batiushko	Father, used of priest, tsar, natural father; also Batiushka
Bliny	Russian pancakes
Bogatyr	Warrior, especially in the byliny
Bylina	Epic song
Chernomor	Wizard, his name means "Black Death"
Foo, Foo!	An expression of disgust
Green wine	Vodka
Gusli	Stringed, plucked instrument resembling a small harp
Hegumeness	Head of an Orthodox nunnery
Kaftan	Long gown traditionally worn by merchants
Kalin Bridge	Folkloric bridge, often associated with serpents
Koshchei	Skeletal ogre, sometimes a wizard
Lapti	Boots made from bast
Lubok	Chap book, often made from bast
Matushka	Priest's wife, tsar's wife, "little mother"
Mukhomor	Wizard, his name means "Poison Mushroom" (Fly-agaric)
Patronymic	Second name, based on father's first name
Pood	About forty pounds
Rus'	Ancient and folkloric name for Russia
Sazhen	Length equivalent to 2.13 meters
Tsarevna,	TsarevichDaughter, son of a tsar
Verst	(Versta) 3500 feet

Introduction

The folktales in this volume grew out of my *The Complete Russian Folktale*, published 1999–2006. In that series and in the subsequent *Anthology of Russian Folktales*, I included some tales that seemed typical Russian folktales except for one thing: They were inordinately long. Further research uncovered a considerable number of these long tales, which are of sufficient quality and interest to warrant publication in a separate volume.

The seventeen tales included in this volume are representative of the narrative art of five men, all of them from Karelia in the extreme northwest of European Russia. Three of them (including a father and son combination) are from Pudozh, affording the reader an opportunity to compare tales across generations. The other two are Pomors, as the inhabitants of the White Sea Coast in Karelia are termed. The Pomor M. M. Korguev, who was undoubtedly the master of the long tale, told the majority of the tales included in this volume.

The narrators often referred to these tales as "dolgie skazki," simply "lengthy tales." The word "dolgii" is usually employed in Russian with reference to time and not distance, but none of the tellers is recorded as having referred to his tales as "dlinnyi," the usual term for length. For reasons that will become immediately apparent, I have chosen to refer to these tales as "serial tales," as they were apparently most often told that way—serially, in parts. But I must remind the reader that this collection of serial folktales merely presents some of the better examples of the form. The volume is by no means exhaustive, and many such tales may well remain in written sources—in particular in the archives of Karelian folklore maintained in Petrozavodsk—to which I did not have access. Yet all seventeen of those included are authentic and traditional folktales. They were thus told and not composed in written form, although it is possible that the narrators may have been influenced directly or indirectly by written sources. I may add that this is the first time any of these tales has appeared in English.

Furthermore, the tales included in this volume fall under the rubric "wondertales." These works are popularly referred to as fairy tales in English, although fairies are not an element in the Russian tradition. The English word is derived from *faerie*, which meant "enchanted." The Russian tales in this volume contain no fairies in any case, and enchantment is not always an important element.

What, then, are "serial tales"? As I have stated, the narrators themselves referred often to "long" or "lengthy" tales—and that is certainly what these stories are, especially when compared to the ordinary Russian folktale. Thus, I use the term "serial" to refer to the manner in which the tales were told, rather than specifically to their length. M. M. Korguev, the accomplished narrator of the long tale, described how he told his tales. According to him, such a tale might be told over several nights while he was at sea with a fishing crew. And indeed, one can occasionally sense possible breaks in the narration, although these tales were probably told to the ethnographer A. N. Nechaev without a break. Korguev would tell tales to weary fishermen in the evenings after supper. After a period of time he would ask the crew, "Are you asleep?" If someone answered, he would continue his tale, but if he received no answer, he assumed that all slept and he would continue the tale another night. His tales were thus told serially.

Stepanida Ivanovna Golovina, when asked about her own, shorter tales, stated: "What do you mean, women [to the transcribers of her tales]? What will you do with these tales? A tale is good only when it is really long. And are there many such tales? Bah!"[1] K. V. Chistov, who actually knew some of the Pomor tellers of tales, seems to have been of the opinion that the long tales were characteristic of the White Sea tradition.[2]

This practice of telling tales over several periods of time seems to have been the custom with other narrators. The naturalist writer Mikhail Prishvin happened to meet a certain Manuilo Petrov, who was a hunter and trapper and not a fisherman. "In the long winter evenings, Manuilo would keep on telling [his tale] until he was convinced that every single man was asleep. To ascertain this he would from time to time shout out: 'Are you asleep, Christians?' And if even one responded, he would fix the reed light and continue his tale."[3] Prishvin went on to add that this Petrov was a fervent believer in the occult.

V. Dmitrichenko, who collected four tales from O. I. Dmitriev in 1939, reported, "Dmitriev's tales are long, most often fantastic, and the heroes have the most extraordinary names. Perhaps some of them were taken from the lubok tradition. He loved to tell tales, making asides to interest

1. Razumova, A. P. and T. I. Sen'kina, *Russkie narodnye skazki Karel'skogo pomor'ia*, p. 12.

2. Chistov, K. V., *Russkie skaziteli Karelii*, p. 192.

3. Prishvin, M., *V kraiu nepuganykh ptits*, p 73.

the listeners. He knew the introductions and endings, in which it was often stated that those who didn't pay attention ought to be punished."[4]

All the tales in this collection—and therefore the narrators of these tales—belong to a type referred to by Russian scholars as "epic" and which I have termed serial. These tales feature well thought-out introductions and endings of the traditional sort, many folktale formulae, triplication of actions—sometimes even speech. They were apparently told in the traditional manner: solemnly, without gesture but with varied intonation. One feature stands out: As far as can be ascertained, all five of the narrators whose tales make up this volume began learning folktales from a relative, usually but not always a male relative.

The best of these tellers of tales, M. M. Korguev, was somewhat atypical. He first heard folktales in the Karelian language spoken by his mother and then heard them from his aunt, but the serial tales for which Korguev is justly famous seem to have been learned from his fellow villagers in Keret' in eastern Karelia, where he was born. Later on he heard and adapted tales he heard in his various occupations—fishing and hunting mostly, although he also herded reindeer, strung telegraph lines, and worked on the Murmansk railroad. According to Sen'kina, Korguev would listen to a story two or three times, even when it was read to him, and then retell it in his own fashion.[5]

M. O. Dmitriev emphasized the physical setting in which he told his tales: winter evenings or nights—and never during the lengthy Orthodox fasts—in a secluded place, with no women or children present, beneath a fir tree or in a forest hut. For Russian scholars these features all point to ritual, although in the case of Dmitriev ritual seems to have played no role at all.[6] Another storyteller summed up the situation very well: "We would sit for awhile and then take up the songs of old and folktales so that a winter's night would pass more quickly."[7] Oddly enough, I have not been able to find any of these exceptionally long tales in the old collections of tales from the North. There are none in the collections of Onchukov or Karnaukhova, and the single example in Azadovskii's Karelian tales is suspect on a number of grounds. This may be due to the exigencies of tale

4. Sen'kina, T. I., *Russkaia skazka Karelii*, p. 32.

5. *Ibid.*, 56

6. Razumova, A. P. and T. I. Sen'kina, *Russkie narodnye skazki Pudozhskogo kraia*, p. 24, and Karelia, p. 44.

7. Pudozh, p. 12.

collecting in this remote area, where narrators may have been loathe to spend the time telling long tales to outsiders—which is how they viewed the ethnographers so keen to record their every story.

Apparently, this type of tale, the serial tale, developed spontaneously and only in the restricted area of the former Arkhangel'sk guberniia in what is now Karelia. Nechaev long ago argued that this region, because of the peculiarities of its population, was different from other Russian regions where folktales were widely collected. In his introduction to the works of M. M. Korguev, published in 1939, he suggests that the Pomory (as the residents of the western White Sea coast were called) enjoyed a higher level of cultural development compared to residents of many other regions of Russia.[8] This difference was due to the role the many monasteries in the region played in introducing literacy and Muscovite culture to the vast region. Equally important, it was through the small but crucial ports and their trade with western nations (England and Holland especially) that residents of the area became acquainted with Western Europeans and were subjected to cultural influences scarcely felt in Muscovy itself. Nechaev also suggests that the serfdom that retarded the development of so much of Russia until the second half of the nineteenth century was of a different, less oppressive, sort in the White Sea coastal area than in the central regions. Finally, he points to the presence of two social groups who brought new ideas to the area: exiled revolutionaries on the one hand, and on the other the skomorokhi, representatives of the pre-Christian religion, which survived in a much-altered form. All of these factors may indeed have played a role in the development of folk narratives, and to them one may add the relative stability of the population. Until the advent of industrialization—most prominently in the early twentieth century—the population lacked geographic mobility, and this stable way of life certainly aided the preservation of traditional aspects of everyday life. The extent to which non-Slavic but neighboring cultures may have played a role has never been investigated, although in the case of Korguev this influence is perhaps likely.

Who were these five raconteurs? Unfortunately, we have at best scant biographical information. The most outstanding and the most prolific of them was Matvei Mikhailovich Korguev, born in 1883 in Keret', Karelia

8. *Skazki M. M. Korgueva*, ed. and intro. A. N. Nechaev, p. xxxiv. See also, Robert O. Crummey, *The Old Believers and the World of Anti-Christ: The Vyg Community and the Russian State, 1694–1758*. Madison, 1970.

(formerly the Arkhangel'sk guberniia). His was an extremely poor family, and when his mother died in 1890, the boy was forced to go out begging for alms. At the age of nine he began laboring as a herder, at thirteen he became a cook's apprentice on a merchant ship, and finally he was a paid storyteller on board fishing and hunting vessels in the White Sea. He apparently knew some byliny (the Russian epic songs), and even some Karelian runes, (here, Karelo-Finnish oral verses), which he learned from his mother. He had twelve children, not all of whom survived infancy. In 1938 he became a member of the Union of Writers (!), and in 1939 he was awarded the Medal of Honor (Znak pocheta).[9] He died in 1943, having performed in Archangel, Moscow, St. Petersburg (Leningrad), and Petrozavodsk, but A. N. Nechaev, who recorded Korguev's tales, stated that Korguev lacked the presence and voice to command a large audience and was at his best telling his tales to small groups of fewer than a dozen persons.[10] As will become apparent, Korguev's tales relate motifs not usually encountered in the Russian wondertales: infanticide, fratricide, regicide, matricide, and—very obviously and frequently—the usually taboo subject of sexual relations between unmarried characters.

P. Ia. Nikonov was a Pomor from the village of Sukhonavolokskoe. Investigators recorded only four tales told by Nikonov, the son of a bankrupt ship owner. His tale "The Enchanted Tsardom," included in this volume, was taken down by I. M. Kolesnitskaia and M. Shneerson in 1938, when Nikonov was fifty-one years of age. Collectors of Nikonov's tales report that he claimed to have heard most of his tales from his father, a well-known and outstanding teller of tales. One of the villagers said, "Iakov Nikonov [P. Ia. Nikonov's father, JVH] loved to tell the long tales and would go on with one for several nights; and you didn't want to go to sleep."[11] Nikonov was a perfectionist and related his tales carefully, with great attention paid to content and expression. "The Enchanted Tsardom" is an excellent example of his art. Combining four traditional story lines (themes or sujets),[12] Nikonov nonetheless manages to introduce new elements into this familiar story. Those who observed Nikonov when he was telling a tale noted that he was extremely attentive to detail and to his use

---

9. Kiuru, E. S. and A. P. Razumova, *Fol'kloristika Karelii*, p. 132.

10. Nechaev, liii

11. Pomor'ie, p. 388.

12. *Ibid.*, p.13. For Russian folklorists the sujet is a movement, a complete theme within a tale.

of language, thinking through expressions and unhesitatingly substituting another word or expression for something he found unsatisfactory.

Fedor Kabrenov was born in 1895 in the village of Lariushino, Pudozh region. His parents were both farm laborers, and his father had several siblings. He went as far as the third grade of the village school, but when his father died, his brothers forbade him to continue. He went to work as a carpenter and lumberjack, but he was also a hunter, and it was apparently in forest camps that he first heard folktales.[13] Most of the tales he told are wondertales, often enough combined with subjects borrowed from the tales of everyday life. Commentators have noted that his popular renditions of tales were known for their strict adherence to traditional norms. Kabrenov was apparently literate and loved to read, as his occasional use of words from the literary language shows, although his source for these words was mostly the bast (lubok) books.

Also from Pudozh was Osip Ivanovich Dmitriev, from the village of Ragnozero. He was born in 1859, and is thus the earliest of the storytellers featured in this volume. He participated in the Civil War (1917–22) on the Red side. Although he apparently never learned a trade and remained unskilled—as well as illiterate—to the end of his life, he had been in his youth a hunter, fisherman, and trapper in the great forests of Karelia. Dmitriev apparently learned his tales from family members or perhaps from his compatriots, but we have no direct evidence of these tales' origins. He was, however, known for telling long, serial tales at night. According to his son, "No matter in which village he spent the night, a full hut of people would be found specifically to listen to tales. . . . He had such a memory that if someone told a tale and you asked him a year later, he would retell it word for word."[14] One bylina was recorded from Dmitriev, but he apparently knew no others. He is said to have known about sixty tales, but few recordings have survived. Dmitriev died in 1939.

Dmitriev's son, Mikhail Osipovich, was also born in Ragnozero. Born in 1905, he was living in Avdeevo, Karelia, in 1975 when his tales were recorded. He was then seventy years of age but still working as a fisherman. He stated that he had learned his tales from his father, but that for thirty years (that is, since circa 1945), he had not told tales and thus his repertoire was much diminished.[15] His serial tales are neither as long nor

---

13. Pudozh, p. 334.
14. Kurets, T. S., *Nositeli fol'klornykh traditsii: Pudozhskii raion Karelii*, p. 59.
15. Pudozh, p. 287.

as complicated as might be expected; this is perhaps due to the fact that over the years he had lost his original ease with telling tales.[16]

A. P. Razumova and T. I. Sen'kina devote considerable space to M. O. Dmitriev in their introduction to the Pudozh tales, noting his predilection for telling the tales in the evening.[17] This timeframe contributed to the magical function of telling tales, warding off evil spirits—although Dmitriev said he told the tales in the evening owing to his audience's need to work during the day. But the first characteristic of Dmitriev's tales that the scholars noted was the stories' great length. They state that some of his tales reached twenty-five typewritten sheets. Although they correctly say that this length does not distinguish Dmitriev's tales from other "serial" tales, and that the combinations of tale plots (sujets) do not represent anything particularly unusual, "for the increase in size of his tales, the performer prefers other folktale devices, for example the introduction into the narration of a large number of tale attributes, the strict observance of the laws of folktale poetics, the artistic use of traditional folktale formulas."[18] Razumova and Sen'kina offer no further comments on Dmitriev's tales.

◈ ◈ ◈

More than a century has passed since Antti Aarne published his *Verzeichnis der Märchen mit Hilfe von Fachgenossen* (Helsinki, 1910). This seminal work, greatly enlarged and edited by Stith Thompson in *The Types of the Folktale*, first published in Bloomington, Indiana, in 1961, established the basis for classification of folktales used throughout the world. Most scholars of the folktale have noted that the A-T (SUS) index is far from perfect. Many tales must be classified under more than one rubric, making the index cumbersome and difficult to use. In the absence of some better system, one is forced to rely on it. I have relied on the version applied to the East Slavic tales in this volume.

There are in fact two works devoted exclusively to the Russian (East Slavic) folktale. The most recent of these, the *Sravnitel'nyi ukazatel' siuzhetov. Vostochnoslavianskaia skazka* (A Comparative Index of Sujets. The East Slavic Folktale), abbreviated as SUS, was published in Leningrad

---

16. Haney, Jack V., *The Complete Russian Folktale*, vol. III, pp. xxxii–xxxvii.
17. Pudozh, pp. 23–25.
18. *Ibid.*, p. 23.

in 1979. It covers most of the tales included in this volume. All of these indexes—the A-T, SUS, and the most recent English A-T-U, as well as indexes compiled for other national folktale traditions— attempt to classify folktales on the basis of perceived similarities of structure and coincidences of motifs.[19] Thus tales numbered 1–299 are Animal Tales, 300–749 are wondertales, etc. For reasons that are far from clear, the narrators of the tales in this volume preferred—almost without exception—stories classified as wondertales (*volshebnye skazki*).

Little needs to be added about the structure of the wondertales. V. Ia. Propp established in his *Morfologiia skazki* that there is but one structure for the wondertale, and his theory is born out by the tales in this volume.[20] Subsequent scholars have emphasized the necessity for a transformation in the middle of the tale. More recent scholars attempt to use statistical methods to define certain qualities inherent to the worldwide folktale.[21] In part, the tales in this volume seem to bear out Gottschall's observation that reference to the leading female and male characters' attractiveness is essential—although in the Russian tales this reference is almost universally expressed as superhuman strength for the males rather than physical beauty, a quality usually reserved for female characters. This feature is emphasized by the fact that in these tales the hero's opponent, the villain, is always described as being physically repulsive.

There are no new character roles in these tales. One meets the hero, a female whom he will seek to marry, a villain whose task it is to try to obstruct the marriage, sometimes helpers and donors to assist the hero, and sometimes parents of the bride or groom. All is as it should be in a wondertale. The only character who is absolutely essential here is the hero (true heroines are rather rare in the Russian tales and there are none in this volume). The narrators recognize this. As Korguev states in one of his tales, "Without an Ivan, a tale rarely exists." Not that the hero is always named Ivan. In two of Korguev's tales the hero is not Ivan, but Ondrei (Andrei) or Sergei. In fourteen of the seventeen tales, the hero either is a tsarevich or becomes one and becomes the tsar at the end of the tale. In the other three tales he must await the death of his grandfather and father to become tsar, but the pattern is clear.

---

19. Uther, Hans-Jörg, *The Types of International Folktales. A Classification and Bibliography, Based on the System of Antti Aarne and Stith Thompson.*
20. Propp, V., *Morphology of the Folktale*, 2nd edition.
21. Gottschall, Jonathan, *Literature, Science, and a New Humanities*, part II.

In these Russian tales it is generally not the physical appearance of the hero that is his chief attribute, but rather his superhuman strength. He can literally move mountains, and he is definitely a dragon slayer long before he encounters the true villain of the tale. Although in Russian tales the serpent may occasionally breathe fire, in these Karelian tales the dragon's outstanding feature is multiple heads. As a rule the hero slices them off with his trusty sword three at a time and with consummate ease. He may then burn the serpent's skin to destroy it forever before proceeding to his ultimate encounter with the villain. As the serpent in these tales is invariably pursuing the hero's prospective bride, the serpent is male. In other Russian wondertales the serpent may be female, and the hero may come to an agreement with her, rather than destroying her. Male dragons are always killed. Despite their threats they never succeed in permanently harming the hero.

But it would be wrong to think that all our heroes begin their careers as tsareviches. Two are merchant's sons. Another is born of a fetish carved from pine, another because a bitch ate some magic soup destined for a hero's barren mother, and still another is abandoned by his parents after his mother develops a hatred for him. And so on. The important thing is that the heroes, without exception, all become tsareviches and are ready to become tsar when the tales conclude. In one tale where the hero must wait for his grandfather and father to die before he can become tsar, his father-in-law, a wealthy foreign merchant, gives him substantial wealth upon the hero's marriage to his daughter.

As I have stated above, none of these seventeen tales has a true heroine, although in several a maiden is the focus of much narrative action. Olena Sorokoumovna (Elena of the Forty Minds) is typical of the wise maiden type who frequently resists the hero's blandishments. But owing to the hero's need for a bride, she eventually acquiesces. The leading female character is most frequently Elena (the Beautiful) or Maria, often diminutively called Lenochka or Masha, and so on—although in one Korguev tale we meet an Anastasia, and M. Dmitriev introduces us to a Svetlana. Without exception these female characters are "beautiful," even when they enter the tale as an old crone or even as a frog! In such cases the heroes' task is to help these potential brides undergo the transformation they require to become beautiful.

In several of the tales the role of the mother is important. Far from being a nurturing parent, she may attempt to kill the hero, or she may force his father to leave him on an uninhabited island. In tales included in *An Anthology of Russian Folktales*, Ondrei the Shooter, the hero, actually returns to his mother's home and just before his wedding kills her. And Fear-Bogatyr also kills his mother. In other tales, however, his parents welcome their son to his own wedding. It is of course convenient for the tsarevich if his father the tsar dies at the end of the tale, so that he can be married and become tsar immediately, thus ending the tale. In one tale ("The Prophetic Dream"), however, the rightful heir to the throne must be eliminated, so the hero and his new wife—a sorceress who has in fact married the hapless tsarevich—proceed to do so with dispatch.

In the tales, mothers who try to kill their sons one way or another are not usually the villains, as Propp understands the term.[22] For Propp, the villain may appear twice in a tale. The villain makes a sudden appearance, perhaps commits a crime or some other villainy (theft, kidnapping, etc.), and then disappears. Later on, he is the object of a search on the part of the hero, who finds and disposes of the villain with the guidance of a helper or donor. In many of these Karelian tales the villain is Koshchei the Deathless, an ambiguous figure from the otherworld, who perhaps personifies death. Such is the case in six of the tales. Other villains include a tsar, the wizard Chernomor (Black Death), Mukhomor (Poison Mushroom, "Amanita muscaria"), the devil, and the hero's parents. In the more novelistic of the tales (Shkip, Peregar, Liubodei), the villain is poorly defined.

Koshchei (sometimes Koshchai) is undoubtedly the most complicated figure in the tales. It is clear from the stories themselves that he is a skeletal figure, that he flies (or perhaps rides) a flying horse, but also that the hero can overcome him by learning and obtaining the secret of Koshchei's death. This secret is usually contained in a duck's egg, inside a duck, inside a hare, or inside a casket that may be buried in some place where the hero can easily find it—perhaps even on the bottom of the sea. That Koshchei's death and Koshchei himself are separate entities does not surprise anyone familiar with Slavic mythology, where one frequently encounters a belief in the separate existence of soul and body, a belief that continues to the present. Some scholars connect the figure of Koshchei from ancient myths about an underworld god (*koshchiuy*), but even this association does not entirely explain the image and role of Koshchei the Deathless in the Russian wondertales. He seems to be a composite villain with a Russian twist.

All the tales included here can be classified as wondertales in which the element of magic is still strong. But with the exception of Koshchei

22. Propp, p. 84.

the Deathless and other such wizards (Chernomor and Mukhomor), the supernatural characters one meets in so many Russian wondertales are notably absent. There is no Leshii, that shape-shifting tsar of the forest, and even the Russian witch, the infamous Baba Yaga, is generally absent. To transport the hero from place to place we do have his magic steed, or a flying carpet—and that marvelous twentieth-century invention, the airplane, although it's just a two-seater. These features of the twentieth-century Karelian tales permit one to conclude that the wondertale per se was definitely on the decline, replaced largely by tales of everyday life. Magic, family conflicts—even physical combat with the monster or villain—all seem to be relegated to lesser status as the tales increasingly focus on pure adventure.

The purpose of presenting this volume of long, "serial" Russian folktales is to highlight a form of narration neglected in the Russian literature about the folktale, and to present what may have been the last stage in the lengthy development of the European folktale. As far as I know, no other tradition produced such tales, and clearly in Russia these tales represent the twilight of the centuries-long tradition of the wondertale.

THE TALES

◈ ◈ ◈

1

DAWN LAD

M. M. Korguev

In no certain tsardom, in no certain land, there lived and dwelt a merchant, and in the evening his son was born, and they gave him the name Evening Lad, and he was the oldest. And then a second one was born, at midnight, so they gave him the name Midnight Lad. The third was born at dawn as it were, and they gave him the name Dawn Lad. So these boys began growing, as it's said, so quickly and not by the day but by the hour. They were so strong that they didn't even know how much strength they had. Dawn Lad ordered a mace weighing three hundred poods for himself. When they had made it for him, he said to his brothers, "Well, brothers, let's go throughout the wide world and search for duels."

They said farewell to their father and mother and set off. They walked far or near, high or low, and they came to a steep mountain. It was such a steep mountain that they couldn't even climb up it. They went up to this mountain, and Dawn Lad said: "Well, lads, we ought to climb up this mountain and find out who lives there. Someone's there, someone lives there, probably wizards. We ought to find out."

Well, they didn't know how to climb it, but next to the mountain lay an anchor with its chain. And then he spoke, did Dawn Lad: "So now then, brothers, who among us will pull that anchor and chain up the mountain so that we can all climb up?"

Nearby stood a very stout, thick oak. So then the oldest brother, Evening Lad, takes up the task. He took the anchor and threw it, but it flew only half way up and fell. Then the middle brother took up the task: He grabbed hold of the anchor and threw it. The anchor flew up, but there was nothing for it to be anchored to. So then Dawn Lad took the anchor, and he said, "Now, brothers, I'll try it."

And so he threw the anchor high and it caught behind some trees, solidly. "Now, brothers, now we can go up the mountain." And holding on to the chain, the brothers went up the mountain.

"Now then, leave the anchor so that we'll be able to lower ourselves back down this mountain."

So that's what they did, they went up that mountain. They went and went and went up along that mountain. There was some kind of wide road or other, but no dwelling was visible along the way until they suddenly spied a little house. There stood a fine little house. And they entered this house and there sat a maiden, a beautiful maiden.

"Why have you brave lads come up this mountain? On this mountain there live just three serpents, three brothers. No one has as yet laid down a path back down, and it's the second year since I was carried away. I am a merchant's daughter."

"Well, all right, if you were carried away, you were carried away, but we'll have a look at this three-headed serpent and see just what he is like."

"He'll come flying back soon, and it will be too bad for me."

Then Dawn Lad spoke: "You hide two of us brothers, and the third will stay here to talk to him."

So she took Midnight Lad and Dawn Lad and hid them, and Evening Lad stayed there sitting at the table. "If there's a need, just shout and we'll come out," he said.

And then, not long after, the serpent came flying in. "Foo, foo! There's a Russian smell in my hut. Evening Lad is in my hut. We'll take a drink today; I've known of you three brothers for a long time, but I've never once seen you." He brought up three 40-gallon barrels of wine. And he began drinking from each in turn. He poured some out for Evening Lad too, and he drank. And so this wine, they drank it all, and the serpent said, "Now come for a walk with me in my garden; I'll show you my garden."

Evening Lad took his club, and as if on a crutch, set off with him. He walked along, leaning on it. Then suddenly the serpent said to him, "Now then, Evening Lad, we need to test our strength." And he roared as serpents do, so loudly that all the leaves fell from the trees.

And Evening Lad said to him, "Don't frighten me, you pagan monster! I'm not afraid."

And he struck the serpent with his club. Two of his heads flew off. He struck the serpent a second time, and the third flew off. Of course, he killed that serpent.

So then he came back, and that merchant's daughter was full of joy, and she said, "Well, Evening Lad, you will be my husband, only there are still two more serpents here."

"Oh, so there are; that's fine. There are three of us brothers. Each of us will acquire a bride."

So she let out the other two brothers. They sat down to drink some vodka, and they slept through the night. Then Dawn Lad spoke: "Well, Evening Lad, you stay here with your wife, and we shall go forth. Don't come for two full days, don't come for four full days, but come on the fifth. When you see your brother, get ready and come on ahead, and we'll pick up our brides on the way back."

So they left Evening Lad, and they went on ahead. They walked on, and it was no small place, and they saw where an even more beautiful house was standing, even better. And they caught sight of this house, and they entered this house, and they saw a girl sitting there who was even more beautiful. This girl was the daughter of a certain king. They sat down at the table, and she began feeding them, and she said, "Where are you going, brave lads? That six-headed serpent will come flying up, kill you, and that will be woe for me. I've been living here for two years already."

So then Dawn Lad said to her, "Listen, Beautiful Princess, don't be sad; you will certainly be rescued from this serpent. We've come here, and we'll deal with that serpent. Hide me here, and my brother will stay with you."

So she hid him in a special room, while Midnight Lad sat at the table. Then the serpent suddenly came flying up. "Foo, foo! It smells of a Russian soul. Midnight Lad has come to visit me. He and I will have to take a good walk, have a drink and get acquainted. So now then. Come on, mistress, bring us some fine little bites to eat, and I'll go get some wine."

He rolled out six 40-gallon barrels of wine. "Now then, Midnight Lad, sit down with me and we'll drink." They sat down at the table, drank up all the wine, and ate. "Now then, Midnight Lad, let's go out into the garden for a walk."

So they set off. They walked and walked about the garden. Midnight Lad walked with his club, leaning on it. Then the serpent spoke up: "Now then, Midnight Lad, we need to test our strength." And he roared with all his voices so loudly that the earth shook.

"You don't frighten me, you pagan monster, I'm not afraid of you!"

He struck the serpent with his club and three of his heads flew off. He hit him a second time and knocked off the rest, and then he returned to the palace. "So now then, your serpent has been killed and so you are freed."

"Since you have freed me, then you are to possess me and take me where you know best," the beautiful princess said.

So then she let out his brother and they sat down at the table to have a drink. When they had drunk up, Dawn Lad said to his brother, "Well, Brother, now you stay here with your wife, and in about three or four days our brother will come to you and then you and he come to me."

And then Dawn Lad said good-bye to his brother and his brother's wife, and he set off. He walked and walked, and then he looked and saw a little house, something shining very brightly. He didn't know whether there was a light burning, or whether it was a palace standing there. He came up closer and saw a silver palace standing there, and it was as fine as if it had been polished. You couldn't even see whether it had doors. When he had approached the palace, he tried to find them, but he couldn't find doors or windows. There was nothing there. He felt for a button and pushed on it until a door opened. He went in and started going upstairs in the palace. So then he came out, of course, in one dining hall, and that dining hall was already furnished. And in that dining hall there was on the table absolutely everything you could possibly want. He had just settled into a chair when such a beautiful maiden came in, there was no more beautiful girl in the whole world. She was so attractive to him that he was left speechless. And Dawn Lad wasn't so bad looking himself. His cheeks were rosy, and he was cheerful and youthful, just like a berry.

She gazed at this youth and said, "Tell me, young man, where have you come from and why have you come here?"

And he answered her: "Listen, my beautiful, from what family are you and what is your name? Then I'll tell you about myself, but until then don't ask me any questions as to why I came here."

She answered him: "Well, good lad, I can tell you that I am a beautiful tsarevna from a certain land, the daughter of the tsar of that land. But I have been kidnapped by a serpent, and I have been living here for this the third year. And I'll also tell you that I don't take account of myself—I'm already done for—but that serpent will soon come flying here, and he will devour you. And I pity you. And now tell me who you are." And then she added, "And I'll also tell you, good lad, that there has never been a trace of people in our mountains; I've never seen a single one."

So then he started talking. "Listen, beautiful tsarevna, I am not from the common folk, of course. I am the son of a merchant, a well-known one, too, and we are three brothers. We set out to find out about this mountain, to learn who lives here. My brothers stayed with their wives, and I went on farther. I am Dawn Lad."

"Oh, I am sorry for you, Dawn Lad, but there is nothing to be done; that serpent will soon coming flying here, and I won't dare talk with you any more. And I don't know, I'm afraid of what will happen next. Perhaps neither of us will be alive any more. He will kill you for he is very powerful."

"All right, now listen, beautiful tsarevna. None of this is very terrifying until I see him. And when I have seen him, I still won't be afraid of him right away, and he'll be visible there. And I won't leave here until I do see him."

Suddenly the serpent came flying up. When he arrived, he said, "Now then, Dawn Lad, you are here, and I've been wanting to see you for a long time. Now let's drink to friendship and on the occasion—as much as is needed."

And he rolled out nine 40-gallon barrels and said, "Well, now, mistress, bring us something to nibble on, and he and I will drink." And so, of course, she brought out everything they needed. Well, they drank it all up. Dawn Lad drank and watched out, waiting to see what would come next. Well, the serpent drank more, because he wasn't paying attention. And when they had drunk their fill, the serpent said, "Well, Dawn Lad, come with me into the garden for a walk."

"Let's go."

Well then, Dawn Lad felt he had drunk quite enough. So he walked out, leaning on his club. They approached the garden, and the serpent roared in all six voices, so strongly that the leaves fell from the trees, and the little saplings bowed down to the ground. Then Dawn Lad said to the serpent, "Don't try to frighten me, you pagan monster, I'm not afraid of you."

So then the serpent roared in all nine voices so strongly that the earth beneath them shook. But Dawn Lad stood there, leaning on his club. And the serpent said to him, "Well, Lad, Dawn Lad, now we'll have to test each other's strength."

And so they attacked each other at full tilt. And Dawn Lad struck the serpent with his club, the first time so hard that he sliced off five heads at once. The second time he swung and struck and there remained just a single head, the ninth. Eight had been chopped off. Then the serpent said to him: "Listen, Dawn Lad, why did you come here to our mountains? Up to now there had been no trace of humans here. Take whatever you want from me, only just don't kill me. Leave me alive, and you and I can consider becoming friends."

And Dawn Lad answered him: "I came here to find out who lives in these mountains. Now I've found out. First we'll finish the fight and then we'll become friends."

And so he lopped off the serpent's last head. And then he returned to the beautiful tsarevna. When he came to her, she saw that Dawn Lad had returned and the serpent was no more. She threw her arms around his neck. "Oh, my dear Dawn Lad, now do with me whatever you will, only just don't leave me in these mountains. You have saved me, so now take me with you and I will be yours forever."

"Well, beautiful tsarevna, that's why I came here, to find out who was living in these mountains and whether there were any maidens who had been kidnapped. We are three brothers here, and in two days they will come here to me." Then he said to her, "Listen, my dear beautiful tsarevna, I will not abandon you here, only I have to explore this mountain to see who lives here, and then I'll come back and it will be clear that I won't leave you here."

Then she said to him, "Listen, my handsome Dawn Lad, don't go away—you'll see such marvels that even you and your brothers won't be able to overcome. You will overcome two of them, but the third you won't be able to overcome. It would be better to take me away from here before they find out. Let's all go together to some other land or to your merchant business."

Then he said, "Oh, all right, I won't go away until tomorrow, I'll wait the night out and wait for my brothers, and then I'll tell you."

So then they began spending the night, of course. And when she had slept through the night, they got up from their sleep and she said to him, "Listen, my dear Dawn Lad, turn back from where you came, and I will give you all the precious things which the serpent acquired and which were brought here—I don't know from where. He comforted me with them so that I wouldn't wish for anything."

She still wanted to talk with him about many things, but suddenly his brothers arrived. When they came, of course, he rolled out three 40-gallon barrels of wine for their enjoyment. And they had a little drinking bout! When they had drunk up all this wine, he said to his brothers, "Well, brothers, we aren't going to be such cowards that we won't go on, that we won't find out what's going on ahead of us."

Well, the tsarevna didn't say anything. She just stood there in tears and thought about how they wouldn't be able to overcome the wizards. But, of course, the brothers decided to go on ahead anyway. The tsarevna stayed behind, waiting. There was nothing else for her to do, as she couldn't restrain him. So then Dawn Lad took his leave of her and said, "Well, good-bye, my beautiful tsarevna, I'll come back. I won't leave you here."

And he and his brothers set off. So they walked and walked and walked and came out onto a small clearing. And then out of nowhere a three-headed serpent flew at them and said, "Well, lads, even if you killed our masters, you won't get away from here alive."

Then our lad said to his brothers, "Well, brothers, let's go." And he struck the serpent with his club on the shoulders, and a head fell off. Then Midnight Lad repeated it for the other ones all at once.

Then he said to his brothers, "Now you stay here, brothers, and I'll go on ahead alone. But I'll probably be back soon; wait for me. If you see anything, don't step back from it." And so he went on ahead. First we'll follow him, and then we'll come back to the others.

And so he came to such a luxuriant garden as he had never seen before. And there were smells that sated him—he didn't have any desire to eat. Then suddenly he saw a beautiful maiden. She approached him and said, "Greetings, Dawn Lad."

"Greetings, greetings! What is your name and how do you know mine?"

"How could I not know? I know all the mighty warriors on earth, and you most of all since you and your brothers have gained fame here on the mountain. But you have come late." And then she said, "Well, let's go visiting now; I'll tell you a thing or two—only just a little, because you are now occupied with another beautiful tsarevna."

So then they set off together. First she led him into a tunnel and into the underground, and then to her palace, which was a palace of gold. She began giving him something to eat and drink, and then she said, "Well, Dawn Lad, I thought that you weren't taken, but now I see that you are occupied with a tsarevna. I see that because I know everything that is done on earth. I have lived here with a certain Chernomor for twenty years now. I was carried off when I was still small, and apparently I'll never manage to get away from here."

"That's a pity, my beautiful, but there's nothing to be done. You yourself know that once I'm in love with a tsarevna, it would be unconscionable and uncomfortable to go back on my word."

"I believe . . . I believe you," she answered him. "Well, all right, Dawn Lad, spend the night with me, and then go. It's going to be bad for you with your brothers. Maybe you can deal with them through cleverness, because with brute force you won't overcome them. I think that without me you won't get down off this mountain."

She said nothing further to him. So then he agreed to sleep with her. They spent the night and got up in the morning, and she said to him, "Well, Dawn Lad, I'll feed you right away, and then go quickly to your brothers."

He ate and then began getting ready to depart. And she said to him, "When you get there, your brothers will be fighting with Chernomor. This Chernomor has a beard that they can't even chop through. And you also won't be able to chop through it, because there isn't a sword that can do it. He lives in a separate tsardom, and he has three beauties such as no one has ever seen. I haven't seen them either, but I know that they exist. Now, when you get there, tear out an oak and bring it down to the earth. Then cut it with wedges, but not all the way through—leave a crack with the wedges—and say to Chernomor, 'Well, Chernomor, go to that oak and if you can raise that oak with your teeth, then we won't fight anymore with you. But if you can't, then we'll fight you as long as we are alive.' And then watch as he raises the oak with his teeth, and his beard will get into the crack. You pull out the wedges, and his beard will be caught in that oak. When his beard is caught, he will weaken, but you still won't be able to kill him. You get away from there."

And thus they took their leave of each other. "Well, goodbye, my dear, I'll be off," he said.

"Go, go now, Dawn Lad, but nonetheless you will come back to me. Your brothers will leave you on the mountain, and you won't come back."

So he went. And he came to that square where his brothers were fighting with Chernomor. He went up, and then he said, "Well, Chernomor, let's stop fighting and test our strength in another way." Chernomor said, "Well, all right, let's. I'm agreed to that."

Dawn Lad took hold of the oak and felled it, and that oak was three spans around. He felled it to the ground. He pounded in two wedges, and when he had pounded in the two wedges, he struck them with his club and split it, then widened the split. Then he said to Chernomor, "Well, Chernomor, if you want to compare strength with us, come here and pick up this oak with your teeth."

Chernomor went up to the oak, and Dawn Lad directed him to the place. "Here, lift it at this place." As soon as Chernomor had grabbed hold of the oak, Dawn Lad saw that Chernomor's beard had gone completely into the crack. He immediately pulled out the wedges. Chernomor began lifting the oak, but he had to lift it on his beard. "Well, now you will always be with that oak, carry on with it, if you are stronger than we are," said Dawn Lad. But then Chernomor said to him, "Well, Dawn Lad, if you so easily got around me, then you are free. But you still won't manage to kill me. Go wherever you will." Then Dawn Lad said to his brothers, "Well, brothers, let's go."

And that Chernomor rose up and set off with the oak through a meadow, and so they parted. And Dawn Lad came back to that palace where his tsarevna was and said to his brothers: "Well, brothers, now go to your own wives and we'll meet back here in two days, and then we'll go up to that mountain where the anchor is chained up."

So when that beautiful tsarevna caught sight of her Dawn Lad, she really rejoiced. She fed him and gave him and his brothers something to drink, and then his brothers went home. Dawn Lad and she remained together. When the brothers had departed, he slept through the night, and in the morning she asked, "Well, Dawn Lad, I didn't think you would trick that wizard Chernomor. And what did you do with him?"

"Well, although it was difficult, we of course overcame him, but we didn't manage to kill him dead."

"Now tell me, probably you were with that enchantress and lovely maiden. Already I know that you didn't restrain yourself, you didn't just go there and come back."

"Oh, my beautiful tsarevna, I was there. When I was walking through that splendid garden, I saw her, but I didn't speak a word with her. I only asked her what she wanted, and she ordered me to go out against Chernomor. And so I went out and she knew me. Then I tricked that Chernomor, and then I came back and came here. And now we'll get ready to go home."

"Good! We'll stay here another day and then we'll set off." Then she took her ring from her hand and said, "Now then, Dawn Lad, this ring—keep it as you know best how to do so."

So when they had collected their things together, she brought a chest and brought out some clothing. "Look here, Dawn Lad, look at this dress of mine for when we celebrate our wedding—just look how it's sewn."

Of course, he started looking at it, but he could see no seams. Everything was done so perfectly.

She closed it up again and said, "Now we have to take the palace with us."

"How will we take the palace?"

"I'll arrange it immediately."

She brought an egg, blew on it, and the palace was no more. She gave him the egg and said, "Put it in your pocket, and when we get home, we'll make a palace for ourselves, and everything will be as it was."

And they set off. They came to Evening Lad and said, "Well, Brother, get ready, you aren't ready yet; I've already got everything with me."

Evening Lad got ready the same way, and they went to the third brother. When they came upon that third brother, he already had everything ready, and all together they set off. On the road they came upon the serpent corpses and the birds had already scattered them about. And then of course they came to the very steep mountain. Dawn Lad spoke: "You go on down ahead, and I'll hand over your wives and mine, too, and you pick them up there appropriately."

So then his brothers went down and down, and when they had got down, he let down the first maiden. Then he let down the second also. Then he began letting down his own beautiful tsarevna. She said, "Listen, Dawn Lad, you go down first, and I'll go down last."

"No, why?"

"So that they won't leave you on the mountain."

"What are you saying, my dear? Is it possible that my brothers would leave me on the mountain?"

"Well, as you know best, but afterwards it will be too late." And she began letting herself down.

When she had let herself down, his brothers looked at her. They saw that she was so beautiful, and they became envious. And this is what they did: They grabbed hold of the chain and yanked the anchor from the mountain. So Dawn Lad remained on the mountain. And there was nothing he could do about it. "Well, brothers, that's a fine thing you did to me," he said, and he continued on farther.

His brothers went home with their wives and there they were married and began living, while that other tsarevna went away to her own tsardom.

So then he [Dawn Lad] walked for a long time over that mountain, and he came to a little hut, where he ate and spent the night. "Well, where shall I go now? I'll go back to that luxuriant garden to that beautiful maiden and ask her whether she doesn't know some way for me to get off this mountain." And he decided to set off immediately. When he came to that little garden, he entered it, and there was this wonderful smell. Then he immediately saw the maiden, and she saw him and took him by the hands.

"Let's go now to my place, Dawn Lad. I said you'd be back here. And here you are!"

So she led him into the underworld, where stood a most attractive palace. When she had led him there, she began treating him to fine food, and she said, "Well, Dawn Lad, you can give me your consent to live here with me forever. Once you have left your tsarevna, she will soon be at home. And you'll have to forget about her, even though I know that she's more beautiful than I am."

He thought a little about it and said to her, "You know what I am thinking now, my beauty?"

"Yes, I know, but you say it anyway."

"Well, when I left home—and I haven't been home for a very long time—I had this desire to see my parents regardless of what happens, and that's all I know."

"Yes, I believe you have this desire to see your parents, but greater is the desire to find out how that tsarevna is and live together with her. Well, if you don't want to, I won't hold you here by force."

Then she said, "Well, just spend the night here with me, and then I'll lead you away." And so he agreed to spend the night with her. So they spent that night, she fed him, and said, "Well, Dawn Lad, let's go now, and I'll lead you out through the tunnel, but don't be upset that it's so dark. It's dark because you didn't agree to live here with me. You are forbidden to know everything and that's why it will be dark."

So she went ahead and he walked behind, and they descended down into the tunnel. They walked together no fewer than ten days. And then they came up to a stone wall, and they stopped. And she said to him, "Well, listen, Dawn Lad, you are a strong lad, so now tell me: Will you take me with you or not? If you'll take me, then say so, and if you won't take me, then I won't cross the threshold, and there'll be no way for me to return if I do."

"Listen my beauty, how can I marry you or take you with me before I have visited my parents and asked them and received their blessing? How could I take you?"

"Well, good, I already see that you have no desire. Kick the wall with your foot and you can see what happens."

And he kicked the wall and saw light and there were people riding horses. She said, "Well, Dawn Lad, farewell! You are down from the mountain now." And the door, which had been invisible before, closed, and up above was the steep mountain. So then he went out and set off along a wide road. He walked and walked and walked, and he himself didn't know where he was going. When he had been walking through that dark tunnel for about ten days, he had been upset. He kept thinking, "I don't know whether I'll get there." And when he came out of there, he had lost much weight and his face had altered such that anybody who met him wouldn't have recognized him.

And he came out exactly in that land where the tsarevna was, and she was then living with her father. And so, of course, he rented a room in an inn and took up living in that city. There were many suitors for that tsarevna, and she sent out a call throughout the city: "I shall marry the one who can bring me that little house in which I used to live, and also my wedding dress."

And there was one prince who was courting her and she, of course, didn't promise, but she invited him, and they put on a feast and invited all to the feast who wished to come. Then all the guests gathered—the groom came there, too—and she gave this order: "Now all you guests, hear me! I will marry only the suitor who will bring me the little house in which I used to live and my wedding dress." And she herself thought, "And if someone fetches the little house, then my ring will be found."

She made this announcement, and then all who were present, including the suitor, asked her, "Well, what sort of palace do you have and whatever sort of dress do you want—I can buy it for you, can't I?"

"Of course not, it's not what I want; it's what I had. And the dress was sewn so perfectly and the palace was of the sort that you don't have in your country."

Dawn Lad heard all of this. Then she, of course, began treating her guests to vodka. When she was treating them, she didn't pay attention, and she offered it to him—she brought him a little glass, but she couldn't recognize his face in any way. So then he drank up the little goblet, of course, and placed a ring on the tray. And she said, "Is it you I see, my Dawn Lad? Why have you changed so much?"

"Yes, I changed a lot when I stayed on that mountain."

Then she came out from behind the table, took him by the hand, kissed him, and said to her father, "Well, Papa, this is my promised, who let me down from the mountain and killed the serpent and tricked Chernomor, and who remained alone on the mountain. I don't know how he got down—he himself will have to tell us. His name is Dawn Lad."

Then the tsar spoke: "Well, Dawn Lad, since you have managed to win my daughter and defeat the serpents, you will receive half the tsardom and live with us."

And thus they began to feast in real fashion. She said, "Well, Dawn Lad, build the palace. You have that egg, and I need to have that wedding dress."

And of course they left the feast, and she led him out onto a fine square where he broke the egg and a palace appeared. And everything in that palace was just as it had been in the past, like it was on the mountain.

Then he said to her, "Listen, beautiful tsarevna, now I'm going off to sleep. I've never slept so sweetly as I did those two nights with you. Afterward I won't tell you anything, and you mustn't ask me. Let your father prepare the wedding."

Then she led him into her bedroom and lay him down on her bed, and she herself lay down with him. When he had slept, he said, "Well, now we can go to your father for the ball and then to the ceremony. Put on your dress." She got dressed and they went to the wedding ceremony.

Soon, of course, they were married and came to the ball. All the guests were amazed by the dress, which had not a seam, not a cut, and they were astonished, wondering who had obtained such a dress. Of course, he didn't tell them everything right then, he said only that he had remained on the mountain and had got down from there through a tunnel, becoming weak as a result.

Then the tsar said, "Well, fine, the affair is still young. Live for the present, and then later you will receive the entire tsardom when I am really old, and you will be my heir." And all the guests began departing, and he took his leave of all the guests and went to his own palace.

And they lived on into deep old age, and in due time Dawn Lad received the throne and began his rule.

(SUS 301A + 301B)

2

ELENA THE BEAUTIFUL

M. M. Korguev

So in no certain tsardom, in no certain country, there lived and dwelt a tsar. The tsar had three sons. The oldest was Vasilii, the middle one Fedor, and the youngest, as is always the case in stories, was Ivan. (Without an Ivan a tale rarely exists.) So when these sons were already grown up, the tsar summoned all three and announced this thing:

"Now, my young sons, my dear ones, do you know what? Before I become old, I have a desire to marry you off and look upon your little children as my little grandchildren."

The sons answered: "Well, that's fine, Father, bless us; whom shall we marry?"

Their father answered them thusly: "So now then, my sons, you yourselves choose your own brides. You will have to live with them, not I. That is my advice."

"But of course not, Father, we would like to find out who it would be desirable for us to marry."

"Well then, I'll likely say this to you: Take, make yourselves a self-shooting arrow each and shoot; wherever your arrows land, there you will find the one you are fated to marry. Let it fall into a peasant's yard or a priest's, or even into a prince's—wherever that arrow falls, there will be your fate to marry."

So, the lads thanked their father. They set off, and each made himself a self-shooting arrow. They shot them off, and set off after the arrows to find out where their brides were. The oldest one's, Vasilii's, arrow landed in a king's courtyard. The middle son's, Fedor's, landed in a prince's courtyard. Those two set off after their arrows and got married there. But the youngest one's, Ivan's, rose up and flew away, and he himself didn't know where. He had to go out in its direction, following his arrow. So he walked, and he walked. He went out of the city and headed off in the direction of the forest. And he saw that there was a large swamp in the forest. And in the swamp was a small hut, and he saw his arrow on that hut. So yes, he went up to that hut and got onto the roof, took it down from the roof and was about to return home. As he was about to leave, suddenly an old, really old woman came out and said, "Well, Ivan Tsarevich, since you came here for your little arrow, it means that fate has drawn you to me. You are obliged to marry me according to your father's benediction."

He looked at her and said, "Can it be that I've come to such an old woman? Why, you don't have a single tooth in your mouth, and you can't even walk. I don't need you, I won't take you."

"Well, don't take me then, as you wish. But once your father ordained it, you have to take me. And if you won't take me, nonetheless you won't get away from me."

And he said, "No, I won't have you. I'll go away."

And he set off. But he couldn't get away; he was stuck in the swamp. So then she came up closer to him and said, "Well, you'll take me or else you'll drown; and if you won't take me, nonetheless you'll drown. You won't go anywhere away from me." And so he thought about it for a little while. "Well, so I'm to perish here, but I've a desire to live a while. Oh, the devil take her, I'll marry her, but I'll never cohabit with her."

Then he said, "Well, all right, go on, the devil take you, I'll marry you."

And then immediately he was on firm ground. So they went along, and she said to him along the way, "So, Ivan Tsarevich, although you took me, you don't know how to keep me." (Why she said that will be clear later on.) He went on ahead and didn't even look about, and he thought to himself, "It's all the same, I won't live with you."

And then soon they came to the tsardom. He led her into a room, left her, and then went to his father to explain his unfortunate situation, what had happened to him. When he had come to his father, his father asked him, "Well, where have you been wandering for so long, and where did you find your bride? Your brothers are already married: one to a prince's daughter, the other to a king's."

He answered his father: "Oh, Father, don't ask about my marriage. What an unfortunate youngest son of yours I am!

"But what is it with you, my son, tell me, and I'll listen; whom have you married, whom have you brought here?"

So he began telling his father how he had shot the arrow and set off in search of it. And then how the arrow had flown into a swamp and that he had set off in that direction in search of the arrow.

> Then I came to the swamp and caught sight of this little hut and then my arrow was on its roof, and I fetched it, and then I wanted to get away from there. Just when I got there, out came this old, really old woman from that hut and said, "Well, Ivan Tsarevich, it is our fate, in accordance with your father's benediction, for you to marry me." Of course, I refused her and wanted to get away from there, but I began sinking into that swamp and no way could I get out. Then she approached me and also said, "If you take me, you won't drown, but if you don't take me, you'll drown and you'll never get away." So I, Father, took her and brought her here. I had no desire to drown in that swamp—do what you like with me.

Now Ivan's father spoke: "Well, Vania, what's to be done? Obviously, that's your fate. Let her live. If nothing can be done, that's nothing. Let her live all the same, and perhaps she'll die soon since she's so old. Then you can marry another."

And then suddenly the other brothers came to their father. And their father said: "Now then, my dear sons, come to me tomorrow, and I'll put on a feast for you. And each of you bring a shirt, let each of your wives sew a shirt, and I'll find out which of the three is the best at handwork, and I'll give the tsardom to that son."

So the brothers said: "All right, Father, we'll go and instruct them."

Then his said to Ivan: "Let your old woman sew too, if she can, but if she can't there'll be nothing to do with the old one."

Then Ivan hung his head, and set off. So he came to that room where she was sitting, and very sadly sat down on a bench, not even looking at her. She approached him. "Well, Ivan Tsarevich, what is it? You're unhappy, you've let your wild head hang low. What did your father tell you to do, what sort of order did he give you?" (But she already knew—she's a witch.)

So then he said to her: "What can you do? Father ordered all the brides to sew shirts, but what can you sew since your hands shake and you can barely walk. And it's better to refuse, not to get alarmed for no reason." And he lowered his head even farther.

Then she spoke: "Listen, Ivan Tsarevich, do not lower your head and go and bring me ten arshins of silk. Even if I'm weak, I'll do it. Don't spare the silk."

So. Now he thought: "Oh, the devil take her; let her." He set off and brought her ten arshins of silk. "Let her do it."

And then he set off to wherever his eyes might take him. But these brides, when the brothers had brought them the silk, came to see how the old woman would sew—they came to see! But when she got the silk, she took it, ripped it into little pieces, and threw these pieces out the window. "Oh, wild winds, make Father a shirt without a single seam so that he won't be ashamed to wear it in the presence of guests." And suddenly—not even a few minutes passed—and the shirt was ready! It was done up and starched. She took it, wrapped it up, and sat down in her place. The other brides ran away from her home.

(Now this tale is told in two ways. In the other way she was a frog in the swamp, but he still had to marry her.)

Well then, they did everything in the same manner: They cut up the silk into little pieces and threw them out the window. Then they started waiting for all to be ready. They also said these words: "Wild winds, sew up a shirt for Father." No matter how long they waited, nothing came of it. So they said to their husbands: "Well, husbands, nothing came of it. Quickly run to the market and buy the very best shirts that there are there, to take to Father."

The husbands, of course, got ready and set off for the market. And at the very best shops they bought the very best silk shirts. They carried them home. Then they immediately got ready, as they had to go to their father by nine o'clock. And Ivan also knew this, that they had to go. So suddenly Ivan went to his old woman and said: "Well, and what have you done?" And then he turned his head in the other direction so as not to look at her. She answered: "Here in this towel, Ivanushko, I have a shirt wrapped up for Father. Perhaps he'll like it, then present it to him, but let him not criticize it, it's as it is."

And so all three brothers went to their father. Right away when they had just appeared, their father asked the eldest son:

"Well now, Vasilii, show me what kind of wife you have when it comes to needlework." Vasilii immediately took out the shirt and laid it on the table. When he had examined the shirt, their father shook it and said, "Oho, you can buy shirts such as this, as many as you like, at the market. Your wife is a poor needle worker. Our servants wear such shirts as these on holidays, even grooms wear them. But now then, Fedor, show me the work of your wife. What sort of needle worker is she?"

Then he looked at the shirt too and unfolded it. "So simple, as if they had come from the same factory. Probably both shirts are from the same shop."

Then the tsar went up to his youngest son and said, "Well, Vaniusha, show me the needlework of your old woman. I'm not going to inquire much of her, just what she did, and with that I'll be satisfied." Ivan gave him the rolled up bundle and said,

"Look, Father, I myself haven't seen it, but she said 'let Father not criticize it, it is what it is.'" So then the father unfurled the shirt and said, "Well just look what sort of shirt this is! There's not a single seam. It's as if alive. For this shirt, Ivanushko, it'll be necessary to give the tsardom to you and your wife and seamstress, but I already know that she's too old! But this shirt! One would not be ashamed to wear it when guests are around."

Then their father spoke to his sons: "Now then, my sons, tomorrow each of you bring me a loaf of bread, and according to this baking I'll find out how your wives will feed you."

And with these words the brothers parted. The older brothers came and said, "Well, wives, Father didn't praise your needlework; he only praised the shirt that Ivan's old woman sewed. It was really a well-sewn shirt. But now Father demands that you each bake him a loaf of bread, he needs it for some guests. So now try, and we'll bring you some flour."

Then Ivan also went up to his old woman, sat down on a chair, and hung his head. He was silent. So she came up to him and said, "Why, Ivan Tsarevich, are you so unhappy? Why have you hung your wild head, or did father not like the shirt, or did he give you a new command? I will try and maybe I'll be able to do something."

He said to her, "He certainly didn't criticize the shirt—he even said thank you and praised you—but now he demands that you each bake a loaf of bread. But how are you to do that when your hands shake so and it's even horrible to look at you?"

"Now, then, listen, Ivanushko, don't even regret the ten pounds of flour. Just bring it to me and somehow I'll make the bread. However it turns out, that's what we have to do."

So then he brought her the flour, and he himself went away so he didn't have to look at her. So she right away then started out to leaven the flour. The dough was started. She fired up the stove. And then at that same time, the other brides came running to see how she would bake. When the oven was heated up, she raked over the coals in the oven, poured the dough onto the coals, closed up the stove, and kept it in the oven for two hours. Earlier, it seems, they also baked by hours! So two hours passed, she opened the oven, and such an aroma passed through the entire hut. You could be fed by it alone. So then she pulled it out. And such a beautiful loaf and so elegant, just like a picture. So the other brides ran home. They immediately heated up their ovens. They raked apart the coals, poured the dough on the coals and closed the oven by its handle. (They didn't guess a thing; they hadn't gone there [to watch the old woman] for that!) So two hours passed, and they opened the ovens but there were just coals—no bread, no dough, there turned out to be just coals.

And then suddenly their husbands came. They asked: "Well now then, wives, are the loaves ready?"

"No, nothing turned out right for us; everything burned up. We'll have to buy some at the market, since the time has already passed and we can't patch it up here now."

So the brothers went to the market. Ivan, without a care, didn't go out anywhere. So they ran to the market and bought the very dearest raisin breads, brought them home, and their wives wrapped the loaves in a tablecloth and the brothers carried them off to their father. Ivan saw that it was time to go, so he went to the old woman: "Well, now, if you've prepared it, give it to me and I'll carry it off, it's time to go."

She brought a cloth and the wrapped-up bread and said: "Well, Ivanushko, take it. Whether your father will like it or not, I don't know how to bake any better."

Ivan set out somewhat after his brothers. When they all got there, the tsar said to his oldest son, "Well now, show me the work of your wife. What is she going to feed you with?"

Vasilii handed over the bread right away. The tsar unwrapped it, looked at it, and then said himself, "Oh, such loaves as this the servants and grooms eat on holidays. Well then, Fedor, show me yours."

He unwrapped the cloth. "So Father, just look!"

"Oh, it's all the same, either they came from the same factory, or you took them from the same market. Now then you, Ivanushko, show me. Your wife is old so I won't be too severe with her."

Ivan undid the cloth. "Well, Father, look—I haven't even looked at it myself. She asked that you not be too severe."

When his father had undone the cloth, the aroma of the bread spread throughout all the rooms. Then the father said, "Now here's a loaf you'd be pleased to give to guests. You eat a bite, and you couldn't get a second out of your mind; you eat a second, and you'll already be wanting a third." Then he went on to say: "Well, my son, if your wife were younger, I would hand over the throne for her needlework, but she's already so old so that for now I won't say anything. Now all three of you come here tomorrow with your wives, and let them each send me a carpet in their own work, let them make it just as they know how."

The brothers all went home. And at that time the tsar began to gather together guests for a ball. The brothers said to their wives, "Now wives, each of you sew a carpet and tomorrow we'll all go together to Father's to a ball."

Ivan also went to his old woman, hung his head, and thought, "Well now what am I going to do since father has given such an order. So how am I to take her, such a one, even to a ball. I'll be conscience-stricken in front of my brothers and the other guests, and everybody will look at her and laugh."

The old woman came up to him. "What is it, Ivan Tsarevich, you're not happy, you've hung your wild head? How did your father insult you? Or did I make something bad for him, or did he give another order?"

"Father really thanked you for your work, but now he has given this order: By tomorrow you all must sew carpets with your own hands and also come to him with the other wives to a ball. So how am I to take such a one as you, for all my brothers will laugh, and the guests, too."

"Well, fine, Ivan, what is to be done? Go and lie down to sleep. I'll make the carpet for you before morning, and you go to the ball alone. Why should I go just to amuse people?"

Ivan left and tumbled off to sleep. And at that time those wives each sewed a carpet. In the morning they got dressed in their royal outfits and prepared for the ball, and Ivan went to his old woman. When he came, she handed him the carpet and said, "So, take the carpet to your father." He looked at her and asked, "And you, old woman, will you come?"

"Of course not, I won't go. Why should I go just to amuse people?" He took the carpet, and she said to him, "When you've brought the carpet, lay it out on a table, and there it can be seen."

So he took the carpet and turned to leave, but then she said, "Listen, Vania, I'll add several words to you. When you come to the ball, your brothers will immediately say:

> "Why didn't you bring your old woman so that people could see what a beauty she is!" And you say to them, "Stop your laughing, brothers, why should you laugh at an elder?" And then look about and just sit there. A little shower will come, and you say, "Well, my little wife washes in rain water." Your brothers will laugh at you even more. Then there will be a roll of thunder, and you say, "My little wife is beginning to get dressed." They will laugh even more than before and say, "Our brother is going nuts." And then

> lightning will flash, and you say "And here comes my wife," and you go out onto the porch to await me.

And with these words Ivan went out. He didn't even feel his legs as he went into the palace. So he walked along, laid out the carpet, and the carpet jumped up from the table and began leaping about, dancing, and playing music. When his brothers brought their carpets, they were only worth tossing beneath your feet and walking on.

So then their father spoke: "Well, Vania, for the handicraft of your old woman, why didn't you bring her? She could have sat here with us." He answered his father, "But she didn't come, yet perhaps she will come. I don't know."

And so after that they all sat down at the table. And Vania sat down with his brothers. Then the eldest brother Vasilii began talking: "So why then, Vania, didn't you bring your old woman so that people could look at such a beauty?" And Fedor right away agreed. He said, "Oh stop it, brothers, stop laughing. Why, not everyone can be beautiful."

And suddenly it started raining. Vania looked and spoke up: "So now then, my wife is washing herself with rainwater." And Vasilii said to Fedor, "Just look, look! That Ivan and his old woman are starting to go nuts. He muttered something about her washing herself in rainwater."

Then there was a roll of thunder. Ivan said, "Now my wife is putting on her best dress." Fedor said to him, "You stop it, Vania, it's not such a good idea to make jokes in front of guests." But Ivan reaffirmed what she had said to him, while at the time he still didn't know anything.

Then lightning flashed, and he said, "That's my wife coming here," and he jumped up and ran to meet her. He ran out and looked, and there came dashing up a troika of white horses and in it sat such a beautiful woman that you couldn't take your eyes off her, only gaze and rejoice. She drove up to the porch and grabbed Ivan by the hand, and they went up. And Ivan was so happy that he thought, "Can this be my wife, or can it be that I'm dreaming all this in a dream?"

They went up to the table, and his brothers', his father's, and the guests' eyes all popped out. Ivan's wife was so beautiful, they all looked at her unceasingly. Then he got up and said, "Now then, brothers, will you laugh at my wife because she's an old woman?"

And the brothers fell silent as though they were dead. All were sitting at the table. Then their father came up to his son and to his bride and said,

"Give me your hand, thank you very much for your handwork. And now, Vania, I am saying, and all these guests will affirm it, that I am giving you half the tsardom, and after my death, you shall step forward as tsar over all my tsardom."

Then he asked his son, "Well, Vania, tell me, what is your wife's name?" And Ivan answered, "Father, I don't know myself because she was always just the old woman. Ask her yourself." He went up to her. "Well, bride, tell me what your name is, what shall we call you?" She answered, "My name is simple and easy. I am called Elena the Beautiful."

Now further along. The guests began eating, and all stared at Elena the Beautiful, even the other brides. So she took a bite into her mouth and put another up her sleeve. And the brides did the same thing, but the same thing wouldn't happen to you that happened with those bites of hers! And the guests kept watching and were amazed, and some of them couldn't even eat, she was so beautiful. To say nothing about Ivan—he sat there quite out of his mind with such a wife. And when she laughed, gold came rolling out, and when she cried, pearls rolled. Then afterwards, they began to dance. Ivan went out with his Elena the Beautiful to dance. And so she danced for a little time, then she waved her sleeve. The window opened, and out the window the River Neva flowed by, and on the river swam various little ducks, drakes, and eiders, and they all trilled in their various voices.

Then out came the brothers, and they went to dance with their wives. They also danced for a little while, and the brides shook their sleeves. From those sleeves poured crumbs and bones, which flew at the guests and the father. The tsar shouted out, "What are you doing? What are you doing? You could knock out the eyes of all these guests!"

They became ashamed. When all had quieted down, Ivan remembered, "Where did my wife put her old age? Maybe, I'll just go and have a look." And so he set off to go there. And then she asked him, "Where are you going, Vania?" She had guessed where he was going, only she didn't think that he would actually do anything.

"Oh, I won't go far."

And he ran away. He went into the room where she had been living. He searched and searched, but there was nothing. Then he went into the washroom and saw her costume lying there. Without saying anything, he stoked up the stove and in an instant threw it in. "Let it burn up so that she will never, ever put it on again." He thought it was for the best!

When he came back, she asked him, "Where were you, Vania?"

"Oh, I wasn't far away." He wasn't saying!

"Almost certainly, you were at home and you burned up my costume. If you burned it up, tell me the truth, and we'll go home immediately."

So then he said, "Yes, Elena the Beautiful, I burned it up."

"But you do know what you have done; you have disclosed me to Koshchei the Deathless. My father blew all his capital on this costume in order to hide me for seven years from Koshchei the Deathless. I had to wait only three more days for him to forget me, but now he will swoop up and take me. Let's go quickly; maybe we'll have time."

They had only just gone out onto the porch when down came a black whirlwind, snatched her, and Ivan was left alone. So then he went home, neither drank nor ate, hung about, and started crying. He thought, "What have I done now! I couldn't wait three days."

His father waited, waited to see what sort of explanation his son would come up with. But he couldn't wait any more, and on the third day he himself went to visit Ivan and Elena. When he got there, he saw that his son was lying on the bed alone.

"What is this, Vaniusha, you haven't appeared before me, and you are lying in bed alone. Where is your wife?"

"My wife," answered Ivan Tsarevich, "well here's what I've done, Father." "When I ran away from the feast and began searching where she had put her old age," Ivan began telling him,

> I searched and searched and found the old woman's costume, so I went and heated up the stove and burned it up. When I had burned it up, I ran back, and Elena the Beautiful asked me, "Vania, where were you, and did you burn up my costume?"
>
> "I was at home and I burned your old age."
>
> "Well, let's go home quickly, otherwise Koshchei the Deathless will seize me."
>
> And she also said, "You couldn't even wait three days when Koshchei the Deathless would have forgotten me altogether." And so then we went out onto the porch, darkness came down and seized Elena the Beautiful, an unseen force carried her off. So now I've been left alone and I'm lying here and crying.

All that was dear to him had flown away.

Then his father said, "You are a fool, Vania, because you couldn't wait for three days. She would have afterwards been yours all your life, but now what will you do—there's nothing I can do to help you. And the whole kingdom is gone for you because you aren't married."

Then Ivan said, "Well, all right, Papa, let Mama bake some pastries for the road. Even though I may die, nonetheless, I'll go looking for her. There is no life for me without her."

So now then, they immediately prepared a sack for him. He said farewell to his father and his mother and set off on the road. So he walked and he walked, far or near, and he kept on walking down the road. And he walked so far that he couldn't walk any farther, and he had no more food left. And he thought, "So now then I'll die hungry on this road in any case."

And just at that time he saw a little hut standing there. It stood and revolved. He went up and said, "Little hut, little hut! Turn to the woods with your eyes and your gates to me. I have no time to waste, just to spend a night. Let in this passerby."

The hut stopped. Ivan went in and saw an old woman standing next to the stove. "Foo, foo, I've never spent time in Rus' and never smelled a Russian soul but now I smell one. I'll eat you up, young man. I haven't eaten human flesh in thirty years."

He spoke up: "What do you mean, Granny, you'll eat a cold and hungry one. You should give me a drink, feed me, heat up the bathhouse, and bathe me in the bathhouse, and then I would be softer to eat."

Then the old woman looked at him. She gave him a drink, fed him, and at the same time heated up the bathhouse. She bathed him in the bathhouse, put him to bed, and let him sleep. And then she went up to the bed and said, "Well then, tell me, young man, of what family and clan are you, and what is your name? Tell me, where are you going, where is your path taking you?"

"I am called Ivan Tsarevich, Granny. And I am going half of my own free will, and secondly not of my free will, and thirdly by my own desire. And I got married by chance to a certain old woman, and she turned out to be Elena the Beautiful. I went and burned up her old woman's costume. And Koshchei the Deathless carried her away. And now I am going to search for her."

She replied:

> You are a fool, Ivan Tsarevich, you are my nephew-in-law, and she is my very own niece. And you didn't manage to hold her. Why, in three days she would have been yours forever, but now I don't know. And there's no way I can help. You know how her father hid her from Koshchei the Deathless, he

> put all his capital into it so that he could hide her for seven years. Maybe her aunts know, they are witches, perhaps they helped her father themselves.
>
> But now go to her father. If he forgives you, then that's fine, but if he doesn't forgive you, then probably you won't be among the living. He lives not far from here. So go, and when you see a large house, and an old woman will greet you and give you a drink and something to eat. That will be your mother-in-law, and if he himself should be at home, I don't know what will become of you.

And so Ivan and the aunt said their farewells, and he set off. He walked and he walked, and he walked and he walked, far or near he himself didn't know. And suddenly he saw a house—huge, really big. He went up to this house. He had only gone up onto the porch when he saw an old woman coming out to greet him. She opened the door and said, "Come into the hut, young man."

So yes, when he went into the hut, she immediately set the table, gave him something to drink, fed him, and put him to bed. And she herself sat down next to him and started questioning him: "So then, tell me, young man, who are you and where are you going, even if you aren't descended from the family?" (But she already knew, the aunt had informed her.) "If you weren't from the family, then I know Auntie would not have let you go. Not a single bird flies by here nor a single beast trots by, and no youth can pass."

So then he began: "This is who I am: I am Ivan Tsarevich. I am going half of my own free will, and the other half by my desire on account of a great need." So he told her his entire situation. She just gasped.

"Well, you are lucky that Father isn't home just now. My unfortunate Elechka has been taken by Koshchei the Deathless. So now rest, and when Father comes, I'll awaken you. You will go up to him, fall on your knees, and beg his forgiveness. What he will say to you I don't know."

Ivan, of course, slept. Suddenly the father entered the house and said, "Who is that in our hut, tell me, or it will go badly for you. Whom have you let in?" She said to him, "Listen, Husband, this is not some other person. I have let in our son-in-law. Do you know what situation he is in? He's going about, crying bitterly." And he said, "Well, bring him here; I'll talk with him, since he came here. He'll receive no mercy from me of any sort for what he's done."

Suddenly she came. "Well, Ivanushko, go. Father has come."

So Ivan went up and, not quite approaching him, fell on his knees and said, "Father, forgive me, I have committed a great sin!" Father said to him, "Well, son-in-law, stand up, sit at the table with me, and I'll explain everything to you."

So Ivan sat down at the table, and his father (in-law) said to him:

> Do you know what you did when you burned that costume? I flew around the world my whole life and gathered wealth, and put it all into that costume, and you burned it up like some old rag. I can't help you with anything else, because she is now living at Koshchei the Deathless's, and I can't deal with him at all. Well, go to Koshchei, since you committed the sin yourself. Of course, you will ride up to Koshchei's territory, but he won't let you in, he'll burn you up with his curses. Then you take off your helmet and start waving it at him. Then he'll let you in and you talk with him there. Maybe you can approach him as some sort of laborer, or servant, and then it just might be that in some circumstance you'll see her there. If you do see her, or get to her, then come to me, but if you don't get to Elena the Beautiful, then don't come back here. Otherwise, you won't be alive.

So then he led out a horse for Ivan, gave him a sword and helmet. Ivan said farewell to his father-in-law and mother-in-law and set off on the road. So he rode, he rode, he rode, and he rode to Koshchei's territory. And at that time Koshchei was sitting in the place where his sword lay. Then Koshchei began cursing him roundly. Ivan removed his helmet and began swinging it. Then Koshchei let him approach and saw that he had ridden with some sort of request. When Ivan rode up to him, he asked, "Well, tell me, youth, why have you come, on account of what need?" And Ivan answered him, "I've come to you, I want to serve as some sort of worker or servant, to serve in faith and truth."

Then Koshchei said to him, "But only those can serve me as my slaves who are equal to me in strength."

Then he spoke, did Koshchei the Deathless: "I do not know your strength. First of all show what sort of strength you have. The one who is equal to me in strength can throw my sword straight up, and it must fly for six hours. Such a one will be my equal in strength." Then Ivan said, "Listen, you first show me, and then I'll do it for you."

So then Koshchei got down from his place, took his sword, and threw it up. He handed Ivan a watch. "So now, look."

Exactly six hours passed, and the sword fell at the very same spot. And it went into the ground so that only its handle was visible. He took back the watch. "Now go, and here's my sword."

Ivan Tsarevich went up to the sword, but he couldn't even move it from its place, and he stood there. Koshchei asked, "Well, why are you standing there? Why don't you throw it? Time doesn't wait."

"Well, wait, in a minute a little cloud is coming, and I'll throw your sword beyond that cloud."

Koshchei looked at him, took him, blew on him, turned him into a nut, and threw Ivan Tsarevich into the open steppe. And so Ivan Tsarevich lay there. There was no way for him to move inside that nut. And so he lay there a day, then two. To his great fortune, just at that time an eagle flew over. An eagle flew over and saw that nut and pecked it. Ivan Tsarevich hopped out and said, "Well, glory be to God, I'm alive now, thanks to you, Father Eagle." The eagle answered him: "Now, tell me, Ivan Tsarevich, how did you get into that nutshell, explain it to me."

"Well, Father Eagle, Koshchei the Deathless dragged off my wife, and I went to him but I couldn't lift his sword and he became angry with me, breathed on me, turned me into this nut, and threw me into the open steppe, and that's how I turned out to be here." He told him all this very briefly.

The eagle answered him, "Yes, I've known that for a long time, Ivan Tsarevich, but if you want to be of equal strength with Koshchei, then come and be my worker for three years, and I will endow you with such strength that you will be equal to Koshchei." (Although he knows, nonetheless he has to ask!) Ivan Tsarevich thought for a little while and said, "Well, so now then, Father Eagle, I'll go with you."

So then the eagle sat him on his back and flew off to his home. (So, the poor chap, he has to suffer for ten years.) When he had flown home, he turned into an old man, and led Ivan Tsarevich into the kitchen and said, "So now bake and cook for me and for you, that's the work for you, and in a year I'll pay you for it."

So Ivan Tsarevich started in at his work, and very quickly he had lived a year with the old man. When he had lived there a year, they sat down to dine. The old man went down into the cellar and brought up a bottle of wine (vodka). He poured the wine out into a cup and said, "So, Ivan Tsarevich, drink up, this is for an entire year, for your work." Ivan Tsarevich looked at the cup and said, "Grandfather, I ought not drink this. Since my birth I've drunk very little at all." But Grandfather answered him, "This isn't anything to make you feel ill. You drink and it will be better for your health."

Then Ivan Tsarevich took up the cup and drank it down in own gulp. When they had eaten, the old man said to him, "Let's go into the steppe, Ivan Tsarevich; I'll show you my sword. It's the same as Koshchei's."

They came to that sword. The old man took the sword, handed a watch to Ivan and threw the sword up. The sword flew up for six hours and fell in the same place. And the grandfather said, "Do you see, Ivan Tsarevich, the old man has strength as in olden times. Give me the watch. Can you lift up or throw my sword?"

Then Ivan Tsarevich handed him the watch and took the sword and threw it up only for two hours. The sword flew for two hours and fell in the same place.

"Now all right then, Ivan, let's go home and you will continue the same work with me."

They came home and Ivan began doing what he had done before. And so he spent the second year. And again he and Grandfather sat down to eat. When they had just sat down to eat, Grandfather brought him two bottles of wine and said, "Well, drink, this is for your second year of work." Ivan didn't even begin to refuse, as he had found out the first time what sort of wine this was. He took it and drank it all at once. When they had finished eating, Grandfather said to him, "Now then, let's go into the steppe. We'll take a look and find out what strength I have, whether it's like before."

Grandfather went up to his sword, handed Ivan the watch, and tossed up the sword. The sword flew for six hours and fell in the same place. Then Grandfather took the watch and said to Ivan, "Now, you throw it."

Ivan threw it and the sword flew six hours already and fell in the same place. So he said, "Let's go. You live with me for one more year." They went. On the road Grandfather said, "So. Live with me for one more year, and you'll have half again as much strength as Koshchei. Now your strengths are equal because my sword weighs the same as Koshchei's."

So again they came home, and Ivan went back to the same old place and lived there a third year. When he had lived there the third year, again they sat down to eat, and Grandfather brought a whole quarter barrel and said, "Now, Ivan, drink up your salary for the third year." (In place of the wine he was giving him strength.) So he drank it. After dinner Grandfather said, "Let's go into the steppe, Ivan. I want to try again to see whether I have the strength I used to have."

So they went up to the same place. Grandfather took the sword and handed him the watch. He threw up the sword. The sword flew for six hours and fell in the same place. Grandfather took the watch in his hands and said, "Now then, Ivan, you toss the sword now and we'll see what happens."

Ivan threw it. Six hours passed and there was no sword. Seven, then eight hours passed—still no sword. Grandfather spoke up: "Well, Ivan, misfortune is near. If the sword doesn't fall by nine hours, I'll no longer be alive, and you will perish together with me."

Suddenly eight and a half hours passed and then nine, and the sword fell. Grandfather said, "Well, Ivan Tsarevich, I won't let you throw my sword any more. You know that I can't live more than three hours without seeing it, as my soul is in the sword, just as Koshchei's is in his, and that's why I can't live without my sword. My sword will not cut through Koshchei's sword, but Koshchei's sword won't cut through mine either. So now let's go home. And I'll tell you everything, how to ride to Koshchei's for your Elena the Beautiful. Now you have one and a half times the strength of Koshchei."

So they came home, sat down at the table, and Grandfather began speaking to him.

> Listen, Ivan Tsarevich, I'm going to give you my very own horse, one that neither a bullet can touch nor fire burn. This horse won't drown in water and won't burn in fire. And he will get you to Koshchei the Deathless himself. And in addition, I'm giving you my sword. And when you gallop up to Koshchei the Deathless, he will become furious with you and say, "Who are you, young man?" And you answer him, "Do you remember how once you sealed me up in a nutshell and threw me into the open steppe?" He will turn to take a look, and you leap down from the horse and strike him with your sword—only not mine but yours. When you hit him, then servants will shout from one side, "Hit him again, dog." And you say, "No, we in Rus' only strike once." If you were to hit him a second time, he would overcome you, and you'll never ever kill him, and he'll kill you. After that, drive your sword into the ground with all your might, and the sword will disappear through the earth, and then pieces of it will fly. Then jump on your horse, take my sword in your hands, and then twelve mighty bogatyrs will come riding at you, but you'll deal with them easily, only strike with my sword. Yes, when you've killed these bogatyrs, then go up to his castle and there you'll find everything locked up. Beat on these locks with my sword and go seek out your Elena the Beautiful. When you reach Elena the Beautiful, bring her here. I know that right now she's very weak, but I'll right her. And you'll have to live another three years here and not sleep with her, because she's very weak. And now you're very strong, and it must be that's she's strong too.

(Now that's a misfortune for Ivan!) Then right away the old man led him out onto the porch and the sword and the horse already stood there next to it. "So mount up and ride off, but remember what I have told you."

And Ivan had no sooner sat on the horse than it tore off. And he saw Koshchei the Deathless sitting there cursing a blue streak. And his horse ran like nothing before. And Koshchei the Deathless began raising up a lake, wishing to drown him with water. The horse ran even more powerfully. Koshchei began firing, hacking, shooting. But nothing touched the horse. Ivan galloped up to Koshchei the Deathless himself and stood there opposite him. Then Koshchei shouted out, "Who are you riding like that, you smart aleck, and you stand against me! Tell me, who ever are you?"

He jumped down from the horse and pointed with his hand to the steppe. "Do you remember how you locked me up in a nut?" (He pointed with his hand in the direction). "And then you threw me there into the open steppe?"

Koshchei turned and looked into the open steppe. And at that very moment, Ivan Tsarevich leapt down from his horse and struck him with his sword and sliced him in two. The servants shouted out, "Hit him again, the dog, another time!" He answered, "No, we in Rus' only strike once."

He swung and threw the sword into the earth. The sword disappeared through the earth, and pieces of Koshchei the Deathless just flew off there. So he leapt onto his horse and took Grandfather's sword in his hands. He looked, and suddenly twelve bogatyrs rode out. Not an hour passed before Ivan Tsarevich had destroyed these twelve bogatyrs. He galloped up to Koshchei the Deathless's castle, leapt down from his horse, tied her up, and went up to the first door. He looked: A heavy lock hung on it. He struck it with his sword, opened the first, then the second, and finally the third door. He went into the dining room of Koshchei the Deathless, where he always drank and ate. He looked. On the table was a festive tablecloth, and on it were such foods as you could only imagine. Now he really wanted to eat! He sat down at the table and thought, "Where can my beautiful Elena be now?"

And then he casually looked under the table and saw a human head beneath the table on the floor—only the head was visible. So then he asked, "What sort of person are you? Tell me, are you alive?" The head thought a little and said, "I am Elena the Beautiful, but what sort of man are you, and why did you come here? Go away before Koshchei the Deathless comes."

"I am Ivan Tsarevich, Elena the Beautiful, and I've come for you, and now I'll take you, and there'll be no more mention of Koshchei the Deathless. I've killed him, so there's no reason to think any more about him."

"If that's so, Ivan Tsarevich, and you have come after me, let me tell you this. For seven years I have sat here with Koshchei the Deathless, and every day he asked me to marry him, but I fought him off with my talisman so that he couldn't even approach me. And so I've lived here for seven years, and in these seven years he has covered me over with seven floor layers, but somehow get me out. And today he was going to lay down an eighth layer, and I would have died. He fed me on nothing but bones."

Ivan said, "Never mind, Elena the Beautiful, I'll hack out all the floors, but I'll get you out alive."

And she said, "No, Ivan Tsarevich, I can't be brought out from the shaking. I'll die. So you go along this wall and push on a button there that is like a pin. Press it and a door will open. When you have opened the door, you'll see there so many keys that you can't count them all. And then you take these keys and sort them and try all the doors and remove the floor levels. Only then will I come out safely."

He immediately stood up and felt with his hand along the wall, found the button, and pressed it. The door opened. He looked, and there were truly so many keys you couldn't count them. He took the keys and began trying them to the locks. He kept trying them, and he opened all seven layers. When he had opened them, and raised them up, he had opened all seven layers. So when he had opened them, Elena the Beautiful came out of there, but she was so sickly that she could scarcely stand up. He said, did Ivan Tsarevich, "Well now, let's go, Elena the Beautiful, I'll sit you on my horse, and we shall go to Grandfather, and there you'll get well."

So they got on the horse and set off for Grandfather's house. They got there. When Grandfather saw that Ivan Tsarevich had brought Elena the Beautiful, he went out onto the porch and said, "Oh, how weak you are, Elena the Beautiful. But all right, you will live here with me for three years and you will get well."

Then he spoke to Ivan Tsarevich, "So now then, Ivan Tsarevich, when you came upon Elena the Beautiful, you didn't know her. And when you saw her true beauty and burned up her costume, you hadn't managed to sleep with her, but now you are forbidden to sleep with her for three years until I have brought her the strength that she is going to need."

And then he took her by the hand and led her into that same room. "So, Elena the Beautiful, you can bake and cook for me and Ivan Tsarevich, and also for yourself, and that will be your only work. And each year I will pay you a salary for this."

She didn't refuse, of course. So she spent a year. And that day arrived when she had finished the first year. So they sat down to eat dinner, and Grandfather in the same fashion brought out a bottle and said, "So now this is your salary for one year, Elena the Beautiful, drink it."

She said, "What do you mean, Grandfather, since birth I have never drunk. How am I to drink an entire bottle?" And he said to her, "Drink it, Elena the Beautiful, it's for your own good." So then she drank it all.

After dinner Grandfather said, "So now then, children, let us go and look at my sword. Can an old man still throw it? Do I still have the strength I had in the past?" So they came to the sword. And so Grandfather took the sword and gave his watch to Ivan Tsarevich. Then he threw the sword. They stood there six hours, and the sword fell in the same place.

"Well, obviously, the old man has the same strength as before. But you, Elena the Beautiful, can you throw it as far?"

She grasped hold of the sword and raised it up chest-high. But she couldn't throw it, even if she did raise it up. "All right, let's go, and you, Ivan Tsarevich, I won't give you my sword because it would fly for nine hours and that's too long for us to wait. And maybe it would fly even longer, and that would be my death." (He already knows, he was once in such a pickle!) So then they came home.

And Grandfather spoke, "Now then, Elena the Beautiful, how do you feel? Have you gotten a little bit better?"

"Yes, Grandfather, I am getting better now."

"Now then, live here just two more years and you'll be completely fit."

So she spent the second year. When they sat down to dine, Grandfather brought out two more bottles and said, "Here you are, Elena the Beautiful, your salary for the year. Drink up!" Well, she drank it. Then Grandfather said, "Now then, let's go into the steppe to look at my sword."

They came, of course, into the steppe. Grandfather took his sword, and handed Ivan Tsarevich his watch. He threw it up. The sword flew for six hours and fell again in its old place. "Grandfather's strength is just as it was of old."

So then Grandfather said, "So now then, Elena the Beautiful, throw up my sword." She took the sword, raised it, and threw it up. The sword flew for three hours. Then Grandfather said, "Now then, good, live with me one more year and you'll be completely well."

And right away they set off home. She took up her old responsibility, and the third year passed quickly. So again they sat down to eat dinner, and this time Grandfather brought out three bottles: "Here, Elena the Beautiful, drink." But he didn't give any to Ivan Tsarevich; he already had had enough of it. So she didn't refuse. She drank that wine. After dinner Grandfather said, "So now then, let's go once more and look at my sword, but this will be the last time."

So they set off for the steppe. Grandfather went up to his sword and threw it up. The sword flew six hours and fell in its former place. Then Elena the Beautiful took this sword and threw it. The sword flew six hours. Grandfather said, "So, Elena the Beautiful, you have the same strength as I have, but Ivan Tsarevich has half again as much. Now you can live with him and sleep with him and live as you wish."

So all went away from that place. Ivan Tsarevich took Elena the Beautiful by the hand, and they went to Grandfather's house. Again Grandfather spoke, "So, if you should have children, they will be just like you, Ivan Tsarevich, strong."

So they lived with Grandfather a week. But Ivan Tsarevich got bored. He began to long for his father and mother and also for his brothers. Why, he hadn't been home for ten years, and he was interested in finding out who would get the tsardom or who had got it. Then Ivan Tsarevich went up to Grandfather and said, "What about my going to my homeland, Grandfather, to see my relatives? I haven't been there for ten years, as you yourself know."

Grandfather said, "Well now then, what is to be done? Go! I'll give you a horse. And I'll give it with the condition that if you wish to come back, then feed the horse. But if you aren't coming back, then don't feed it and immediately send it back here." (Maybe Grandfather will be the horse himself, wait and find out. Maybe he rode to Koshchei the Deathless on Grandfather because after that he asked nothing at all about the matter.)

Then Ivan Tsarevich remembered his father-in-law's order that he was to bring his daughter back with him. Once more he had to ask Grandfather for permission. "So now then, Grandfather, tell me one more thing. I ask you, when I was at my father-in-law's, he said to me 'If you get Elena the Beautiful, then come and visit us.' Can we not stop by to visit him?" Then Grandfather said, "Well, what's to be done? If he ordered it, then let

Elena the Beautiful visit her father and her mother, but for no longer than four hours." (Such a time limit he gave!) Just so.

Then Ivan Tsarevich thanked Grandfather, as did Elena the Beautiful. And they went out into the yard, where the horse stood. He placed Elena the Beautiful on the horse, leapt on it himself, and rode off. The moment they got on, they were at his father-in-law's. When her mother saw her son-in-law and daughter, she ran out onto the porch and began crying and kissing them both. Then she led them into the house. Yes, she led them into the house, where her father met them, and he began embracing them with tears, and caressed his son-in-law and daughter. Then they all sat down at the table. Then he said to his old woman, "Well, old woman, bring to the table whatever we have; bring out everything."

And so she brought it all out—eat what ever you see! When they had eaten, the father-in-law said, "Well, now tell me, Ivan Tsarevich, how did you get Elena the Beautiful?" And he answered, "Listen, Father, if I were to tell you everything about how I got Elena the Beautiful, it would take us a very long time, and Grandfather-eagle ordered us not to remain for long; that was the condition under which he gave the horse."

"I know, Ivan Tsarevich, I am an eagle. So then he was the one who helped you?"

"Yes, it was he."

Then Ivan told him something in brief, how the whole business had gone. His father-in-law said, "Well all right, you're quite a lad, Ivan Tsarevich, live happily with my daughter, and off you go. I had thought you might spend a year with me, but if that's what Grandfather said, then go."

They said farewell to Father and Mother, got on the horse, and rode off. And they had just set off when they were already in his country; not a day passed. When Koshchei the Deathless had carried off Elena the Beautiful, that carpet, which had sung and danced—and also the River Neva and the ducks and drakes—all had been destroyed. And the carpet lay motionless. But when Ivan Tsarevich and Elena the Beautiful came to his country, the carpet again began dancing and playing, and once more the River Neva began flowing. Everything was just as it had been. And the people became happy. Yes, while Elena the Beautiful hadn't been in that country, the whole tsardom had been in deep sorrow. And the time had run out. And the father and tsar was near death, just waiting until Ivan Tsarevich came. And just at that time on that day he had decided to transfer the throne to his oldest son. But when Elena the Beautiful came, the tsar immediately became cheerful, and throughout the whole tsardom smells and odors burst forth. And the people became cheerful, even though no one knew yet that they had come. So then, when he and Elena the Beautiful entered the tsardom, all the rooms shook and the floors crackled, and all the people looked at them and were amazed. They were like two mighty bogatyrs. When Ivan Tsarevich went into the hall where the guests and his brothers were sitting, his father and mother threw themselves at their necks and really rejoiced. Then the father said to his eldest son Vasilii, "Well, Vasia, whatever you like, but now you will have to give way, since Ivan Tsarevich has come, and he is to rule the throne."

Vasilii didn't protest and left the royal place, and Ivan Tsarevich sat in his place. Then Vania remembered about the horse. When Ivan Tsarevich had sat at the table with his Elena the Beautiful, he remembered and said, "Listen, Elena the Beautiful, you and I have totally forgotten Grandfather's instruction. Once we decided to remain, we have to go and let the horse loose." So then they ran out into the yard, untied the horse, and said, "Well, our dear little horse, thank you very much for bringing us to the tsardom, and tell Grandfather for us thank you very, very much for helping us in everything."

And then the horse disappeared from sight. They came back, sat in their places, and their father and brothers began questioning him: "You let your horse go, Ivan Tsarevich, but with us you ought to have fed him first, watered him just like you eat and drink. They would have watered and fed you." And he answered, "I was forbidden to keep him any longer. I had to fulfill Grandfather's instruction." Then his father said, "I nonetheless will dare to ask, my son, how did you get Elena the Beautiful?"

Ivan began telling him, what happened to him, how he was locked up in a nut, how Grandfather helped him, and how he fought with Koshchei—he told him everything that had happened. They all listened, and many even cried at his adventures. (We won't repeat all this; I never repeat what has already been told.) So then, Ivan Tsarevich received the throne and all rejoiced that Ivan Tsarevich became tsar.

And they began living and were so into deep old age.

And here's the end.

(SUS 302_1 + 402)

3

ISLAND OF GOLD

M. M. Korguev

In no certain tsardom, in no certain land, there lived and dwelt a well-to-do peasant, and for a long time he had had no children. Later he and his wife were no longer young, and a son was born to them. When the son was born, at first the mother loved him very much and cared for him and caressed him, and brought him up as best possible. And the father even more so. When the boy began growing, he learned to read and write, but when he was about thirteen, his mother stopped loving him. And she didn't love him so much as she began hating him, and she said to her husband, "Send the son off wherever you like; I can't stand the sight of him any more. Otherwise I'll simply collapse and end my life." And she began harassing her husband. Finally, he couldn't take any more, and he said to his son, "Well, my son, let's go out hunting." He answered, "Yes, Papa, let's."

They took some things to eat and set off in a boat to an island. This was a really marvelous island, and he [the father] didn't know what sort of island it was. When they had arrived on their boat at the island, he said to his son, "We'll walk along the shore, only I'll go in one direction, and you go in the other." They went up a mountain, of course, and the son took his rifle and his father took his, and they set off, one in one direction and the other in the other direction. The son didn't know any of the evil thinking in his father and what had occurred with his mother and father. He hadn't been in on it. It had all taken place secretly.

So. Now he walked back a little and saw his father running toward the boat. He took the boat and was off. He left his son alone on the island. When he had run up to that place, where the boat had been moored, he saw a basket hanging on a fir tree, but all trace of the boat had gone cold. So then, of course, he started crying and he said, "Well, probably my parents have abandoned me here to perish. Probably I am alone on this island.

I do have a small amount of supplies, but nevertheless with these supplies I won't live."

It was already approaching evening, and he didn't dare go away from the shore, even though he had his rifle. Twilight came, and then there was such a terrifying roar on that island that it was difficult to stand upright. He became afraid. "Well now, I'll probably perish." And he sought out a thick tree and began climbing up this tree. He climbed up in the tree, and the groaning, and shouts, and racket on the island continued until morning itself. In the morning it became somewhat quieter. But nobody came to him. When it was already completely daylight, he began going down the tree. "Well, in any case I'll have to get down this tree."

When he had climbed down the tree, he thought: "What am I to do now?" He thought for a little: "I'll have a bite to eat, and then I'll go around this island. Whatever that groaning and roaring, anyway I was brought to this island to perish."

Meanwhile all was peaceful. So he decided to go up that high mountain. When he had climbed up this tall mountain, he walked over a great plain. And he saw two devils fighting there, not groaning. But in the night they groaned; it was a devil fighting with a forest spirit. They were cousins, dividing their father's possession, a magic mirror, and they had been fighting over it for a hundred years. But they couldn't divide it equally because it was in one piece. Vaniusha thought about it: "I need to get up close."

And so he went up really close. But he didn't know what sort of people they were. When the forest spirit saw him, he shouted out, "Vaniusha, save me from my cousin and I'll give you a mountain of gold!" And in answer to that the devil shouted, "Vaniusha, save me, and you and I will divide father's capital and mine too—only save me!"

Then he thought, but he didn't know which one to shoot, which one he might need. And he decided to shoot that forest spirit, who had promised him a mountain of gold. So Vaniusha aimed his rifle, and the mighty bullet lay in the chest of the forest spirit. The spirit fell down dead, and right away that devil came up to him: "Well, Vania, good lad, you figured out which one to shoot. Now you will be happy. And now go back to where you were, where your father brought you. You have supplies to last you through some days, and then you will have everything you could only wish for."

The little devil disappeared, and Vaniusha set off for that place where his father had brought him. He opened his satchel and began eating. Just so. When he had eaten, he lay down to sleep and slept the whole day through until evening. He didn't hear a thing. When evening came, of course, it was all quiet on the island. Vaniusha laid a fire, a bonfire, and said, "Well, now I've nothing to fear. I have a comrade on this island who has promised to pay me all this."

So he lit the fire, surrounded himself with branches to keep the wind out, and lay down to sleep peacefully, not thinking about another thing. When it was already light, he thought, "My comrade isn't here. There's no answer, and whether I'll live here or not, I don't know." So then he lay there a little longer and then he looked back and he saw from the rear a large palace standing there, with a garden around it, and he set off for that palace. He went into the palace, and there on the tables was food, a lot of it, wherever you looked—just sit down and eat. Ivan sat down at the table, ate with joy, and lay down to rest on a divan.

So then he lay there for a little, and so the doors opened and in came that same comrade, the one he had saved. It was the devil himself. And the devil said to him, "Greetings, Vania."

"Greetings, greetings. I don't know your name."

"Call me Imp. I am the devil himself, the master of this island. There were two of us, but the other is no more." He asked, "Well then, Vania, how are you going to live now? Do you have food, and how is the lodging or merriment, how are you thinking about yourself—will you be able to live here or not?"

Yes. So then he answered, "Live here, comrade-friend, I can, but in fact it's boring living on this uninhabited island alone. You know yourself that it's very boring, because there's no one here, not even an animal, not a dog or a cat!"

"Well, now then, my friend, if that's what's the matter, then you need a comrade, and we can fix that. So what do you desire? Just tell me. Maybe you want to get married? What do you think, are you young or not? You could get married. If you want to get married, whatever you decide, I'll marry you off and help you in any way you want. If you wish, I'll marry you to some tsarevna or to a princess, wherever you like, and you will live happily."

"But my friend, since I am only seventeen years old, is it time for me to get married?"

"Well, you can get married, as it be. I'll marry you to a certain tsarevna and make you a gold boat in which you can sail around this sea. Only never leave me and you will be happy."

Then the little devil went away, and Ivan lay down to sleep until morning. When Ivan woke up, he saw a beautiful girl walking about the room, so beautiful that you couldn't look straight at her. When Ivan saw the girl, he ran up to her, of course, and took her by the hands. And he kissed her and led her into his own room. The beautiful maiden looked straight at him and said, "Yes, in my own tsardom I was the tsar's daughter, and then one night I turned up on some island or other married to a young man. And now there's nothing more to be done. You have to live."

So then they went into the buffet and sat down at a rich table and began eating. And suddenly his friend came in. He came in and said: "Well, Vania, now I see that you are married and I have provided you with everything, so live and you know well how to, only don't tell your wife the whole truth."

So he lived an entire year with this tsarevna, but he didn't know from which land she was, because this was all unknown. Then one splendid day he took his rifle and set off walking about the island just for the pleasure of it, but in fact to see whether he couldn't find some sort of game. In the beginning he was walking through some large, dense forest, and then he came out on a little hill, and he climbed up on this hill. As he was going about this little hill and on its sides, the whole place didn't seem very nice to him, just mountains and big ravines. He kept on walking and walking on. And then on one side he caught sight of a door, like a cave. A cave and something like a door. Just so. Then Ivan went up to that door, opened it, and looked in, and in that room sat an old woman. He began asking her: "Tell me, Granny, have you been living for a long time on this island? I haven't seen you, although I haven't been living here long, and maybe I haven't been in these parts."

"Yes, young man, I've lived here for a very long time. I am a merchant's daughter, who was kidnapped. And then my husband died, and I remained here alone. This husband is the very one whom you shot. Now listen, Vania, and I'll tell you something: The devil still hasn't given you what he promised. You ask him, but without it you won't be able to live on the island. He promised you everything that you wanted, and he should give it to you."

"I don't know what, Granny. At the moment I'm living well. He married me off, I'm living with my young wife, and I have everything. What I should ask for more, Granny, I don't know."

"Here's what, Vania, I'll instruct you, for without it, it will be bad for you on this island. Ask that magic mirror of him, the one they were fighting over, my husband and the devil. And with that mirror you will have everything that you wish. You can look in it, and it will tell you. And he should give it to you because he promised."

Then Vania said, “And if he gives it over, then I’ll ask something of it.”

“Well, of course, he will give it to you because he promised.”

So Ivan and the granny said good-bye, and he set off home. He came home to his wife, of course. They ate supper and tumbled off to bed. In the morning they got up, drank tea, and set off sailing on the golden boat. They came home, of course, ate dinner, and then he said, “I wonder why my friend hasn’t been here for so long.”

Suddenly out of nowhere he appeared. “Well now then, Vania, how have you been getting along?”

“Oh, all right. I’m living well, but listen, I’ll explain everything to you, and you most likely won’t refuse me.”

“Of course I won’t refuse.”

“Then let me tell you. Listen, my friend, you promised me that favorite thing, the one you and your cousin were fighting over, that magic mirror. Give it to me, it may be needed.”

Just so. Then he said to him: “All right, Vania, I’ll hand it over—only you don’t know how to handle it.”

“Why not?”

“Simply so. And you still don’t know about it, someone on the island probably told you because you have asked me for it. And you have nothing to do with that mirror on the island. Why? Because you have everything. If you need something, you will have everything. If you need your relatives, tell me and I’ll fetch them here.”

“No, at the moment I don’t need them.” That was because he was angry with his mother and father for abandoning him on this island. “So now, my friend, you don’t want to hand over that mirror to me, but you promised; you said you’d give me everything that I wanted. Now I wish for it, but you don’t want to, you are refusing my request.”

“All right, Vania.” So then he immediately unbuttoned his pocket and drew the mirror out of the pocket. “But now, Vania, know how to handle it, and afterwards don’t be angry with me for what happens. You know, Vania, it seems you saw with your own eyes how my cousin and I fought a hundred years, so it’s worth something. Well, remember and always keep it with you. Don’t leave it for a minute away from you.”

So Ivan said, “All right.”

Then the devil left him. So Ivan got the mirror and kept it with him all the time, day and night. He lay down to sleep, and put it away, he didn’t tell his wife about this mirror. And she didn’t know.

Yes. Then one splendid time he went off into the woods, and she—even though she was living well, of course—she also went into the woods. She was interested in finding out what sort of island it was. She also went among the steep mountains, the same ones he had walked among. And she saw that same cell that he had gone into. So then she went into that cell, and there she saw the old granny sitting there.

"Oh, my beauty, you've been living here for two years and you haven't once dropped by to see me. You are late, my dear."

"Granny, I didn't know where you lived. I accidentally chanced upon your cell and found out that you are here, and so here I came."

> Oh, I've been living here. Do you know how long I've been on this island? No less than fifty years. And then it happened that your husband came to this island, and he killed my husband and I'm left alone. And I don't know how to get to the island on which I lived. And although I probably have no more kin, I would still like to get back to my native city. I wasn't there when you were born, my beauty, but I know from which town you are, and I lived there too. And I know from which tsardom you are, because all that is known to me. So now tell me, my beauty, which of the two will you choose: Do you wish to live here with your husband, or do you wish to see your family and go back to your land and also take me out of here?

She answered her: "I would live here and it would be fine, but I long for my family. I would very much like to see them."

"But how do you think? Do you want your husband or not, or do you think that you can leave him here?"

"Granny, I don't know what to say to you. He is still young and hasn't been anywhere, and he knows nothing. I am accustomed to my cities and tsardom, and he knows nothing. So I would like to leave him here just to get to my country. So now you have it!"

"So now listen, Anastasia Tsarevna, I know you on account of your father. Your husband has this certain thing: He has a magic mirror. Watch out for it, and when he leaves it, take it and bring it here to me. And do whatever you want with your husband. We'll leave him here and fly to your country. But only if you bring it here to me."

So Anastasia and the old granny said good-bye, and she went home. Her husband was already at home, waiting for her to see where she had gone. So he asked, "So, where were you, my beautiful Anastasia?"

"I was out walking about the island, and I got lost, but finally I came back."

"Well, all right, never mind, let's have something to eat."

She laid the table, and they sat down to eat. They ate, of course, the day passed, and they lay down to sleep.

And so she started keeping an eye out for that mirror to see where her husband hid it. She kept looking and looking. And he lay down to sleep, and then she saw how he took out the mirror and placed it on the shelf. When they had lain down to sleep, then in the morning they got up from their sleep, and he went in the morning as was his custom into the woods, and he completely forgot it on the shelf. And so she immediately took that mirror and at that moment set off to that granny. When she had brought her the mirror, the granny immediately took it in her hands, gazed in it, and thought, "Let you immediately take me and the tsarevna to that tsardom in which we lived."

And then later she asked her, "And what do you want to do with your husband now?"

"Oh, I don't know."

"Here's what I think. Even though your husband is perhaps not the cause, I'll take revenge on the both of them because together they killed my husband. That's what I think. We'll drown this island with water, and let him and the devil perish."

So the old woman looked in the mirror and thought, and that's what was done. Suddenly out of nowhere the water poured forth, there was a banging and shouting and crackling, and the island began sinking beneath the water. Ivan saw that the water was running all over, and he began climbing up the mountain. Ivan kept on running, but the water was right behind him. And he climbed to the top of this high mountain, and there was no higher one. On the mountain there stood a stone somewhat higher than the mountain. And suddenly the water came halfway up the stone. Ivan climbed up on the stone and stood on it, while all around the island was water. And he thought, "Probably I'm done for!" When Ivan had climbed up on the stone, water was all around it and it was half way up it. Then he started crying, "Well, I'm done for, and somewhere my friend is perishing too."

Suddenly he saw a cat swimming toward the stone. The cat swam up, climbed out on the stone, and said,

> Well, Ivan, you didn't keep that mirror I gave you for long; I said you wouldn't be able to hold on to it. So now death has come to both of us. Well

> so be it! Now I know who did this. It was my cousin's wife who did it. And we shall have far to go to search for her. She told you and now your wife. Now do you know what? A ship will come sailing by. You ask to get on that ship and they'll take you, only they won't take me. And you say, "If you are going to take me, then take my cat too, and if you won't take my cat, then don't take me either." They'll take you and thus we won't perish there if they take us.

So they waited a little and suddenly up came a ship. Vania began waving a piece of cloth, and the ship began approaching. The ship came up, and the crew gave him a rope ladder.

"Come on board!"

So he went on board and after him came the cat. The captain said, "No, no, we won't take the cat, it's such a monster."

"Listen, comrades, if you take me, then the cat, too. And if you don't take the cat, then you won't take me."

Then the captain thought for a moment: "All right then, the devil take it!"

So they went on board the ship. And when they had boarded the ship, the captain came up to him: "Well, my friend, tell me who you are and how you happened to be on that stone."

He answered, "Of course. My name is Ivan, and I happened to be on that stone by accident. It was an island, but then there was a flood and it covered the island with water. And that's how I happened to be on the stone."

"Now tell me what is your specialty, what work can you do, or what trade do you desire?"

And then the cat whispered to him, "Take to being a cook; they don't have a cook and I'll cook everything that you need for you."

So then he said, "It's true, I don't know any trade, but in the past I was a cook and I would be one again—that's my specialty."

Then the captain: "That's very good that you know how to cook. It just so happens that we haven't had a cook for these three days because our chef died, so you can become the cook." The captain also asked, "What wages do you want?"

The devil whispered to Ivan, "Don't bargain with him. We have money enough. Say 'whatever you give will be fine.'"

"So here is your kitchen, here are the pots and plates and tea cups, forks, spoons, and everything else on earth. Here's the pantry where the supplies are kept. Now then let's go on. Here are your dinner, tea, and breakfast—three times a day—and all the rest, as you wish it."

Ivan, of course, took it on and he thought, "How will I cook? The devil knows because I've rarely seen a pot before my very eyes."

And the devil whispered to him, "What are you thinking? You won't have to do any cooking here; all is at the ready. When they ask for tea, just tap with the teaspoon, or if they ask for breakfast, just the same. And when they order dinner, strike with a jar, and all will be ready—only just pour."

So then a month passed, two and then three, and soon they had been sailing for half a year. And Ivan kept on at his work. You see, all the sailors, and the captain, and the quartermaster all praised Ivan and thanked him for his work, saying that he was cooking very well.

And then they sailed into that city where the tsarevna and the old woman were. So they sailed in, came up to the quay. And suddenly twelve ships also docked at the quay. And all these captains, when they had docked, got together to talk things over with each other. And finally it got to cooks, who had what kind of cook and how much he was paid. And it came to the captain on whose boat Ivan worked. The captain began speaking: "I have this cook, and rarely are such cooks as he to be found because out of little or nothing he can make a real repast."

So all these captains agreed that they should order their cooks to make what each could. The first did three, the second six, and the third nine. But more than twelve dishes not a single cook could prepare. So Ivan's turn came. The captain came to him: "Listen, Vania, how many dishes can you make for a dinner?"

"I don't know."

And the cat whispered to him, "Tell him we'll make him one of sixteen."

"That's the lad. You do it, and you'll exceed all the other cooks. Now tell me, how much money do you need and what should be bought?"

Then the cat said to him:

> Now listen, Vania, take three rubles from him and go shopping; take a basket but don't leave me behind. You and I will go into a shop, and I'll hop onto a shelf and break a decanter. They'll beat me, but you say, "No, don't beat my cat—I'll pay whatever it costs." They'll say, "It costs a ruble." Then give them a ruble and say, "Here, let me collect the glass in my basket." Then collect it, leave the shop, and we'll go into another shop, and in the same way I'll make my way onto a shelf and push off another decanter. Again they'll beat me and chase me away. In the same way you say, "No, don't beat it, I'll pay." And then you collect the glass and leave the shop. And then we'll go into a third shop, and I'll make my way onto the very top shelf and toss down a crystal

dish. They'll beat me and chase me out. You say, "No, don't beat it." Pay, collect up all the glass yourself, and leave the shop. Then we'll come back onto the ship and cook.

So then Ivan said to the master, "Well, I need three rubles."

"And what can you buy for three rubles?

"I don't need any more."

The captain gave him the money, and he and the cat set off for the town together. So then they went into the first shop. The cat leapt up onto a shelf, as if after a mouse, and dropped a glass decanter off it. When the shop assistants saw such a naughty deed, they gave chase, beating and cursing the cat. And he saw it and said, "No, comrades, don't you beat my cat. I'll pay whatever is necessary, and I'll even collect the broken glass."

The assistants said, "It'll be a ruble."

He handed it over and gathered up the glass and left the shop. He went to the second. He entered the second and just the same: The cat dropped a glass bottle. The assistants began cursing and chasing after it, and they said, "What a dirty trick it played on us here!"

He said, "Don't beat my cat and I'll pay whatever is necessary."

The assistants answered, "Give us the money."

He gave it to them, gathered up the glass, and went out of the shop. And so now he goes to the third shop. The cat made its way onto the very top shelf, and threw down a dish. So those assistants got mad and started chasing it.

"You, comrades, don't beat my cat. I'll pay. How much does it cost?"

They answered, "A ruble."

He paid, gathered up the glass, and left the shop. And so they walked along and the cat said to him, "So now we've bought everything that we need for dinner, we have everything on the ship. Do you think, Ivanushko, that for three rubles you could buy so little? We can now feed all twelve boats. Let them come to us. We can feed them, and there will be some left over, but only the twelve captains are coming."

So he came to the boat, and the captain asked him, "Well, Vania, did you buy up everything?"

"Yes, we bought it all. Come and see what I bought."

The captain came over and looked in his pantry, and he just couldn't take his eyes off it. "Well, you did very well in your purchasing, but how could you buy up all this?"

And the cat whispered to him, "Don't say anything right now; just answer a few words."

So then he said, "Sir Captain, I'll tell you about all this later on, but I don't have time right now. I have a lot of work to do to prepare dinner."

And he said to the cat, "Now, my friend, how do we do this? You tell me, as I don't know anything about this business."

And the cat said to him, "Ivan, don't you fret about it. Just go to the frying pan, bang on the jar, and pour it out for the first dish. And then come, and all will be prepared for the various dishes. You just serve them out and carry them out, and I'll worry about all the rest."

So then the captains began gathering, as they had agreed, and he was ready to serve all the captains. Then the captain said, "Well, Vania, serve us our dinners." So he went up to the frying pan, struck on the jar, and thus produced the first dish. And then he continued on further. He carried out all, up to twelve, and then they asked Ivan, "How many more can you produce?"

He answered, "I can produce up to sixteen, but for the time being I can't produce more. I haven't been ordered to."

So Ivan produced all up to the sixteen. He finished the dinners. Yes. Afterward the captains ordered Vania to go into the cabin. Then he came into the cabin, and the captains thanked him and gave him gifts. The cat had already said to him, "Don't take those gifts; only take a letter of praise." So when he came and the captains began presenting him with various gifts, he said, "No, comrades, I don't need your gifts, but write me a letter of praise so that I can at any time go wherever I like as a cook. That would be better for me."

So the captains agreed to that and wrote him a letter of praise. "Here, Vania, as you wished." He took it and went back to the cat. When all the guests had departed, the captain came to Vania and said, "How much money do you need, Vania? I'll release you to go into the city. You can celebrate for three days."

Before that the cat had told him, "Take only sixty rubles, we don't need more." So the captain gave him sixty rubles. Vania took the money, and he and the cat left the ship. So then they walked about the city. The cat said to him, "Well, Vania, now let's go into a shop. We'll buy an accordion, which will cost fifty five rubles."

So they came into the shop, but at that instant the cat turned into Ivan and Ivan became a cat. Yes. So they came into the shop. And he said to the shop assistant, "Show me an accordion." The assistant began pulling whichever ones he had, and gave the various prices. And the prices he quoted were from fifty rubles to a thousand rubles. "No," he said, "I don't need such accordions. I need one for sixty rubles."

He left that shop and went into a second, and again he asked the assistant, "Assistant, show me accordions and give the prices." Again the assistant pulled out the accordions and said the prices: "We have them at prices from one hundred fifty to two hundred fifty." Then the devil said, "No, I don't need any such accordions."

They went into a third shop. And they ordered them to pull out an accordion. He selected an accordion for sixty-five rubles, but he had only about sixty and it cost sixty-five. So he said to the assistant, "Now then, give it to me for sixty rubles and I'll buy it."

"No, we haven't any such prices so as to give it to you for sixty. It costs sixty-five."

"Well then let me play it and then I'll think about it and maybe I'll buy it."

But the devil already knew. The assistant let him. The devil took the accordion and began playing. He played so well that all the assistants were dancing, and all the dishes and all the assistants and all the accordions that were in the shop also started playing. The devil played for a little bit and finished. And he said to the assistant, "Well, give it to me for sixty."

"Oh, all right. Since you played so well, here, take it."

The devil took the accordion and left the shop, with the cat close behind. As they went about the town, the cat said to Ivan, "Now I'll start playing." And there was such an audience in the city that it was difficult to pass through. When the devil began playing, all the people began dancing, and the horses, and the cars stopped—everything came to a halt. No one went anywhere; they all just danced. Then they found out that he was such a fine player, and they forbade him so that the people wouldn't stand on the boardwalks and dance. They forbade him to play any more or he would be punished. The devil stopped playing. "Well, let's go on farther. And then they're going to throw us into such a pit that we won't be able to get out of it. But anyway, we'll get out. When they throw us into the pit, we'll nonetheless have to go on, and there we'll search out what we came for."

So they went on a little farther, and again the devil began to play. When he started playing, the public came to a halt, and the horses and automobiles. Then a troop of soldiers came, took and led him and the cat to that pit. When they had led him there and pushed him into that pit, the devil said, "Well, Ivan, now we are here and we have to find some sort of miracle, then this business will be fine." So then the devil turned him back into Ivan, and he began running about the pit as a cat. He ran for a long time about that pit, found nothing. And then somehow he found a rat he needed, and he brought it to Ivan. He brought it and said, "Well, rat, do this little service for me. You have many mice, rat, and then I'll let you go."

The rat thought about it a little. "Then you let me go, and I'll serve as you wish."

"No, you summon your mice and rats, and then when you have fulfilled everything, I'll let you go. Don't be afraid—I won't do you any harm."

The rat immediately ordered the mice, and also the rats, to come running out. An enormous number of mice and rats gathered, but one of them was senior to the others. They all shouted in one voice: "Let our master go. We'll do for you and serve you in whatever you wish."

So then Ivan said to the mice, "Well, lads (and the devil had already told him in advance), you gnaw through three little walls, and there is a small room, and in it an old woman, and she has a small mirror. And she keeps it under her pillow. And she never sleeps so that it won't get lost. Bring it to me. You have sharp teeth, and you can dig and gnaw through."

The mice and rats all answered, "Well, all right, if it's like that, we'll do it."

And they all ran off to do it. Ivan remained with his cat and the rat. So they began digging at the first walls and the underground. They knew where that old woman was living. And they broke through into the hut where the old woman was lying, although she wasn't sleeping. The rats all at once leapt onto the old woman's neck and chewed her up, and then they brought back the mirror. When they had brought the mirror, they gave it to Ivan, and he let the last rat go and thanked it.

Then Ivan said, "What are we going to do now?"

"Well now we'll get out of this dungeon and then return to the ship, and then we'll find out what we have to do next."

So the devil right away thought, and the pit fell apart and in an instant they turned up in the city. And so that pit fell apart, and they went to the ship peacefully.

When they came onto the ship, the captain asked, "Well, Vania, how was it in and about the city?"

"Well, we had a good time, and what was necessary, I did."

Then the devil said to him, "You tell the captain this: 'Let's reckon up, as I won't be living here anymore. I'll be better off going into the city as a cook.'"

"Well, Vania, you won't survive, but I won't keep you here by force." He counted out his money and handed it over. "Well, Vania, it would have been good if you had lived here longer, but our crew will often remember you now."

"Well after this, I'll cook you one more dinner. We'll all eat together and then I'll leave."

The captain was really pleased.

"And I'll also tell you what I bought in the city and even show you."

He went up to the frying pan and banged with the jar, and the dinner was already ready. He asked the captain to the table, and the captain invited him—Ivan himself, and his cat—to that last dinner. And he came. When he had come, he said, "Well then, captain, I bought an accordion."

"That's fine, Vania. Do you know how to play it?"

"Yes, I know how a little."

"So then, let me ask you to play this accordion."

So he handed the devil the accordion, and the devil instantly changed into a human and sat down to play. When the crew, and also the captain, heard it, they started dancing, and they danced for a full two hours. And the boat rocked from side to side, and you just wouldn't know what was happening on that boat. When he began playing, all the sailors started dancing and they went up to the captain. And so they approached him, some in rowboats, and they danced. When they came out onto the decks, they started dancing without asking anything at all. And the captains came with the sailors onto the decks, but the devil stopped playing and went off. And the devil stopped playing and all came to a halt. When they had all halted, the captain said, "Well, Vania, you are a fine lad. You may be a fine musician; it's a pity only that you are going away."

So then Vania said good-bye to the captain, and the captain stuck his hand in his pocket and gave him another five hundred rubles as a reward. Then he went to his quarters.

And again they asked that captain, "What sort of musician is that you have, and where did you get him? From our very birth we've never heard such playing, and likely we never will."

"That's my former cook who, as you know, prepared a sixteen-course dinner. But now he's leaving me."

"We didn't know that."

"And after all of that, I gave him leave for three full days. He went into the city, bought the accordion, and at our farewell showed me that he's a good player."

And he began saying good-bye to those captains. And the captains gave him what they could in their farewells.

Ivan disappeared from view, together with the cat. They went out onto the quay, and the devil thought, "Now let us right away return to that island, and all will be as it was in former times."

Some hours passed and Ivan was already on that island with the devil, sitting with his wife at the table. And he questioned his wife: "Well, how was your visit at home, my dearest Nastasia. Was it good? Tell me."

She began apologizing and said to him, "Listen, Vania, I'll tell you everything with all my heart, everything that happened here on the island with me." So she related her entire situation, how the old woman had deceived her, and how she had flown back to her own tsardom.

"Oh, all right, my dear, I won't blame you for this, we know about this witch and that she is no longer alive. We got everything from her that we need, and therefore you returned back here together with me. But we were in a dangerous situation; probably you know yourself how you left us on the island."

And she stood there and asked for his forgiveness. "It wasn't I who left you; it was all that old woman, and she thought it all up."

He said, "Well all right, all that will be forgiven."

And then suddenly his friend came. And again they had these conversations.

"Listen, my dear friend, give me my little mirror now." He wasn't even shy in front of his wife.

"No, listen Ivan. I'm not going to give it to you. If you were to lose it a second time, we'd perish, and we wouldn't be able to get it back."

"Listen, my friend, I really need it. I need to fly to see my father, to visit him, and maybe bring him back here. But without it I won't be able to get off the island."

Well, he said, "Well, all right, I'll give it to you but only for a short time while you fly there and back, and then you'll give it back to me so that we don't lose it a second time." So he gave the mirror to him and said, "Well, watch out and don't make any mistakes, Vania. Keep hold of it as best you can. But now you can fly to your father."

So Vania took the mirror, thought deeply that he needed to fly to his father, and immediately he turned up in his village. He went into his father's house. He entered the house and saw his father sitting on a chair. He was sad, and his mother was no longer there. And he couldn't work any longer, and he just kept thinking about his son: "Where is he, the poor lad, probably he is no longer alive."

Ivan's aunt lived with him, and he had this sister. He came right in and greeted them. "Greetings, Father!"

"Greetings, greetings, good lad. Sit down. Where are you from?"

He didn't recognize him, of course. He sat down next to him and began discussing things. "Tell me, old man, how old are you, and did you ever have any children?"

And then he said to him, "Any family? From the very beginning I had but one son, and a wife, who hasn't been alive these past five years. And I myself am seventy years old."

"And what happened to this son—did he die or what?"

The old man gazed into his eyes, and immediately tears formed in his eyes. He wiped away the tears and said to him, "Tell me, my good man, what is your name?"

"My name is Ivan."

> Well then, I'll explain to you about my son. In just such a way when we were living together with the old woman, our son was thirteen years old. In the beginning his mother really loved her son, but then later she became angry with him and then couldn't stand the sight of him. Finally she said to me, "Take your son wherever you like and either kill or drown him, but I won't have him living here any more or else I'll kill myself." And she gave me no peace. So then what was I supposed to do? I came to my son and said, "Well, Vania, let's go out into the woods." We got in a boat and set off, although I pitied him being abandoned on that island where we had gone. That island was the most terrifying and very wondrous, although I myself had never seen much of it but I had heard a little.

His aunt was sitting there weeping and listening.

"Well, go on, Grandfather."

"When I took him to that island, I set off in one direction and he in the other. When I had walked around the island, I got in the boat and rowed away, and he remained there. And since then I don't know where the poor lad perished."

He looked him in the eye. "Well, Grandfather, would you recognize him now if your son came to you?"

He looked at Ivan and said, "How could I recognize him? About twenty years have passed, and he's no longer young—he's more than thirty."

"Now then, Grandfather, you are my father and I am your son, and I've come for you."

The old man stood up, rejoicing. He flung his arms around Ivan's neck and embraced him. He said, "Is it you I see, my Vania?"

"Don't you cry now, Father, and if you desire, then come with me to the island. I live well on the island, everything turned out fortunately for me, but I'll tell you everything about my journey. And you, Auntie, if you wish, I'll take you with me too."

Then he said, "Well, Vania, it's as you wish. I'll go."

And his aunt said, "All right, it's all the same where my brother and I die. Why, we've already lived."

At that moment he drew the mirror out of his pocket and thought deeply that they might instantly turn up on that island. And at that very minute, he and his father and aunt were thrust upon the island. And suddenly his friend came to him.

"Well, Vania, you have brought your father and an old aunt here. And that's fine. Live here now, and it will be fine for your bride because if you go away, she won't be lonely."

Then he said to him, "All that will be fine, only listen, friend. It would be good if you settled people here, and we had a decent city, and we would name it the Island of Gold. Then I would be content."

Well, so then he said, "I'll do that for you, only give me back the little mirror and don't ask for it again. And then everything will be for you." Ivan handed him the mirror, and he said, "Good, now in a day you'll find out what will be."

So the whole day passed. Then on the second day they got up, and on that second day everything was altogether different. Such a city had been made that you couldn't take your eyes off it! There were shops everywhere, and trade, and there was a port, and in that port were various foreign ships, and all kinds of baubles from abroad in this city. Ivan looked, walked about the city, and saw the sign: Island of Gold. There stood a single palace, and the same was written on the palace. So Ivan came home and he went up to his wife: "Well, Wife, you won't have to long for a city anymore or for some tsardom or other. Now you have everything. You can walk or stroll about the city, and when you come home, you know, it will be yours to rule."

So afterwards they lived, and they had children, and they led their lives until old age.

(SUS 518 + 560)

4

IVAN SOSNOVICH

M. M. Korguev

In no certain tsardom, in no certain land, there lived a peasant, and of course he lived neither in riches nor in poverty, but just in the middle. And he lived—the two of them, he and his old woman. And so they lived well, only they had no children. One fine day, the old woman said, "Listen, old man, we have no children, and there won't be any. But I've heard that in this one place you can get children."

"Tell me now, Granny, how we are to get hold of children, since we are now old!"

"Here's how: you go into the forest and cut down a piece of pine and carve a lad from the pine. It won't be alive of course, but out of pine, and then you'll bring it to me and I'll place it in a cradle and rock it for three years, and then a lad will be born to us. Believe me, this is what I've heard. We'll try it."

So the old man obeyed her and set off for the woods, where he made a lad from pine, you see. He brought it to her. "Now, old woman, don't be lazy. Rock it for three years."

"I'll try, I will."

So now then. The old man, of course, worked in the field, and she rocked away. She prepared dinner, and then she rocked some more. She rocked and rocked, and then the three years passed. It all happened toward spring when the old man had to plow and sow, to do his own thing. So then. Once the old man went away to the field to plow, and the three years were up. So she rocked away, and then suddenly their son came out and said, "Greetings, Mama, I've been born!"

She was overjoyed, and he stood right up on his legs, climbed out of the cradle, and began speaking. She said, "You were born as you ought and have started speaking, but I don't even know what to call you."

"Call me Ivan Sosnovich, Ivan the Pine's son."

So then she prepared dinner. And so dinner for the old man was ready, "But you still can't carry it to him because you're too little. I'll have to carry it to him myself."

"Well, Mama, get it ready and I'll carry it. I'll find him, wherever he's working in the fields, I'll find him."

She got everything ready for him in a basket. "Well, carry it to him, if you can." She showed him the rows that he was to follow. Ivan Sosnovich set off. He walked and he walked and he walked, until he saw this old man working in the field. He recognized him, of course.

"Greetings, old man, you must be my father."

"I don't know you, son; you are still so small. Tell me who you are, and then I will know you."

So then he said, "Here's the way it is, Grandpa. I'm Ivan Sosnovich, my mother rocked me for three years, and then I grew up. And I've brought you your dinner."

"That's fine, even if you're still so small and yet you brought me my dinner . . . Well, sit down and we'll eat together."

"No, I don't want anything; just give me the mare and I'll plow."

"What are you on about, my son? You are still small. You can't."

"No, I'll plow a little."

"Well, give it a try."

And then the old man thought, "Once he's asked to do it, there's nothing to be done. Let him try."

So he took the plow and hitched up the mare while the old man ate. He took that plow and dug it deep into the earth, such that the mare couldn't pull it.

"Listen, Ivan Sosnovich, you won't be able to plow with my mare, as you've dug the plow so deep into the earth. She can't manage such strength. You're really strong. Let her go and nibble some grass for a bit and sit down with me and have some dinner. Then after dinner I'll rest a little. Afterwards we'll go and bring her back."

So of course he let the mare go nibble some grass, and he sat down with him. The old man ate and went off to sleep. When he got up from his nap, he said, "Well, Ivan Sosnovich, go and lead that mare over here, and then you go back to your mother. I'll come back a little later."

So then, you see, he went after the mare. He was just coming up to the mare when he saw that an old bronze-headed wolf had just eaten their mare. And he rushed at him. "Now I'll eat you!" He let him come up close, grabbed him by the legs, and threw him onto the ground such that there remained only a wet spot from him, and the earth shook from it all. Then he went back to the old man. He came up to him and said, "Well, Father, bronze-headed wolf has eaten our mare."

"Oh, Ivan Sosnovich, how is it that he didn't eat you?"

"Well, he didn't eat me, and I killed him. He won't be eating anybody's mares anymore."

"Well, let's go home then."

They set off. The old man thought, "I'm not going to have to feed him. Since he killed that wolf, he's going to be a proper bogatyr."

He came to the old woman. The old woman asked him, "How did it go, old man? Did you bring our son back with you?"

So the old man started telling her about their son and the wolf.

> So our son brought me dinner and I sat down to eat. I sat down to eat and he said, "Let me please, I'm going to plow." Well, I couldn't refuse him. He took the plow, hitched up the mare, and sent the plow off into the ground so that you could hardly see it and the mare couldn't go. I said to him, "Let her go, let her nibble some grass." So we let her go, and I rested for a little while and then I said, "Well now, Ivan Sosnovich, go and bring back the mare." So right then he went after the mare, but bronze-headed wolf had already eaten our mare. So he grabbed that wolf by the legs and hit him against the ground such that the earth shook. He killed that wolf and that's the reason we came home.

"Listen, Granny," he then said to her, "we're not going to have him to feed. We thought he would live off us, but no. Probably he won't even live with us."

Ivan Sosnovich heard all this that they were saying, although he wasn't standing nearby. And so they all slept through the night. On the next day Ivan Sosnovich said, "Now then, Father, go to the smithy and have them forge me an axe, and then I'll go cut wood for us. We don't have much firewood."

"What kind of axe do you need, Ivan Sosnovich?"

"One that weighs fifty poods."

So the old man set off, of course, for the smithy, and he ordered the smiths to make an axe weighing fifty poods. The smiths said, "We will forge one, of course, but let him come and get it himself. We won't be able to carry it for your son." So then, of course, they began their work. He went to his son: "So now, Son, you go fetch the axe. They're making it, but no one can bring it here."

Ivan Sosnovich went to the smithy himself. When he got there, the smiths said, "Take the axe, it's lying over there. We can't carry it."

Ivan Sosnovich took the axe in one hand and set off for home. When he came home, of course, to his mother and his father, he said, "Well then, let's have dinner now, and afterward I'll go cut some wood."

They ate dinner. Ivan Sosnovich set off to cut wood. He cut wood the whole day long. In the evening he came home and said, "Well, Father, I only cut a little today, just fifty cords—the axe is too light. Tomorrow go to the smithy and order an axe of a hundred poods, and then tomorrow I'll go out and chop wood again." (He didn't chop it: he broke it!)

And so the old man went as he should have to the smithy and ordered a hundred-pood axe. And of course the smiths began to forge it. Ivan came the next day, took the axe, ate his dinner, and set off for the woods. So he came to the woods, chopped until evening, came home, and said, "Well, Father, I still chopped only a little—only a hundred cords. The axe is too light. Go and tomorrow order at the smiths' an axe of a hundred-fifty poods."

And so the old man went as he ought to, and at the smithy he ordered an axe of 150 poods, saying that it was to be ready by morning. The smiths didn't dare refuse, and they forged it by dawn. In the morning Ivan Sosnovich got up from his sleep, ate his dinner, went to the smithy, and from the smithy straight to the woods. He came to the woods, of course, and chopped the whole day. In the evening he came back and said, "Well, Father, I've chopped enough, a hundred and fifty cords, but the axe is too light. Still that will suffice you for a whole lifetime. I'm not going to bother you with this smithy business any more."

He took the three axes and dragged them to the smithy. Oh, do what you will with these axes! Then he came back home, and the next day he said to his father, "Well, Father, go over to the smithy and get them to forge me a mace of three hundred poods—one that won't bend and won't break against a rock—and have it ready in twenty-four hours."

And so the old man set off to order it. He was afraid himself. "If you would just go away; you're obviously not going to take care of me." And so the smiths, that is, worked away at that mace. They forged and they forged and they forged; in one day they had it ready, somehow or other—they were also afraid of what might happen. So he came to the smithy the next day. He came to the smithy, and the smiths said, "Well, then, Ivan

Sosnovich, here's your mace. Take it. We can't even lift it." When he took the mace in his hands, he bent it, and it doubled over like a rainbow. He said, "If you don't make me a good one, it'll be too bad for you. I'll come again tomorrow morning."

So that's how he threatened them, and the smiths quickly set to work. He got through that day, and then he came to the smithy and took the mace in his hands. It didn't bend. He threw it against a stone, and it broke! "So now then, lads, make it so that it won't break against a stone, and then I'll pay you.

He came again on the third day, took the mace, and it didn't bend. He lifted it up and threw it, and it scarcely quivered. "All right, lads, I won't bother you any more." He paid the smiths more than they had ever seen in their whole lives and came home. So then when he got home, you see, he said, "Well Father and Mother, bake me some stuff for the road, and I'll go wherever my head takes me and you won't see me any more."

"Well, what's to be done? Go then, Son!"

The next day all was ready. He said goodbye to his father and to his mother, and he showered them with money. "Here," he said, "this is for your old age, and you've got enough firewood, so live in good health." And so off he went down the road.

So he set off. He walked and walked with his mace. Suddenly he came to two oaks, and between them stood an old man. He stood there and took one and then the other in his hands and struck them against each other. One saw him and spoke: "Greetings, Bogatyr Oakman!"

"Greetings, greetings, good man. No, I'm not the bogatyr Oakman. You see Ivan Sosnovich killed the wolf and all the earth shook. Now he's a real bogatyr!"

"But I am that same Ivan Sosnovich"

"Take me with you, Brother."

"Where?"

"Wherever your nose leads us."

"Let's go then."

So now there were two of them. And they walked along together. They came to two mountains. A man was standing between them, and occasionally he would raise one mountain and strike the other with it. Then he spoke: "Greetings, Bogatyr Mountain Man."

"Greetings, greetings! I am no bogatyr Mountain Man. There's bogatyr Ivan Sosnovich; he killed the wolf with the bronze head, and all the earth shook. Now he's a real bogatyr."

"But I am that same Ivan Sosnovich."

"Where are you off to? Take me with you."

"Let's go then."

So they went on further. They walked and the walked, and they came to a river. There stood a bogatyr, and he was ferrying people across it on his moustaches. Ivan Sosnovich said to him, "Greetings, Bogatyr Moustaches!"

"Greetings. But I'm no bogatyr Moustaches. There's this Ivan Sosnovich, who killed the wolf with the bronze head. Now he's a bogatyr."

"But I am that same Ivan Sosnovich."

"Take me with you."

"Let's go then, only we have to get across this river."

"Well, get on my moustache, one on each side, and I'll take you across."

And so he brought all of them over the river. Then he stretched out his moustache. "You pull me over; there won't be a ferry here any more."

And that's what they did. Then all four of them set off along the road. And they walked and walked and walked, of course, because the place wasn't close by. Suddenly they saw this house standing there, surrounded by a fence, and it was a big house. They entered it. They entered the house, but there was no one in it. They examined the dining room and the kitchen where they prepared the food. Ivan Sosnovich said, "Now then, lads, there are some oxen outside. We'll have to slaughter five oxen and roast them. So who will be the cook today? You stay here, Oakman, and prepare a meal for us, and we'll come back later."

So Oakman went out into the yard, butchered the oxen, and cooked away. When he had cooked it, he tasted a little, but all the while he kept looking out the window, wondering why he hadn't seen his comrades in such a long time. It was as if he were afraid of something. Once he looked out the window, and he saw a little old man running along. He was about the size of a fingernail, with a beard a yard long, and he was pulling forty carts of hay along behind him. He pulled them up, opened the courtyard, began drawing some water, and was about to count his oxen. He counted and counted, but he was short five head. "Hey!" he said. "Who's here in my house? He neither feeds me nor gives me a drink, but he's making use of my interests!"

He ran into the hut and then into the kitchen, where he looked and saw Oakman sitting there. He grabbed him by the hair, beat and beat him, and dragged him around, so that Oakman couldn't move anymore. He ran outside and stuffed him under a corner of the hut. "Let this corner never rot!" And he ran away.

So Oakman lay there for a long time, until he came to. He came to and started moving about beneath the corner. He wriggled and wriggled, and finally he came out. He went into the kitchen and looked: The fire under the kettle had gone out. He lit the fire and then stretched out on the bed. Just then his brothers came in.

"Well, Oakman, is dinner ready?"

"Then let's eat."

"I don't want to, the fumes have got to me."

"Well, if you don't want to, you don't have to."

So they sat down to eat, they sipped their soup, they ate up the meat. But it all seemed too little for them. So then Ivan Sosnovich said to them, "This time, Mountain Man, you stay behind, and Oakman will come with us. You cook dinner and butcher about seven oxen today so that there'll be enough for dinner." Then they went away.

So of course Mountain Man went out into the courtyard, took seven head of oxen, and slaughtered them. He washed them, put the meat on to cook, and he cooked it, boiled it for three or four hours. The meat was nearly done. He took out a piece, ate it expectantly, while looking out the window. "Soon my comrades will come and everything is all ready."

Once he looked out the window and he saw a little old man running along. He was about the size of a fingernail with a beard a yard long, and he was pulling forty carts of hay along behind him. He pulled them up, opened the courtyard, began drawing some water and was about to count his oxen. He counted and counted, but he was short seven head. "Hey!" he said. "Who's here in my house? He neither gives me a drink nor feeds me, but he's making use of another man's interests!"

He came running into the house and began letting Mountain Man have it. He beat and beat him, he pounded him, and then he ran out onto the road and poked him under a corner of the house. "Now this second corner won't rot."

But he didn't look beneath it. This Mountain Man wriggled in the same way beneath the corner. He wriggled and came out. He started running, started up the fire again, and collapsed onto the bed. Soon his comrades came.

"Get up, Mountain Man, let's eat."

"I don't want to. My head aches, the fumes got to me."

Then Oakman answered, "This hut is filled with fumes." But he didn't say that the same thing had happened to him; he was silent. So then they ate the meat, but they thought it was too little.

Ivan Sosnovich said, "All right, Moustaches, today you stay behind. Butcher ten oxen so that we can eat right honorably, and we'll set off."

So the three of them got ready, and they went away. Now Moustaches right away went into the yard, slaughtered ten oxen, and put them on to cook. He took out a chunk and ate it, and it was good. "My brothers have been gone for a long time"—he kept looking out the window. As he was looking out the window, this little old man the size of a fingernail with a beard about a yard long came up, pulling forty carts of hay behind him.

"What's going on here?" He ran into the yard and began counting his oxen, and once more some were missing—this time he was short ten. "What is happening to me; every day it happens that I am losing oxen. He doesn't water them, he doesn't feed them, and he's making use of someone else's property. He ran into the hut and grabbed Moustaches by the moustache and began pulling him around. Moustaches couldn't do a thing with him. He beat and beat him, he dragged him about, and then he ran outside and stuffed him under a corner. "So now the third corner won't rot."

Moustaches thought a little. "This is probably what happened to my brothers. It was probably from this that they were overcome by the fumes. And he began moving beneath the corner. He came out and went into the hut, where he saw that the fire had gone out. He lit the fire and fed it, and then he flopped on the bed—he couldn't do anything more.

Suddenly he heard his brothers coming. Once more Ivan Sosnovich asked, "Well, is the soup ready?"

"It's ready."

"Then let's eat."

"I can't. The fumes have overcome me, and my head aches."

So they sat down to eat. They ate, they ate up all the meat. Ivan Sosnovich said, "This time all of you go, and I'll stay and see what these fumes of yours are."

So they all got ready, set off and said, "All right, but you will have the same 'honor' as we had, Ivan Sosnovich."

Ivan Sosnovich went into the yard. He went out into the yard and butchered twelve oxen. He brought them in, washed them, put them up, and walked through the rooms, singing a song. He looked, and the meat was ready. He took out a piece, ate it, and again he sang a song.

"For some reason my brothers have been gone a long time. What were those fumes they spoke of? There are no fumes here at all." Through the window he saw running up an old man the size of a fingernail, his beard the length of an arm, pulling forty carts of hay behind him. He ran into the yard, began drawing some water to water his oxen. Then he came out, singing a song. The old man counted and counted his oxen. He was missing twelve.

"What is this? Who's moved in with me? He neither feeds, nor waters them, but he makes use of my interests!" He ran into the hut and began struggling with Ivan Sosnovich. They struggled and struggled, but he couldn't do a thing with Ivan Sosnovich. Ivan Sosnovich tore out all his beard, such that just his head remained. He grabbed his head in both his arms, took a hammer and some nails, and nailed him to a wall so that he could only move his head. Then he heard his brothers coming. He pulled the head over and nailed it to another hut and left the door open a crack. They came in. "Well, sit down lads, dinner is ready."

They thought, "What is this?"

He sat down to eat with them, but he left the door open a crack. Through the crack they could see this head twisting. "Look, brothers, there are our fumes!"

Ivan Sosnovich overheard them.

"What is it, brothers?"

"We said that that old man over there, he's our fumes."

"And why didn't you tell me earlier?"

"We didn't say anything because we didn't know which of us was strongest. Now we see that you are strongest of all."

But the old man just kept on wriggling and wriggling, and he tore himself loose from the wall and started rolling along the floor. They went after him. Ivan Sosnovich went after his mace and then after him, but he rolled and rolled and rolled into a pit. They couldn't get him; he rolled away into the underground and there was nothing they could do about it. So then Ivan Sosnovich said, "Do you know what, brothers, this old man will get well and come and make war on us. Now we'll need for someone to let himself down and kill him there."

But the pit was of an unbelievable depth. So Ivan Sosnovich said, "We'll go into the yard now, and make straps. We have to kill him or else he'll come and make war on us, and it'll be too bad for us then." So they went into the yard and slaughtered all the remaining oxen. They cut out the straps and came over to the pit. "Well, who'll go?"

They all refused. Ivan Sosnovich: "I'll go then. Only you wait here until I come back."

"All right."

So they lowered him down into the pit. When they had lowered him down, the straps just reached from the bottom of the pit up to the earth. He set off with his mace. He walked and he walked and he walked, and there stood a little house. He entered the little house. He looked about, and there was a beautiful girl sewing. Whenever she pulled on a thread, a soldier popped out. She'd pull again and out popped another. He began questioning her: "What is this, girl? You're sewing and mending, against whom are you casting this spell?"

"I'm casting this spell on Ivan Sosnovich, because Ivan Sosnovich pulled out my grandfather's beard, and he barely got away from him. So we'll have to cast a spell on him and then make war on him."

"Toss your sewing in the stove, Miss, and I'll marry you, and then we'll go back."

She tossed it, and she was happy that he had said that. He rested a little and ate something, of course, and then he set off to go farther. He walked and he walked and he walked, and then he came to another little house. He entered the little house and there sat another maiden, sewing, and she was more beautiful than the other. Whenever she pulled on a thread, two soldiers popped out. She would pull another, and out popped two more.

"What are you sewing, Miss? Against whom are you casting this spell?"

"I'm casting a spell on Ivan Sosnovich because Ivan Sosnovich pulled out my grandfather's beard, and he barely got home. So I have to cast this spell, and then we'll make war on him."

"And where is he now?"

"He's far away. There is this third girl, and he's with her."

"Throw your sewing into the stove. I'll marry you and set off home."

So she tossed her sewing away. He rested and went on farther. So he went on farther, and he came to the third girl, and she, too, was sitting in a hut, sewing. Whenever she pulled a thread, three soldiers popped out, and when she pulled on another, out popped another three.

"What are you sewing and mending, Miss? Whom are you casting this spell against?"

"I'm casting a spell on Ivan Sosnovich."

And then he said, "Listen, Miss, toss that sewing into the stove, and I'll marry you."

She obeyed him. Then she set the table and began feeding him. And she was most beautiful of all. Then he said, "I'm going to kill him, this grandfather of yours."

She replied, "Oh, Ivan Sosnovich, you won't kill him! Even though he's battered all over, and you yanked out his beard, he's lying in the bathhouse wounded now, and we are preparing a spell now, just as he ordered us to do. But right now you can't kill him."

"Why not?"

"You won't be able to kill him if I don't teach you how."

"Tell me then, beautiful miss, teach me. If I don't kill him, then I won't get out of here, and I won't rescue you."

> Well, since he's lying in the bathhouse, and the bathhouse is being watched, you must really not go to him right now. But right now you should go to the orchard. In the orchard there's a small room, and in this room there's a little cupboard. Open the door, and there are two little bottles standing there to your right and two to the left. Those on your right hand contain the living waters, and those on the left the dead waters. Take the dead waters and put them where the living waters stood, and put the living waters where the dead ones stood. Then drink a little of the living water, but don't drink a lot of it. When you have drunk it, go over to the bathhouse where he'll be lying on a bench. He doesn't look like he did when you saw him. He's a huge old man lying on that bench, so big that he'll frighten you. But what are you going to hit him with? Do you have something with you?

"I have a mace weighing three hundred poods."

> Then hit him, although the first time you won't even wake him up. But then after the second or third he'll get up and say "Ivan Sosnovich, are you here, have you come? I'll deal with you here." He'll whistle for the two-headed serpent to come to his aid. And this serpent will leap out and come running to the hut. He must drink the living water to gain his strength, but he'll drink the dead water and die. And that's why I told you to change the bottles. Then you can do with him what you like, though he'll whistle for an army, but there'll be no soldiers, and you can kill him easily. Now go!

So then Ivan Sosnovich, of course, listened to all this, and then he set off. Right away he went to the orchard. And he entered the little room. He saw the cupboard, opened it, and looked at both sides at the little bottles.

So then he moved the living water to where the dead water was and the dead water to where the living had been. He drank the living water and set off again, and he went down to the bathhouse. So he went down to the bathhouse, opened the door and looked. The old man was lying there, and he was so huge that it was really frightening. He went up to him. He went up to him and immediately struck with his mace. The old man turned from one side to the other, but he said nothing to him. He struck him again, even harder, and a third time even harder still. From the blow the ceiling jumped up! The old man leapt up.

"Ah, Ivan Sosnovich! You've come to visit me. Now you are mine. Let's go outside," and he began whistling. He began whistling, and the serpent got up and burst into the little room where he drank the dead water rather than the living, and he expired. There was nothing: no armies, no serpent. The old man said, "Oh, those bitches! They've tricked me! Well all right, but I won't give in to you alive. First we'll fight, and then you'll kill me." So then that old man wanted to fight with him, but Ivan Sosnovich struck him with his mace on his head, and the old man fell to the ground. Ivan Sosnovich struck him a second time, and knocked his brains out. He left just a wet spot. Then he went back to the maiden.

"So now then, Miss, I've killed that old man."

"Yes, you've killed him, Ivan Sosnovich, and now let's go. I agree to marry you."

So they got their things together. She gave him a ring and said, "Now then, Ivan Sosnovich, keep this ring until we come back to the tsardom." She was a tsar's daughter. And she said, "The others, you'll take them too, won't you?"

"Of course, we'll have to take them, too. There are three more of my brothers, and they're waiting for us all."

Then he went to the next one and said, "Well, beautiful princess, let's go." She got dressed, and they set off. But that one didn't give him anything. And so they came to the third. They came to the third, and he also said, "Well, get dressed, Miss, I'm going to get all three of you out of here as you did me a favor. I'm going to get you all to Rus."

So they set off, and then they said: "I am a tsar's daughter," "I am a king's daughter," "I am a duke's daughter."

And he said, "I'll marry you all to my brothers, but this one I'll take for myself. But we're one short."

So then they came to that pit where the strap was. He began pulling on it, and he said, "All right, let's go. We'll take turns, and I'll go last. They'll lift you out of here."

And so they began to be lifted up. The first was the duke's daughter. They said, "Oh, such a maid! Fine indeed!"

Then they lifted out the second. "Really fine. Now if we can lift up the third."

And he said, "Now, Tsarevna, it's your turn to be lifted up."

And she said, "Listen, Ivan Sosnovich, you get out first and then lift me out; otherwise, they'll leave you in the pit."

"What? Would they really leave me?"

"Look out and mark my words! There are three of them and three of us, so just you see—you'll be left behind. Listen, you get me out, or all your efforts will be in vain. You killed the serpent, but I won't be yours. They'll leave you in the pit for ever and ever."

"No, they'll raise me up."

"Wait and see."

So he nonetheless stood her up. "Get up, beautiful Tsarevna, up you go!"

And so they raised up the third and said, "Now there's one for each of us, if he has another one. If not, then we probably won't raise him up." They asked the girls, who said, "We don't know."

But Moustaches said, "No, we still have to pull him out of there." They let down the strap and began pulling. Then Oakman said, "No, I won't be married." He took the strap, cut it in two, and he went flying back down there. When he flew back into the pit, the tsarevna of course didn't say a word to them, but she thought to herself, "I told him so, and now all his efforts are in vain."

So they took these beautiful maidens and set off for the city. But Koshchei the Deathless found out about these beautiful girls. When he found out that they had come to the tsardom, he attacked the tsardom, took the beautiful maidens away, killed two of the young lads, and wounded the third. And then he flew away with the maidens. And that tsardom was completely turned to stone.

(For the time being we'll leave off about these and take up about Ivan Sosnovich.)

So now then, when Ivan Sosnovich hit the earth, he lay there half a day unconscious. Then he came to. "Now where am I, damn it! I didn't pay attention to that beautiful maiden, and I'm in the pit again. So that's what those brothers of mine did to me. Well, all right." And so he walked back into the underworld.

Then he came to that little hut. So there was nobody there. He sat and ate, and then he went on. Then he came to the third, and he felt like sleeping. He slept a little, ate a little, and then went out into the square where he had killed the old man. Then he went into the orchard. He looked around, around that little house where the serpent had been felled, and there it lay. Well, so what, there was no one there. He went on, out into the open steppe. He came into the steppe, and there he saw standing a big pine tree. And he saw a herd of oxen walking about of themselves, without a herder—a huge herd. So he went up to that big pine and sat down, and he heard some eaglets crying out from on top of that pine tree.

"Save us, young lad!"

"How can I save you, what do you need?"

"We are hungry. Our mother flew off to Rus and hasn't been here for a long time. So we are hungry; we can't even raise ourselves up."

"So what is it? You want to eat?"

"Yes, we want to eat."

He grabbed an ox, dragged it over, and tore it into little bits and gave it to them.

"Thank you, Ivan Sosnovich. When our mother comes back, she will repay you, she'll do whatever you need to have done. Only hide when she comes flying back so that she won't swallow you up—she's really big."

So he stood there. He stood and he stood and he stood, and he saw some sort of mountain. It was a bird. The children cried out, "Watch out, Ivan Sosnovich, that's our mother coming. Hide behind a tree so that she won't see you." He skipped behind an oak and she came flying up. They began crying and said, "You abandoned us and we almost died. If it hadn't been for a kind man, we would have died."

"And how did he save you?"

"He fed us, and we are alive!"

"And where is this man? Who is he?"

"This man is Ivan Sosnovich, he was left behind in the underworld."

So she spoke to him: "Greetings, Ivan Sosnovich! So what do you need for having fed my children?"

"I don't need anything. Except do me a little favor, if you can."

"Well, Ivan Sosnovich, what favor can I do for you?"

"Carry me out of here back to Rus. That's all I need."

"So, Ivan Sosnovich, it's a long way to fly from here to Rus. We'll have to have plenty of supplies. And you aren't so light, Ivan Sosnovich, so we'll have to have an even greater supply."

"But I don't know what sort of supplies are needed, tell me."

"First of all, you'll have to kill forty oxen for me for the road. And as we're flying along, you'll have to toss half an ox into my mouth at a time. And then forty buckets of water. And when you throw the half ox, I'll devour it, and then the bucket of water. And then, did you kill our old man here?"

"I killed him."

"Then you go round to his hut and bring some of the living water. Give me a little of it, and bring the rest with you. You get all of this ready, and bring it here, and I'll be ready. I'll do you that favor, since you saved my children."

So he went to that herd and butchered forty head [of oxen], dragged over the meat, and went to the orchard. He took a vial of the living water with him and came back to the eagle. She came down, down from the big treetop, and he tied everything to her wings. He got on and they flew off. They flew and flew. She looked around, and he would give her half an ox and a bucket of water. They flew and flew, as they had to fly over three seas. And as he flew, he tossed things to her. They flew over the second and flew out over the third. He didn't have many oxen left, maybe just ten, and they had to fly over the whole sea. He started throwing her smaller pieces. As he threw her smaller pieces, she began turning around and flying lower. Then the shore became visible, but he only had half an ox left. She said, "I want to eat, otherwise I'll throw you off."

He gave her the last half ox and a little of the living water. She gained strength from it. She flew on a little and said, "I want to eat." But he had nothing left to toss to her. She said, "Well, Ivan Sosnovich, cut out at least a little morsel from your legs and toss it to me. Otherwise, we won't get there."

Without saying a word, he cut a little bit from his leg, and then a second, and he tossed them to her. Thus they got to the shore. When they had crossed over the shoreline, she came down to earth, but he couldn't stand on his legs, and he said, "Now where will I go since I can't stand on my feet, do you hear me, Eagle?"

Then she said, "Very well, Ivan Sosnovich, since you didn't begrudge giving me some bites of your muscle, I'll give them back to you." And she coughed them up. "You put them back in place and rub them with the living water, and you'll be healthy." He put the muscles back in place, rubbed them, and got up.

"Now give me the rest of the water to drink, or else I won't be able to fly back. I had to lug you over here as well as your mace of three hundred poods. You won't need it any more, even though you are going to have much grief along the way."

And thus did Ivan Sosnovich take his leave of the bird. She drank and flew off.

And so he walked and he walked and he walked, and then he looked and there lay an army, all dead. He walked about this army and saw Mountain Man, dead. He looked at him and went on farther. He went farther, and he saw a second army, lying there all dead. He went up to it and saw Oakman, also lying there and also killed. And so he went on farther. He saw not far away some sort of burnt-over area and then another army, all dead— everything was burned up. When he went up to this third army, he saw Moustaches sitting on a bush, his legs and arms chopped off and covered in wounds, scarcely alive. He went up to him. When he saw him, he said, "Greetings, Bogatyr Moustaches."

"Greetings, greetings, Ivan Sosnovich, how did you get here?"

"Oh, I just got here somehow. And where are your brothers?"

"My brothers are dead, and look at the situation I'm in."

"And where are the beautiful maidens I got from the underworld? Tell me, why did you leave me in the underworld, throwing me back and not pulling me out?"

"Listen, Ivan Sosnovich, I'm not guilty of that, I begged my brothers to pull you out, but Oakman cut the strap because he wouldn't have a bride otherwise. And of course, we ended up with no one."

"And where are they now?"

"Koshchei the Deathless carried them away, and the entire tsardom has been petrified. He slaughtered all three of our armies, burned everything, took the maidens and flew away, and I don't know where he is now."

"Well, Moustaches, I'll hold no ill will against you, and since I have no means of curing you, forgive me and I'll kill you so that you won't suffer any longer."

Then Ivan Sosnovich once more came forward. Suddenly he saw two men approaching with mauls. He went up to them and asked, "Where are you going, lads?"

"We've set off for the high mountains to find out where Koshchei the Deathless's death is; otherwise, we can't kill him. We set off looking for it because he has destroyed our entire tsardom."

"Take me along as one of your companions. I'll help you. I need him."

So they went on farther. Then they met up with two men who had shovels, off to do the same thing. An entire group was gathering.

"Where are you going?" he asked.

"We are going to the high mountains to find out where Koshchei the Deathless's death is. We have to get hold of it."

"Take us along with you."

"Let's go then."

They went on farther. As they went they saw two drillers and a third man carrying a bag with an explosive substance. And he asked them, "Where are you off to, lads?"

"To such and such mountains. We have to kill Koshchei the Deathless by some means or other."

"Then let's go together."

And so they set off. Then they came to such a high mountain that it would make your head ache! The last of them, the one carrying the bag, said, "Well, lads, we have to take apart this whole mountain, and there is a chest there, and in it is Koshchei the Deathless's death. And we have to smash that chest, and in it is an egg, and we have to break that egg open. But no one among us has strength enough for that."

"So you, lad, you tear it, tear that mountain apart, and I'll break open the chest. I'll help you now, too."

So they all set to work. And those drillers set about their own work, drilling. The sapper blew open a hole, those with the mauls worked with them, the diggers dug with their shovels, and Ivan Sosnovich dug out the huge stones with his hands. In three days they had taken apart the whole mountain. Finally they got to that base of the slope where the chest lay. That chest didn't stay in one place. It whirled from side to side when it had been freed from beneath the mountain. Then a driller said, "Well, lads, who among us can smash that chest? Don't waste time. If Koshchei the Deathless flies up (he'd found out, you see), he'll grab the chest and we won't kill him. He's strong, you know."

So then Ivan Sosnovich dragged out his mace and struck it so that the chest popped open. Thunder passed throughout all the woods, and just a wet spot remained there in that place. Then the sapper said, "Now let's go to Koshchei the Deathless, although he's not there. He's flying about somewhere. So we'll go to him and take away those maidens he kidnapped. Although it's your affair, Ivan Sosnovich, you did all this. You be the senior of us, even though we helped in part."

So they set off. He went ahead. They came to Koshchei the Deathless's dwelling. Ivan Sosnovich went to search out the maidens, and they remained behind to look over the house. And just what didn't they find there! Ivan Sosnovich walked about the dark castle for a long time, but he didn't see anything. Finally he saw a door, and he went in. And then there was a crystal door, and there sat the three maidens. And the self-playing gusli was playing, too. When he went in, they immediately recognized him.

"Oh, Ivan Sosnovich, why did you come? Koshchei the Deathless will surely kill you."

"No, don't worry about it, beautiful maidens. He is no longer, and I've come to rescue you for the last time. I've come from that place where my brothers left me, and I saw them all killed there."

"Well, Ivan Sosnovich, take the self-playing gusli now, because our city is petrified. And when we go there, play the self-playing gusli, and the whole city will come alive. We shall live and I'll marry you. And as for the other maidens, it's up to you: Marry them off to somebody else if you can, or just release them."

So he took the self-playing gusli and left. And he saw his brothers frolicking in gold and taking much money for themselves. And he said, "Well, take as much as you need. I don't need any; I won't be poor in any case."

So they all left Koshchei's dwelling together, and they approached that petrified city. Ivan Sosnovich started playing the gusli, and the whole city came alive. Everything was as it had been, and they immediately went to the tsar's palace along with those maidens. The tsar was sitting on his throne.

When she had come to her tsardom and went up to her father, she said, "Well, Father, look at my rescuer. First of all, he rescued me from the underworld. But his brothers abandoned him there, and now he got me away from Koshchei the Deathless."

Then that tsar said, "Very good, daughter. Since that is the case, and he even rescued you a second time, he has endured enough."

So they immediately had a feast. They put on a wedding. Then Ivan Sosnovich told them everything that had happened to him—how he had been born, everything from beginning to end. After that, the tsar made him his heir, and after his death he left him his throne.

And he and his tsarevna began living and dwelling until deep old age.

And that is the end.

(SUS 301B)

5

SHKIP

M. M. Korguev

In no certain tsardom, in no certain land, there lived and dwelt a tsar. He had a son and a daughter. The daughter was called Maria, and the son, of course, Ivan (like all other Ivans—just so!). So of course they came of age. And the father said to his son, "Here's what, my son," he said, "I feel within myself that I will soon die. You have to get married and occupy the throne."

"Well now then, Father, bless me, but who am I supposed to marry?"

And then he said: "Well, my son, I'll give you a ring, and you take for yourself as a wife without paying heed to whether she's a peasant's or a merchant's daughter, or even the daughter of some widow It's all the same."

And so then not long after, the tsar got sick and died. The tsarevich remained unmarried. He remained with his sister. But he, of course, well, he had to get married and mount the throne. So at first he tried the tsars' daughters, then the kings', but none of them did the ring fit. It was either too small or too large. There was no one who fit his father's blessing. Finally, he went among the merchants' daughters and the peasants' too. In a word, he went through them all, but none did it fit, whatever you like!

Then once he was sitting with his sister, drinking tea. "Listen, Sister, try this ring on yourself."

"But Brother, even if this ring were to fit me, I'm nonetheless no wife for you, because you are my brother."

"But try it anyway, Sister. After all, I'm not asking for you to be my wife."

And then she said, "Well, so then, let me just please you. I'll try on the ring."

So she took the ring, put it on her hand, and it was as if it had been made for it. Then he said to his sister, "You know, Father gave his benediction that whoever's hand this ring should fit, that is the one I was to select. It fit no one except you; that means that Father's blessing must be fulfilled—and you must marry me."

She immediately said to him, "Listen, Brother, how could I marry you? Our law does not permit that a brother should marry his sister."

"Well, as you wish, Sister, but think about it now and decide. We have to fulfill our father's benediction once he pronounced it."

His sister thought about it a whole day. He asked her: "Well now, Sister, have you thought it through?"

"Of course not, give me three more days."

So she thought about it from all sides, but nothing came to her. "I must run away!" She went to her brother and said, "Well, I'll think about this ring for three more days. Then if I put it on, I'll marry you."

"Well, very well, Sister, in three days we'll start the wedding ceremonies."

"All right. Good."

So then she went off, got together sufficient money, and secretly rode out of town. When she had ridden out of town a little, the second or third village away, she stopped and bought a little house. She bought the little house, took in a widow to live downstairs, and she began occupying the upper floor. And this widow had a son. They called him Ivan, and he was already grown up.

So then she, of course, bought up some goods and began trading. She hired some assistants, and she took on the widow's boy as a seller. Well, in the beginning, of course, as an errand boy, a helper. So she started trading and business grew. When this lad had grown up, she promoted him to senior assistant, and he learned to trade so well that she praised him sky high for his work. Just so. When this Vaniushka became twenty years old, she often went to him to talk. She invited him upstairs to her rooms, she gave him tea, and she liked him more than all the other assistants. And then one fine day Vaniushka so much liked his mistress that he told his mother. But he didn't know that she was a tsar's daughter. "Well, Mama, I want to get married to the mistress. Do you think she'll marry me?"

His mother said to him, "What are you doing now, you fool? If you say anything, she'll take offence and drive you away. Do you live so badly? She'll drive you away right out of your rooms."

She began cursing him and even beat him, and in general there was a great uproar at their house. And she heard everything upstairs there, all their conversation. Suddenly she came down to him and said, "Well, Granny, what's going on with your son?"

"Oh, the devil with him! The fool! He keeps going on about the same old thing, and there's nothing more to be said."

"Tell me, anyhow."

"Well, listen, Mistress, there's nothing to be said. He's been talking nonsense, the fool, and I won't say another word."

So then she didn't say another word and went out. And of course he didn't say anything.

So then the next day he went off to the shop and traded. And a month passed. Again he went to his mother and said, "Listen, Mother, I'm going to get married to the mistress anyway." And again she beat him and cursed him. "What the devil, you fool, do you live so badly? She feeds you, clothes you, you have everything, and you say that and she will get mad and drive us all out."

Once more she had heard everything and she came down to them. "What does he keep on asking you, Mistress, and what won't you give him? Perhaps it's to get married that he's asking?"

"What do you mean, Mistress? To get married? He is still young, and there's nothing more, nothing at all more, to be said about it. I won't let him do anything of the sort."

So she went away again. And he went off to the shop again. Another month passed. No more. He fell into thought: "Let be what will be, I'm going to." He came to his mother: "Just so, however you like it, I'm going to get married." And she started beating him again. But he kept on: "I'll get married, I'll get married."

She came down again. "Well, tell me now, Granny, what are you and he in an uproar about this time?"

"What do you mean, Mistress? Here's what it's all about. He wants to get married, but can you insult people? And why not? I'm ashamed even to say it. The fact of the matter is that he wants to get married to you, only I beg your pardon. You will be insulted and drive us out and drive him away from his work."

"Why do you say that, Granny, that I might drive him away from his work? And what if I do get married to him? Whose business is it? If I marry him, then it's my affair. But if I don't, why should I drive him away from his work? There's no insult at all here that he wants to marry me. You don't have to raise an uproar, Granny, you don't have to put your son down. If he wants to get married, whose business is that?"

"But then, Mistress, my son is proposing that I set off courting you for him. If you want to marry him, so be it, but don't take offence if I ask you to marry him."

"Good lad, that Vaniusha, he's figured out how to start a marriage! I'm agreed: Tomorrow we'll start a small wedding, and then we'll live. Only there's much to be done. Each has his own tasks."

So the next day they started the wedding. They went to the wreathing and had the marriage. Then another day or so, and they went back to their work as before. And so they lived together a year, and in that time a son was born to whom they gave the name Shkip. And as soon as he was born, he immediately started talking and could read and write. So he learned quickly, even while still in his mother's belly. And thus this boy was so clever that when he wanted to eat, he would ask, and when he wanted to sleep, he would also ask. But still, most of the time, his grandmother spent her time with him, and therefore she had no rest.

So then one fine day Granny went out to milk the cows, leaving him in his cradle alone. At that time, this one little old man came riding into the yard on his horse. So the old man came and went into the hut. And the boy wasn't asleep, and he spoke up: "Grandpa, where have you come from?"

"I've come from my house, my child."

"If you want something to eat, take what's in the cupboard and sit down, eat. Since Granny isn't at home, help yourself."

So the grandpa ate, and then he again spoke to him: "So, Grandpa, do you have any sons or daughters?"

"No, certainly not, my child."

"And a cow?"

"I have a cow, and a granny. Other than that, I have no one else."

"Then take me, Grandpa, as your son. My name is Shkip. You have a cow, and I'll drink the milk. I don't need anything else. Do you have a big sheepskin coat?"

"I have. But you, Shkip, are a child. You're still young— why, you'd freeze."

"No, I won't freeze. Wrap me in your sheepskin."

"But if they catch me, an old man, they'll clobber me for it."

"No, no one will catch you."

"Well, all right, if they won't catch me, I'll take you to Granny. You can live with Granny."

He brought the sheepskin, wrapped him in it, and rode off home.

When Granny came from the barn, Shkip wasn't there. They searched for him and searched. Where had he got to? He was no place, and so they remained like that.

So then the old man brought him home and said, "Well, Granny, I've brought a son. The son begged me, and so I brought him. God gave him."

"Well, just so. Live as God wishes it. There's milk as he's still young, just six months old."

"But he's a clever lad, he can say everything. If he wants something, he just asks for it."

So now he was living with the Granny, this Shkip. And when he wanted to eat, he would say: "Granny, give me some milk."

And so he lived there a full month. And once he said to the grandfather:

> Now then, Grandpa, I'm going to give you some instruction, and you will get a lot of money. Go right away to where the ruler has his square, and in this square is a pillar, and on that pillar there are a thousand rubles hanging, and whoever climbs this pillar gets the money. There is also a general's clothes. So whoever climbs the pillar and gets the money, then they'll also give a general's clothes to. There are lots of brave lads there. All kinds of knights on horseback come here, but no one can get the money—they just don't know the trick. But I'll tell you how, and you'll get it really easily. Here's how you do it: Go to the market right now and buy a number eight weight and a spool of thread. And then a piece of small rope and go to this square. And when your turn comes, look around and there at the top is a ring. And you look around, and you'll see that ring and tie the number eight weight to the thread and toss it through the ring. When you get that ring, then tie on the rope and pull it through, and then on this rope you can climb up and get the money.

"All right, I'll go and try it."

"Go on, go on! You'll get it!"

So that's what the old man did. He went to the market, bought everything, and went to the square. He saw the fine lads there, some on horseback, some climbing, and all failed. When the old man came up, all said, "Now then, that old man will get it." The old man walked and walked about, and then he caught sight of the ring. He immediately took the number eight weight, tied on the thread, and threw it. He at once guessed that he had managed to get it in the ring. Then he drew the rope through and climbed up. He climbed up, got the thousand rubles and the general's clothes, and climbed back down. "Hey, some old man! No one could get that money but he got it!"

A general came up and said, "Good man, Grandfather, take the money and the general's clothes." The old man took the money and the clothes and set off home. And this general came, of course, to the tsar and said, "So, Your Highness, we had so many riders and brave men, but none could get the money. And then this old man came and got it. Understand, I don't know who told him, or whether he came to it on his own, but only that he got it."

The tsar said, "Summon that old man here!"

Now that tsar still wasn't married. But they immediately sent for the old man. "The tsar has ordered us to deliver you there right now." The old man took fright. "Well, I probably did something that wasn't right."

So then Shkip spoke up: "Go, don't be afraid. He will ask you, 'Who told you how to do this, or did you think it up yourself? Speak up, or I will sentence you to a cruel death or put you in a dungeon.' You say to him, 'No, Your Highness, I thought it up myself.' Then he won't believe you in any case and will say, 'I'll execute you in any case.' Then you say, 'If you're going to frighten me that way, I have this seven-month- old boy, and he thought it all up, and his name is Shkip.' And what will he say to you? So go now."

So he came to the tsar. "Greetings, Your Highness!"

"Greetings, greetings, Grandpa, valiant old man. So tell me how you were able to get the money and the general's clothes, did you think that up yourself or did somebody help you? No, I won't believe it if you tell me that it was you yourself. If somebody helped you, I'll execute you or put you in a dungeon."

The old man was frightened. Then the old man said to him, "I have this seven-month-old boy, and he can read and write and he can say everything. His name is Shkip, and he told me how to get everything."

Then he said to him, "Well listen now, Grandpa, is he your own or taken from somewhere?"

"No, he's not my own, but he asked to go with me when I was in this one town, and I took him to my place."

"Then bring him here."

The old man, of course, went home and said, "Well, Shkip, the tsar himself has summoned you. He doesn't believe, he thinks that I probably kidnapped you. You tell him yourself."

"Well, carry me to the tsar, wrap me in the sheepskin and carry me, and I'll tell him."

So he immediately took him and carried him to the tsar. The tsar came out and Shkip said, "Well, greetings, Uncle, I'll be your nephew."

The tsar smiled. "What sort of nephew are you? True, I had a sister, but she went off, and no one knows where. Perhaps you are my nephew!"

"Yes, yes. Nephew. My name is Shkip."

"Now tell me, Shkip, did that old man steal you from your home. Where did he get you, or did you yourself wish it? And where are your mother and father? I've a desire to know this."

"My mother is married, she trades, and she lives by herself. But Grandpa didn't steal me. I myself wished to come here, and I instructed him in getting the general's clothes and the money. But Grandpa isn't guilty of anything. I myself would have gotten them, but I'm still too small. But since you have brought me here, now I'm going to live here with you, if you will take care of me. And you wanted to marry my mother, well, it's good that she went away. But I'll find a bride for you if you will carry out all that I say."

Then he said, "Well, fine, Shkip, I'll take you. I would agree to hire a nanny, but since you wouldn't agree to it, I'll take care of you myself."

"Good, but you must let the old man go and reward him for taking me. Otherwise, I wouldn't have come here to you."

So he, of course, gave the old man some money. The old man set off home.

"Well, old woman, that Shkip was a fine boy. They gave me some money so you and I can live without worry."

And so they began living.

And Shkip was now with his uncle, the tsar. And so he lived with his uncle a full year, and said to his uncle, "Well, Uncle, now I'm a year old. Bring me some paper and a pencil. I'll draw you a plan according to which you will build a ship and go to get married. Your bride is there, but you thought of marrying your sister, although that you didn't manage."

His uncle thought, "Never mind, you have a clever head, little nephew."

And so of course his uncle brought him a large sheet of paper and a pencil, and he sat down and began drawing up the plan. He worked at it for three days. On the fourth day he gave the plan to his uncle. "Well, Uncle, here's your plan. Hire the workmen, and let them make the ship. And if they don't do it right, it will be necessary to take it apart and start from the beginning. And let them work at it for a year, and then take me there and I'll see whether they've worked properly or improperly."

And so the uncle next day set off to hire the workmen and he said, "So now then. Work according to the plan as it is indicated here, and in a year I'll come and look. You're not to work more than three years." And so these workmen took the plan, of course, and set to work. Soon it was already a year that they had been working. He said again, did Shkip, to his uncle: "Well, Uncle, wrap me up, set me on a horse, and lead me there. I'll go over the whole ship and look at the plan and see whether they are working properly. I still can't run after you on my own legs. I'm only two years old."

So his uncle, of course, took him, wrapped him up, and brought him to the ship. They got there and went around. "Uncle, here something's been built not quite right, in my opinion: The bow isn't correct. "Workman, bring the plan here." The workman came with the plan and he started showing him: "Here, you see, this isn't right, it's built crooked. You have everything shown you on the plan, but you didn't follow it; it's not right. Take the ship apart down to the keel."

So they took it apart and they started work for the same pay. And thus another year passed. And then he spoke to his uncle again: "Well, Uncle, now I can run a little. Let's ride before it's too late, before they've gone too far with the work. If it isn't satisfactory, we'll hire another foreman. This one doesn't know how to work."

So of course they came riding up and they came to the middle part. He ran about a little. "Uncle, again the ship is of no use. It won't hold together. The underwater wings are no good; we could all perish. [This is apparently a sailboat cum submarine, JVH.] Take apart the entire ship down to the keel, and get rid of these workers."

So of course he got rid of the workers and others started working. He was already three years old and into his fourth. They worked a fourth, another year. "Well, Uncle, now I can run. Let's go while it's not too late, and if it's not correct, then we'll have to destroy it again."

They came. "Well, Uncle, let's go look." The uncle thought,

"What's going on here, he's bringing me so many losses." But he didn't say anything. They looked the ship over. "Well, Uncle, this time I haven't noticed anything. Although it's correct, we'll wait another year."

And the second year he also didn't notice anything. More than half of the third passed and there remained only four months. "Well, Uncle, let's go. I'm already six years old, in my seventh. Now I can do it by myself."

They came on the ship and looked.

> Well, Uncle, everything, everything is good, only the rigging isn't quite satisfactory. But that's all right. You've been waiting to get married for a long time; we won't delay any longer. So now, Uncle, get all your foodstuffs on board, and I'll go and fetch you a bride, although she's far away, in the

> thrice-ten kingdom, the enchantress daughter of a king. This ring will only fit her; it won't fit anybody else. So you stay here, and I'll go alone, and I'll bring back a beautiful princess. But only on the condition that I will sleep with her the first night. That's the only way I'll go, as you wish. Otherwise, I won't go, or you go yourself. I'm already seven years old, in my eighth, I am all ready.

Well, even though he was seven years old, and in his eighth, he was very big in size, strong like a well-built man. Even his uncle was amazed at his growth. "So, Nephew, even though I won't go without you, I am not agreed to that proposition. Why? Because I haven't seen my sister for ten years, and for thirty years I haven't been married, and you would take away from me the most precious thing. I can't agree to that in any way."

"Then listen, Uncle, she won't live with you if you don't give me the first night. If it's otherwise, you'll never get married."

Then he said, "Well, all right, Nephew, go, but I won't go. I'll grant it to you, it's all right, so be it."

"Now permit me to say this: Hire the captains, hire the navigators, but I must have power on the ship, and what I order them to do, they must fulfill it, even though I'm still considered young."

So then the tsar sat down and wrote out an order: "The captains are to fulfill Shkip's orders. Whatever he wants, you are to sail there."

He took his leave of him and set out for the ship. "Well, Uncle, wait for two years and then I'll come. Wait that long, then wait two more years, and you'll be the master of all your world."

Then Shkip came onto the ship, and they immediately began raising anchor and sent the ship into the sea. They were soon under sail at full speed. And Shkip pointed in which direction to go and the captains obeyed him. And when they had been sailing nearly a year, the captains were bored. It seemed such a long journey and they didn't know where Shkip was going; they didn't know themselves. And they soon began . . . the captains were obliged to ask Shkip, "Well, will we soon come to that tsardom?"

"Listen, captains, soon we'll be there, soon land will be seen."

Not even a month passed before they sailed into that country. And when they arrived at that tsardom, he docked his ship, and in that town there was no such ship ever. And all were amazed at such a ship, and all came to see it. And he was in his cabin occupied with his curiosities, playing his gusli, which no one had ever heard before. And that princess found out that this ship had docked. She went and looked it, heard the singing, and then invited Shkip to appear before her, and there she began to entertain him and question him. "Why have you graced us with this visit and what are you going to do?"

He said, "I am going to offer my goods, take on others, and then I'll go. But there are some goods that no one has ever seen, and these I won't show here."

When the tsarevna learned that he had such goods, she said: "Listen, Shkip, wouldn't it be possible to see these goods? Of course, I will not come alone."

He said, "Listen, beautiful princess, if you wish to examine the goods, then come tomorrow. Otherwise, we'll soon be gone from here. Bring your nannies, your father, bring your mother. Bring them all to have a look."

Then they said, "Fine. We will come at ten o'clock."

"All right. We shall await you."

And the tsarevna didn't know the sort of villainy that was in this Shkip. Well then. He came to the ship and said:

> So tomorrow the tsarevna will come to the ship with her retinue, and at that moment you cut the hawsers, raise the anchor, and send the ship full sail to sea. And I'll give you the signal: I'll start playing the gusli. I'll make a small break and then start playing a second time, and then the ship will already have gone far from the shore. Then the royal retinue will all come out on the deck, and only the princess will remain below. You gather them all in rowboats and send them off into the sea, but don't stop the ship. And I'll play, and she won't go away until they have gone. And then I'll start playing the gusli the third time, and she'll come out herself, and then it will be all my affair.

And so all stood at their posts, both the captains and the sailors. And then suddenly on the second day they saw that all the princess's retinue was coming on board the ship. So Shkip immediately went up to them, bowed, and immediately led them into the cabin. And they came in, and no one noticed any deception on his part.

The guests all sat down at the table and he right away took his gusli into his hands and started playing. And he heard the rigging squeaking, and the ship was already in motion. He kept on playing. They moved off a little, and the ship was already rocking, and so he started playing a second time. And then the entire royal retinue came out on the deck. When they had come out, the captains and sailors were no longer yawning. They lowered the rowboats, put them in the rowboats, and shoved them off from the side. And he played on.

She asked, "Why is the ship rocking so, Shkip?"

"Oh, it's just like that."

"And where are all my kith and kin?"

And then she stood up and went out on deck. She saw that there was nobody there and the land was no longer visible. She saw she was deceived and immediately turned herself into a swan and tried to fly away. Well, Shkip grabbed her, turned her back into a maiden, and said, "No, beautiful princess, you have deceived many, but you won't deceive me. You've never come up against such a lad as me before. And I'm taking you to get married to a certain tsar. You will live with him."

When that king got home, back to the shore, he sent off a steamship to give chase, to grab back his daughter and return them all to the kingdom. So that steamship immediately set off after them, of course, and was already close. It could see them. Then the crew all took fright. "Well now they'll either drown us or capture us. They'll execute us all!"

Then Shkip saw that they were all aroused, and he said to them, "Well, put out those underwater wings and we'll hide beneath the water." So they hid themselves and went under the water. That steamship saw that the vessel had sunk. "We probably shot it up." They went back and forth and back and forth, and then returned to the kingdom.

"Such and so, Your Highness, we began shooting, shot it up, and the boat sank.

"Well, my unfortunate daughter perished along with that fool Shkip."

They went off a decent space, and he gave the order to draw in the underwater wings. They rose up and were already close to their country. And the crew and the captains were amazed at the build of the ship, that it could go so far under water—this they had never seen.

So they sailed into their own land. The tsar saw that his nephew had sailed in, and now he went down to the pier. When he had got to the pier, his nephew came out. "Well, Uncle, your desire has been fulfilled. You can take your bride, whom I promised you."

She came out of the cabin, he took her by the hand, they went right away beneath the wreath, and the feast was all ready. When the church wedding was over, they had the other wedding, and after that it was time to lie down to sleep. Then Shkip came up to him and said, "Well, Uncle, now fulfill my order: You are to grant me the first night, since I obtained the beautiful princess."

But the princess looked Shkip in the eye, said nothing, but thought, “It’s all the same if I go off to sleep with the tsarevich. I’ll go.”

Then his uncle said to him, “Listen, Nephew, no way can I let you go off and sleep with my wife. You know yourself that you can now get married to any princess or duke’s daughter, and I’ll help you.”

“Well, all right, Uncle, if you won’t grant it, then don’t be annoyed at me. I will not fetch her a second time. My life is dearer to me than your wife. I’m still young. I don’t need your wife. If you won’t give her to me, then go, sleep.”

And he left. And so he had only nestled in next to her, and she put a hand on him, and it was so heavy that he fell asleep. She crawled across the tsarevich, turned into a swan, and flew away. Farewell!

When the tsarevich woke up, his wife wasn’t there, and he immediately remembered: “Oh, what a fool I’ve been that I didn’t let Shkip sleep with her. Maybe she would have been here now, I didn’t know for what purpose he asked for her.”

He got up, washed, went into his study, and summoned Shkip to him. He got no answer. A second time, a third. Finally he set off himself. He came, and Shkip said: “Well, Uncle, are you married now?”

“Yes, I’m married,” he said.

“Well, and where is your bride?”

“Well, I don’t remember. She threw her hand on me, I fell asleep, and she left.”

“Well then, it was already well known to you that she wouldn’t live with you, and now it’s as you see. I’m not going to fetch her here a second time, my life is dearer.”

Then his uncle started talking again: “Listen, Shkip, let’s go talk privately.” He led him into his office and said, “Listen, nephew, get her for me. Maybe you can.”

“No, Uncle, I told you that I wouldn’t go get her. My life is dearer—dearer, understand. It’s no longer possible to go on that ship to her now.”

“Then how can she be fetched?”

“Now it will be necessary to go overland—and not unarmed, but with an army. Send whoever you like, but I won’t go.” His uncle pondered it deeply. And Shkip looked at him and said, “Well, Uncle, if that’s the way it is, I’ll go, I’ll serve you once more. I’ll go only on the condition that you grant me the first night to sleep with her. If you won’t grant that, and say so right away, then I won’t go on any account.”

Then he said, “Well, nephew, only go then. I’ll grant it.”

"Well, will you stand by your word?"

"I will stand by my word."

"Do you regret it?"

"I don't regret it."

"Well look then. But if you regret it, then a third time no one will go, and I won't go. But this time I'll go. Well, all right, if that's it, then gather an army of thirty thousand for me, and I'll go. And don't expect any time less than in a year."

So then an army was gathered, and our Shkip set off on the road. He set off. To walk a year is not little, of course. About a year passed, and he came to that country. And when he came to that country, he said to his troops:

> Now, lads, divide the army into three parts: a right, a left, and a middle. I'll ride off into the city and there, of course, I shall have discussions with the king. That will take just one full day. When that princess sees me, she will be very suspicious of my face. She will take her magic book and find me out. Then on the second day, she will send me immediately to the gallows. When she sends me to the gallows, I'll stand on the first rung, and the tsar will allow me to smoke my pipe and blow my whistle. And that whistle can be heard for about fifteen versts, and you immediately hurry up, and I will smoke my pipe for not less than half an hour, perhaps more. And then I'll stand on the second rung. When I stand on the second rung, and whistle, and I'll smoke my pipe, you will already be around the city. When I get onto the third rung, you pour into the city—don't wait for the third whistle. If you wait, I'll already be hanged.

And when he had told them all this, he rode off. He rode into that kingdom as a knight, and went to the king. The king, of course, admitted him as a regular knight, sat him down at the table, and began to entertain him and ask him who he was, where he was going, and for what purpose. He told him everything. And then in a little while his daughter came in, and his face was immediately suspicious to her. "Isn't that Shkip?" She took down her magic book and checked it, "Yes, that's who he is."

She carried back the book, put it in its place, came back, and said, "Father, do you know what I'm going to tell you?"

"Well, speak up, Daughter."

"Well, do you know with whom you are sitting right now?"

"Well, with a knight as you can see."

"Oh, with a knight?"

"Yes."

"And this knight, do you know who he is, Father?"

"I don't know. He's a neighboring knight, he told me, not from far away. I need to get acquainted with him."

And Shkip sat there, silent, knowing what was coming.

"And do you know what kind of knight, Father? I'm going to tell you now. You've got to get rid of him immediately. This knight is that very Shkip who kidnapped me the first time. He must be handed over to the gallows tomorrow, but now he must be locked up."

They immediately seized him and imprisoned him. They imprisoned him, and he was sentenced to be hanged on the next day. They led him out to the gallows, and so he went up on the first rung and stopped. When he was on the first step, he said, "Your Royal Highness, let me smoke my pipe and blow my whistle. My life is already in your hands."

"Oh, all right, go ahead, smoke and whistle away, where would you go to now?"

But his daughter stood up and said, "Listen, Father, don't let him, or it will turn out badly. Don't let him."

"Oh you, a man has got to smoke. Where would he get to? Guards are standing around, executioners. Go on and smoke, I permit it."

So he blew on his whistle and started smoking his pipe. And he smoked for an entire hour. And his army moved up closer and closer. And then he stood on the second step and said, "Well, Your Royal Highness, let me smoke just one more pipe and whistle."

So he smoked an entire hour and saw that his army was already near on three sides. Well, the public knew nothing about this. When he got on the third step and began asking, "Let me smoke my pipe and whistle," his army attacked. They immediately seized the tsar, bound his hands, and the executioners' and those of his daughter, and they freed Shkip from the gallows. This Shkip grabbed the executioner's sword and set off immediately to slice off that tsar's head. And he ordered them to hold the tsarevna while he went for his horse. He went for his horse and said to his troops, "Well, you can gather your troops and head back." They gathered the troops and turned back. They put her bound on a horse, and he led his armies far from that tsardom so that they couldn't catch up to them. And then he said, "Well, lads, now you go back and I'll ride back with the princess."

He untied her and rode off. She didn't say anything with him, she just thought, "Well, I've been captured again." And then in short order he came back to the tsar, to his uncle, and said, "Well, Uncle, I've got your wife back for you, and now grant me permission to go to bed with her. And if you are not agreed, if you don't permit it, you will forever be unmarried, and you won't see your wife."

Then his uncle said, "Well, all right, Nephew, if it's not against your conscience, lie with her." And he went out.

And so he tumbled into bed with her, and she laid her hand on him, but he threw that arm against a wall and the entire hall rang out. She put her leg on him, and he then threw off the leg. They made such a thundering noise that the tsar couldn't sleep at that time. He heard everything, wondered what would be next, what was going on there with the young ones. And then she thrust her entire self over him, hopped out onto the floor, stretched out her wings and got ready to fly. But he grabbed her by the wings and ripped her in half.

Then his uncle came in: "What is this thundering, Nephew, no one can sleep." And he saw his wife, ripped in half. When he had ripped her in half, serpents poured out of her, just a horror how many! His uncle said, "Well, now what have you done this time, you've ripped my wife in half, and again I'll stay unmarried."

"Uncle, that's not your affair. Go away and order them to bring me two tubs of water."

The water, of course, was brought, and he immediately took half the princess and washed her clean, squeezed out the serpents, and placed her in the tub. He took the other half and washed it in the same way. And then he put them together, blew on it, and she grew together. And then he carried her into the bedroom and covered her with a blanket. Then he went out and said to his uncle, "Well, Uncle, go now in an hour and lie with your wife."

"But why lie with the dead when you have killed her. You didn't do it for yourself or for me, but you have left me unmarried."

"Never mind, I have not left you unmarried, Uncle. I've only fixed it so that she won't leave you. Go and have a look, and then go to bed."

He came and looked: What a beauty lay there. And he fell down next to her. They spent the night. In the morning they got up, you understand, cheerfully, and everything went well with them. He then summoned his nephew: "Well, thank you, Nephew, now I'm quite peaceful with my wife."

"That should have been so long ago, Uncle. If you had listened to me the first time, you would long ago have slept with your wife."

And she said to him in answer, "Well, good, this time, Shkip, you convinced your uncle to let you go to bed with me. If you hadn't convinced him, there wouldn't have been a living tsarevich, and you, too. And I would have turned into a swan and flown away. But now all that of mine has gone away, there's nothing left, and I'm at your mercy."

"Well, that's what had to be done with you," answered Shkip.

Then the tsar began to put together a real feast, but Shkip said to him, "Do you know what, Uncle, I'll go and look for my father and mother, to find out where they are."

"Well, now then, go, and on the way ask my sister to forgive me, and ask her to come to the feast too. But I don't know where she is living."

So then the tsar put on the feast, he invited all the princes, boyars, and fine maidens also, so that Shkip might select a bride, although Shkip hadn't suggested to him that he would get married.

Then this Shkip came to his father and to his mother, but they didn't know him at all. He came into the house and greeted them: "Greetings, Master and Mistress!"

"Greetings, young man. Sit down and enjoy our hospitality."

So then they started their conversations. This and that, and then he said to his father, "Tell me now, Papa and Mama, did you ever have children? You live here the two of you, this old granny with you? But you are still young."

And then the master said to him, "Yes, young man, we had this son, but I don't know just how. We weren't at home, and I don't know where he went. He was called Shkip."

When he began speaking, his mother looked at him very intently in his eyes. But she said nothing, and Shkip said, "Well, Master, bring a little vodka, and I'll tell you about your Shkip. He is now serving a tsar, your brother," he began telling it, "and he married him to a king's daughter. And he suffered a lot, the poor dear, and it was difficult, difficult for him, but nonetheless he has remained alive."

When the master heard about his son, he brought some vodka and poured out two shots.

"Drink, Master, and pour out one for the mistress and Granny. Although I don't drink vodka, I'll have to for the sake of honor, and then I'll tell you about your son."

So the master poured out some for all. And then he said to the granny, "Granny, come here, you drink too. I'll tell you how they spirited Shkip away from you."

The old woman was overjoyed. She came up to the table and said, "Well, all right, let's drink, although I don't drink anymore. But in such joy I'll drink a shot."

They all drank together. And when they had drunk, he said, "Well, Papa, you are my father, and you are my mother, and you are my grandmother. An old man carried me away as a six-month- old as he wished."

And he told them everything: how he had lived, how he had married off the tsar, how she had first of all gone away and he had fetched her back, and how they were living now. Then his mother began crying, threw herself around his neck, and embraced and caressed him, and his father did too.

"Well now, Mama, don't cry. I won't leave you again. I'll live with you. But now my uncle is making a feast, and he has requested that you come to it."

So. And then his mother said to him, "Listen, my son Shkip, I of course won't refuse to go, but for that insult, that he proposed marriage to me, I won't go there until he himself comes here and apologizes. Likely I don't live beyond the seas. It won't be far for him to go."

"All right, Mama, I won't beg you to go. What you say is true, that it is my uncle's duty to apologize for his transgression. I'll go now and tell him."

And so he rode off. His father and mother were so happy that they forgot to find out about their son's life even. And he came to his uncle and said, "Well, Uncle, if you are yourself guilty, then go yourself and ask your sister to come. She didn't come with me. Go yourself and apologize for your transgression. She of course won't refuse."

The tsar immediately mounted his horse and rode off to his sister. He entered her house and began apologizing. "Well, forgive me, Sister, if I committed a sin. Do not be angry and come to my feast, and we'll marry off Shkip all at the same time, even though he hasn't asked to get married. But he's already done me such a great favor."

And they immediately got dressed. "Well, all right, Brother, if you have confessed it, I won't be angry at it."

And they all rode off together. But Granny had to remain at home because there would have been no one there. When they arrived then, all the guests had gathered, and then Shkip said, "Listen, Uncle, you must try the ring on your wife, to see whether you are married according to your father's blessing." And right away he gave the ring to his wife. His wife put it on—and it fit!

"So now you can get on with it!"

And so they started the feast. And then the uncle said to his nephew, "Well, Nephew, now choose from all these tsars' and kings' daughters. You are already incredibly clever; your fame has gone throughout all lands. When you were born, you could talk and read and write. And so from this table you can select a bride for yourself; there are many maidens from various lands. Don't even think that they would refuse."

And he answered, "Well, Uncle, as I am still young, I am not even thinking of getting married." He was uncomfortable saying this in front of all the maidens, where he wanted to get married. "And I'll tell you after this feast that the time has not passed."

When all the guests had departed, only his father and mother remained, and he with his wife. And then Shkip said, "Well, Uncle, now I will tell you whom I wish to marry. Then I was embarrassed to say in the presence of those maidens, as I didn't want them to think that I did not want to take one of them. And I won't," he added, "but now I'll tell you about marriage. And I'll tell you now why I don't want to marry a king's or tsar's daughter. Because my mother got married, got married to a poor peasant, it means that she didn't take into account the country or his wealth. And I'll marry the daughter of just such a peasant, one from this very city. And I won't take one of a wealthy family. It's because my mother married a peasant."

Well, of course, his uncle was confused, but there was nothing to be done once Shkip had agreed. So Shkip immediately rode over to that peasant, took his daughter, went to the wedding wreath, and put on a ball. After all of this his uncle promoted him, Shkip, to be his heir to the throne. And then his uncle spoke once more: "Well, where do you wish to live, here with me, or will you go home to your father?"

"No, Uncle, I won't live here with you. I'll go home to my father and mother. I will live with them, and then we'll see."

And so they said their farewells, of course, and set off home. His father and mother were overjoyed that their son and his wife were going with them, and Granny was too. He lived with them a certain time, but then his uncle began to demand urgently that he come. And so he went to him and he said, "Well, now, Nephew, take the throne, rule the throne, for I am already old. I can't rule the throne any longer."

And Shkip began ruling from the throne, and he lived and dwelt until deep old age.

But he didn't neglect his father and mother. He provided for them very well.

(SUS 516**)

6

SON OF A BITCH

M. M. Korguev

In no certain tsardom, in no certain land, there lived and dwelt this tsar. He had no children. And he pondered deeply: "To whom shall I hand over the inheritance? I'm already quite old, and I have no children." And so then he gave this order: "If there be found any old man or old woman who could fix it so that there should be born to me a son or daughter, or some other offspring, I shall reward them." And there was no one to be found in this city who could respond to this notice. He thought even more deeply. Then he got on his horse and rode off to some village or town, and he thought: "Maybe there will be found someone who could aid me in this affair."

And so then, of course, he mounted up and rode out of the city. And suddenly an old man came out of the woods. He stopped. He stopped and said, "Greetings, Grandfather. Perhaps I'll ask you something and you'll tell me."

The old man looked at him and saw that it was the tsar. He said, "Yes, Your Highness, perhaps I know. Tell me what you are in need of."

"Well now, old man, the problem is that right now there is this sadness: I have no heir. I somehow need to obtain a son or a daughter because I have no one to pass on my tsardom to."

So then the old man said to him, "Well, Your Highness, I can help you in your misfortune, although nothing, no words can help. It will all come from you. Your Highness, now you must immediately ride home, and take two fishermen and catch with your own hands some sort of fish. Any one that happens along, a pike or some other sort." The old man also said to him, "The first time you cast out your net, you'll have a lot of fish. Throw them all out. The second time you cast it out, throw them all out. But the third time you cast it, you'll catch only a pike, and you take that one. When you've caught it, take it home and order it cooked. Eat yourself and give some to your wife and anybody else, if necessary. Then offspring will be obtained."

And then the tsar said, "Well, thanks, Grandfather, for your good advice." Of course, he took out some money, but there, I don't know how much he gave him. He thanked him. They said their farewells, and the tsar went home. When he got home, he said to his wife: "This is what, Wife: Tomorrow I'm going fishing, as this grandfather ordered me, and then we shall have some heirs."

So then on the next day he immediately sought out two fishermen with nets, and they set off to fish, he together with them. They came up to a lake, of course. They cast the net and caught a lot of fish. The fishermen were delighted. And he said to the fishermen, "Now we have to let all those fish go." They cast them a second time, and this time they caught even more than the first time. And they let them go. They cast them a third time, and caught a pike. "This is the fish we have to take."

They got ready to go home. They set off, taking the pike. Then, of course, he paid the fishermen some money. The fishermen went home and said, "Why didn't the tsar take all the fish?" Well, they didn't know this riddle; they just talked among themselves. When he came home, he right away said to his cook, "Now then, make a soup. Prepare it for me and the mistress."

It was all prepared, of course. They brought it to the table. He and his wife sat down to dine. They ate the fish, of course, and also the soup. When they had finished eating, there was some left. Their servant ate some, and he gave some to his wife (they gave them the remaining bones). This servant had a dog, a mother-bitch, and they also gave her some bones to eat. So then when all had eaten, the tsaritsa immediately became pregnant, and the servant's wife and also the bitch became pregnant. And when nine months had passed, three sons were born: to the tsaritsa, to the servant's wife, and to the bitch, who didn't deliver a puppy but a boy. The servant saw that the bitch had delivered a son, so he took the boy away from the bitch and fed it together with his own son. And then these lads began growing so quickly, not by the day but by the hour. Every hour they were bigger.

When the tsar found out that the servant had two sons, he came to him, "Tell me, servant, by which means do you have two sons and I only one?"

And he said to him, "Your Highness, by this means: When I had eaten, I gave the bones to my dog, and she also gave birth to a son and not a dog. Then I took him in. Just by such means do I have two sons."

And they named all of them Ivan—except the one they called Son of a Bitch because he was of a dog. And so all these lads grew and went to the palace grounds to play. And they didn't omit Son of a Bitch; they also included him because he was also a human. So these lads grew quickly and really soon learned to read and write. And then once the tsarevich came and said to his father, "Papa, give us brothers, which we are, of course, each a horse to go riding around."

Their father didn't refuse. He gave them, of course, each a horse. They went to the stables, and the groom said to them, "Well, Tsarevich, choose a horse for yourself and the others for themselves." And each began choosing. The tsarevich chose a horse for himself, and so did Ivan the servant's son, but Son of a Bitch no way could choose a horse. When he put his hand on a horse, the horse would go down on its knees because he was so strong. Later the groom said to him, "Wait, Son of a Bitch, I'll choose a horse for you."

And he set off to choose one. He led a horse to him, and the brothers were waiting for him. The moment he led it out of the yard, put on a bridle, and got ready to leap on, the horse fell down. In his bitterness he took it and tore it into several pieces. "Take that, Crow, a gift from Son of a Bitch." And then the brothers rode off, but he remained there. He walked home and said to his father, "Here's the deal, Father, can it be that in this tsardom there's no horse that I can ride on?"

"Wait until tomorrow, Son of a Bitch, something will turn up."

When the tsar found out that Son of a Bitch was very powerful (which his father had told him), then the tsar said, "Tomorrow we'll find him a horse." And towards evening the brothers came riding home. Then the next day Ivan Tsarevich and Ivan the servant's son went riding, and they asked Son of a Bitch, too. He got ready. So they went to the stables. And the tsar had given this order: "Search out the very best horse for Son of a Bitch!" They immediately led out a horse for Ivan Tsarevich and also for Ivan the servant's son. Then they led out a beautiful, spirited steed. "Well," thought the groom, "Son of a Bitch will ride away on this one."

But the moment he took the horse, put on the bridle, and struck it on the chest, the horse collapsed from the blow. He became angry and went and ripped it up. "Take that, Crow, a gift from Son of a Bitch."

And again the brothers rode off. And he came home unhappy and gloomy. His father asked him, "Well now, Son of a Bitch, it's obvious that you didn't ride again, did you?"

"Yes, how could I? It's obvious that in this country there's no horse for me."

Then his father said to him, "Well, all right, Son of a Bitch, just wait. I'll go around and talk with the tsar. Perhaps they'll still find a horse for you."

So the father, of course, went to the tsar and told him what had happened with Ivan Son of a Bitch, and he said, "Well, all right, we've already chosen from two herds and it didn't work out, so from the third, probably, one will turn up."

So then the brothers got ready to go home in the evening. The next day they again went out riding. (It was already the third day or so.) So the groom, of course, led out for him the very best horse—better than this one there wasn't! It was a dappled gray. So he led out this horse and he said, "So here's a horse for you, Son of a Bitch, ride it!"

But he, not even putting on the bridle, struck it on the shoulder, and the horse collapsed. Then Son of a Bitch was so angry that he tore it into tiny bits. "Take that, Crow, a gift from Son of a Bitch!"

His brothers had already set off. And so he walked out of the city. He walked out of the city and came to the very edge of the city, and there stood a little hut. And in this hut there lived a sorceress. He knew this. So he went in to her. He went into the hut and greeted her: "Greetings, Granny."

"Oh, greetings, Son of a Bitch, you haven't been here for a long time. I haven't seen you for a long time. Come on in and tell me, why have you come?"

And so he answered her: "Listen, Granny, I can't find myself a horse that could carry me anywhere. My brothers have already gone into the steppe this third day to ride, but no horse has turned up for me in this tsardom."

"Well all right, Son of a Bitch, as you're in need of a horse, I'll show you one and perhaps you can manage it. I'll teach you how to hold it. Now then, when you go out of this hut, shout 'Sivko-Burko, magic steed, stand before me as a leaf before grass. As you served my father, as you served my mother, now serve me, Son of a Bitch.' And he'll come flying at you with the force of a whirlwind. Only don't be afraid. Strike him on the shoulder, and if he doesn't trample you, then he'll serve you."

So then Son of a Bitch went out of the little hut and shouted, "Sivko-Burko, magic steed, stand before me as a leaf before grass. As you served my father, as you served my mother, now serve me, Son of a Bitch."

He had only just shouted when he saw a horse rushing up to him, like a whirlwind. It galloped up. He struck it on the shoulder, but it stood there as if rooted. And the horse started speaking to him in a human voice: "All right, Son of a Bitch, I will serve you in faith and truth since you knew how to take me."

And then the granny came out to him. She brought a saddle, a bridle, a bogatyr's armor, and she gave him a club. When Son of a Bitch had got dressed, he leapt onto the horse, of course, and said good-bye to Granny and immediately caught up to his brothers. Yes, you see, he caught up to his brothers and said, "Well, brothers, keep close behind me and I'll ride on ahead."

Of course, he didn't let his horse go at full strength so that they wouldn't fall behind. They came out onto the main road, looked, and there stood a bridge across the road, dividing two roads. The bridge was enchanted; no one could ride over it. So he said to his brothers, "Well, brothers, let's go on, no matter how enchanted it is, and we'll get to the other side in any case."

His brothers, of course, could not contradict him. They knew that he was very strong. So they crossed over the bridge and rode out onto a glade. He spread out a tent. When he had spread out the tent, he said, "Well, brothers, who will stand watch tonight? We have to know who rides across this bridge. Or shall we draw lots to see who will ride over this first night?"

So they drew lots, they tossed for it. And the first night went to Ivan the servant's son, the second to Ivan Tsarevich, and the third night to him, to Ivan the Son of a Bitch. Yes. So, of course, when they had to ride out, they said, "Listen, Son of a Bitch, you go, as we don't dare." Both brothers refused. Then he said to them, "Well, all right, brothers, if you are so afraid, then you remain here—only don't sleep. If anything happens, come running out to help me. I'll be alone; I'm going without my horse."

So he took his club with him and set off. He came to the bridge, sat down, and just sat there. Suddenly midnight approached, and a three-headed serpent rode up and started speaking with its tongues: "Who from those lads has settled down here? We've been settled for thirty years and haven't seen anybody." Son of a Bitch immediately jumped up, took his club in his hands, and immediately cut off all three heads, threw them under the bridge, and then headed back to the tent to his brothers. He came to his brothers, and they were asleep, although they had been forbidden to sleep. He woke them up. They started asking his forgiveness: "Well,

Brother, forgive us, we won't do it next time, but forgive our going to sleep this time."

Then the brothers asked him, "Listen, Son of a Bitch, tell us who rode on that bridge, even though we ought not have to ask. But tell us anyway."

He said, "A three-headed serpent came riding by, and I killed it. But tomorrow a six-headed serpent will come. So now as you wish, Tsarevich, you ride out, it's your turn."

The tsarevich was very frightened. "How should I go, Son of a Bitch, with the three-headed one we couldn't manage it. Where would it be with the six-headed one? You ride out, Son of a Bitch, as you wish. Take my place."

He said, "Well, all right, brothers, I'll go. If I shout, come running to help; only don't go to sleep. I'm going without my horse."

Well, they promised. "Well, Brother, you go, we won't fall asleep, forgive us."

Son of a Bitch set off for the bridge without his horse, sat down with his club, and just sat there. About midnight something came. "Whoever has settled down here at my place has clobbered my brother—none other than Son of a Bitch. I'll take him now, put him on the palm of my hand—whop—and there'll just be pulp and water." Son of a Bitch immediately jumped up and struck him with his club three times. He cut off his heads, tossed them under the bridge, and headed back to the tent. When he got to the tent, his brothers were sleeping. And he said, "Why have you been sleeping again, as you were forbidden to?" They began bowing at his feet and begging forgiveness. He said, "I'll forgive you just this once more, but the third time I won't forgive you."

So evening came and he said to his brothers, "Well, brothers, I'll be setting off today. And I'll go without my horse. My horse will remain next to the tent. If I shout out, let my horse go to my aid, and you come running yourselves. If this isn't done, and I return, you won't be among the living."

And so he came and sat down near the bridge.

His brothers had promised, "All right, we'll do it." And his brothers sat there for a while. Then they became bored and— even more—frightened, and they fell asleep. They fell asleep, and then about midnight the serpent came.

"Foo, foo, foo," he said. "Son of a Bitch, you may have killed two of my brothers, but you won't get away from me alive." Son of a Bitch jumped up immediately. And like the first time, he struck with his club and knocked off three heads. And his horse stamped his feet, but his brothers slept—for no reason. His horse roared, but his brothers didn't hear. When he struck a second time with his club, he took off two more heads. Then his horse tore away and set off running, but his brothers still slept.

The serpent said, "Well, Son of a Bitch, now you are mine, since you didn't figure out how to lop off my one remaining head."

Just then, up galloped his horse. As the serpent rushed at Son of a Bitch, Son of a Bitch just barely managed to leap onto his horse, but at that moment he was wounded in the hand. Although the horse gave him such a push with his hooves, he still managed to jump. He took his club in his hand and chopped off the serpent's last head. He chopped him into little bits, threw him under the bridge, and then galloped back to the tent. He tied up his horse, gave him some wheat, and then went into the tent.

"Well brothers, now I'm going to kill you."

His brothers leapt up and fell at his knees. "Well, Brother, do as you wish, of course. We fell asleep. It's your choice." They began saying farewell and crying.

Well, then he said, "Well, all right, brothers, I'll have nothing more to do with you."

They slept one full day and night, a second, and then they rode on further to see who lived on ahead. Well, the brothers, of course, didn't dare say anything to him. Just the opposite; they had to make it so that he led them, and they thought, "How are we ever going to get home?"

And so they rode and rode and rode, and they came to a great big house. He settled his brothers and the horses and left them, and then he himself went up beneath the window to listen to what they were saying inside. And this was the house where the serpents had lived together with their wives and father and mother. They were expecting them.

When he had sat down at the window, he listened. The father spoke, "Listen, my sons have been killed by Son of a Bitch, but he won't ride past us, and if he does, we'll have to do something." And he asked the eldest bride, "What can you do to Son of a Bitch?"

"Well, Father, this is what I want to do: When they ride away from here, past us, into the steppe, I'll turn myself into a bed, and put such a sleep on them that they'll lie down on the bed and be finished. They'll die."

"Well, all right, that's a good idea. Now middle bride, what do you know? Speak."

"And I think, Father, this: When they ride up, I'll turn myself into an apple tree. They will want to eat. They will eat the juicy apples, and they will die immediately."

"Well, and you, youngest one, what have you thought up? Tell me."

And she said, "Father, this is what I've thought up: When they come, I'll turn into a well, with water. And then I'll put such a great desire to drink on them that they won't be able to hold back. They'll drink and they'll die."

"Well, that's fine, Bride. You've figured it out. That is the very best one of all."

Then the mother spoke: "This is all your nonsense. They'll just pass by. But I'll fly behind them; they won't escape me. I'll catch up and swallow them up."

And so they decided and went their ways. Son of a Bitch went back to his brothers. He came up to his brothers and said, "Well, get on your horses, and let's ride."

And so they rode off. They rode and they rode and then they rode out into the open steppe, and there such a deep sleep fell upon them that they could ride no farther. But Son of a Bitch held on. And then suddenly they saw this bed. And the brothers spoke up: "Son of a Bitch, let's lie down and rest. Probably you want to sleep."

"Wait, brothers, I'll go and find out what sort of bed this is, and then we'll lie down."

He climbed down from his horse and struck the bed with his club and just blood remained, and the brothers desire to sleep passed. They went on farther. Again they rode and rode and rode. And they had such a thirst that they had no spit to swallow. They rode up to the well. They rode up to the well and said, "Son of a Bitch, we've such a thirst that we really want to drink."

And he said, "Wait, brothers, I'll go on ahead, and then I'll let you."

He just got down from his horse and struck the well with his club, and blood appeared, not water. His brothers' thirst disappeared; they didn't ask to drink. They rode on farther. Again they rode. They rode and rode, and then they rode up to the apple tree. They had such a desire to eat that they couldn't stand it. "Brother, let's each take an apple."

But Son of a Bitch said to them, "Wait, lads, I'll go and pick them, and then I'll give them to you."

He got down form his horse, struck it with his club and blood was formed, but no apples. They no longer had any desire to eat. They rode on farther. Then they asked, "Listen, Son of a Bitch, why does it happen that we want to eat, to sleep or an apple and you strike them with your sword and blood appears and we no longer have any desire?"

"This is why, brothers: I already knew beforehand. And now we'll ride out on to the main road. You ride on ahead, but I'll have to go on first."

So he right then rode out onto the main road and said to his brothers, "Well, now good-bye. Go home. You won't see me any more."

And his brothers said farewell to him and rejoiced that he had sent them home. They came home, told about everything that had happened with them. But where Son of a Bitch had gone, they didn't know. So Son of a Bitch had already turned his horse around, and he rode on farther. He rode for a long time, he rode and he rode, but he encountered nothing on his way. Then his horse stopped and said, "Well, Son of a Bitch, now I'll be leaving you. I am no longer needed; you go on alone. I served you as much as I could, but now release me."

So of course he released him. He set off on foot with only his club. And at that time the old woman turned herself into a witch and chased after Son of a Bitch. So then Son of a Bitch came up and saw standing in the road an iron smithy. He went into the smithy, and he said to the smiths: "Close this iron smithy. A witch is flying over here, and she'll ask for me, and then I'll tell you what to do, but don't let her in here."

They immediately closed up, but the witch was already at the walls and shouting, "Will you give up Son of a Bitch?"

He said to the blacksmiths:

> Give me an iron rod, and let that rod have a screw, and make it quickly. I'll help you. And when you've forged it, say "Wait a little and we'll roast him for you and give him on the end of this rod. You'll just have to eat him!" And she'll wait. When everything is ready, let him out end first, and then make a wheel. And then when she is eating this wheel, it will spin her. She'll swallow it in her greed. When we start turning it, you hold her, and then we'll all go out of the smithy, and I'll know what to do. And I'll pay you for all of this.

Of course, the smiths took on the work. They forged the rod, made up the wheel, and handed it out the window to her. "Now then, we have prepared it all for you and heated it from the end." When they handed it over, she grabbed the red-hot iron, and they started turning it. They turned her hard and she let go. Then they all left the smithy, all three of them. So they went out of the smithy. He took his club, struck her, and said, "You were a witch, but now be my trusty steed." And she immediately became his horse. Of course he then thanked the smiths, and paid them as was appropriate. They handed him his bridle and saddle. He saddled her and rode off. And then he thought, "Now I'll ride back to my own country."

But this horse, the old woman—whatever he was thinking— turned up at her old man's, at the wizard's. He rode up on the old woman to where the brides and serpents had been slain. And when he had ridden up, the old man immediately saw that he had ridden on the old woman. He went outside. He stepped up and said, "Well, Son of a Bitch, you have killed my three sons and their three brides. You have killed my old woman and ridden up on her. Now then, you won't get away from me alive; you've come yourself. If you perform a little service for me, I'll let you go alive, but if you won't serve me, I won't let you go alive, because I no longer have the old woman, and I need to get married."

There was nothing for Son of a Bitch to do. "Well, all right, what can I do? Tell me, what service is it you have for me?"

"Well, only I won't give you my old woman as a horse, but this is what you must do: When you have fulfilled this deed, then I'll give her back to you as your horse. Now go to the thrice-nine seas to the thrice-ten tsardom and fetch me a beautiful tsarevna. I'll get married to her, and then I'll give you my old woman as a horse, as you made her. But if you don't bring her here, it's your head from your shoulders."

Then he left him. Suddenly he was walking, walking, walking, and he himself didn't know where he was going now. The road went on and on before him. And he saw a herd of horses on the road. An old man was watching over them. He went up to him. "Greetings, Grandfather."

"Greetings, Son of a Bitch." And he asked him, "Where are you off to, Son of a Bitch?"

"I'm off to the thrice-nine seas, the thrice-ten land, to fetch a beautiful tsarevna."

"Take me with you."

"All right. Let's go, Grandfather."

"Well, all right, but just think of me, and I'll be there, when I'm needed."

And so he set off again. So he walked and walked and walked, and he saw a shop. He went up and looked, and two men were standing there, and it was a bread shop. And they were poking bread into an old man, who kept on shouting, "I want to eat, I want to eat."

He went up to him: "Greetings, Grandfather."

"Greetings, Son of a Bitch, where are you going?"

"Well now, I'm going to the thrice-nine seas, to the thrice-ten land, to fetch a beautiful tsarevna."

"Take me with you."

"All right, let's go."

"Well, just think of me, and I'll be there."

And he set off farther. Then he walked and walked and walked, and there lay an old man beneath seven fur coats, and he kept shouting, "It's cold!"

He went up to him and said, "Greetings, Grandfather."

"Greetings, Son of a Bitch, where are you going?"

"I'm going to the thrice-nine seas, to the thrice-ten land, to fetch a beautiful tsarevna."

"Take me with you."

"Well, let's go."

"Well, just think of me and I'll be there."

So he set off farther again. He walked and walked and walked, and he himself didn't know how far he had walked. Suddenly he saw an old man lying beside a creek, and the water was streaming into his mouth, but he kept on shouting, "I want to drink."

"Greetings, Grandfather."

"Greetings, Son of a Bitch. Take me with you!"

"Let's go!"

"Well, all right, just think of me, I'll be there."

He himself went on. He walked and walked and walked, and then he saw an old man standing there. And in a garden there were flowers such as you've never seen on earth. Flowers and apple trees stood there, and the old man stood there.

"Greetings, Grandfather."

"Greetings, Son of a Bitch, where are you going?"

"I am going to the thrice-nine seas, the thrice-ten tsardom, to fetch Elena the Beautiful."

"Take me with you."

"Let's go."

"Well, just think of me, I'll be there."

He himself went on farther. He looked and there sat an old man in the road, looking at the sky.

"Greetings, Grandfather."

"Greetings, Son of a Bitch."

"What are you doing, Grandfather, looking at the sky?"

"I'm looking, counting the stars, and I know how many there are, it's all known to me. But where are you going?"

"I'm going to the thrice-nine seas, to the thrice-ten land, to fetch Elena the Beautiful."

"Well, take me with you."

"Well, let's go."

"Well, just think of me, I'll be there."

So now then, he walked and walked and walked, and he came to that tsardom where the beautiful tsarevna lived. And of course he went up to the tsar. When he got to the tsar, he greeted him, and the tsar said, "Well, what sort of young man are you? Why have you come? Tell me, what is your name?"

"I've come on such and such an errand. I'm called, of course, Son of a Bitch, but why I've come I'll tell you. I want to court your daughter, if you can give her up."

"Why not, let you be my son-in-law. But the fact of the matter is that first you have to fulfill my task, and then you'll be my son-in-law. However much bread there is in our city, in our tsardom, the surpluses, you must eat all of it in one whole day. If you can, then the daughter is yours, but if you can't, then it's your head from your shoulders."

He said, "Well, only not today, tomorrow. I agree. Let it be like that."

Right away, the next day, he set off. They led him to a shop. There was a mile-long row of loaves. Of course, he took up one loaf and recollected, "Where is that old man who could never get enough bread?"

He immediately appeared. "Well, what is it, Son of a Bitch?"

"All this bread has to be eaten. Help me!"

They dug in, they dug in, and three hours didn't pass before the shop was completely empty, and the old man still hadn't eaten half what he could. He shouted, "I want to eat."

They opened a second. And so thus they went to a second shop. Not two hours passed and he had emptied it, and the old man shouted, "I'm not half full yet. I want to eat, let me eat!"

They went to a third shop. And so the old man went up, and two men began to stuff his mouth full, and he swallowed it. And so then in three hours the shop was completely empty. He said, "I want to eat, I want to eat. I've only eaten a little. I'm just half way through my meal."

Then the servants answered, "There's nothing more to feed you with, all the supplies are gone."

And the old man disappeared. And Son of a Bitch went to the tsar and said, "Well, Your Highness, I've fulfilled the first task, so everything has been eaten as was ordered. Now I ask that you hand over your daughter."

"Very good, Son of a Bitch, now you must fulfill a second task. No matter how much water there is in our streams, you have to drink it all up. If you can drink it all, then we'll give you our daughter."

He said, "Well, all right then, only not today. I'll fulfill that task tomorrow."

So on the next day they showed him the river and began gathering to see how he was going to drink it. So then he went up to the stream and drank a little bucket, and he thought to himself, "Where is that little grandfather who wanted to drink?"

"Well, Son of a Bitch, I'm that very one."

"Well now then, Grandfather, help drink up all the water in this stream."

The grandfather threw himself next to the rapids and opened his mouth, and all that water poured right into his mouth. And no matter how much he drank, he kept on shouting, "I want to drink!" The stream, finally, was all dried up, but he kept on shouting, "I want to drink, I want to drink." Then he asked, "Is there any more water here anywhere?"

Then the courtiers answered him: "You, it seems, will drink up all the water from our storage wells, and our tsardom will all dry up."

With these words the grandfather disappeared, and Son of a Bitch went to the tsar. When he had come to the tsar, he said, "Well now, Your Highness, now I've fulfilled your second task, so you can give me your daughter."

"Good that you've done that, Son of a Bitch, but now you have to fulfill one more task. Only then will I hand over my daughter to you."

He answered, "Well, what is it?"

"Now you have come from a long journey, and you have to bathe in our bathhouse. It is located three versts beyond the city, but you can't go closer than a hundred sazhens to it; it's heated up red-hot. If you can bathe in our bathhouse, then I'll give my daughter to you."

He said, "Good. Tomorrow morning I can go out."

He set off in the morning, and they all went after him to watch, to see how he would bathe. When he approached that bathhouse, he couldn't go any nearer, it was steaming so. The servants hung back, but he remembered that grandfather. "Oh, Son of a Bitch, what do you need?"

"Well now, Grandfather, how can I bathe in this bathhouse?"

"Wait, we'll do it right away. Follow right behind me."

The old man went ahead and he behind, and the others just watched. The old man just went up, blew, spat, and it all froze over. He went into the bathhouse, and the grandfather just stood on a little stone and said, "I haven't seen such a frost in my whole life." And the servants stood there, looking at him. When he came to the servants, he said, "Now let's not have the tsar laughing at me. He's heated up the bathhouse such that we all froze!"

The servants went back to the palace, the grandfather disappeared, and he also went to the tsar. The servants came to the palace, reported everything that Son of Bitch had done. He was astounded. Then in a little time Son of a Bitch came and said, "Well, Your Highness, now I have fulfilled the third task."

Now it was necessary to think over how to marry off his daughter. So then he said to him, "Well, Son of a Bitch, you have to fulfill just one more task. You must train an unbroken horse of mine by tomorrow. Train him and I'll give you my daughter, but if you don't train him, he'll kill you in any case."

"Well, all right, tomorrow I'll ride him."

So he slept through the night, got up in the morning, and the grandfather who trained horses was already there.

"Well, Son of a Bitch, let's go, it's time"

"That's good, Grandfather, let's go, but probably I won't be able to ride him."

So they set off and Grandfather said to him, "Well, Son of a Bitch, this horse, now he's summoned up all his strength, and this tsar has turned him into a horse to deceive you. You won't get on him. I'll mount him and break him, I'll rid him of all his desire, and you'll get the tsarevna. But remember that there'll be two more incidents along the way as you ride with her. Well you, Son of a Bitch, stand back, and I, looking just like you, will go and come back."

So Son of a Bitch remained behind, and the grandfather, looking just like him, went up to the royal palace. When he approached the horse, the horse roared like mad. The grandfather, despite that, mounted him, took an iron rod and began letting him have it between the ears. And he rose up into the sky. He completely broke up the rod. Then he took out a copper and started letting him have it with that. The horse began quieting down and then descended to the ground, reducing his pace. And he completely broke up the copper rod. The horse set off completely quietly. Then he took out a lead rod and started off with that. This rod didn't bend, didn't break. At every joint it was twisted and strengthened. And when he had broken up this rod, he spoke to him: "Well, Son of a Bitch, let me go alive and let's ride back to the palace." So then the old man came up to Son of a Bitch and said, "Well, Son of a Bitch, go to the palace now. I've knocked out of him what he knew of wizardry. Now he'll marry her to you."

So Son of a Bitch went to the tsar. He came to him, and he was lying on a couch, all beaten up and in bandages. He began explaining everything.

"So now then, Your Highness, will you now marry your daughter to me?"

"I'll marry her off. Come tomorrow, I'll arrange a ball, marry you, and you can go home."

So he immediately went home, of course, and the next day he came back to the palace. At the tsar's, everything was all ready for the wedding. He got married. After two days had passed, they gave him a fine horse, an expensive one, and he and Elena the Beautiful rode off on it. But this tsarevna was a real enchantress, and she started questioning him: "Now then, Son of a Bitch, tell me the whole truth, don't hide anything from me at all."

"And what, beautiful Tsarevna, shall I tell you about?"

"Here's what: Was it for yourself, or did you bring me here for that wizard of an old man?"

"For myself."

"You are lying, Son of a Bitch, you are likely deceiving me!"

Just then, they rode up to that garden where the apple trees and flowers were growing. And in that garden she immediately turned into a flower. Son of a Bitch was left all alone. He right away recalled that old man, rode up to him, and he asked him, "Well, Son of a Bitch, did you obtain Elena the Beautiful?"

"I got her, but then she flew away to you in this garden and probably turned into a flower or bloomed out as an apple tree."

"We'll find out right away, Son of a Bitch."

He went into the garden and saw that one apple tree had just bloomed out with fresh blossoms. "That's probably her!"

Because he knew all the flowers. Then the old man came to that apple tree, ripped it out by its roots, and turned it into Elena the Beautiful. He said, "Well, now then, Son of a Bitch, she won't come into this garden again."

So he set off farther but he thanked the grandfather. So then they were again riding down the road. And she asked, "Tell me, Son of a Bitch, only don't lie, you are probably taking me to that old wizard. He's really old. In any case, I'm not going to live with him."

"No, I'm taking you for myself."

But then she made one more attempt—maybe it would come to something! So she turned herself into a star and flew off into the sky.

And he thought, "Well now, what shall I do? Again I'm left with nothing." Afterward he recalled that old man. The grandfather was lying in the road, gazing into the sky.

"Well, Son of a Bitch, how are things? Did you get the beautiful tsarevna?"

"I got her, but she flew away from me as a star into the sky."

"Wait until evening. I'll fetch her because I know all the stars."

So they waited until evening. As soon as the stars started shining, Grandfather said, "Aha, there's where she's sitting!" He immediately soared up and flew into the sky. The grandfather came down and brought him the beautiful tsarevna. "Well, Son of a Bitch, here's your beautiful tsarevna. She'll never fly away from you anywhere again."

So they said farewell and rode on farther. And again they were riding along the road, and she said, "Now then, be open and tell me the pure truth. It's all the same even if you are hiding it, I know it."

So then he spoke again: "Well, listen, beautiful Tsarevna, I'm taking you of course not for myself but for that old wizard. Then he'll free me."

"That's just it: He won't free you, he'll kill you. Well, I'll help you, and we'll live together. You got me and so you can possess me. Now listen, Son of a Bitch, when you came from there, did your horse remain there?"

"He remained there. He wouldn't give him to me."

> Now listen: He's prepared a pit for you, and there are poisonous snakes and every vile thing in this pit. The pit is covered with canvas, and there's a layer of earth covering it. And he will order you to walk over this. And he will already know that you've got me. And this layer of earth, when you start over it, he'll ask, "Did you dally with my wife along the way? If you didn't dally, you will pass over, but if you did, you won't." Now next to this bridge there's a wheel, he'll turn it, and you'll go flying. But you say to him in answer, "Listen, Grandfather, I don't believe that you rode my horse. If you didn't ride it, then of course you can walk over it. But if you did, then you won't be able to." And then let him go ahead. When he sets off over this layer of earth, you stop. And when he gets to the middle, you turn the wheel, and he'll fly off. And afterward this whole business will be ours.

In very quick time he rode up to that old man, the wizard.

And he said, "Well, Son of a Bitch, you have fulfilled my task. Now I need to test you." And directly from the road, as it were, he led him to that pit, where all was prepared. When he came up to the pit, he said, "Now listen, Son of a Bitch, along the road you, likely, dallied with my wife?"

"No, I didn't play with her."

"So now, it's necessary to test that. If you dallied with her, then you won't be able to cross this earthwork. But if you didn't, you'll pass over it."

And he said, "Listen, old man, I also don't believe about my horse. You were supposed to keep it and feed it, but no way can I believe that you didn't ride it."

"No, I didn't ride it."

"If you didn't ride it, then you can cross over this bridge. Whoever believes that you didn't ride it, you'll test it. And I don't believe it. You go across first."

Then the old man got it: "Of course, he doesn't know my trick. Of course I'll cross over."

And he set off. And Son of a Bitch ran to the other end and watched, standing there. And just when the old man got to the middle, Son of a Bitch turned the wheel, and he flew into the pit and burned up. Then he took the beautiful tsarevna by the hand and led her into the palace of the old man. There they spent an entire day, and he said: "Well, beautiful Tsarevna, I'll go look for his old woman, who was a horse. She must also be destroyed together with the old man."

And so he went out to the stables to look for the old woman. He found her in a stall. He quietly led her back from there, led her up to the pit, and pushed her in. And so she burned up with the old man. So then he destroyed all their family: sons, fathers, mothers, and wives. Then he asked the beautiful tsarevna, "Listen, do you wish to live in this place, or do you want to go to some other place with me?"

"Yes! It wouldn't be bad to go away. Why? Because this is such an enchanted place that anything might happen. And we can take any thing valuable with us and ride away, if you have some other place."

"Well, beautiful Tsarevna, then ride with me to my tsardom where I was born."

So they gathered all the valuables, as many as they needed, got on the horse, and rode away. In a short time they came to that tsardom where he had been born. His brothers and father caught sight of him. They met him and found out that Son of a Bitch had returned already married. When the tsar learned of this, he rejoiced that his son Son of a Bitch had come back, and he put on a great feast. This feast lasted for three days, and all the brothers participated. He told them everything at the feast—where he had been, how his brothers had ridden away. The tsar gave him a stone palace where he could live with his wife. And thus they lived their life until ripe old age.

(SUS 402 + 400A + 302)

7

THE AIRPLANE

(How an Airplane in a Room Carried Off the Tsar's Son)

M. M. Korguev

In no certain tsardom, in no certain land, there dwelt and lived a tsar. And in this land there was a goldsmith who repaired gold watches and fixed all sorts of other gold objects. Now, once he was walking about the city, and he met a certain fitter, and, of course, this fitter bumped into him, shoved him, and got him dirty. Of course you know, that fitter wasn't in the same sort of clothes as the goldsmith. When he had soiled him a little, the goldsmith started cursing: "Why have you mussed me up? You know who I am, everybody knows me, the whole tsardom does."

"Maybe everybody knows me, too, even though I'm all dirty."

And so they started quarreling and quarreling, and the thing almost went to a fistfight. Just at that time, the tsar decided to go out. He met them. When the tsar noticed that the goldsmith was standing there with some unknown person, quarreling, he questioned them: "Why are you quarreling?"

The goldsmith turned to him and said, "Your Highness, he has soiled all my things and me, too, and so we started quarreling. Judge this matter for me, please, and ask him who he is."

Then the fitter spoke: "Your Highness, I'll tell you everything. You know that I am the only fitter in the whole city."

"Well, what's this business all about?"

And both craftsmen insisted on their own version. The tsar said, "It would be better for you not to quarrel. I'll give you this proposition: Whoever can outwit the other will win. In a week, you come to me and bring the piece you've managed to make. Then whoever outwits the other will do to the other what he wants."

So they stopped quarreling and went to their own homes. The goldsmith came home and thought, "What sort of thing could I make to outwit that fitter?" So he thought and thought, and he made him a golden dove. It was as if alive—only it was made of gold.

And that fitter really liked drinking vodka. So for five days he drank vodka. And then he remembered on the evening of the fifth day: "Hey, tomorrow I have to appear, and I haven't thought of anything. Well, all right, I'll make something." And he immediately started making an airplane in a room.

In one day he had made the airplane. It started flying about the room—and farther, if necessary. He wiped it off with some old rag, wrapped it up, and carried it to the tsar. And at the appointed hour, the goldsmith and also this fitter gathered at the tsar's. The tsar asked the goldsmith, "Well, what sort of intriguing thing have you brought? Show me."

So then he unwrapped it and let out the golden dove. The dove was just like alive, only it didn't fly. The tsar was really amazed that he could make such a thing, a rarity, and he said to the fitter, "Well, Fitter, show me what you have brought."

Well, of course, the fitter dragged out the rag, gave him the airplane, he gave it to him. "Fine, this is also a fine thing, but in fact show me how to fly in it."

He said to him, "So now then, you take hold of this lever, and wherever you need to go—to the right, the left—act in accordance with this lever, wherever you need to go. If it needs to fly farther, it will fly farther. Only no more than two persons can fly in it, because I worked on it for a short time."

And so then this tsar joyfully sat down, flew all about the room, got out, and said, "Well, Fitter, you have outwitted the goldsmith with this amusement—do with him what you want. Either mock him, or just do as you want!"

He said to him, "Your Highness, I likely don't want to do anything with him. Let him live as he lived. Well, in fact I want to take over that firm so that he won't be a goldsmith any longer. More than that, I don't need anything."

Of course, the tsar fulfilled that for him. He fixed it so that he wasn't a goldsmith, and he rewarded the fitter with money and said, "Well, all right, Fitter, live as you wish. Maybe I'll order you to do something more." And he went off.

Now this tsar had a son whom they called Sergei. And he was a twelve-year-old. And he often watched as his father flew in this airplane, and he observed how to operate it. And once his father, the tsar, went off somewhere. And he saw where his father had put it, and he had put it under the bed. So the tsarevich went into the bedroom and took this airplane. Of course, there was no one in the room; just his mother was sitting there. He sat down in the airplane, flew about the room, but there was a window open. And so he decided to fly out the window. He flew out and started flying around, and he himself didn't know where he was flying. He flew across the city, and then across another the airplane flew.

But he didn't know how to let it down. He was already flying over the tsardom. Then he started thinking about how to let it down. So somehow he kept trying, and finally he began to go down. And then this airplane just landed in another tsar's courtyard! He let it down in the tsar's courtyard opposite the royal stables, and there stood an oak. So he got out of the airplane, wrapped it in the rag in which it had been, went up to the oak, stuck it beneath the oak—beneath its very roots—and headed for the stables. When he had approached the stables, the grooms caught sight of him, such a handsome lad, and they questioned him: "Why have you come here, boy? From which tsardom are you, and how old are you?"

He answered, "I don't know myself from which tsardom I am. By accident some airplane brought me here. It brought me here and then flew off itself, and I don't know from where."

The grooms looked at him, such a handsome boy, and explained to the tsar, "So it's like this and that, this handsome boy came flying here, and I don't know where he is from."

Then the tsar ordered, "Well now, then bring this boy here, and I'll ask him where he's from."

So right away the grooms led him to the tsar, and he said, "Greetings, Your Highness!"

"Greetings, greetings, young man!"

And he saw that he was properly turned out and handsome. And so he started questioning him: "Well now, tell me, young man, from which city are you, who are your parents, and by what means did you get here?"

"Your Highness, I don't even know myself. I poorly remember the city, because accidentally some sort of airplane seized me and carried me off, and I've forgotten about that, about everything."

"Well then, so you don't even know your city and who your parents are. Maybe you would like to live here with me?"

"Yes, Your Highness, if that is possible. I would like to live here with you."

"Well then, for the time being live with the grooms, and then we'll see what will become of you."

So he went back to the stables with the grooms. And he lived with those grooms for a whole year. He got to be thirteen years old, then fourteen. And then, accidentally it happened that he was herding there at the stables. And this tsar had a daughter. Her name was Tatiana. So then she saw this handsome lad and she went up to him and said, "Tell me, young man, from what land are you, and how did you come to be here among us? Tell me, don't hide anything at all, you will be fortunate. I've heard of you for a long time now, and I kept on intending to see you, but today I'm seeing you for the first time."

And he said, "Listen, beautiful Tsarevna, I'm uncomfortable talking outside. If there is somewhere private, I will tell you what I haven't told anyone about who I am."

She said, "Right now there's nowhere for us to step aside. My nannies go after me everywhere and follow me. Perhaps you know some place?"

"Listen, beautiful Tsarevna, if you wouldn't oppose it, this night open a window to me, and I'll fly in and tell you who I am."

"Well, fine, but what is your name?"

"I am called Sergei."

"All right, I'll open the window, and you fly in."

So he spent the evening, and it got dark, and all were quiet—the grooms and all the rest. He went up to the oak, got into the airplane, and flew. And he saw an open window, flew straight to her, and she was waiting.

When he had then flown into the room, she saw that Seryoga had flown to her, and she went up to him, gave him her hand, sat him down at a table, and began questioning him: "Well, now, tell me!"

So he began talking to her. "Listen, beautiful Tatiana, I am a tsar's son, Sergei, and I flew on an airplane from some tsardom, only don't say anything to anybody. I'm just telling you privately, and don't tell anybody."

Then she said to him, "Well, listen, Tsarevich Sergei, you know how I love you, but do you love me?"

He answered, "Listen, beautiful Tsarevna Tatiana, how should I not love you, as I have never seen such a beauty. You are most attractive to me, although I am still young."

"So now then, here's what, Serezha, come flying to me right after this, and we'll have more fun. I'm also very young. I'm thirteen, in my fourteenth year. I have really fallen in love with you. Without you it will be very tiresome—only fly to me at night time."

So then they talked about everything, and the time passed until five in the morning. And he said, "Goodbye, Tanichka, otherwise people will find out." So they parted. He flew away, placed the airplane beneath the oak where it had been earlier, and went himself quietly into the stables.

So then a day or two passed, and then he flew to her again. And he flew to her throughout the whole year, and no one knew anything about the fact that the tsarevich was flying to her, and who he was until once the beautiful tsarevna Tatiana said to him, "Do you know what?"

"I don't know anything, beautiful Tsarevna."

"Here's what: I sense that I'm pregnant. If my father finds out about this, it will be bad for me. I don't know, Tsarevich, what ought to be done from your side."

He said to her, "Listen, Tanichka, don't you think about a thing. We have certain means by which I'll take you away to my country. This airplane of ours will carry two, I'll test it."

So when he flew off from her, that same day he left the town and captured a ewe, to see whether the airplane would carry two. The airplane carried them. "All right, it means that it can carry two." Up until then he hadn't known. He came to that place, again placed the airplane away and continued his work. He thought, "Now what will become of me?"

And rumors made their way to the tsar. Apparently the servants and nannies told him, "Your daughter is pregnant." He fell into deep thought and said, "We must place a watch around the palace and find out what sort of beast is flying to her and seize it." He immediately summoned his daughter. When he had called her to him, he said, "Tell me, Tania, in all good faith, who is it who flies to you? If you don't tell me, you will nonetheless not enjoy a good life. When you give birth, I will order the both of you executed."

She answered him: "Listen, Papa, I won't tell you until I have given birth, and when I do, then I'll tell you. But until then, better not to ask. Do as you wish."

And so then a guard was mounted. But the tsarevich came again in the night by the same route. The guards of course didn't hear. He flew without a noise in at the window. Then she said to him this thing: "Listen, Serezha, they are watching out for us now. Everywhere there are guards except in my bedroom. It would be better not to be caught, or else they'll shoot you. Tell me better how I am to fly with you, or else it will be bad for us. My nannies have reported about me that someone is flying to me, and he yesterday questioned me and threatened me with execution."

He said, "Listen, Tania, don't you think about a thing. There'll be a time, and we'll fly! It will carry the both of us, but it won't carry three."

So then the servants began to watch her hard and reported to the tsar, "Your guards are of no account, but there's somebody there with her. He flies to her in her bedroom."

Then the tsar ordered them to do a piece of work: to put daggers in her window from all four sides. "Either he'll be cut up, or his clothing will be cut, and afterwards we'll discover this beast." And that's what they did. During the day they put the four daggers to the window. She lay down to sleep and thought, "Oh, my dear Serezha will perish, I'll never see him any more, and I'll have to finish myself off."

But then he that very night flew off, and he didn't know what had been done there. The windows were all open, and so the airplane carried him through calmly and no dagger hindered him. And she was overjoyed that he remained whole. She spoke to him: "Now listen, Serezha, you managed to fly here, but I don't know how you'll fly out—come and see what they've done here. Now the both of us have fallen into a trap."

Yes. So he said, "Listen, Tania, even though we're trapped, it's not entirely. I won't be able to take you right away, as we both can't fly through here, but I'll try to take you soon. I know we have to fly."

So he got in his airplane and flew back, and there were no marks on him. He placed the airplane in its old place beneath the oak, and then he tumbled off to sleep. And he didn't know what was left there. When the servants came, they examined all the daggers, and they saw that on one dagger there remained some material from some sort of shirt. And not even the tsarevna knew this. When they came, they saw the pattern, showed it to the tsar, who then ordered them to go throughout the entire city to search for the person and fetch him and put him in a dungeon. Well, where? Right away they set about to examine all the subjects in the palace, and then they later began to look at the grooms. When they began examining the grooms, they examined them all and finally came to the young groom. He was still asleep. He had played about through the night, and he had to sleep!

So then they woke him from his sleep and began examining him, and in his outer garments they found nothing. But then in his frock coat they discovered where the hem was cut off. They compared the clothing, ordered him to get dressed, and presented him to the tsar. When they had brought him to the tsar, the tsar asked him, "How did you manage to fly there? You flew here as a young boy, and now you're pulling such stunts that now I'll have to execute you. Tell me, how did you fly?"

And he answered, "Your Highness, well, I won't tell you how I flew, but you can do with me as you wish."

And they ordered him to the dungeon for three days and then execution. And so they led him off to the dungeon. And so his young life was to end! Just so. When they had led him to the dungeon, they removed all the daggers from the tsarevna's window, and there was no longer any guard.

Thus they kept him in the dungeon for a whole day. And the second day the tsarevna learned of it and started weeping bitterly. "My Serezha is finished. Well, it's all the same. I won't give myself up into their hands alive. When they execute him, I'll take matters into my own hands that very day."

The second day some ragged man walked by the dungeon where he was sitting. Now he had this little window looking out onto freedom. And so he started calling this man over. "Hey, my good man, come here! I've a couple of words to say to you." Then he spoke to him: "Listen, my good lad, go to the court yard and there you'll find an oak, and beneath this oak is an object in a rag. Stick in your hand, and bring it here. And I'll give you twenty-five rubles. No, fifty—I won't spare. Only bring it here."

"Well, all right," he said, "I'll go." But he thought, "Probably there is a lot of money there; I won't bring it to him." So he went to the tsar's courtyard, went to the stables, and there he was opposite the oak. He stuck in his hand, brought out some sort of object, unwrapped it, and there was just some iron. "Well," he thought, "all right, I'll bring it to him and get some money for it." So he brought it to the window, of course, and handed it over to him through the window.

"Well, young man, many thanks to you," and he handed him the money. Then he looked to see that everything was in order. Everything was just so. He waited for nightfall. And when he had awaited nightfall, all the people had quieted down, and then he got in his airplane and flew off already on the third day. This was the day when he was to be executed. He flew to her, but the window was closed. He knocked, she guessed, and opened up and threw herself around his neck, and said, "Well. Serezha, now it's the last minute. Carry me off as quickly as possible, or else it will be too late!"

Then he asked, "Listen, Tania, bring me a pencil and paper and ink. I shall write your father and leave it here. Sometime they'll see it." He, of course, left a small note, who he was, of which country, whose son he was, and what he flew on. He sealed it and left it on the table, and said, "Well, Tania, get ready, we'll fly off now. Collect just what you need, don't take a lot. You yourself know that our airplane isn't very big. It's only got two places."

She took what she needed. And so when they were ready. They got in the airplane, flew out the window, and flew off.

They came looking the next day, but the tsarevna was no longer there. They just found the letter lying on the table. And they presented it to the tsar. When the tsar had read in this letter what had happened with the tsarevich, that he was a tsar's son, he said, "I wouldn't have dealt with him so. Now it's late, if he had only written who he was . . . Well, now I don't know where he has carried her off to." With that he quieted down.

So they flew on farther. They flew up near a city and she said, "I feel that today I might give birth."

He said to her, "Listen, Tania, what shall I do? You know that our airplane won't carry three. I already said that earlier." So then he calmly began lowering the airplane to that city. On the very edge of the city, there stood a little hut all by itself. When they had landed, he said, "Well, Tania, get to this hut, if you can, the last one."

They went up to the hut and knocked hard. Out of the hut came an old woman and asked, "Where have you come from, my children?"

"Don't you ask. First let us enter your hut."

And when they had entered, he said, "Well, Granny, let us spend a day here, and then I'll tell you everything—who we are and where we've come from."

He sat his Tsarevna Tatiana down on a chair and began explaining to the old woman who they were and how they were going. "Well, Granny, here's what happened: We are flying from a certain tsardom, and Tsarevna Tatiana feels that today is to be the birth day, that she has to give birth. So if you can, help her with this."

Then she said, "If you won't oppose it, Sergei Tsarevich, then I'll take Tatiana Tsarevna into a separate room, and you will stay here." Then a little time passed and she ran out and said, "Well, Sergei Tsarevich, you have just had a son born." He really rejoiced at this. And she went back, took up the child, washed it, and then brought it to Tsarevna Tatiana.

"Listen now, Granny, and you, beautiful Tania, either I have to stay here or you must, Tsarevna Tatiana, or we must leave our son with the granny, because our airplane can't ascend with more than two persons."

Then Tania thought a little and started weeping tears: "Well, we'll have to leave someone from the two of us." Then she also said, "Listen,

Tsarevich Sergei, this is my final word: I won't leave you. I'm willing rather to leave our son with Granny for safekeeping."

So then he said, "Well, all right, if that's the way it turns out, we'll have to accept it. Tell me now, Granny, how much will you take for the safe-keeping of our son while we fly home? Afterwards I'll fly back for him, as she still doesn't know how to pilot an airplane."

So Granny spoke up: "Listen, Sergei Tsarevich, I don't know, you would better give me as much as you can, but don't worry about your son. Is it possible that I don't know how to bring up children, in the best way of course, according to the old fashion? Don't you worry about a thing."

Just so. Then he handed over five thousand rubles to her.

"Well, Granny, maybe that will be sufficient while we fly home."

"Why of course, children, it's sufficient but you his parents know your own needs."

So they spent three days there, and then said goodbye to their baby. Of course, he was yet dumb and didn't understand a thing. They said goodbye to the granny. With tears the granny said, "My children, don't you worry about a thing. I'll keep your son for you as is proper, if God grants him health."

They said farewell to their granny and departed. They flew off. And in a short time they flew to his country. When they had arrived at his country, his father and mother rejoiced that their son had returned, and with a young wife, Tsarevna Tatiana. And they put on a big feast. And so they were married there, and he and the tsarevna began living there.

And now we shall leave them and start talking about their little son. When they had flown off, and a whole year had passed, they still weren't there. He had already started to walk, but they still weren't there. And when they had flown away, they had still not given him any name at all. Either they were too dismayed, or something. And so a year passed, another year, and the boy began running about. Granny didn't know what to call him. There was nothing else to be done, so Granny gave him the name "Know-nothing." When the lad was five years old, he was already a big, strong lad. And he spoke to Granny. He called her "Mama." "Mama, do you know what? I want to learn."

So Granny spoke to him:

"Listen, my little son, don't call me mama. Just call me granny, because I am already old. I can't be a mama to you. But wherever you want to study, I'll get you there."

So the granny registered him in the village school to study. And the lad so quickly began learning that in a year he surpassed those who had studied three years, and he went into the third class. And so he studied for five years and went through all the town schools, and there was no place else for him to study. He would have to move to another city. And all his teachers praised him and were amazed at his learning, saying that they had never seen such a boy. He read and wrote and was adept at all such things.

So now his granny said, "Well, now your name will be Know-nothing." And all the teachers called him Know-nothing.

"Listen, son, I received from your father five thousand rubles, but only one thousand are left, or even less, and you know yourself that we have to live. You can't go on with your studies. You had better go to a merchant in a shop."

And he, of course, was agreed. "Well, all right, I am agreed. What's to be done—we have to live."

So he went to a merchant in a shop. He came there, of course, to the merchant and spoke. Of course they didn't call him "comrade," they called him "master." "Master trader, take me on, of course, not as a senior but as some sort of junior. I can do accounts, mark goods, or count."

Of course, the merchant looked at this youth and said, "Whose child are you and what is your name?"

"I don't know my name, only my granny knows. They call me Know-nothing, but I am schooled. I will serve you."

So of course the merchant looked at him and took him on at the beginning as a shopkeeper's assistant. So then this boy served three or four months, and then he became a most exacting order clerk, such as is rarely to be found. The master made him an order clerk. And when he had served a year, they gave him a separate shop, and he became the manager. He kept all the accounts himself. And so this merchant loved him so that he promoted him and raised his salary, and he raised it to one hundred rubles. And so he began serving in that shop. And so many people started going to that shop that there weren't enough goods. The merchant sent over everything and sent over the most expensive goods, and he himself was amazed. "From my twelve shops not a single order clerk can deal with goods and sell so many as this Know-nothing."

Now this merchant had three daughters. And once the youngest daughter had to go into the city. And she had earlier heard that one of the order clerks was very handsome and traded best of all. And she went to have a look at him. She came, looked at this order clerk, and asked for several goods there. And so she liked him so much that she couldn't live without him, but she didn't say a word to him. He spent that whole day in his trading, went back to his granny, drank and ate. And Granny said to him, "Well, Know-nothing, now it's much easier, now we don't need your father's money so much, but as you are living on your salary, it's fine."

He said, "What were my parents like, and why did they abandon me?"

"I know that your father was Sergei Tsarevich," she said to him, "and this is why: They flew in an airplane and landed here. And you were born here. Then they flew away and left me with five thousand for your upbringing."

"Well, all right, what am I to do? Maybe they are no longer among the living now."

In the morning he arose and opened his shop. He had just opened it, when at twelve o'clock that same merchant's daughter came in and said, "Listen, young man, what is your name?"

"They call me Know-nothing."

"Then come this evening." And she told him the address. "I'm uncomfortable here, and you and I have much to talk about." Then she asked further, "When do you close your shop?"

"At six o'clock."

"Well, all right, then I shall await you after six o'clock."

After that, he spent that day. But a shopper kept walking and walking about. She didn't buy anything new, only gazed at the order clerk. Five-thirty came, and he started to count up the money and goods. The master came at six. He gave him the money and closed the shop. Then he looked at the address and set off. He came to a big corridor. She ran out, took him by the hand, and led him away. How she had expected him! So she led him into a parlor, brought out all sorts of snacks, and began treating him, and then questioning him herself. "Tell me, Know-nothing, of what people are you and have you lived with our father for long?"

He said, "I don't know who my people are. I live with my granny. As she says, my father and mother flew in an airplane. The airplane wouldn't carry three, so they left me with the granny for my upbringing. Now I've been working at your father's for about two years."

She looked at him in the eye and said, "Well, tell me, how old are you, Know-thing?"

"Now I'm thirteen years old. It's the fourteenth since I was born."

And she said to him, "Listen, Know-nothing, I've fallen deeply in love with you, so you come to me every day when you finish your work. Come right away."

So he ate a little there, of course, and he drank absolutely little. She took him by the hand and led him to a tunnel. As she was leading him through the tunnel, he saw there such a beautiful hall and music everywhere. From it two very young maids came up to meet them. She said right away, "Greetings, sisters, meet my partner. He will be mine."

They greeted him, of course, and said, "Well, Marusia, now we each have a partner, and we shall all live well." They called the youngest one Marusia.

Suddenly out came two other young partners. They greeted each other. Then there began dances and merry-making and all sorts of good things. They danced, and then departed to separate rooms. Know-nothing stayed there until four o'clock in the morning, and then said, "Listen, Maria, I've got to get out of here before someone sees me."

She said to him, "Listen, Know-nothing, sit quietly here. As yet no one knows about this house and underground, even our father doesn't know. I'll soon lead you out and acquaint you with this area. Only we know about this, and you are not to tell anyone about it so that no one will know anything." And so she took him by the hand and led him out to the edge of the town. Not far away was his little hut, where his granny lived. She led him out and said, "Listen, when you want to see me, or come to me, you come to this door, press the button, and open it."

Well, that door was so cleverly made that it wasn't even visible from the outside. So they said good-bye. She said to him, "But, Know-nothing, come to me every night, and we shall have a good time."

When he had come home at five o'clock, his granny asked him, "Where have you been so late, my son?"

"Oh, playing about, Granny. You see, I'm young, I want to play." More than that he didn't say, he just added, "Wake me up, Granny, at nine o'clock."

She woke him up. He sat down at the table and drank a cup of coffee. His granny asked, "Why have you drunk and eaten so little?"

"Well, all right, Granny, I'll eat there today."

Then he went, opened up the shop, and began trading. And then suddenly at eleven o'clock in came his master. "Greetings, Know-nothing, what kind of goods do you need today?"

"Well, so such and such goods are going with me. There are a lot of customers, as you yourself can see."

Then the master ordered him to get all the goods and was really happy, as such an order clerk he had never, ever met.

And then again that evening he closed the shop at six o'clock and set off walking. And this went on for a whole year. Then once she said to him, "Do you know, Know-nothing, I sense that I am pregnant."

"Well, so what? I don't know anything."

"Well, you know how my father values you as the very best order clerk, so try your luck: Ask to marry me, and see what he says. But don't you say anything about your coming to me or even that you know me, and don't show it."

So again he spent the night and went home. The next day he opened the shop. When he had opened the shop, just like every day, to that very first shop his master came and questioned him as to what goods he needed. When the master had come, Know-nothing said, "Well, Master, because you value me so much, and appreciate my work, what I'm going to ask you, please don't refuse me."

And he said to him, the master did, "Well, what, Know-nothing? Speak. What idea do you have? I know you well, and perhaps I won't refuse you."

He said, "Do you know what, Master, I want to marry your daughter. Will that be possible? You see that I am young and that I live with my granny."

The master looked at him and slapped him on the cheek: "How dare you? I don't know whose son you are, and is it likely that I, a millionaire, could give my daughter to some sort of Know-nothing!"

He didn't say another thing and continued his work. So again he spent the day until six o'clock, counted up what he had sold, and carried the money to the master. He closed up the shop and went off. The master wasn't angry; he took the money, and said nothing more to him.

When he came to her, she again asked him, "Well, did you ask my father?"

"I asked him."

"And what did he say to you?"

"He struck me and said, 'How do you dare, you are no one's son, some Know-nothing.' Therefore he won't marry you to me." He spent the time with her until about two, went home, and went to bed.

Now up until then, his father and mother had forgotten about their son, how they had abandoned him. Then once there was this conversation between the tsarevna and Sergei Tsarevich:

"Listen, Sergei Tsarevich, we loved each other passionately when we were united. And now fifteen years have passed and up until now we have had no children."

When she said that they had no children, he held his head with both his hands and said, "But don't you remember in what condition you were when we flew away from your tsardom? Where we left our son?"

Then she immediately remembered and broke out weeping. "What have we done, Serezha, if fifteen years have passed and we, the parents, have not been concerned for our son and have not thought to visit him."

"Well, what will you do, I'll have to fly after him, and you will remain at home. I'll fly."

Just then their father and mother came. And they saw the bride in tears. "Why are you so tearful today?"

She began explaining everything, how they had abandoned their son.

"Perhaps he is starving there, even if alive. But now go and search him out, son."

So he gathered up some really fine clothing—regal—for his son, and all sorts of good things: two suitcases, some money, of course. So, of course, he knew in which city he had been left. He flew to that city, landed his airplane by that hut in which he had been left. So when he had come up to that hut, he knocked. It was about eleven in the evening. He knocked, and the old woman came out.

"Granny, may I spend the night here?"

"You can."

Well, Granny didn't recognize him because it was fifteen years ago. So, of course, Granny saw such a guest and thought he was some sort of merchant. She put on the samovar. He opened his suitcase and got out some wine and snacks, and said:

"Well, Granny, sit down and eat with me."

The granny, of course, didn't refuse, and she sat down to eat with him. He poured out some wine and said, "Well, Granny, drink up, even though I, of course, drink little. But straight from the road I can. Drink up, and then I'll tell you for what reason I came to this town."

Granny drank a glass, and then he poured her another. And then he started talking. "So now then, Granny, how do you live alone, don't you have any family?"

"No, I'm not alone, I have this boy."

"But is he yours, or where's he from? Where did you get this boy?" (He was questioning this granny now.)

"No, he's not mine, but I'll tell you about this boy, how the business came about."

And so she started telling him. "So now then, this time was already fifteen years ago. Once a tsarevich happened to fly over this city. Sergei Tsarevich they called him. And his wife, it happened that she had to give birth at that time. But their airplane couldn't carry three persons, and the child was left with me."

And he listened.

"So then, of course, she gave birth to the son here, and they left him, and they gave me five thousand, and I raised him on this money. Although it wasn't enough, I raised him and taught him to read and write. And now he works for a certain merchant in a shop. And this merchant praises him highly."

"And where is he now?"

"He's asleep now."

"Now then, Granny, listen, only don't say anything to anybody and not even to him. But what is his name?"

"Well I don't know, they didn't leave a name for him, so I've called him 'Know-nothing,' and that's what he's called. But he's a very smart boy—handsome—fifteen years but as if a grown man."

"So now, Granny, I am that same Sergei Tsarevich. And we've just remembered him after these fifteen years. And he is my son. Only don't you say anything to anybody now; I'll find out his situation with the merchant. I came here to have a look, to buy some goods. First I'll sort out everything. But now, do you know what, Granny? Is it possible to wake him? I want to have a look at him."

"Yes, it's possible, only he just went to bed. But since you're his father, then it's possible to awaken him."

"Only now don't say anything to him, just that a merchant has come and wants to buy some goods of him, and what kind of goods does he have, and he wants to get acquainted."

So the granny went into a separate space and started to wake him up. "Get up, Know-nothing, just now some merchant has come and wants to buy some goods from you and get acquainted with you because you know all the goods."

Of course, Know-nothing got up, washed, and dressed, and went up to this merchant. When he had gone up to him, of course, he greeted him politely. And he asked him to sit down on a chair. He sat down next to him, and then Granny sat down with them together. And then he began questioning: "Well, and how do you live here? What kinds of goods are there in the shop? How much does the merchant pay you?"

He told him everything in detail. He let him know everything.

"Well, do you know what, I came to you to buy some goods worth one and a half thousand, the very best."

"Well, well, that's very good for our master, that will have great significance for him. He will praise me!" And so Know-nothing was very happy.

"Now I will bring you a book and show you all the goods that will please you most, and tomorrow I will order them from the merchant." And he brought a book and calculated up to a thousand, and then he looked at him and said, "You are well taught, my boy, how much does he pay you? How quickly you calculated all that, and what bookkeeper could add it up so quickly!"

"I receive from the merchant a hundred fifty rubles."

"He pays you very little for such learned work. Well, all right, Know-nothing, let's drink a little something."

So he poured out a shot for himself and for him and for the granny, and all of them, of course, drank up. When they had drunk a little, it became a little noticeable in him, and also in Sergei Tsarevich. Of course, he gave no sign that he was a tsarevich.

He said to him, "Yes, Know-nothing, your name isn't so great, but what can you do? Your parents didn't give you a better one, and your granny called you that." And again he questioned him: "Tell me, Know-nothing, what do you do to amuse yourself? Why, you're very young, so do you dally with the girls, or no?"

And so he said, "Up until now I haven't told a soul, and people don't know anything. But if I were to tell you, I would ask you and Granny to say nothing to anyone—where I have been, when I started going to the merchant. But I've been living with the merchant's daughter just short of two years. And she's in a condition from me. And I once asked the merchant to marry her to me, but he struck me on the cheek and said 'How do you dare, Know-nothing, say such a thing to me?' Since then, I haven't spoken of it to him."

"Well, what will you do? You've endured it, haven't said a thing. But I will speak of it later with the merchant. Maybe you'll still have her as your wife."

Then Know-nothing was really happy when he heard these words from the merchant, and he said, "Listen, dear merchant, if it's like this, I'll show her to you, only you mustn't say anything—nor you, Granny."

"Well, what's to be done; we won't speak of it."

So then he immediately got dressed and ran to that tunnel where he had always gone. He pushed the button, the door opened, and he went through the tunnel to her. "Well, Marusenka, get dressed. Now I'm going to lead you to Granny. Don't be afraid, nothing bad will come of it."

She quickly got dressed, and they set off. And he brought her there in something like a half hour. And she was such an attractive young lady that the merchant looked at her simply with amazement. She immediately greeted him. And he said, "Well, sit down at the table, I will question you and perhaps you will tell me something."

They sat down together at the table. They sat for a little time, and she told them everything about herself, how she had become acquainted with Know-nothing. When four hours had passed, she said, "Well, Know-nothing, I must go. Look, you yourself know that."

So then she, of course, said good-bye, wished them all well, and Know-nothing accompanied her to that tunnel and then came back. When he came back, then his father asked, "When do you open the shop?"

"At ten o'clock."

"Well, go to sleep. It's now six o'clock. Sleep until ten, and if you are late, tell the merchant 'I was busy with some merchant.' Then he won't say anything to you."

So he went away to sleep. And he and the granny remained there. "Listen, Granny, right now don't say anything, but his name is Nikolai. But don't say anything right now, and then later all will become clear."

And so the merchant also went off to have a little rest. And so it went to nine-thirty. She woke him up.

"Granny, I haven't overslept?"

"No, you haven't overslept, but if you had overslept a little, you'll explain everything."

So. Then he immediately put on his shoes, got dressed, and went to the shop.

When he had managed to open up, the merchant came, his master. And when the master had come in, he said:

"Oh, I almost overslept today, I was busy with this one merchant."

"And what's going on?"

"Well, this one merchant came, a buyer, and he wants to take goods worth one thousand five hundred. Such buyers as this we've never had before."

"Well, good lad, Know-nothing, get the goods ready."

"Yes, I know already."

The merchant simply rejoiced; he ran about the shop, joyfully. And then not long after that other merchant came, but still the merchant didn't leave the shop.

"Well, and how much will you be wanting to take?"

"Well now, as I said yesterday."

"Well, let's go then and you have a look. Will you be taking everything right away, or shall we pack it for you?"

"No, I won't be taking them right away. Let them be for a day or two, and the order clerks can pack them."

So they packed up all these goods. He took the money and this merchant, the master, invited the merchant to be his guest. So they set off. And at that time Know-nothing remained to trade. And when he [the visiting merchant] came to his place, he was seated at the table, and they began treating him, giving him drinks, and so forth. They sat there and talked. And this merchant, Sergei Tsarevich, asked, "Has this Know-nothing lived with you long, and how much do you pay him for such speedy work, as I note."

"I am paying him a hundred fifty rubles."

"You pay him little. With us such order clerks receive at least three hundred rubles in shops. And, if he wishes, I'll take him and I'll pay him three hundred rubles. I consider that he'll agree to go with me for three hundred rubles."

And then that merchant said, "Well, even though I pay him a hundred fifty rubles, I won't let him go. And I'll give him three hundred rubles because such order clerks are nowhere to be found. He does the restocking for all eleven shops. And I meet all his conditions and fulfill them as he wishes."

So then he again said, "No, you don't fulfill all his conditions. I heard from him himself, from Know-nothing, that he wished to marry your daughter, and you gave him one on the neck. For that reason he became really angry, so you don't fulfill all his requests as he wishes."

So then they talked a little more, and he went away. His wife came out to him. He said to her, "Here's what that merchant said to me: that I pay Know-nothing very little, and that he will take him on himself; that I don't fulfill his request to marry him to my daughter, though he's of no known parents and it will be a great disgrace to me. But I've no wish to release him because he's a very valuable worker."

Then his wife said to him, "Listen, Husband, you haven't judged this correctly. If he's such a valuable worker, this Know-nothing, then that's all nothing, and you must give him our daughter, if he wants to take her. I've heard some unpleasant rumors about her going around. That is my advice, and there, it's as you know best."

"Well, what kind?" her father asked.

"Well, like this: One cook related to me that as of yet no one knows that she's in 'a condition'. And moreover, she can't be controlled."

"Now, if that is it, then call Know-nothing here from the shop, and I'll tell him something."

They immediately ordered Know-nothing to go to the merchant. And he went about a little and then closed the shop. The merchant sat him down next to him and began talking with him: "Now, listen, Know-nothing, this merchant wants to take you and pay you three hundred rubles. And I will pay you three hundred rubles—only live here." And he went on to say, "You told him that I struck you on the cheek because I wouldn't give you my daughter. But if you were from any sort of family—even peasant stock—if you had a name, then, you understand . . . But I don't know you, you understand. Why, I'm a merchant, a millionaire, and I would be shamed. It would be a disgrace to all!" He looked at him, got angry, and said, "Well, get going, do your trading. Go to the shop."

Wait a minute! You'll give her up, you yourself don't know! Then he began trading again. And the merchant sat for a long time at the table and thought. After that he ordered them to summon his littlest daughter. She came, he looked at her, and he said, "Tell me the truth now, Daughter, with whom have you been playing about? Who's got you pregnant? Don't hide it."

And she said, "Father, I'll tell you only when you marry me to the one who I played about with. Otherwise, I won't say; even if you kill me, I won't say."

Then her father looked at her. "Well, go on then. If you won't say, I won't speak!"

And then this Know-nothing spent the day again, closed the shop, set off for her, and went down into the tunnel. When he came to her, she told him what her father had said to her, and he had told about himself. Then she also said, "So you go home now and invite that merchant here. Let him see our valuables, but let him not say anything to anybody. My father is not to know of it. And you come with him."

So he went and said, "Well, here's what" Listen, comrade merchant, let's go now to the underworld, where there are these three daughters, and I'll show you all their valuables, if you wish."

And so they got dressed and set off. They came to that door, pressed the knob, and passed through so that nobody would know of it. So then they came to that hall, and all three sisters came running up, greeted them, and began entertaining them. So there was music, joy, and the merchant looked at all this that was going on.

The two young partners came, and they all began having fun together. And after these dances he went to the merchant and said, "If you want to get acquainted with one of these girls, you can."

"Good."

And they went away, each to their own rooms. And then after this, he went to get acquainted with his girl friend, and they spent until four o'clock in the morning. Then Know-nothing came out, got dressed, and they went right back home. When they got home, they lay down to sleep. They got up at nine and drank their tea. He went alone to his work in the shop, but the other simply went into the town. So he opened his shop, the master came, and he began trading. Then this merchant came again to that merchant. Again they had a conversation. The merchant's talk was all about the same thing: about goods and riches.

So again he spoke up: "Well, did you talk with your order clerk, Know-nothing?"

"Yes, I called him in, and he is agreed that I will give him three hundred rubles."

"Well, and are you giving him everything that he requested of you?"

And he answered him: "Of course not, you will yourself understand that I am a merchant. Could I possibly marry my daughter to such a Know-nothing? Why, it would be a disgrace."

"You think that way in vain; I wouldn't even hesitate for such a valuable worker. In any case, I'll take him away for myself. I'll pay him even more. Well, all right, we won't talk about it anymore. If you wish, come be my guest, and where I take you, endure it all. And if you can endure it, then I'll pay you two millions—yes, please, the money is on the table. Only be silent, whatever you see. You need great patience. Only give me your answer now."

He looked at him, shook his head, and said, "Yes, that's a lot of money, I'm likely agreed."

"But only on the condition of silence, whatever you see."

He even gave him an oath.

"But if you can't endure it, then your money is lost. Well, so, now then come to me at about seven o'clock or at six." He gave him the address. "At the house of some old woman, and come to me only as a merchant so that no one will recognize you, will know you are of this city. And there we'll do everything."

Then he said, "Well, all right, I'll come."

So he went off to make himself up so that no one would recognize him, and he got ready to appear like a merchant. Most of all he was interested in finding out what it was that he knew, what sort of rare thing it was. And so he was ready at six o'clock. "Well, I need to go now!"

And he set off. Just at that time, Know-nothing had closed the shop and was coming home, where the other two were already sitting. So then Know-nothing caught sight of an unfamiliar merchant sitting there. And the merchant said to him, "Greet such and such a merchant."

They sat down at the table. Sergei Tsarevich brought a suitcase and took out various wines, which were up to then not available in that town, and he began treating that merchant and Know-nothing. When he had treated him, Sergei Tsarevich said, "Well, now I have treated you as you treated me."

Then he and Know-nothing went to one side and he said, "Listen, now you can invite this merchant to go with us, too. I already know you'll be going."

"Yes, that's possible. Only he mustn't say a word to anybody."

"He won't talk; he's promised to be silent."

And so then at about nine o'clock or ten they set off. He came up to that door, pressed the button, they descended into the tunnel and set off. The merchant was amazed that this was taking place and happening in the city, and he didn't know about it. So he led them into the hall. Suddenly out came running his three daughters, and they greeted them. The music started up and they began entertaining. And he saw that Know-nothing was with his youngest daughter. And he thought, while sitting there silently, "So somehow, well, I've got to keep my promise."

So they drank, of course, were entertained, went off to dance. And Know-nothing said, "Well now, guests, whoever wishes, choose a maiden for yourself and go dance." Well, that was unbearable. And he said, "I don't want to, let my comrade go, he's a little younger."

So when they had danced a little, they finished that game, and the girls came up to the table and said, "Now then, you can choose from among the girls for yourself and spend the time until morning, but we are going."

And they all went to their own rooms. But the merchant was still amazed and thought, "What's going on here, and who is this being done by?"

So when they had left, the one merchant said to the other, "Well now then, my friend, are you going? I'm not going and I would like it if you remained here with me to talk about something while they go out."

"All right, I won't go."

So they remained sitting there together. When the two of them were sitting there, then that merchant said to the other merchant, his host: "Well, what you see, what is going on here, you see your order clerk Know-nothing with your daughter? Can it be that you won't marry your daughter now?"

"No, I will marry her, it will only disgrace me that he is called Know-nothing."

"Well, what's to be done? And in addition you will receive two millions."

So they spent the time until four o'clock. Know-nothing came out and said, "Well now, guests, let's go. I have to be at work by ten o'clock."

And they immediately got ready and went out to the old woman. When they had come again, they sat down at the table, had some refreshments, and he said: "So now, comrades, you know what sort of person I am, I have to go to work by ten o'clock, so I'll go to sleep for a little while, because I have always been on time, and I wish to today also—otherwise there will be unpleasantness from the merchant."

Then that merchant said, "Listen, Know-nothing, you already really worry about these goods. I also have come to buy goods. He will say nothing to you if you open at twelve, so sit a little with us—at least an hour."

And so then he added:

"Well, how then, will you live with this merchant, Know-nothing? Or will you go with this merchant who has made you the offer?"

"I don't know. If only he fulfills my proposals, then I'll remain. But if not, I'll leave because there's nothing for me to do here. And I won't leave my wife Maria, but I'll take her away with me in any case."

"Well, all right then, don't get upset. Maybe the merchant will marry her to you. Perhaps that merchant doesn't like it that your name is Know-nothing, but otherwise he'd marry her to you. And today he'll give you his answer."

So he wished them all the best and anyway went off to rest. The two of them were left alone. Then afterwards he went off, and that merchant asked him, "Well, I saw what was going on there and I endured it. Well, young man, take your two millions, and I'll come to you later."

They ate and drank. He came, and he lay down to sleep. And that Know-nothing, the old woman let him sleep until ten thirty.

"Well, get up, Know-nothing. You've already slept a long while today."

"Oh, Granny, how late I am today. That merchant won't praise me for certain."

He quickly washed and set off. He came, of course, and opened the shop already in the twelfth hour. His master came, and he said: "Well, master, forgive me, it never was before. I've let my time pass today."

"Never mind, never mind, Know-nothing. I heard that you were with that merchant this night, and for that reason I'll forgive you."

And then after that he went home and began discussing it with his wife. "Listen, Wife, you don't know what sort of treasures we have in our tunnel, but I found out and have received two millions for it. How our daughters carouse! And Know-nothing carouses with the youngest one because she is pregnant and we'll have to marry her off—it's all the same."

"My advice was that you should have married her off a long time ago."

So then he ordered them to summon Know-nothing.

"What do you require, master?"

"Well if it's like this, Know-nothing, that you've managed to do all this, then you're some lad, and I'll marry my daughter to you. Now go to the shop."

So he went to the shop, and the merchant called his daughter in and said, "Well, beautiful Maria, I will marry you to Know-nothing. Is that what you wish?"

"Of course I wish it, I've been telling you that for a long time."

"Well, you can tell him that."

She immediately ran off to the shop. And at that very time his father came to the shop. She came in one door and he in another. When his father had come in, he said: "Well, listen Know-nothing, I will tell you something but you are not to say anything. You are not Know-nothing, but Nikolai, and your second name is Sergeich, and I am your father. But you are to say nothing to anybody."

So then at that time she came running into the shop and said: "Well, Know-nothing, Father will marry me to you."

"But I am not Know-nothing; I am Nikolai Sergeich, a tsar's son."

She took fright and fell into a faint. "How could Father refuse a tsar's son and strike him on the cheek for asking to marry me!" Then right away she said, "How my father will be embarrassed when he finds all this out. Listen, Kolia, I am even more embarrassed! What will become of me now?"

"Don't you bother about a thing," his father said to her, "Don't you think about a thing; now we'll close the shop and put on a wedding. I shall go to your father. I know how to handle it. I was only fifteen years old when I married a tsarevna. Since you love him, let it be so."

So he went to that merchant, and she ran off home. The merchant right away ordered them to call Know-nothing and close the shop. When Know-nothing had closed the shop, he immediately went home to the old lady. When he got there, there sat his father. "Listen, my son, now we are going to put on a wedding. But first you must take that case with the royal clothing that I have in readiness for you."

And they also asked the old granny to get dressed and go with them. And for the granny he also had everything brought there. And so they got ready all three of them and went to that merchant for a ball. And so, of course, they came there and were invited to the table. They sat down to be entertained. They began putting on the wedding. So then they sat there for a little while, and then Sergei Tsarevich stood up and said, "Listen, comrades, and I will explain something of myself and of my son to you." So then he began talking: "Do you know what sort of merchant I am? I am Tsarevich Sergei from such and such a country, and this Know-nothing is Nikolai Sergeich, my son."

The merchant immediately fainted. How could it have happened that he had treated a tsar's son that way! He immediately got to his feet and began begging forgiveness. Here's what the tsarevich said: "Well, it is too late for forgiveness but I'll forgive everything and now give me a separate room where I can go with my son; he and his bride must change their clothing."

So they went into a second room. He got them all some clothing—for the bride as well as for his son, the heir to the royal house—and for himself, and they all went back to the table. So they all came back to the table. They sat down but all the guests got to their feet and began honoring Sergei Tsarevich, and like the merchant, they all began asking forgiveness for not having known it up until then. Then the feast continued. And the feast went on for three days. Then all the guests departed.

And he said to his son Nikolai Sergeich, "Well, Kolia, get ready; we'll leave your wife for the time being because I told you that the airplane would carry only two. Then you can fly back for her, if she still hasn't given birth. But if she has, then you'll have to leave the baby and bring her first."

Well, of course, his wife didn't want to be left behind, but there was nothing to be done, and she said to her father that the granny who had looked after Nikolai Tsarevich would go to her if she wished, while she was there. Then Nikolai Tsarevich said to the granny: "You, Granny, calm her, remain with her while I fly off, and then it shall be as you wish it: if you wish to come with us, or if you wish to stay here."

"Well all right, Nikolai Sergeich, I'll stay here with her."

So they said their goodbyes and flew off. Suddenly they came to their own country, and he brought his own son. No way could his mother recognize her son. When he said it, she fell into a faint. When she regained consciousness, she threw her arms around his neck and begged forgiveness for having abandoned him. Then he said, "All right, Mama, don't cry now, you have your joy now as we'll all live together."

Then his grandmother and grandfather came, and all rejoiced when they saw their grandson Nikolai Sergeich. They sat down at the table and of course began questioning him. How had he spent those fifteen years? He told them everything, even that he was married. They all greatly rejoiced: his mother, his grandmother, and his grandfather. And they asked him when he would fly off for her.

Then he began asking his father, "Tell me, Father, do we not have a little bit bigger airplane so that I could not only bring me and my wife, but also whoever is born there, and my father-in-law and his wife, and the granny?"

And he said, "Listen, Kolia, we don't have such an engineer; he died long ago. And for that reason we didn't order another airplane. You will have to carry them in this one, one at a time, as you yourself know."

So now his father showed him how to control this airplane and what he had to do, and then he got ready and flew off to that city. He flew into that city, came to the house, and she immediately ran out to him and said, "Well, Kolia, I gave birth to a son, and now three of us can't fly at once."

"Well, all right, Marusia, get ready yourself. I'll take you and then fly back for our son. And let Granny look after our son until I fly here for him."

(I've omitted something here: When the merchant found out what was going on—that there were three cavaliers—he immediately married his daughters to these lads and let them then live as they know how, with God.)

Then they went to the granny and told her everything. "Well, all right, my children, fly away, and I'll make an effort. Only don't forget what your father forgot; I'm already old and I might die."

"All right, Granny, don't worry, I won't forget."

And then in a short time they flew to that tsardom. When they—the mother, and grandmother, and grandfather—saw the bride, they were overjoyed, and they received her very well. And so he stayed there several days, and then said, "Well, Marusia, you know I have to fly after our son, or else Granny might get tired."

And so he got ready to fly there a second time. When he had flown there again to that city, he dropped in at Granny's and said, "Well, Granny, I've come after my little son."

"Thank you, my child, here is your son. He's well, healthy, so you can take him."

And he said to the granny, "Granny, don't you want to see our country and live with us? If so, I'll take you, too, and fly here a second time for you."

She said to him, "Listen, Nikolai Sergeich, I am already old, the grave is there for me. I've a desire to die here at home."

So he took out some money and gave her a good bag of it, without even counting it out. "So this is for you, Granny. Live on as long as you can, and it's all the same. While you're alive, we will visit you and find out whether you want to fly to us."

So he took his leave, of course, and took his son. They flew off. Soon they landed in his own country. There was even greater joy from his grandfather and grandmother when they saw their grandson. After all that, Sergei Tsarevich said to his son, "Well now, Kolia, we shall put on a ball, and we'll have to invite your father-in-law and mother-in-law; in any case we'll have to fetch them. And meanwhile, we'll have the guests."

So then Nikolai Sergeich immediately flew after his father-in-law. And so, of course, he flew to their home, and they greatly rejoiced, sat down at the table, and began eating and drinking.

"Listen, Father and Mother, now I have flown here after you. I beg you not to refuse, but I will only be able to take you one at a time. Whichever wishes to go first, we'll fly off." So then, of course, there was no way that they could refuse. "Well, whichever one wants to go first."

Then he carried off his mother-in-law, but he said to him [the father-in-law], "Well, Father, don't be insulted, I'll fly back for you, but know that three of us can't fly together."

So they quickly flew there. They landed and went into the palace. They entered the palace, and they received her as if she was an honored guest, and they began entertaining her. And Tsarevich Sergei said to his son, "Listen, Kolia, you stay here now and I'll fly there. I'll take your place at least once. So since we are both the fathers, I'll fly and bring him back, and you and your mother-in-law do as you wish, because she was good to you, probably, and you took her first."

So then he got ready to fly. He flew to him and said, "Well, Kinsman, now you will fly to be our guest; we have something to entertain you with. Only first, I'll drop in on the old granny. I'll look in on her."

He went to her, and they exchanged greetings. "Greetings, Granny!"

"Greetings, greetings, Tsarevich Sergei. Have you come to look in on me?"

"That's it, Granny, one must call on you. Well, how is it, Granny, do you have enough money while your old age is carrying on?"

"But of course there's enough; more than enough. I've had enough already from you. I need nothing more."

"I'll tell my kinsman, that merchant, to look after you."

"Thank you, Sergei Tsarevich, I've already had enough from you." And so they said farewell, and he went to the merchant.

"Well, Kinsman, get in, let's fly!"

And so they flew there, and then the honorable feast began. And they feasted for three days. After that the merchant said to his son-in-law and to his kin, "Listen, I have shops, trade. I don't need to live here any longer. It would be good if you took me away from here. I no longer have a worker like my son-in-law Nikolai Sergeich in whom to put my trust. And I knew nothing of this. Now I apologize."

And then he said, "Well, Kin, I'll take you back as I brought you here."

So again they got in the airplane and flew away. And then when he had got him there, he flew back and said, "Well, I have fulfilled my duty. Now, Son, you do the same with your mother-in-law."

And he said, "It's not so bad for Mother-in-law to live here, if she wants. Then we'll take her back, but for now she isn't saying anything, so let her live here."

So she lived there for two whole months, and then said, "Well, son-in-law Kolia, it's time to take me home. My old man might be lonely, thinking I've perished."

"Well, all right, I'll take you."

So just then she said goodbye to all her kin, and they got in the airplane and flew away. So he brought her home, spent a day there, and his father said, "Listen, Son-in-law, if you wish, take some of the capital or some shops from me, because I don't have anybody else but you three sons-in-law. If I divide it, you see I'm no longer young."

So then he said to him, “For the time being, I don’t know anything of that. Probably you’ll not go anywhere, as you’ll promise me, but for the time being I don’t know anything.”

They said goodbye and he flew home. And when he had flown home, he began living and dwelling into deep old age. And then he mounted the throne when his grandfather and father died.

(SUS 575)

8

THE PEASANT'S SON AND THE FIREBIRD

M. M. Korguev

Now then, in a certain tsardom, in no certain country, not far away from the tsardom there stood a tree. And in this tree there lived and dwelt a little old man. And this little old man, of course, he was still really fit. Only they didn't have any children. He kept on hunting. He put out traps, caught birds, and from this he fed himself. And then one fine day, a son was born to them. And he began to grow up, and he learned to read— although only a little. Then, when the son had grown up and was about twelve, he said to his father, "Papa, take me hunting, or just let me see the woods."

He said, "Well then, son, let's do it, let's go."

They set off for the woods. Along the road he said, "Now then, Son, when we start going round setting the traps, you ought to set a trap for your own good fortune, even if it's just one. Maybe something will fall into it."

So when the got to the woods, his father showed him how to set a trap. And he set one trap for his own fortune. And they visited all the traps and went home. They had caught a lot of birds. When they came home, the old man and his son, they sold these birds. And of course they lived on just this alone; from this they fed themselves. They sat at home for a couple of days and again went out.

They went, and visited them, and saw what was there. They still hadn't got to his trap when the father said to his son, "Look, at your trap there's a fire burning." He looked. Yes, a fire was burning. They went up closer, and the fire became clearer and clearer. When they got up closer, the old man said, "Listen, my son, a firebird has gotten into your trap."

And he wanted to go up still closer. So the old man went up and wanted to take it, but the bird wouldn't yield to him. It burned him, burned him with fire, and it wouldn't surrender into his hands. Then he said to his son, "Well, you set it, you get it now, as you wish."

And he pushed his son closer to the trap. When he had pushed him closer, this youth took it. She yielded to him. He untangled it and put it in his bag. They set off farther, visiting the remaining traps. While they were going round the traps, they were held up for a long time, and it got dark. When it had become dark, nonetheless the firebird was in the bag and it lit up the path for them, like daylight. And so they came home. When they arrived home, the old man sold some birds, and some he kept for himself. And he said to the old woman, "And where shall we put this firebird? Of course, we can't keep it for ourselves. We'll have to sell it to someone. Perhaps someone will give more for it."

Then the old woman agreed: "Yes, Old Man, you'll have to take it to the city and offer it to a merchant or take it directly to the tsar. Likely, carry it straight to the tsar, and maybe he'll buy it."

So the old man put the bird in a sack. His son helped him, and he set off for the city. He set off to carry the bird right to the tsar. He came to the courtyard of the tsar's palace. There the courtiers asked him, "Grandfather, where are you going?"

The old man answered, "I am going directly to the tsar and I want to offer him a firebird. Maybe he'll buy it from me."

Then the courtiers led him to the tsar. He came in and bowed. "Greetings, Your Highness."

Then the tsar spoke: "Well, what have you to say, Grandfather, why have you come?"

He answered him: "Perhaps, wouldn't you like, Your Highness, to buy this bird from me. It got into my trap."

"Well, then show it to me."

The old man began shaking it out of the sack. When he had shaken it out, everything lit up such that it changed the entire tsardom from this light. Then the tsar said, "Well, Grandfather, however much you need for this bird, that's how much I'll give you."

"I don't know, Your Highness. Whatever you give, let it be your goodness, and I'll take it."

And he said, "Well, Grandfather, I'll give you two ankers of gold and a stone house. Will that be enough?"

Grandfather answered, "Thank you very much, Your Highness, whatever you give, I'll be satisfied."

The tsar immediately ordered his minister to open the cellar and to give Grandfather some gold and a horse and to take the gold to his house. And all this was done. The minister led him, and when he had received everything, he came and stored everything and ran to his old woman. (First we'll quiet down the old man and then we'll go on further.) He came up to the old woman and said, "Well, now we're rich, Old Woman. Let's go. We'll leave this house, Son, and go to a new one. We've enough for all our lives for bread and everything, and now we'll live without needing anything."

So, of course, they came to this stone palace, and they went in. The old man and old woman lived there until deep old age. Afterward the son got married. And now this part is ended. We'll leave them and go on to the tsar's son.

When this tsar had received the bird, he assigned it a special room and began himself to feed it whatever it wanted and what he ate himself. And he didn't entrust the keys to this room to anybody so that no one would let it out. Then one fine day he said to his wife, "Well, Wife, now I will go to all lands and gather all for a feast. At this feast I'll show off this firebird. Let all evaluate everything, how much it would cost. No one has seen it." And he added also, "So, Wife, I'll entrust the keys to his room to you. And don't you give them up so that the bird is safeguarded."

And he himself rode away to all the lands to let them know about this bird and invite them to a ball. Let them view and he will show it. He rode away, but he had a son. They called him Vaniusha. He ran about and played in the street. And it happened that he saw that firebird in the window. When he had seen it, the firebird started speaking in a human voice: "Well, Ivan Tsarevich, let me out of here. I'll be of use to you. I'll pay you back for it with whatever you wish."

And he said, "Well then, Firebird, how will I let you out: I don't have the keys, and I don't know where they are. Probably I won't be able to let you out."

"Now listen, Ivan Tsarevich, if you want to let me out, I'll instruct you as to how to do that. Go now to your mother, and ask her to look about your head. [For lice, JVH] And then untie the key. Then come into the room, open the window, and I'll fly away. And then ask your mother again to look about your head, and tie the key back in its place."

So he immediately went to his mother. And as he was her only son, she always humored him. He went up to her and said, "Mama, I've got something itching on my head, look about my head."

"Just so, lie down on my knees and I'll search."

And while she was searching, he untied the keys. So she finished. And he right away went to that room. He came and opened the lock, opened the door, and opened the window. "Now fly, Firebird. Don't be offended with me that I let you loose."

It perched on the windowsill, spread its wings, and said, "Well, Ivan Tsarevich, leave the window open for six hours. If I can't fly really high, I'll fly back here within six hours, and then you can close the window. And if I don't fly back, also close it."

He came in six hours and she had already flown back. "Well, Ivan Tsarevich, I could only fly one third the way. Keep me for three more days, and then let me go."

He locked the room and went to his mother. Once more she searched about his head, and he tied up the keys. And so three days passed. Again he went up to his mother: "Search, Mama. Again something has started itching on my head."

And she didn't know her son's tricks and said, "Well, all right, my son, lie down."

And she began looking. And just then, he again untied the keys. And just when she had finished, he again set off. He came to that room and opened the room and window. The firebird said to him, "Well, Ivan Tsarevich, this time keep the window open for eight hours. If I don't fly back in eight hours, then I can fly up, and I'll fly away."

When he had let it go, he went home, leaving the window open. He came in eight hours, and it was already sitting in the window, and it said, "Well, Ivan Tsarevich, today I flew up more than halfway. But I have to fly up to hide the whole earth; only then can I fly away to my own tsardom. Now you keep and feed me for six days."

So it went on living there for six days, but he had already tied the keys to his mother. The six days passed and he again went to his mother. "Well, Mama, search my head again, obviously, something has shown up again. And then I won't force you to again."

So she finished searching. He took the keys, went, and opened the window. It said to him, "Well, Ivan Tsarevich, if I don't fly back here within nine hours, it means I've flown away. And then, if you have a need, just think about me."

Nine hours passed—no firebird. He immediately closed the window and locked the room. Then he came to his mother. "Well, Mama, search once more." She started searching, and at that time he tied the keys in their place.

Not long afterward, the tsar came. And then from all the lands about, the tsars and also the kings, princes, and boyars began to gather. When they had all gathered, the tsar came to that room where the firebird had been, but it was no longer there. There remained just a single small feather. Then he came and said, "Well, Wife, tell me, who was in that room and let the bird out? Otherwise, I'll immediately execute you."

His wife answered, "Well, Husband, do what you wish with me, but I don't know where it has gone. I visited it myself only once a day and didn't give the keys to anybody."

Then the son came up. He saw his mother in tears. He pitied her. "Father, it's all my fault. I let the firebird go. Do with me what you wish, but don't upset Mother unjustly."

Then he said to him, "Now listen, Son, how did you dare to let it go? And you, Wife, how did you dare to give him the keys?"

"No, Papa, she didn't give me the keys. I took the keys myself. How I managed it, that is my affair, but Mama didn't give me the keys. When the firebird began asking me, it told me how to untie the keys Mama had, and that's what I did. I asked her to search my head, and at that time I untied the keys and let the bird loose. And in such a manner I tied them back in their place, and she knew nothing of it. So now do with me what you wish."

"Well, if that's the case, you've committed such a crime I'll execute you."

His mother started crying even more. Then the tsar said, "Well, all right, go for discussion to all the tsars and kings. They will tell your punishment."

So they went, but he grabbed and took that feather with him. Then he led him in and said, "Comrades, here is my son, and he has committed this crime: He has let loose the firebird, and nothing remains of it except this feather." And he placed the feather on the table. "I want to execute him. What judgment will you deliver him?"

They answered him: "Your Highness, you, as you yourself know, that the tsar's family is not to be executed, nor hanged, but you may only banish him to all four corners. But you may not take his royal title from him. And this is our only decision."

Then he said to his son, "Well, son, now leave the tsardom and go wherever you like, and you shall have no inheritance. Go in what you are standing there."

His mother wept bitterly, bitterly, so much did she pity her son. And she spoke up: "Listen, you are the father of your son. How can he go away without a servant, without even a horse? In any case, first of all he ought not set off alone."

Then the tsar ordered them to search out the poorest horse in the stable and he gave him a servant. That servant was also called Ivan. And so they set off on the horse, Ivan Tsarevich and the servant Ivan. And that tsar remained with his tsars and kings, and they could only believe him because he had that feather from that firebird. And when the feast was finished, they all went back to their own countries.

Now let's go after Ivan. So this Ivan Tsarevich went off with his servant. Whether far or near, they rode and they rode. So they rode and rode, and then their horse tired and fell down onto the road, and they were forced to abandon it and go on on foot. For a long time, they walked along the road. Well now, the tsarevich was young, and he couldn't go as quickly as the servant, but he nonetheless didn't give up. So they walked and walked, and then they came up to a well. Ivan Tsarevich said, "Well, let's stop, have a taste, and rest a bit." The well was very deep, but Ivan Tsarevich wanted a drink. And he said to his servant, "Well now, Servant, let yourself down into the well and get me some water."

And that servant spoke out: "Listen, Ivan Tsarevich, if I go down there, you won't be able to lift me out. It will be better if you go down; it will be easier for us."

Of course, he wouldn't alter his words. The servant tied his belt to him and let him down into the well. When he had drunk his fill, he said, "Well all right, Vaniusha, pull me back up now. I've drunk enough."

And he said to him in answer, "No, Ivan Tsarevich, I will not pull you back up. If you give me your royal clothing and will serve me as the servant Ivan, and I will be Ivan Tsarevich, then I'll pull you out. But otherwise, you will stay in the well."

And then he said, "Well, then I'll serve you as your servant and hand over my royal clothing." And he swore an oath to him with everything on earth. And so he pulled him out. Ivan Tsarevich didn't go back on his word; he immediately began undressing and handed over his clothing to him, and he himself put on a servant's dress. And so they set off farther. And they walked and they walked and not long after, they came to a certain tsardom. When they had just come into that tsardom, they immediately went to that tsar in his palace. There the people saw that a tsarevich of some sort was approaching, and they met him with joy. They questioned the tsarevich as to what he was called. And he told them everything: that he was Ivan Tsarevich from such and such a tsardom.

Then the tsar said, "Well, Ivan Tsarevich, where do you order us to put your servant—what sort of job, or what will you do with him?"

"Your Highness, isn't there some sort of little job for him—perhaps herding the hens, or some sort of shepherd. I am agreed that he should not fiddle about here with nothing to do."

The tsar answered him: "Here's what, Ivan Tsarevich, we don't have anything like herding hens or like that, but we do have three hundred hares. Perhaps he could herd them so as not to lose them? And he'll have to herd them for three years. And as he is herding them, if he loses even one in the course of three years, then he will be punished for it."

"Well, let him herd them."

And so, they gave him a room. The next day they handed these hares over to him. He counted them, of course, and drove them out to pasture the first time (every pasturing equaled a year, and at the end of the year he was to drive them back). So he drove them out beyond the city and drove them into the forest. And he had only just driven them into the forest, when the hares saw the bushes and ran away, each one somewhere. He ran about a whole day, he ran after them, but he couldn't catch sight even of one! By evening he thought, "Now I'm doomed to die."

He caught sight of a large boulder. He fell on it and started crying. And he cried to the point that his faced swelled up from the tears. Then he remembered: "Oh, if only the firebird would help me!" And this affair took place at night. And suddenly he looked up and saw the sun was coming up. And this sun came closer and closer. But it was no sun. The firebird flew up to him. It flew to him and said, "Why are you crying, Ivan Tsarevich? Get on me and fly to my tsardom. All your hares will be quiet, only just get on me."

It sat him on its back and flew off. And it rose up so very high that he could scarcely see the earth. And suddenly it flew to a high mountain. The mountain parted into two parts, and it flew into that mountain. Ivan Tsarevich looked, and there was a large tsardom, and so rich that all about was gold and silver. They entered a house. The firebird seated him at a table. "Right now I'm not going to ask you anything, Ivan Tsarevich, until you've eaten and had something to drink." And it went away.

In a short time the tsar came in. "Well, greetings, Ivan Tsarevich, what you wished for you have received. I am not the firebird, but I am the tsar of this country. You know how fate dragged me into your country: I was at war with your neighboring tsardom and lost my strength completely and fell into a trap. And I recovered my former situation only because you fed me and released me, and I'll pay you back for that with whatever you wish. Live here with me for about six days, and then I'll lead you to my oldest sister. And you'll stay there. You'll remain there for eleven months as if it were one day, and you'll forget all your sadness and troubles."

So he lived there for six days. And it seemed to him it was six hours. When the six days were finished, then the tsar called him to his oldest sister. He led him to that sister and said, "Well, Sister, treat Ivan Tsarevich to whatever he wishes, and ask him what he wants from you. Keep him for eleven months and then bring him before me."

She accepted Ivan Tsarevich with joy and began giving him something to drink and to eat, and she entertained him and indulged him. And he had such a happy life that these eleven months seemed to him but eleven days. And then in the eleventh month, she began to question him (formerly, you see, she hadn't asked him anything) when she had dressed in the most expensive clothing. And she asked him, "Well, Ivan Tsarevich, tell me, what can I pay you back with, what can I repay you with for my brother? Tell me only what you would like, and I'll give it all to you. Take some gold, Ivan Tsarevich, as much as you need. Take some silver, take some pearls, some precious stones—take what you need."

But he refused it all: "I don't need anything."

"Well, if you are going to refuse everything, then at least take this self-filling tablecloth, as you are living in that tsardom in poverty. Don't refuse it—it will be useful to you."

He took the self-filling tablecloth, and she said to him, "When you come home, lay it on the table, and you will have as much as you need. Don't think that it will be diminished; it lasts forever."

And then she immediately presented him to her brother after this. When she had presented him to her brother, she said, "Ivan Tsarevich will take nothing for rescuing you, Brother. I only gave him this solitary self-filling tablecloth. More than that he wouldn't take."

"Well all right, and thank you for that, Sister," the tsar answered her.

Then she took her leave and went away. So then that tsar spoke: "Ivan Tsarevich, why tomorrow it's already a year you've been living with us. (See how he spent that time so quickly!) Yes, Ivan Tsarevich, I'll now give you an accordion and take you away to the city. You start playing this accordion, and every one of your hares will gather together; just let them count them. You don't need to think about a thing."

Then he immediately turned into the firebird, placed him on his back, and rose up. He rose up so high that the whole world disappeared. And he had soon placed him in his own tsardom. Then he himself flew away, and Ivan Tsarevich with his accordion went into the city. He had just approached the city when he began playing the accordion. He watched as from all directions, one after the other, the hares began running. Just count them! So they opened the gates and began counting. When they had finished counting, all the hares were there—absolutely! And how fine were these hares! They reported to the tsar that they had come in so smooth and fine. When the tsar came, he looked and said, "Well, we'll have to give this herder the finest food, the same as we ourselves eat." And then he added, "You can now go and relax for three days and rest, and then you can drive them out again."

Just then, that other Ivan came, the servant of Ivan Tsarevich, as Ivan Tsarevich, and he said, "What, good food for him? Give him bread and water; he needs nothing more."

Then Ivan Tsarevich said nothing. He went to his own room. They brought him the bread and water. He took the bread and gave it to the beggars, poured the water into a basin, and spread out the self-filling tablecloth. Well then, of course, there was something for him to eat and drink! So he started to eat. He ate and took out his accordion, and he began to play—such that all the courtiers gathered to watch. And the tsar's daughter heard it and said to her nannies, "Nannies, Mommies, who is that playing so well? Let's go, I have to see. I've never heard such playing in our land."

Of course, they couldn't refuse, and they set off with her. They walked through the courtyard, toward that accordion, and they came up to that little hut, where Ivan Tsarevich was sitting and playing. She ordered her servants to open the door, and they all went in the hut together. Ivanushko was sitting and playing his accordion, and in front of him was his self-filling tablecloth. So now then, she came and greeted him: "Greetings, Herder, have you been herding our hares for long?"

He said, "A year, and soon the second will come. Now here's what, Your Highness, it's not a good thing for me to be sitting here at the table with your nannies, is it?"

But she didn't refuse, because there was no one from their tsardom standing by his table. When they had sat down at the table, Ivanushko began to play his accordion. And as she listened to him, she thought that only two hours had passed. But meanwhile two days had passed, and she was still sitting at the table there with her nannies.

And these nannies spoke up: "Listen, beautiful Tsarevna, is it not time for us to go now? So much time has passed already."

So then she stood up. "Yes, perhaps we'll go now."

She and Ivanushko said goodbye, and they set off for the palace. She said nothing to her father about this and did not permit her nannies to speak of it. She forbade it. And to herself she thought, "If I manage to go again, I won't take those nannies with me. Probably he'll tell me who he really is. He's certainly of no simple calling if he has such objects with him." And she began guessing.

So the three days passed, and Ivan again had to drive out the hares into the forest. He closed the room, went up to the gates, counted the hares, and chased them out. He took the accordion with him. He herded them only up to the forest and watched as the hares, one after another, began vanishing. And they all disappeared—not one could he see. Evening came. He came to that boulder and thought, "Well, all right, now I'll play the accordion, and probably all the hares will come here together."

He began playing the accordion. But all his labors were in vain. No matter how much he played, he couldn't see a single hare. He played and played, and then lay down on that boulder and started weeping bitterly. "What am I to do now?" So he cried a little and then he looked up and saw that the sun was coming up. Then he thought, "That is no sun. It's nothing less than the firebird." He looked: closer and closer, and finally it flew up to him.

"Well, Ivan Tsarevich, why are you crying? Likely you are in a bad situation. Get on my back!"

"But why should I not cry? I've lost all the hares. I played and played on the accordion, but I can't see a single one."

"Nor will you see any. Better get on my back and we'll fly to my tsardom."

And so he got on the firebird's back, and they flew off. From the beginning, they rushed so high that the earth disappeared. Then they flew to its tsardom. Again the mountain parted into two parts, and it flew in there. It led him into its house, gave him something to drink, fed him, and said: "Well, Ivan Tsarevich, stay with me for a day and a night, and then I'll lead you to my middle sister. And she will give you what you wish for, because you let me out."

And that's what he did. The next day he led him to his middle sister and told her everything, just as the first time. "Greetings, Sister. Now then, I've brought Ivan Tsarevich to you. Give him something to drink, feed him—you yourself know why—and do everything that he wishes."

And then he went away. And then he lived so happily, so happily that he didn't know how the eleven months passed just like eleven days. After the eleven months this sister also dressed herself in her best clothes, and she was more beautiful than the first, and she asked him: "Well tell me, Ivan Tsarevich, what do you need for having saved my brother? Tell me the truth. You are still young now, your thoughts may go in any way."

More she didn't say. And he said, "Listen, my beautiful one, I need nothing."

"Well, take a bag of gold, take a bag of silver, or of pearls."

"No, I don't need anything. The first sister already gave me a lot."

"Well, look, I do have something more to give you."

Then she went away into a certain room and brought out a whip. "So then, Ivan Tsarevich, this will be useful to you in the first place. When you come up to the palace and you don't have any hares, then just as soon as you've got there, strike the road three times crisscross and see what happens. They will come running one after the other—only shout so that they open the gates and count them. Now let's go to my brother. You have lived with me for eleven months."

She took him by the hand and led him to her brother. She led him to her brother and said, "Well Brother, Ivan Tsarevich took no gift from me. I only gave him this little whip. This little trifle will be useful to him when he is gathering the hares."

"Well, all right, Sister, good that you figured out to give him this."

Then she and Ivan Tsarevich said goodbye and she went home. After that he said to him, "Well, Ivan Tsarevich, tomorrow I'll carry you back to the old place, but tonight sleep one more night and listen to what I say to you. This time I won't give you anything. If I were to give you the strength of a bogatyr, it would be too heavy for me to carry you. And this time I won't show you where the bogatyr's horse is—or armor or the damask sword. I'll tell you all about these when you come here for the third time. There's no way you can avoid being here with me a third time."

When he had slept through the night, they got up, and he again turned into the firebird and was carried off. The firebird flew to the tsardom, let him down, and said, "Well, my sister gave you a little whip and told you how to handle it. So do it." And then he flew away.

He came to that city and began striking with the whip. He struck about three times crisscross and looked: The hares were running as they twisted the latch. He shouted, "Open the gates, count the hares!" They immediately opened the gates and began counting. Every hare was present. And they were so pink, so filled out, and they had grown to twice the size. And so right away they reported this to the tsar. So the tsar came, examined the hares, and said, "Well, I've never had such herders. We must give this herder the same such good food as we ourselves eat. Now, Ivan the Herder, we are giving you four days rest. Enjoy!" He added a day this time.

Just then Ivan Tsarevich came out and said, "My herder Ivan needs nothing. Just give him a crust of bread and some water."

So again they brought him some bread and water. He gave the bread to the beggars and poured the water into the washbasin. He spread out the magic tablecloth, ate, then took and drew his accordion apart. He began playing so that the entire tsardom rejoiced. When Tsarevna Oleksandra heard it, she didn't say anything to her nannies and ran straight away to her herder Vaniushka. She came running and opened the door. He right away said, "Well, beautiful Tsarevna, sit down and eat with me!"

She immediately sat down at the table with him. So then, Brother—a second time, and more daring——she had finally come then! "Tell me, my dear Vania, honestly, you are not of simple origins, are you? Tell me the whole truth, reveal it, perhaps you will be happy then."

And so he said, "Yes, beautiful Tsarevna, I would like to know what your name is."

"My name, Vania, is Oleksandra Tsarevna."

"Thank you for telling me."

Then he poured out a goblet of mead for each and said, "So, beautiful Tsarevna Oleksandra, drink this goblet, and then I will tell you. But before then I won't tell you anything."

She cheerfully took up the goblet and said, "Let's drink, Vania, although I've never drunk before. But I'll obey you; I'll drink."

They clinked goblets and drank.

"Well, I'll tell you, Oleksandra Tsarevna, but don't you say anything to anybody until the time comes. Yes, and listen. I am of course in truth Ivan Tsarevich, and he is my servant, just my lackey. When I went down into a well to have a drink, he didn't want to lift me back up, and in just such a manner I handed over my royal clothes to him and took his place and he mine. And now for two years I've been herding hares in your tsardom. And I'll tell you why I was exiled from my tsardom: I was exiled because I let out my father's firebird. And for that reason the firebird is helping me now and gives me whatever I wish. Only don't you tell anything to anybody about this, so that my lackey won't find out—your so-called Ivan Tsarevich."

Then she said to him, "Well, all right, Ivan Tsarevich, in any case I won't marry him—I'll marry you!"

She took a ring from her finger and gave it to him: "Here is my ring. Take it and consider me yours!"

So the three days passed, and she just sat there with him, and he played his accordion and gave her pleasure. "Well now, beautiful Oleksandra Tsarevna, you must go, and tomorrow I must drive the hares out to pasture."

And so then when she had gone home, she thought more and more about Ivan Tsarevich, but, of course, she was silent, and she kept it all to herself. On the fourth day, he went out and in the same manner began to count the hares. And when he had counted them all up, he drove them out. And he had just driven them out to the forest, when the hares ran away in every direction and he couldn't see them (he did a poor job of herding the hares!). First of all he chased after them and chased, but then he said, "Why should I chase after them, I have this little whip!"

The time passed until evening and he began striking the road criss-cross with that whip. But no matter how he struck, he could see no hares. So he resented this, sat down on a boulder, and started crying: "Well, if the firebird won't help me this last time, then it will be my ruin." And so he cried for a little time, and he looked, and it was as if a fire were burning far away. "Well, that is probably nothing other than the firebird flying to help me." The fire came closer and closer, and it flew up to him and said, "That's enough crying, Vania, get on me and let's fly!"

So he perched on it, they rose up, and flew away. Again the mountain divided, and they flew into its tsardom. It led him into its house, sat him down at the table, gave him a drink, fed him, and said to him: "Well, Vania, stay here with me a full day. And I will give you everything that I promised. And then I will lead you to my youngest sister."

So he stayed there a full day, and on the second, it led him to its youngest sister. He led him there and said, "Well, Sister, I have brought Ivan Tsarevich to you. Entertain him. Give him everything that he wants. You yourself know that he is young, and so give him what you can."

She immediately went away and dressed in her very best clothes and came back. The other two sisters were beautiful, but this one was still more beautiful. Ivan immediately took a liking to her. When she came, she sat down next to Ivan and began speaking. "Well, tell me, Ivan Tsarevich, tell me what do you want for saving my brother? Do you need gold, silver? In a word, whatever do you wish? I will give you everything. I will stint you nothing!"

He just kept sitting there, he was silent, and he gazed at her. He, of course, refused the gold and the silver, and he said, "I need nothing." "You already know, probably, my beautiful one, what I need," he said finally.

She got the point right away. "Listen, Ivan Tsarevich, you are young. Perhaps you want to get married, I can find a bride for you, whatever kind you wish."

She remembered the words of her brother then. Then he looked at her. His heart was overflowing with joy. "What if I marry her?" But he didn't say anything to her; he only thought to himself. And then he remembered Oleksandra Tsarevna, who had promised him and whose ring he had, and he said to her. "No, beautiful Tsarevna, I am still young, and it's still early for me to marry. But perhaps you will help me with something else?"

Then she thought for a little: "What can I give to you, such a dear guest?" She went away into another room. She brought out some clothes and said, "Well so, Ivan Tsarevich, take off your clothes and put on these, and then put your old ones on top. And don't show anybody these clothes. Such clothes nobody has. I prepared these for my husband, but you take them now for saving my brother. No way did things turn out right for me. (She didn't reveal it to him directly, just gave a hint.)

Ivan got undressed right away, put on those clothes and his own on top. And just then, the eleven months passed. Afterwards, she said to him, "Well, Ivan Tsarevich, let's go to my brother. He'll also give you something." She took him by the hand, kissed him, and said, "Well, I didn't manage to live with you, as you yourself refused." There—she was sorry to say it to him.

She led him to her brother and said, "Here I've brought Ivan Tsarevich to you. Well, he didn't take any gifts from me. I only gave him those clothes that you yourself know."

"Well, all right. Thank you, Sister."

She said good-bye and went away. And then the tsar came up. "Well, tell me, Ivan Tsarevich, were you bored? You have flown three times to us and lived with us for three years. Tell me the truth."

He said, "No, Your Highness, I wasn't bored living here. These three years seemed perhaps like three days."

> Well, good. I wanted to give you everything that's dear, but you yourself refused. Of course, without it you won't live, but since nothing came of it,

> we'll say nothing more. My sister took all measures, but you yourself refused (he had wanted to marry him to his sister, but it didn't happen). So, now what was promised, I'll say, but listen, Ivan Tsarevich. So Ivan Tsarevich, when you arrive home, the tsar will give you five days of rest. On the sixth day, the tsar will suffer a misfortune: A serpent will come out of the lake and ask for a human every day to devour, and then they will condemn the tsar's daughter to be taken to him. The first serpent will be a six-headed one, and there are three in all: six, nine, and the last a twelve-headed one. The six and nine you will deal with easily, but with the twelve-headed one you will have difficulty. You'll take off the first ten heads easily, but the last two heads will be very difficult. You will fight for two whole days with it. And then on the second day think of me. When the sun rises, you shout at him, "Look, you cursed monster, your house is on fire!" He will look back, and only then can you chop off the remaining two heads. Watch out, and don't drag this on into the third day, or he will kill you.

Then he said, "Here, Ivan Tsarevich, are two little bottles: Drink a small glass from one of them and from the other two. Only don't drink now. Drink when you have to. And then that stone on which you lay and cried—do you remember that stone?"

"I remember it."

"So now, beneath that stone are a bogatyr's horse, armor, and a damask sword. You drink from the little bottles, and you'll easily be able to turn that stone over."

And then he brought him a horn. "Now then, Ivan Tsarevich, here's this horn for you. When you start blowing it, all the hares will come together. And now perch on me, and I'll carry you away. We shall part and you will never see me again. Only don't forget what I have told you." After that it put him on its back and flew off. "Remember my words!"

After that he disappeared. So, of course, he came up to that tsardom. He blew once, then a second time on that horn. He looked, and the hares were running, just like water pouring forth. "Open the gates, count the hares!"

The gates were immediately opened, and they began counting. They counted them all up and said, "Well, Ivanushko, it means you have finished your task." Then they reported to the tsar that all the hares were present and healthy and in the pink.

"Such a herder we've never seen before, and we've lived a long time in your tsardom."

So when the tsar had looked over all his hares, he said, "Well, fine lad, Ivanushko, you have finished your work well. We'll have to feed you now with the very best food, and I'll give you five days rest."

But again out came that so-called Ivan Tsarevich and said, "Besides bread and water, he needs nothing at all. He has just eaten at home."

Well, and he didn't need it; he didn't require their food. So he went into his room, where they had already brought him water and bread. Again he gave the bread to a beggar, and he poured the water into the washbasin. Then he washed, put his clothes on top, sat down at the table, and took up his accordion. When the tsarevna heard him playing, her heart quaked, and she immediately ran to Ivan Tsarevich. When she came into his hut, when she saw Ivan Tsarevich, he was already in another uniform. And he was so handsome and pink-cheeked and entirely changed. It is well known that you deck out a mortar in fine clothing, and it will be fine—no more so than a man, and a young one to boot! And the clothing on him—why, it would be impossible even to value it. She had absolutely never seen anything like it in her country. She couldn't stand it any more, and threw her arms around his neck.

"My dear Ivan Tsarevich, do with me what you wish. I agree to everything."

And, of course, he embraced her, hugged her to him, and said, "So, let it be, beautiful Tsarevna. We shall live as we can."

And so they lay down to sleep. There was no time to play the accordion this time, and she stayed with him a whole two days. He said to her, "Listen, my beautiful Tsarevna, now it's time for you to go, otherwise someone may find out—the tsar, someone from the servants—that you are here, and that would be bad for me, although I'm not afraid. But it would also be bad for you."

She was really sad, but it really was time to go. When she arrived home, her servants asked her, "Where do you go, Your Highness? Your father is asking us."

She knows the answer to give. You don't have to teach her what to do! "I was visiting a certain princess, a friend. I was invited to a banquet, and there they detained me for a long time."

With that it ended. So a whole day passed. She couldn't wait any longer; she had to run and see Ivan Tsarevich again. She ran away. She came to the doors and knocked. He opened the door, but he already knew. Again she threw her arms around his neck—and did they kiss! She stayed with him another whole day, and then he said to her: "Now it's time to go home, beautiful Oleksandra. We won't see each other soon, because there's going to be a misfortune in the city. But nonetheless you will be mine. As has been said, so shall it be."

She went home, and on the fifth day there came an envoy from the lake and he demanded a person every day for the six-headed serpent to eat, or else he would marry the tsar's daughter. And he threatened that if he were himself to come, he would destroy the entire tsardom. The tsar fell into very deep thought. "Well, if he devours a person a day, then he will eat up the whole tsardom—and take my daughter nonetheless."

And they decided it would be better to marry off the daughter right away. Then the tsar wrote out such a decree: "If there can be found anybody who will rescue my daughter, she shall be give to him in marriage and half the tsardom, too. And later on he will be placed on the throne of the tsardom."

Then up came that Ivan Tsarevich, who was with them. "Your Highness, permit me, I wish a word with you."

"Well, speak, Ivan Tsarevich."

"Well, Your Highness, I want to save your daughter and marry her. Only give me a horse and all the equipment."

This pleased the tsar very much. And in one day all was arranged. For him there was a horse and armor. And they put the tsarevna in a black carriage, and they set off immediately for the lake. But now Ivan Tsarevich heard all this business and knew what to do. He took the two little bottles and went to that stone. He came, unsealed these two little bottles, and drank a shot from one and from the other two shots. And he felt in himself such incredible strength that he himself was amazed. And he went up, moved that stone as if it were a joke. He turned it over and let himself down there. And there stood a jet-black horse, and there hung all its harness. The armor hung there, and the sword. He immediately led the horse out, saddled it, and of course, put on the bridle. He put on the bogatyr's armor, buckled on the sword, and leapt onto the horse. He rode along, and he saw that Ivan Tsarevich was also riding along, but he said nothing to him. He leapt by him like lighting and also drove passed the tsarevna. He rode up to the lake and then rode around. And just when that tsarevna rode up, the water rose up six times. On the seventh time, the serpent leapt out and said, "Foo, foo, the tsar is generous. I awaited only the tsarevna, but he has given me her together with Ivan Tsarevich—now I'll dine!"

And Ivan Tsarevich replied to him, "Don't boast, pagan monster, maybe you'll choke on your dinner. First test, then boast."

And he said, "Well, why argue. So let's go at it, let's ride and fight."

They had only ridden at each other the first time, when Ivan Tsarevich cut off his three heads. The next time they rode at each other, he cut off the remaining three heads, and then he cut out the tongues, put them in his pocket, and rode to the tsarevna. But the tsarevna didn't recognize him and questioned him: "Tell me, good knight, who are you. Perhaps I know you from somewhere."

"So, Oleksandra Tsarevna, you so soon forget. You didn't recognize Ivan Tsarevich!"

She ran to him, embraced him, and began crying. "Well, don't cry, beautiful Tsarevna, I have to ride. But don't tell anyone about me—I still have to save you two more times."

He leapt onto his horse and rode off into the forest to that so-called Ivan Tsarevich. And he had hidden in the woods so that that serpent wouldn't devour him—some savior! As soon as he saw that bogatyr riding up, he began questioning him and found out that it was that Ivan Tsarevich. He started speaking: "Listen, Ivan Tsarevich, wait just a minute, and I'll have a talk with you. Give me those tongues, Ivan Tsarevich, and take from me as much money as you need or whatever else you wish."

He said to him, "You yourself know that they are not for sale. They're for a deal."

"And what's the deal?"

"It's a toe from a foot and a finger from a hand. I'll cut them, and then you take them."

He agreed, gave him his hand, and he cut off a finger from his hand and a toe from his foot with a knife. He gave him the tongues, and then he rode away. And the so-called Ivan Tsarevich came to the tsarevna and said, "Listen, if you say that it wasn't I who killed the serpent, then I'll kill you!"

She said to him, "Listen, Ivan Tsarevich, I agree to be your wife and won't tell anyone that you didn't kill the serpent."

So they rode back to the tsardom. And meanwhile, Ivan Tsarevich came back to the boulder. When he had ridden up, he leapt down from his horse, took off the bridle and saddle, and the horse spoke: "Listen, Ivan Tsarevich, don't send me down beneath the boulder. I should rather nibble grass, and when it's necessary, I'll serve you in faith and truth. But put the bridle and saddle beneath the stone."

Then he: "Well, all right, if that's so, I'll let you go, but you won't try to run away?"

"No, Ivan Tsarevich."

So he put the bridle and all the munitions beneath the boulder. Then he came home and tumbled off to sleep. And he slept for three whole days without waking. And on the fourth day, the alarm came to the tsar again from the nine-headed serpent. This one threatened even more than the first. So again the tsar went to that so-called Ivan Tsarevich. "Well, Ivan Tsarevich, if you're going to take it upon yourself to save the tsarevna, get ready!"

So they set off again in the same manner, and Ivan Tsarevich went after them to that same boulder. He came to the boulder. He got all his armor and began to summon his horse. When he had given a shout, the horse rushed up, just like lightning, and stood before him as if rooted to the ground. He put on the bridle, saddled him, put on his bogatyr's armor, and galloped off. So he galloped up near a mountain, and the tsarevna was already there. And that false one had hidden in the forest. The water began to rise. It came up nine times, and on the tenth, the serpent emerged.

"Foo, foo," it said, "You have killed my brother, but you won't kill me. I am two times stronger than he. I'll put you on my palm, and with the other I'll smash you, and there'll just be grease and water!"

He said, "Well, don't boast, pagan monster, riding into the steppe. Why argue, better let's fight!"

And so they rode apart from each other. The first time they came together, Ivan Tsarevich sliced off three of the serpent's heads. The second time they came together, and another three heads he sliced off, and the third time also three. Then he got down, cut out the tongues, stuck them in his pocket, and rode away. He rode up to the tsarevna. She threw herself at him to embrace him, but he said to her, "I have to go, beautiful Tsarevna!"

He got on his horse and rode away. And at that very time that Ivan Tsarevich was waiting for him along the road, and he said: "Well, listen, Ivan Tsarevich, sell me those tongues, or take whatever you like."

"You know that they're for a deal. Here, let me cut off a finger and cut out a strip from your back."

And he agreed to that.

Right away Ivan Tsarevich cut off a finger and cut out a strip from his back. And that tsarevich galloped off to the tsarevna.

"If you say that it wasn't I who killed that serpent, I'll kill you!"

"No, Ivan Tsarevich, it's not the first time I've said it, and I won't say it again—I'll be your wife!"

After that, they set off for the city. And Ivan Tsarevich to his boulder. He took off the armor and bridle, and let the horse loose in the field, and he himself went and tumbled off to sleep. He slept all day. So then six days passed, and the envoy came and again asked for the tsar's daughter's hand in marriage for the twelve-headed serpent. The tsar read the letter, got frightened, and immediately went to Ivan Tsarevich and said: "Well, Ivan Tsarevich, save her once more, and then we'll put on the wedding."

And so he immediately started getting ready. The father and mother went out to see them off and wept. And she also cried and said, "Perhaps you'll find out that I won't be returning. The serpent is twelve-headed, and it will be difficult with him for Ivan Tsarevich!"

Just wait and see whom she was talking about! They set off. But Ivan Tsarevich went to that boulder. He got the bridle and armor and shouted for his horse. The horse came running to him and stood there as if rooted to the ground. And so then he put on his saddle, his bridle, and on himself that bogatyr's armor, and he galloped to the lake. He galloped up to the lake, but the serpent still wasn't there. The tsarevna got out of her carriage and said, "Well listen, Ivan Tsarevich, let's sit, let's sit a bit until that serpent is aroused."

He got down onto the ground from his horse, and a powerful bogatyr's sleep struck him. She tried to wake him. She embraced him, kissed him, but she could not awaken him. And now the water in the lake started to rise up, and no way could she wake him up. It was certain death for both of them. His horse was nibbling grass and watching. Then he ran over and struck him with a hoof on his head. And he woke up! He barely had time to jump onto his horse, when the water rose up for the thirteenth time and the serpent appeared. He rose up and said, "Well, here's luck that he managed to leap onto his horse. Otherwise, I would have swallowed them both immediately."

And just then the tsarevna ran away into a tent.

"Well, fine, even if you killed one of my brothers and then a second, you won't kill me. I am stronger than they."

"Well, so what? Let you be stronger than they were. Only don't boast going into the field; boast coming from the field."

And the serpent answered him, "Well, why argue, Ivan Tsarevich, it would be better, obviously, to test our strength, and there we'll see who wins out."

And so they rode apart. The first time Ivan Tsarevich cut off three of his heads. The second time they rode at each other, and he also cut of three heads. A third time—he cut off three heads, too. There remained three heads more. They fought for a whole day, but he couldn't cut off another head. Yet neither of them wanted to surrender, even though they were both really tired. On the second day, he cut off the tenth head—just one. And so it went on for almost two full days. But the serpent couldn't knock him from his horse in any way. So then the sun started to rise, and they were both exhausted to the very bone. Then Ivan Tsarevich gathered his remaining strength, rode up to him, and shouted, "Look, pagan monster, your house is on fire!"

And the moment that one turned around, he cut off the remaining two heads. And that monster rolled over on him, but he just managed to leap to one side. But as the monster rolled over onto the ground, it brushed against him and scratched his right hand and his horse's right leg. Then Ivan Tsarevich climbed down from his horse, cut out the tongues, gathered them into his pocket, and rode up to the tsarevna, who this time had seen everything—that it had been really difficult for Ivan Tsarevich, but that nonetheless he had been victorious—and she was full of joy. So then he rode up and jumped down from his horse, and she rushed into his embrace. She embraced him, of course, caressed him, and then he said to her, "Listen, my dear, first of all wrap up, bandage my hand. It's wounded and so is my horse's leg."

She immediately tore off a piece of her clothes, ripped it in two, and with one half she bound up his hand, and with the other she bound up the horse's leg so that sand didn't get in it and the wound didn't get infected.

"And now I'll go and sleep. Probably I'll sleep for nine days, and you do what you must. You know what you have to do."

He said goodbye to her, got on his horse, and rode off. He had just ridden to the forest, when there stood that Ivan Tsarevich, waiting for him with a bow again.

"Well, Ivan Tsarevich, now be so good and give me those tongues, and take what you will from me, or sell them."

"But you know already that they aren't for sale by me."

"Well, all right, so what's your deal?"

"The deal . . . well, I don't know now what to take from you—you're all cut up. Be that as it may, give me one more finger from a hand, and a toe, and I'll also cut a strip."

He agreed. He began undressing. He cut a off a finger from each hand and then the strip, and he wrapped them in a kerchief and rode off. And the other one got on his horse and rode to the tsarevna.

He stopped the horse and asked, "Well, beautiful Tsarevna, if you say that I killed the serpent, then all will be fine. But if you even think of deceiving me, then there'll be no more living for you."

And she said to him, almost through tears: "Listen, Ivan Tsarevich, I don't intend to lie. If you wish, then let's start putting on the wedding tomorrow; I'm totally ready."

So then he calmed down, and they rode off to the tsardom. And that other Ivan Tsarevich rode to his boulder, grabbed the boulder, and collected all the equipment, and he said to his horse: "So now go on, Black Steed, while you're free, while you won't be needed."

"Thank you, Ivan Tsarevich, now I will rest. But when it's necessary, I'll come at the first call."

After that Ivan Tsarevich set off on foot for home. And he had only just got to his quarters when he fell asleep in all his clothes.

When the tsarevna came and the tsar found out that his future son-in-law had killed the last serpent, he rejoiced greatly. And when three days had passed, the guests gradually began to gather for the wedding feast. And it took them about six days until the guests had all gathered. And all this time Ivan Tsarevich still slept. On the seventh day, the tsarevna went out with her Ivan Tsarevich to the wedding table. And there all the wedding guests were sitting. And she stood up and said, "Father, permit me to speak a word. Will that be possible?"

He said to her, "Speak, Daughter. Why would it not be possible? Everything is permitted to you!"

And she began speaking: "Here's what, Father. I wish that at our wedding all the grooms, chefs, cooks, hired help, herders would be present. And I also wish that that herder who herded the hares was at the wedding, because I have heard that he herded better than all, so he must also be invited."

Now he already knew what sort of herder he was. Her father spoke to her: "Very well, Daughter, I shall fulfill this your wish. All are already here except only that herder, and you correctly say that he must be invited, since I am very pleased with him because he didn't lose a single one from that herd for three years, and he fed them very well. He must absolutely be invited."

The son-in-law answered him: "Listen, Father, you don't have to invite that herder, because he's my lackey."

"No, Ivan Tsarevich, we shall absolutely invite him."

And right away they sent for that Ivan the hares' herder. The envoy came to the little hut. He opened the door, and that herder was asleep in a sound, unshakeable sleep. No matter how he tried to wake him, he couldn't wake him up. He noticed his bandaged hand. And from his hand blood dripped. And he went back with a response to the tsar. "Your Highness, I was at the herder's, but he is asleep. And he is sleeping so soundly that no matter how much I tried to wake him, I couldn't awaken him. But I noticed that his right hand is bound up, and that from his hand blood was dripping."

And then she knew. She got up from behind the table, went up to her father, and quietly spoke to him, just to him alone: "Papa, let's go look at that herder. I will show you what sort of herder he is, but for now I won't say anything more. You yourself will see."

They immediately set off. And she already knew where the herder's hut was. When they were going off, the tsar said to the audience, "Now then, comrades, you wait just a little while I go after a certain necessity."

They came to the hut, opened the door, and Ivan Tsarevich, of course, was sleeping. "Papa, you see I will explain to you who this herder really is. This herder is Ivan Tsarevich; the other is a lackey. I've known this for a long time, but I didn't say anything to anybody. It was he who rode out three times and killed the serpents. And look here, the last time he was wounded, and I bound up his hand with my birthday kerchief there, at that place, and also his horse's leg. And so the last time he rode out, he told me that he had given the tongues to that so-called Ivan Tsarevich, but that he had taken something in trade for them, but I don't know what."

"So that's it, Daughter? But why didn't he proclaim himself earlier?"

"He didn't proclaim himself because he knew everything earlier, that he would be riding to save me. So now then, Father, he has such precious things that we have never had in the tsardom. But when he gets up, he will prove himself. I'll say nothing more."

"Well then, Daughter, try to wake him so that he'll go with us to the feast."

She fell on his breast and said, "Wake up, Ivan Tsarevich. Wake up, my dear friend, my savior. You saved me and our tsardom from all those serpents."

Finally he opened his eyes. He sat down on a chair and said, "Listen, Your Highness and beautiful Tsarevna, go and complete all that you had to do and let that Ivan Tsarevich, the one sitting there in his place, stay there, and when I come, then I'll explain everything. When I come to the feast and ask to speak, then permit me to tell it."

"Good."

So they went back to the feast and continued the entertaining. But Ivan Tsarevich got up, washed, bound his hand, and dressed. That clothing, which the tsarevna, the firebird's sister gave him, he put on first, and his own on top, and he set off for the feast. And he sat down at the lowest end of the table. But, of course, the tsar saw him and knew then that he had come. They began passing around goblets. And they also brought Ivan a goblet. He drank it and stood up. "Your Highness, do not order me executed; order me to say a word."

"Speak, Herder, speak whatever you wish."

"Now then, I want to ask of you: Why does that son-in-law of yours, Ivan Tsarevich, sit at the table and eat in gloves?" Further he did not question.

The tsar immediately said, "Yes, why, Ivan Tsarevich, as you see, all the people sit without gloves, but you have them on your hands. Well, take them off!"

When he had taken off both gloves, it turned out that on the one and other hands he had only six fingers. The tsar began questioning him: "Well, Ivan Tsarevich, tell me why you don't have all your fingers? It would seem that earlier you had them."

He said, "Well, Your Highness, all these fingers the serpent bit off in battle."

Then Ivan the little herder stood up and undid the kerchief: "Your Highness, and then where did I get all these fingers? Compare them. Won't they match up? He gave me these fingers himself because he took the serpents' tongues from me."

Then the tsar said, "Well then, do with him what you will now."

But Ivan Tsarevich answered, "Your Highness, he not only doesn't have all his fingers on his hands, he also let me cut strips from his back so that I would give him the tongues. He himself didn't kill a single serpent."

The truth, you see, will always out.

Then he put all the rest of the things on the table and showed the tsar and all the guests. And the other one sat motionlessly and said nothing. And then Ivan Tsarevich told them everything—who he was. "I am, in fact, the son of a tsar, Ivan Tsarevich, and because I let out my father's firebird, because of that I was exiled to wander at will. And he is my lackey."

Then the tsar said, "Well, Son-in-law Ivan Tsarevich, deal with him as you wish; it's your choice. And then take his place, and take all that was promised by me."

After that Ivan Tsarevich grabbed Ivan the lackey and said, "Come and see, guests, what I will do with him."

And he dragged him out into an open place. Then he raised him up and struck him hard against the stone pavement, such that there remained only a wet spot—more than that nothing remained. And then he went back into the room and said, "Now then, guests, give me five minutes to change clothing, and then I'll come back."

So then he went to the washroom. Right after him came the tsarevna also. So he washed, took off his outer clothing, and became a handsome lad. After that he and the tsarevna went and sat down at the table. They sat down at the table, and all the guests and the tsar, all were amazed that he was such a handsome lad, and he shone all over as if in gold. There was plenty to eat and drink, and all drank and ate as much as they liked. And he said, "Father, let me bring two more objects, the self filling tablecloth and the accordion, and I will treat you as best I can."

He ran for the tablecloth, spread it on a table, and on the table were such rare foods that had never been seen in the tsardom before. All the guests ate and drank, rejoiced and praised Ivan Tsarevich. Then he took his accordion in his hands and began to play. When Ivan started playing his accordion, the guests sat and thought that they had been sitting for just one day, but they had sat there for six days. It seemed to them just one. When he finished playing his accordion, the guests thanked him, and all departed.

Probably, we too have been sitting a long time.

The guests went their own ways, and they remained sitting with the tsar. Then Oleksandra the beautiful took him by the hand and led him into her bedroom. Then the tsar rewarded him with everything, and consequently raised him to the throne.

And they began living and lived until deep old age.

(SUS 502)

9

A PROPHETIC DREAM

M. M. Korguev

In a certain tsardom, in a certain land, there lived and dwelt a merchant. The merchant had three sons. This merchant built a new home. When the home was completely ready, he said to his eldest son, "Go, my son, and spend the first night in this house." When he was about to set off, his father said to him, "Take the cock with you."[1] And then he said, "Be sure to tell me what you see in your sleep."

So that evening he set off to spend the night. The night passed. When he came back, his father questioned him: "Tell me then, my son, what did you dream?"

And he said to him: "Listen, Papa, I didn't dream anything special at all. I only saw my youngest brother, Ivan, flying about the heavens on twelve eagles."

So the second night he sent the second son, the middle one: "So then, my son, off you go, and whatever you dream, tell me."

For that second night the middle son also set off with the cock. He went off to sleep and slept through the whole night. He came back to his father. And his father asked him, "Well then, tell me, my son, what did you dream?"

And he said to him, "Well, Papa, I also didn't see anything special, only that our favorite sheep has disappeared from the yard."

The third night came. He summoned the third son. "Well, Vaniusha, you go sleep in the new house, and in the morning tell me what you have seen in your sleep."

Vaniusha didn't answer anything to his father; he took the cock and went off to sleep. And all night he dreamed that he was wooing a beautiful

1. The cock was thought to chase off evil spirits with its cry, probably because it crows just at the crack of dawn. Note Gogol's story "Viy".

tsarevna. And then up flew a serpent and tried to sting him. And just at that moment the cock crowed and the serpent flew away.

In the morning he went home to his father. And his father asked him, "Well, tell me, Vaniusha, what did you dream?"

Ivan was silent. He said nothing to him.

"Speak, why are you silent?"

"I won't tell anybody my dream until it comes true. Then it will be told!"

Just so. His father said to him, "No, you must tell it."

"No, I won't say anything, even if you kill me, I won't. I won't say anything!"

His father tried every way possible to get it out of him. He beat him. But he wouldn't say a thing. Then his father decided to strip him naked, and he led him out onto the road and tied him to a pillar. "Now tell me, Son!"

"I won't tell you even though you have tied me to this pillar!"

So his father rode off, leaving his son at the pillar.

After some time the son of a tsar came riding by that pillar. He saw this young man tied up there, and he stopped and asked him, "Who has tied you to this pillar? Tell me, who are you?"

"I am Ivan, a merchant's son, and my father tied me up."

"For what reason did your father punish you so severely?" Then he went and untied him and took him off with him. He brought him in and dressed him as was proper. And Ivan lived with him for a full month. Then the tsarevich came to Ivan the Merchant's Son, and asked him, "Well then, for what fault did your father punish you, Vaniusha, tell me!"

"What is there to tell? I told you that my father had a new house built. I slept a night in it and didn't tell my father my dream, but my other brothers did. So for that reason he tied me to the pillar."

Now that tsarevich was still young, and he was very interested—what had Ivan seen in his dream?

"Listen, Ivan Tsarevich, if I wouldn't tell my father, then I won't tell anything to you! Do what you like with me!"

Then the tsarevich said, "If you won't tell me, I'll lock you up in the keep, and I'll keep you there until such time as you yourself will want to tell me that dream!"

He said, "It's your choice, Tsarevich, do what you wish, but I won't tell you my dream!"

Then the tsarevich led him off to a castle and put him in a dungeon. And so he sat there for a month. And the tsarevich started looking for a bride for himself in neighboring lands. And in one tsardom he sought out a tsarevna named Elena for himself, but he didn't know that she was a sorceress.

The tsarevich ordered them to load up a ship with food and supplies. And he had this sister, and he said to her, "You rule the throne and look after the entire tsardom." So the tsarevich got himself fitted out—the ship was ready—and he set off on his journey.

A month passed, two, and there was no news from the tsarevich. Half a year went by—still nothing. And his sister was greatly saddened, and she began going about the prisons, offering alms to the incarcerated ones. She came to Ivan the Merchant's Son. And Ivan asked her, "And where is your brother?"

She answered him: "My brother has gone off to get married."

"He'll find it difficult to get married without me. And he won't get married in that country where he's intending to."

She heard him out and then said, "Listen, what is your name?"

He answered, "Ivan".

Then she said, "If you know my brother Ivan Tsarevich and wish to help him get married, then do so and I'll let you out of this prison. And for that my brother will reward you with whatever you wish."

"I'll go under one condition: When I return, you'll put me back in this very same place."

She said to him, "Listen, Ivan the Merchant's Son, if you take on yourself the misfortunes of my brother, how could I put you in prison after that?"

"You did not imprison me, and you ought not release me. But that's the condition under which I'll go and help him. And now write the captain of the regiment an order such that I can take with me eleven men, and prepare horses for all of them."

She let him out of the prison, led him off to her palace, and sat down to write an order to the captain so that he would bring out the whole regiment to the square. She gave the order to Ivan the Merchant's Son. "Take this order to the lieutenant and select the soldiers you wish, and we shall prepare everything for you for the journey."

He immediately went off to the lieutenant. The lieutenant brought out the regiment and said, "Well, select the soldiers that you need, Ivan the Merchant's Son."

Ivan walked about in front of the regiment and selected eleven Ivans, the ones he needed, and then he said to them, "Well now, brothers, let's go to the palace."

They went to the palace, and all the horses and clothes were already prepared for them. When they had got dressed, Ivan looked them over and saw that the very best clothing had been prepared for them. He went to the tsarevna and said, "Select clothing that is the same for all of us; I don't need this!" They selected the same clothing for him as for all the Ivans in quick order. He got dressed and said, "Well, brothers, mount your horses and let's go!"

They mounted up and rode off. They galloped and galloped, and then they came to a steep mountain. Ivan said, "Now then, wait here for me. I'll go up that mountain and look out for where we have to ride next." He climbed up the mountain, and there he saw three devils fighting. He got off his horse. "Why are you fighting?"

They went up to him and said, "Listen, good man, these three magical things have been left to us by our father, and we've been trying to divide them for a hundred years but we can't split them up. Please, help us to divide them equally."

"Very well, I'll divide them for you, but hear me out!" He took out a bow and three arrows. "Watch as I shoot. Whoever brings me the first arrow will receive the hat that makes him invisible; the second who brings in an arrow will receive the speed-walking boots; and the third to bring in an arrow will have the flying carpet."

He shot in different directions, and they all ran off after the arrows. And he took the hat that makes you invisible, the flying carpet, and the speed-walking boots, came to his brothers, and said: "Leave your horses, brothers, get on this flying carpet, and let's fly!"

They spread out the flying carpet and flew off. And then in short order they had flown to that land where Ivan Tsarevich was at the time. The tsarevich had just managed to come to the pier. Ivan spoke: "Well, brothers, let's go on the ship."

When they had come onto the ship, the tsarevich asked them, "Where are you from, young men, and how are you called?

"We are twelve brothers, and we are all called Ivan. I've heard that you have no sailors. Won't you take us on as sailors?"

The tsarevich was overjoyed, and he said, "How would I not take you on! I've just now lost twelve sailors in a storm!"

So they went on board the ship. The tsarevich spent a whole day on the ship, and on the next one he got ready to go into the city to have a look at the tsarevna, to see what she was like and whether she would marry him.

He went to the tsarevna and greeted her. She asked him, "Well, Tsarevich, to what do I owe this visit?"

He answered her, "I would like for you to become my wife. That is the reason why I came here."

And she answered him, "Yes, I'm agreed, but only if you fulfill my task. If you don't fulfill it, then it's your head from your shoulders! Guess my first riddle, and then I'll marry you. Come tomorrow and bring it to me. And it is: . . . But you'll have to guess it yourself, and it must be exact!"

The tsarevich went to the ship. He walked about the ship and was sad. Ivan the Merchant's Son came up to the tsarevich.

"Well, Tsarevich, tell me: What are you thinking? Perhaps I can help you."

He looked at him: "Go away, I know it without you."

But he kept on pacing and thinking. Ivan the Merchant's Son went up to him a second time. "Ivan Tsarevich, share your woe with me before it's too late. Maybe I can help you, or else it will be too bad."

Then Ivan Tsarevich led him into his chambers and began telling him all. "Listen then, Ivan, here's the thing: The tsarevna, whom I've been courting, said, 'Guess a riddle, and if you don't guess it, I'll execute you!' But I can't guess it."

Then Ivan the Merchant's Son said, "Very well, just wait a little!"

He put the invisible-making hat on his head, the speed-walking boots on his feet, and he set off for the palace. He came unseen into the palace, sat down on a chair opposite the tsarevna, and just sat there. And the tsarevna knew nothing and called her maidservant. She called the maidservant and said to her, "Well, Maidservant, go and order a slipper of the master. Let him sew it quickly, and bring that slipper here."

The servant girl went off, and Ivan the Merchant's Son went off after her. She came to the cobbler: "The tsarevna has ordered that you immediately sew her a slipper!"

The cobbler immediately set to work. He sewed the slipper and said to the servant, "Wait about five minutes until it dries!" He put it on the stove to dry. He had just put it down, not a minute had passed, when the slipper had disappeared. No matter where he looked, the slipper was not to be found. All his labors were in vain. But that Ivan had taken it.

Once more the cobbler set to work. He made a new slipper and gave it to the maidservant. "Now then, take this quickly to the tsarevna!" The servant girl set off but Ivan was right behind her. They got back, and the tsarevna asked, "Why were you so long?"

"When he had finished sewing the first slipper, that first slipper went off somewhere!"

"Oh, what a lackadaisical cobbler he is!"

She took the slipper and sat down at the table. Ivan sat down next to her, but she didn't see him. And then she brought a box of gold pins and pearls and started decorating the slipper. Ivan did the same: He took some pins and pearls from the box and decorated his slipper.

The tsarevna prepared everything and went off to sleep. But Ivan set off back to the ship, thinking to himself, "Very well, you won't catch us out on this." He came to the ship and gave the tsarevich the slipper, and then he said, "Take this slipper and at ten o'clock go to the palace. We'll see what she orders you to do."

In the morning Ivan Tsarevich set off for the tsarevna. He came there, and all the boyars were sitting at the table, waiting to see what the tsarevich would bring with him. When he got there, the tsarevna came out with the slipper, and her servant girl came out after her with the sword. The tsarevich went up to her and handed her the slipper exactly like the one the tsarevna had. All the boyars stood up, clapped their hands, and said, "Well, this tsarevich is worthy of our tsarevna. He has guessed the first riddle!'

The tsarevna said, "Now, tsarevich, guess my second riddle, and then I will marry you. Bring me tomorrow what I shall have, only a second."

The tsarevich immediately went back to the ship, but he was sad—yet not very sad. "Perhaps," he thought, "Ivan will help me."

But Ivan the Merchant's Son had already gone out onto the deck. "Well, Tsarevich, how are things?"

"Let's go into the cabin and talk a bit." When they had come into the cabin, he said, "Well, she gave me a second task, and if I guess it, she'll marry me. What do you think—can you help me in this?"

And Ivan the Merchant's Son said, "All right, I'll go and have a look!"

He put on the speed-walking boots, the hat that made him invisible, and he set off. He came to the palace and heard the tsarevna say to her servant girl: "Fetch me a gray duck. Let Ivan Tsarevich guess that he's to bring a gray drake."

The servant girl set off, and Ivan the Merchant's Son set off, too. He caught the drake and returned to the ship. He returned to the ship, gave the tsarevich the drake and said, "So here's the drake for you, and the tsarevna will have the duck."

In the morning the tsarevich set off for the palace, as he had before. He came there, and there were all the boyars sitting at the table, waiting for him. Suddenly there was the tsarevna, in her left hand was the duck, and in the right a sword. The boyars saw the duck and said, "Oh, that's a fine duck, but without its mate!" And then the tsarevich pulled out the drake and gave it to them. "Oh, that tsarevich! A fine lad! He's guessed it. You can marry our tsarevna!"

But the tsarevna spoke again: "No, Tsarevich, guess my final riddle: Bring me a hair of the sort I'll have with me."

The tsarevich headed back to the ship and thought, "What sort of hair will she have? Perhaps Ivan can guess it."

He came to the ship and met Ivan. "Well, Tsarevich, why are you so despondent? Tell me quickly!"

"Listen, Ivan the Merchant's Son, here's the thing! The tsarevna has ordered me to bring her a hair of the sort she'll have. Can you do it or no?"

And Ivan the Merchant's Son answered, "I'll have to go quickly!"

He immediately put on his speed-walking boots and the hat that made him invisible, and set off for the palace. He came to the palace, but the tsarevna was just ready to go out on the road. Ivan the Merchant's Son sat down in her carriage, but again she couldn't see him. Along the road he squeezed her hand firmly, but she kept thinking, "What's going on with my hand?"

They came up to the sea. The tsarevna got into a boat and set off, and he went with her. She came to an island, got off on the shore, and began calling out to her old granddad. Suddenly there arose from the sea this old man. He had silvery hair and a beard of gold. So he came up to her and spoke: "Greetings, Niece, you've not been here for a long while. My hair is all twisted and my beard all tangled."

Grandfather sat down comfortably, put his head on her knees, and she began combing out his hair and smoothing out his beard. And she plucked out a single hair. Ivan saw it all. The tsarevna selected about ten hairs. Grandfather fell asleep on her knees. Ivan watched. He watched and then grabbed a whole bunch of hair from his head. The old man leapt up.

"What are you doing? Is that the way to act? What are you up to?"

"Forgive me, Grandfather, forgive me. Your hair is really twisted. Let me comb out your beard."

He turned his beard toward her. She began combing out his beard. She combed it out and in jest pulled out some golden hairs. Ivan saw all this, but the tsarevna had no idea. Ivan crept up and grabbed—he nearly pulled out half his beard. The old man leapt up from his sleep and said, "What are you doing? Can you really act that way?"

He cursed her and rushed off into the sea, not even taking his leave of her. She was really amazed: "What is this? I've never, ever said good-bye to Grandfather like that. What could have happened here?"

She got into the boat and set off. Ivan was with her. They came to the shore, the tsarevna rode to the palace, and Ivan went back to the ship. He came to the ship and said to the tsarevich, "Well now, I'm giving you the hairs just like those the tsarevna will have. Only she has but a few, and we have a whole bunch. Go to the palace tomorrow. The tsarevna will carry out a few hairs, and you show her at the beginning the same number. And then say to her: 'Well, Tsarevna, I'll give you a whole bunch.' Then toss her the bunch. She will order you to tell her whether you have somebody, or whether you are guessing this all by yourself. You say, 'I have Ivan the Merchant's Son.' She will say, 'Send him to me!' And you say, 'I don't know which one to send, as I have twelve young lads. Which of them will guess? But maybe I'm the one.' Then she'll order you to send us all, and we'll set off."

In the morning the tsarevich went to the tsarevna. When he had just got to her, the boyars were already sitting at the table waiting to see what he would bring, whether he could guess the last riddle. The tsarevna came out and brought the hairs and a sword to cut off his head if he didn't guess it.

The tsarevich went up to her and gave her the silver and gold hairs. And then he said, "If you should need them, tsarevna, I'll give you a whole bunch." And he tossed her the whole bunch. Then all the boyars clapped their hands and said, "Well now, that tsarevich is worthy of our tsarevna!"

She was so upset by this that she fainted. She lay there a whole hour, then got up and went away to her room. She entered her room, took out her book of magic and began looking at it. "Who is this that's guessing the riddles? The tsarevich himself, or some one of his servants? This has never happened before! I've had many suitors, but none has ever guessed them. They've all left their heads here." She looked in her book and saw that the tsarevich wasn't guessing the answers himself, and that he had this servant, Ivan the Merchant's Son. And she immediately found out that it was that Ivan whom she had visited as a serpent. "Why is it that he isn't courting me for himself, but for the tsarevich?" The tsarevna came back and said, "Send me your servant Ivan. It isn't you who has been guessing my riddles, but Ivan!"

The tsarevich said to her, "Listen, beautiful Tsarevna, I have twelve lads, and I myself don't know who is doing this. I'll send all of them to you. You guess yourself who it is."

The tsarevich came back to the ship and said to Ivan, "Here's the deal, Ivan: Now you'll have to go to her with all the brothers. The tsarevna summons you."

"Well all right, I'll go. Only, I'll have to call all my brothers." They called all the brothers out, and then he said: "Well, brothers, now we're to go to the tsarevna for a feast. When we come in to her, the tsarevna will ask, 'Which of you is oldest?' Then you shout out all together, 'I'm the oldest, I'm the oldest!' Then she'll pour out eleven plain goblets of wine, but the twelfth goblet will be of gold, the one from which she always drinks. You all try to get that goblet and shout, 'I'm the oldest, I'm the oldest.'"

So they all set off for her palace, to the tsarevna. When they got to the tsarevna's, she right away sat them down at her table and asked, "Now, which of you is the oldest?" And all of them shouted out together, "I'm the oldest, I'm the oldest."

So she didn't manage to find anything out. Then she brought out the eleven plain goblets and the twelfth of gold from which she always drank. She filled the eleven goblets with plain wine and the twelfth with expensive wine. "The one who is the oldest will take that goblet!"

She had just had that thought, when all twelve of them reached for the golden goblet, nearly knocking over the table. And all shouted, "I'm the oldest, not those others!" So once more she didn't succeed.

She decided to get them drunk on wine until they'd fall down. Ivan the Merchant's Son drank, but carefully, and he saw that his brothers were all starting to fall off their feet. Ivan also fell down as if he were soused. The tsarevna noted that all of them were lying there, so she immediately went and brought her book of magic and began saying a charm on them. She charmed and charmed away, and the book pointed to Ivan the Merchant's Son. Then she left her book, took out her scissors from her pocket, and clipped off the hair on his right temple. She cut it off and went out.

"All right! You've had it now, Ivan the Merchant's Son, and Ivan Tsarevich together with you. No one will get away from me alive."

Ivan woke up, and felt: He saw that his right temple lock had been cut. "Get up, brothers, quickly, our misfortune is near. Lie down with your right temple facing up." The brothers turned over, and he cut away all their temple locks. "Now lie there until she herself comes back!" So they lay there, and they managed to calm down a little.

The tsarevna came and looked at the first one, the one lying on the edge—his temple lock had been cut off! "So you've cut off all of them?" she shouted. "You wanted to marry that tsarevich to me? Now I'll kill you all and that tsarevich too!"

But the Ivans said to her, "Listen, Tsarevna, first look: We all have identical temples!"

She looked: "What is this? My book of magic is wrong!" She went and threw that book of magic into the sea and didn't believe in it any more. And she said to the Ivans, "Well, bring your tsarevich here. Let's put on the wedding."

Ivan and his brothers went back to the ship. He came to the ship and said, "Well, Tsarevich, get ready! Now we're going to put on the wedding."

The tsarevich was overjoyed. He called all the crew together and they set off for the palace. They came to the tsarevna, and she seated them all at the table, began feeding them, and they started the wedding. The princes and boyars clapped their hands: "The tsarevich is worthy of our tsarevna; he can control her."

They had the wedding. Ivan Tsarevich got ready to go home with his tsarevna. And just when he was ready to depart, Ivan the Merchant's Son came up to him and said, "Listen Ivan Tsarevich, we'll be leaving you now, the twelve brothers. You sail on without us."

"Why don't you want to go with us, Ivan? I would reward you with whatever you wish."

"No, I can't. I only want to ask you about something—and don't refuse me!"

"Speak, Ivan, I'll do anything."

"When you get home, remember that Ivan the Merchant's Son is sitting in your castle keep. He's my brother. For my sake try and let Ivanka out!"

The tsarevich said, "Well, all right, Ivan. When I get back to my own tsardom, I'll let him out right away. Maybe you and I will see each other again?"

"That will remain to be seen, whether we see each other or no, but just let him go."

And he said to his wife, "Now we don't have twelve sailors. Ivan is going away." She brought him twelve more sailors, and they set off on their way.

And so Ivan the Merchant's Son rolled out his flying carpet and said, "Well, let's fly away!" And the tsarevna immediately grasped that it was Ivan the Merchant's Son, but there was already nothing to be done.

And so they flew to that mountain, where they had left their horses, and he said to his brothers, "Now, brothers, take your horses and let's ride!"

When they rode up, the first little devil came running up with an arrow, and Ivan gave him the hat that makes you invisible. He looked, and the second came running, and he gave him the speed-walking boots. He looked, and the third came running up, and he gave him the flying carpet. They thanked him and said, "If it should be necessary, Ivan, just think of us, and we'll help you."

The brothers got on their horses and rode off. They came to that tsardom where Ivan had been sitting in the dungeon. The tsarevna met them and asked, "Well, Ivan the Merchant's Son, how are things with you? Did my brother get married?"

He said, "Beautiful Tsarevna, all has been done, just as I said. Your brother will be here in four days. And now take me back to the dungeon. Let the others go as you know best."

And she spoke to him again: "Listen, Ivan the Merchant's Son, I don't dare put you back inside. My brother Ivan Tsarevich will come, and he will punish me for it. For what reason should I put you back in? Because you have performed a great service for him?"

And he said, "Beautiful Tsarevna, you didn't put me in the dungeon, and it's not for you to release me. It's not to you that I am to tell my dream."

Six days passed. Ivan Tsarevich came with his wife Elena the Beautiful. The tsarevna was very happy and forgot about Ivan, whom she'd put in the dungeon. And Ivan Tsarevich forgot about Ivan.

They had the wedding for three days. They brought all the prisoners wedding cups. Ivan Tsarevich's sister brought a cup to the dungeon, saw Ivan the Merchant's Son, and immediately remembered him. "Oh, Ivan the Merchant's Son, forgive me for forgetting. I'll tell my brother right away, but if you don't want that, come with me."

"No, he put me here, and he must release me!"

She ran to her brother right away. She came and said, "Listen, Brother, do you know that that Ivan, who's sitting in the dungeon, helped you to get married?"

"And who dared to put him in the dungeon?"

"Listen, Brother, wasn't it you yourself who put him in there because he wouldn't tell you his dream?"

So Ivan Tsarevich went to the dungeon right away, along with Elena the Beautiful. He came to the dungeon and said to Ivan the Merchant's Son, "Well, Ivan the Merchant's Son, come out. Forgive me for things turning out that way. I won't ask you any more about it." He led him to the palace, sat him down at the table, and said, "Now, ask me for anything you wish. I'll do anything for you that you ask, because you helped me court Elena the Beautiful."

He said to him, "Ivan Tsarevich, I need nothing. Only permit me for three years to eat and drink in whatever houses or taverns I go without duties or taxes. More than that, I need nothing."

Ivan Tsarevich said to him, "But listen, Ivan the Merchant's Son, I will grant you that, but what else do you wish?"

"I need nothing more for the time being, but afterwards I'll tell you when the time has passed."

But then Elena the Beautiful started thinking more and more about Ivan the Merchant's Son, even more than about Ivan Tsarevich. She thought about how to see Ivan the Merchant's Son. She chose a time when the tsar wasn't at home, and she called him to her. She sat him down at a table and said, "Why did you, Ivan the Merchant's Son, marry Ivan Tsarevich to me and not marry me yourself? Was it because I flew to you as a serpent when you were sleeping in the new house? You were really very clever then: The cock crowed and woke you up. If it hadn't awakened you, you wouldn't have been alive, and I wouldn't have married the tsarevich! Tell me what you are thinking right now. Be open with me, don't hide it!"

"Right now I don't know what to say to you, beautiful Tsarevna. My time isn't up, and I don't dare hope for you. The tsarevich untied me from the pillar. I felt sorry that he might perish, and I wanted to help him."

"That's the kind of person you are, Ivan the Merchant's Son. You pitied him, but he had no pity for you and put you in the dungeon because you wouldn't tell him your dream, which he didn't need anyway."

And he said, "Then my dream will be told when it comes true."

And then she said, "Listen, Ivan the Merchant's Son, fetch that book of magic for me that I threw in the sea, and I'll fix everything, and you will be my husband and the tsar."

Then he said to her, "Listen, beautiful Tsarevna, I no longer have the magic things that helped me out then."

She then said to him, "Don't tarry, Ivan the Merchant's Son, or else it will be late. Have some concern for yourself."

"Oh, all right, Elena the Beautiful, if that's how it is. I'll do that for you."

"But you are doing this for me and for you."

He said, "I'll go away for about three days, and then I'll come back to see you. Choose the time."

"Very well, there'll be a time."

So then he right away ordered them to lead a horse out of the stables. They gave him the horse immediately, and he rode off to that hill where the three devils lived. When he got there, he thought of them, and suddenly all three of them appeared: "What do you need from us, Ivan the Merchant's Son. We are happy to be of service to you."

"This is what I want to say to you: Does any one of you know where Elena the Beautiful's book is, the one she threw into the sea? I want to get hold of it. Fetch it and bring it to me. I need nothing more from you."

He asked the first little devil, "Do you know this book?"

He shook his head: "No, I don't know it."

Then he asked the second.

"No, I don't know it. I've heard of it, but I don't know it."

Then he asked the last one, "Well, maybe you know it?"

This little devil answered, "Yes, I know it, I have it. Back then you gave me the speed-walking boots, I ran to our parts, and there I by chance caught sight of it. It was being carried along by the waves. I picked it up, and now it's with me."

"Well then, my friend, give it to me!"

The little devil shrugged his shoulders and said, "I've no desire to give it back, there's a lot of good stuff written in there. I'll finish reading it, and then I'll give it back!"

But Ivan the Merchant's Son had no time to wait; he'd promised to come back within three days. The little devil's brothers begged him: "Listen, Brother, if you want, we'll do a trade, take anything you want. We promised to help him, so you'll have to give back the book."

Ivan just stood there, listening to their conversations. Finally the little devil said to his eldest brother, "If you take the speed-walking boots and give me the hat that makes you invisible, then I'll give him the book."

"Well then, we'll do a trade, because we really must help Ivan the Merchant's Son."

He got the book and rode back. Three days had passed when he rode into the tsardom to Elena the Beautiful. But again, the tsar wasn't home. Ivan the Merchant's Son handed over the book of magic, and Elena the Beautiful said to him, "Well, my good lad, Ivan the Merchant's Son, I shall be your wife, and you shall rule the entire tsardom. Just wait for three days and all will be clear."

She took the book and read in it how to destroy Ivan Tsarevich. She put him in a fatal sleep, as if he were really dead. Then they buried the tsarevich, just as everything was supposed to be. And then they put on a feast. And they summoned guests to that feast. They were sitting there, enjoying the feast, which went on for two whole days. Then Ivan the Merchant's Son said, "Listen now, I'm going to tell you my dream."

And he told them everything that had occurred. And then his father asked his forgiveness for once having acted unjustly with him in tying him to the pillar. The son forgave him and began living with his wife Elena the Beautiful into deep old age.

And with that, we'll end this.

(SUS 725 + 518 + (507)

10

THE ENCHANTED TSARDOM

P. Ia. Nikonov

There lived and dwelt this Tsar Ondron. And he lived happily and well, ruling his country, but he had no children at all. For a long time they begged God to give them a son or a daughter for their comfort, but there were no newly born children, and they could wait no longer.

So then finally, and nonetheless, at the last moment of their lives, a daughter was born. They called this newly born daughter Maria. And so this Maria began growing, and she was a beautiful daughter, really fine, such that all the neighbors began envying her beauty. Finally, word of her beauty went throughout the entire world—that she was really lovely. And so as a consequence, finally the wizard Mukhomor learned of this beauty. So then this wizard came to that tsar and began asking for her hand. He turned into a handsome lad, even though he was, perhaps, a hundred years old. The tsar found out that he, this very wizard, was a sorcerer. The tsar had no desire to marry his daughter to such a despised man. The wizard-sorcerer right away got so angry at the tsar that he turned the entire tsardom into a swamp. He enchanted the entire tsardom, such a mighty wizard he was. And he turned their daughter into a frog. So he enchanted that tsardom for three hundred years, and the tsarevna became a swamp frog. The tsardom became an entire swamp, and she hopped about, croaking in the swamp, in her own tsardom.

Now there lived next door to them another tsar, and this tsar had three sons: Makar, Zakar, and Ivan were the sons. So now then, the tsar's sons began to grow up. They grew up to be grownups, and he taught them, and then he had to marry them off. Once he said to them, "Well now, children, you need to, it's time for you to get married. You will rule over the tsardom. I order you each to make a bow (there were bows then, they shot from bows) and an arrow. And these arrows will decide your fate. You will go out into the open steppe," he said, "and shoot in various directions and we shall see whose arrow falls where."

So then the tsar, losing no time, made them bows, and he made them some arrows, and he sent them into the open steppe to let fly the arrows, each to loose them wherever. The day was a splendid one, fine. So they got busy with this work, shooting. The eldest shot, and his arrow fell into the castle of the neighboring king. Now that king had, you see, a daughter. He, you see, should marry that king's daughter. So then the second son shot at a neighboring tsar's, and that tsar had a daughter, so that one was to marry her. But the youngest son let loose his arrow, but it didn't fly anywhere, just right into a bush and in that neighboring swamp where the enchanted tsardom was.

Out from that bush jumped the frog and brought the arrow in her claws. "Croak, croak," she said. "Here you are, Ivan Tsarevich, your arrow fell to me in the bush, into my burrow."

He got furious. "That is my luck," he said. "My arrow fell into a bush to a frog's house. What will happen to me now? I'll be an unhappy man."

So then all three brothers came home to their father and told him where each one's arrow had gone. One said, "Mine went to that king." The second said, "Mine went to that tsar." The turn came of the third. "Well, and why don't you say anything? Where did yours go?" he said.

"I'm ashamed," he said, "I'm ashamed to say where my arrow went, Papa. Mine went to a frog living in a bush in the swamp."

"Well, that's no misfortune. You are a lucky man," his father said.

"How lucky, when it went to a frog?"

"That frog is from an enchanted tsardom. Don't be afraid," he said to his son. "There's nothing dangerous there."

But his brothers started then to make fun of him. "Your arrow went to that swamp hopper! You've shot a swamp hopper!"

So then that tsar lived for a certain amount of time and said, "Well now, children, go to your wives. Let's see what kind of workers they are: Let them each embroider a towel for me."

So then the brothers made fun of him. "We'll go now, one to a princess, the other to a tsarevna, and where will you go, Vanka? You'll have to go to your hopper in the swamp, to that bush. And what will that hopper do for you? Absolutely nothing!"

So off he went to his swamp hopper, and she ran out to greet him. "Croak, croak, Ivan Tsarevich, why are you so desolate, why so sad?"

"I'm desolate and sad because Papa has ordered a bath towel. Can you possibly do that?" he said.

"Well, Ivan Tsarevich, come along after me," she said.

So Ivan Tsarevich set off, and she went ahead. Ivan Tsarevich followed. They came to a big bush. She started croaking, and suddenly that bush turned into a palace. Then she croaked a second time, turned a somersault, and turned from swamp hopper into the beautiful Maria Tsarevna. So then, Ivan Tsarevich just looked. "Something's wrong here, Brother. Now that hopper is that same frog but a person." So then he asked her, "Why were you a swamp frog and then you turned into a beautiful woman?"

"It's like this," she said. "I was the only daughter of a tsar, my father, Ivan Tsarevich, and a wizard, Mukhomor, envied my beauty. But Father found out that he was a wizard and wouldn't give me to the wizard Mukhomor." "This wizard," she said, "got angry with my father and turned our tsardom into this stinking swamp, and I'll be a swamp frog until I am freed. Now if you free me, I'll be the beautiful Maria Tsarevna as before." "But for the time being," she said, "don't tell anybody this secret, that I can turn from a frog into a person."

So right then Ivan Tsarevich either ate or drank with her, I don't know which, and then he tumbled off to sleep. And she began preparing that towel for her future father-in-law. She took some silk, cut various herbs, and carried them outside into the wind. And then she threw them. "Little nannies, little mothers," she said, "little servants true. As you served Father, Mother, now serve Maria Tsarevna, the swamp hopper. Make me a towel," she said, "to give to my father-in-law, such and such a king or tsar (I don't know), one that won't shame me to have it laid out on the table."

So then, and not very long after, they right away made her the towel and wrapped it in paper. So then, in the morning Ivan Tsarevich got up early from his sleep. She of course woke him up. She couldn't remain a human for very long; she had to turn back into her old swamp frog skin, you see. "Well then," she said, "Ivan Tsarevich, take this packet and hand it over to your papa as a gift from me. And say of me 'This is a gift from my future wife, from the swamp hopper.'"

Ivan Tsarevich went home, and his brothers were already at home. And his brothers had brought their gifts. He gave it to his father and said, "Here, Papa, is my gift from my future wife." He said, "Here is the towel as you ordered made."

So then afterwards the tsar began examining the eldest one's, he looked at the towel. "Hand this towel over to the kitchen help in the kitchen to wipe their hands."

And then he looked at the second. "Give this towel," he said, "to the parlor maids wherever they are, to wipe their hands."

So then afterwards he looked at Ivan Tsarevich's from the swamp hopper, and he ordered them to hang it in the dining hall where guests gather and where the tsar puts on balls. Let the towel be there!

A little time passed and the tsar said, "So now then, children, let your wives each make a rug for my sofa." So they went, these brothers: the eldest to the princess; the second to the tsarevna; and Ivan Tsarevich went back to his swamp hopper where his arrow had fallen, for there his fate would be decided. They came and each gave this order to his bride: "So and so, make a rug." The second also said to his tsarevna, "Make a rug; Papa has so ordered it."

But Ivan Tsarevich went back to his swamp hopper, and she again came running to meet him. "Croak, croak, Ivan Tsarevich, what do you need? What has Papa ordered you to do?" (Probably she already knows.)

"Papa has ordered our brides to each make a rug for his sofa."

"Well, all right, that is no task, just a trifling task. The task is still in the future," she answered him. "Wash and dry yourself," she said, "then go to bed, and in the morning get up and all will be ready."

Ivan Tsarevich washed and again tumbled off to sleep. And when it had got dark, she again took and prepared various herbs, threw them, and said, "Little nannies, little mothers, true little servants, as you served Papa and Mama, now serve me," she said, "Maria Tsarevna, the swamp hopper." So then in a short time—and in fact momentarily—the nannies and little mothers did it: They made such a rug that no better could be required. They wrapped it in paper and said, "Here you are, Maria Tsarevna, a gift for your future father-in-law."

Time passed, and again she had to turn back into the swamp hopper from a human. She woke up Ivan Tsarevich, and then she spoke: "Take your assignment here, the rug of my work, and give it to your papa and say, 'Here, Papa, is a gift from my swamp hopper.'"

So Ivan Tsarevich took the gift and went home. His brothers had already arrived, they had brought their gifts. So now then, the tsar began examining these gifts.

"My eldest son's rug," he said, "is for the grooms to wipe their feet on. Put it there, at their feet. And place second son's rug in the kitchen for the cooks to wipe their feet. And now what," he said, "what has Ivan Tsarevich brought from the swamp hopper?" He took it and looked. "Oh, this is it," he said. "You can place this on the little cushion where I sit."

So they placed them all according to his orders. Finally he said, "Well, children, bring me a pie from each of your wives. I want to try their cooking, to see what pies they can prepare for their future household."

So all the sons set off again: one to the princess, the second to the tsarevna, and the other to the swamp hopper. Again Ivan Tsarevich came and the swamp frog ran out, shouting, "Croak, croak, Ivan Tsarevich, what can I do to serve you?"

"So now my papa wants to test the cooking of the future brides, and he has ordered them to bake a pie each."

"So that's it," she said. "It's no task, just a trifling task. The task is all still in the future," she answered him.

She went and turned a somersault towards the bush, a palace was made from the bush, and she became a person, once again a beautiful maiden. "Well, Ivan Tsarevich, wash yourself and then dry yourself," she said, "and then go to sleep. When you get up in the morning, then everything will be ready."

So Ivan Tsarevich went and washed and tumbled off to sleep. And that very time she immediately took what she needed, she mixed the flour and water. She mixed it thoroughly, and then she poured it all out the window. "Little nannies, little mothers, true little servants, as you served Papa and Mama, now serve me, Maria Tsarevna, the swamp hopper. Bake a pie for me for my future father-in-law," she said.

So then momentarily, in no long time, the pie was ready. They wrapped it in paper, handed it to her with steam still rising, warm, even hot. Ivan Tsarevich got up from his sleep in the morning, and she handed it to him. "Now give my cooking to your papa and say: 'Papa, take this from my future wife, the swamp hopper.'"

So then Ivan Tsarevich took it and set off to his papa. He came home and his brothers had already come, all was ready, the pies were set out on the table. "Here, Papa, is my pie from my future wife, the swamp hopper." The tsar took the pies and then he looked them over.

"Crumble up this pie," he said, "and give it to the horses. Let the horses eat what's from my eldest son."

Then he handed over the second pie. "Let the servants break this one up and give to the livestock, to the pigs and cows. Let them eat it."

Then he began looking over the pie from Ivan Tsarevich's swamp hopper. He looked at it and said, "There's no shame in putting this pie on the table."

So all right, some time passed after that. The tsar had to marry off his sons, put on a wedding. And so Ivan Tsarevich kept thinking, "How will mine come here? They'll be with horses and in carriages, but how will I bring her? I'll just have to bring that swamp frog in my pocket."

So Ivan Tsarevich went there, and out to greet him ran the swamp hopper. "Croak, croak, Ivan Tsarevich," she said. "How can I serve you, what is it your father requires?"

"Well," he said, "my papa has ordered the brides, the future wives, brought to the palace. They're going to put on a wedding."

"Well," she said, "that's no task, it's just a trifling task. The task is still in the future." She went into the bush, turned a somersault, and became as before the beautiful Maria Tsarevna. "Now, Ivan Tsarevich, you won't rest here just now. Go home and order your father to cover over all the windows so that there is no light in your palace. And when you have covered all the windows, some time will pass, and there will be some shouting: 'Tsar, your tsardom is burning!' The tsar will run to the doors and you," she said. "You hold him back. Say 'that isn't your tsardom afire; it's my wife come in a box.'" "And then," she said, "this will be repeated three times: Everybody will shout, 'The tsardom is afire,' but you answer 'That isn't the tsardom afire; it's my wife come in a box.'"

So Ivan Tsarevich set off home to his papa. He came and his brothers still hadn't arrived; they hadn't everything prepared, they hadn't managed to get there. So after a little time the brothers arrived and all dispersed throughout the halls, and the tsar caught sight of Ivan Tsarevich: "Where is your wife then?"

"She'll be coming, Papa, in a box. And cover all the windows so that there'll be no light in the palace."

The tsar had to heed his son. He took and ordered them to cover all the windows so that no light could be seen from anywhere. As soon as the windows of the palace had been covered, someone suddenly shouted, "Tsar, your tsardom is burning!"

The tsar leapt up, thinking it was in fact afire. But Ivan Tsarevich said to his father, "That isn't your tsardom afire; it's my wife coming in a box."

Suddenly they shouted again, "Tsar, your tsardom is burning!" The tsar again leapt up, but Ivan Tsarevich said, "That isn't your tsardom afire; it's my wife coming in a box."

Again the tsar sat down, but then for a third time they shouted, "Tsar! Your entire tsardom has caught fire!"

The tsar leapt to his feet, wanting to flee. His son again grabbed him by the arm. "No, sit down," he said, "Papa, my wife has just arrived in a box."

Ivan Tsarevich ran off and met his wife. The tsar was there himself, too. A carriage stood there, shining as if it were a fire burning, all covered over with precious stones. So they led Maria Tsarevna into the rooms, and at night she was a person but in the daylight the swamp hopper. Then the tsar gave a feast for the whole world, as they say. Ivan Tsarevich said, "Well, Papa, arrange your feast so that it's all towards night. In the daylight she's just a swamp hopper."

So that's what the tsar did. He arranged the feast for the night. He invited all the kings and all the neighboring tsars to the wedding, and those other brothers came with their wives. All were beautiful, all were fine, but Ivan Tsarevich's Maria Tsarevna, the swamp hopper, was best of all, most beautiful. They sat down at the table, and they began to bring drinks and things to eat. This Maria Tsarevna the swamp hopper drank only a little from her wine glass, from her tumbler, and the rest she poured into her sleeve, and some bites from her food she also put there. The wives of the brothers found this out and also started pouring out their drinks and putting bites from their food there too. So then the father-in-law saw what she was doing and what they were doing, and then the old man wanted to dance! He invited the eldest wife. When she went out to dance, all the bites of food tumbled out, everything poured out! What a disgrace! So he returned her to her place and took the second. The same thing happened: It came pouring out of her sleeve, and bits tumbled out, too. So then it was the turn of Ivan Tsarevich's wife, the swamp hopper. He invited her, took her by the sleeve, moved it, and out of it poured various gardens, with ponds outside. And then birds began singing, and it was all so happy, the tsar had so much pleasure—more even than before, than he had ever had in his life.

So then that ball, the feast finished, and things moved on toward morning to daylight. At night a human, but in the daytime a swamp hopper. All went with their wives to their own rooms. But she turned into a swamp frog, and she said to him, "Well, Ivan Tsarevich, for three days I will be a hopper, but then I'll be a person. At night a human, but in the daytime a swamp hopper."

So then a day passed and she was again a swamp hopper. In the daytime she went about as a swamp hopper, but at night she was a human. "Well," he said, "let her go to the devil's mother! She's such a beauty but she seems content to live as a swamp hopper." So he took her frog skin there and burned it all up, he threw it in the stove when she was a human. Night passed and day came. She needed her skin to be a frog, but she couldn't be a frog.

"Well, Ivan Tsarevich, you didn't manage to control yourself, you couldn't wait a couple of days. Now you'll see me no more, perhaps forever. Now that very wizard, Mukhomor, will have control over me, the one who cast the spell," she said. "And you, Ivan Tsarevich, shall remain here and travel throughout the whole world. You'll carry three iron lapti, and three iron kaftans, and on your head three iron hats that the rain will strike through, and then three iron staves you'll put in the earth, and only then can you obtain me. But perhaps," she said, "even then you won't obtain me."

At that moment, the wizard grabbed her up into the air and carried her off. So Ivan Tsarevich had had a wife, but he couldn't keep her. So Ivan Tsarevich despaired. Well, what was to be done? As she had said, he had to do all that, to go wandering throughout the whole, wide world. So then one splendid time he went to the smiths and ordered them to make everything: first the iron lapti, then the iron kaftans; then he ordered three iron hats, and then three stakes or staves, also of iron. And then when they had made everything, he set off on the road, the way. For a long way or for a short way he journeyed. One pair of lapti he wore out and also one kaftan. He poked one stake into the ground, and on his head the rain poured through his hat, and it became holey, so he took it off and put on another. And finally he came to an old granny who lived outback, and he told her everything that had happened with him in this whole business.

"Oh, oh, oh, my dear!" she said. "You have far to journey yet. But I will help you, aid you in your sorrow." "Now then," she said, "she is now with the wizard Mukhomor [he's the same as Koshchei the Deathless]," she said. "He lives by such and such sea, and in that sea there is an island, and his palace is on that island, and in that palace is Maria Tsarevna," she said. "And what must you do for that? In the sea there lives the fish-whale, and in that whale there is a coffer, and in that coffer there is a duck, and in the duck an egg, and in that egg is the death of Koshchei the Deathless."

So Ivan Tsarevich set off on his journey. He walked for a long time or a short time, and he came upon the shores of a sea. Finally he found that fish-whale, and he began begging it to spit up the coffer. So the whale spat up the coffer, and he went and opened the coffer. He opened the coffer, and the duck was out of the coffer as if it hadn't been there an age. And it flew off and goodbye! The duck had flown away from him. So he again began ambling along the seashore. What should be done? And on the seashore there sat a kite. "Well," he said, "I'm tired and hungry. I'll kill that kite and cook it." He was already wearing his second set of clothing. He'd worn out the lapti and poked in the staves. He had left just one kaftan, one pair of lapti, and one hat. But he wanted to kill the kite, when the kite spoke to him: "Don't kill me, Ivan Tsarevich, I have little children not yet fed. Let me live, and I'll do whatever you need me for."

So he left the kite there. He walked on and somehow even forgot what he was doing. He was just walking along, thinking deep thoughts. So then he was going along the shore, and on the shore lay a pike. "Now I'll cook it and eat. I didn't manage to kill the kite, but I'll cook the pike and eat it."

But the pike said, "Let me live in peace, Ivan Tsarevich. I'll be of use to you."

Well, all right, so he left it too. Everything went on just as before: His legs would hardly carry him; he was so hungry and cold. "I don't catch anything," he said. "If only a hare chanced by, I wouldn't hesitate. I'd kill it and eat it."

Suddenly out of nowhere there ran a hare. He aimed and was about to shoot the hare, when the hare spoke: "Don't kill me, Ivan Tsarevich, I'll be of use to you."

"I'll let you go then," he said.

But the duck was still flying up—it was hardly to be seen. He thought and thought: "Well, I need to kill that duck." But wherever he went, the duck flew on, and he couldn't kill it. You see, his rifle wouldn't reach there; it was really high. "But likely that kite could bring it down to me so that it would land lower, and then at that point I could kill it. Where was that kite that I didn't kill, that I left alive."

And just then the kite was right there. "Well, Ivan Tsarevich, what do you need? I'll aid you in your misfortune."

"I've got to get that duck, which is flying around up there, and then I'll kill it. There's no other way for me to kill it, as it's flying really high, soaring straight up, you see."

The kite, not saying another word, soared up, and whether it struck the duck or not, it frightened it so that it came down and down, and almost landed on Ivan Tsarevich's head. Ivan Tsarevich right away, "bang," shot, and the duck fell into the sea so that again he couldn't get it. Again a misfortune. Ivan Tsarevich set to thinking: "I probably saved that pike. I didn't cook it, I nudged it back from the dry shore into the water." Just then the pike appeared.

"What do you need, Ivan Tsarevich?"

"I need to get that duck, that wounded duck is swimming in the sea, but I can't get it."

So the pike didn't say another word, it turned back toward the duck. It caught the duck and brought it to Ivan Tsarevich. "All right, Ivan Tsarevich, here's your duck."

Ivan Tsarevich took the duck, in an instant tore it apart, but the duck egg fell out onto the sand and broke. So what sort of grief was that! Nothing was easier. So then somehow, some other way, he fell to thinking: "Well, I saved that hare somewhere, I didn't shoot it, maybe it can help me with this?" The hare immediately came running, splashed it with its paws and the egg was whole. So Ivan Tsarevich took the egg, put it in his pocket, and set off farther toward the sea. He came to the sea where the island was, but he had to get over to that island. How he was to do that he didn't know. "Somewhere there was that whale that gave me the coffer and the duck. Perhaps it might come to me and be of service to me?"

Out of nowhere, that whale came. "Well now, Ivan Tsarevich, what would you like from me now?"

"To take me to that magical island, to Koshchei the Deathless."

"Get on," it said, "get on me, a whale, and I'll take you to that island."

He sat down on the whale, and the whale carried him to the other side. The whale said, "Well, go, Ivan Tsarevich. The wizard Mukhomor isn't there now. He is the wizard Mukhomor, but he is also Koshchei, and now he is flying about the world, fighting with other wizards. Go right to his palace," he said. "His palace is beyond that mountain, and there Maria Tsarevna will meet you."

He came to that palace, and Maria Tsarevna met him. "Where have you come from?" she said. "How did you get here?"

"No matter how I got here, here I am!"

"Soon," she said, "Koshchei the Deathless will fly in, and he will tear you to bits. Where can I hide you? Somewhere I've got to hide you."

She took and turned him into a little pin and stuck it into a wall. And she had just managed to turn him into that pin and stick it in the wall, when suddenly in flew Koshchei the Deathless.

"Foo, foo, foo," he said. "I've never been to Rus', never smelled a Russian scent. Who's here with you?" he said.

"There's no one here," she said.

"It's Ivan Tsarevich, finally," he said. "Aha, but how did he get here? I'll crush him."

She turned him back out of the pin, and Ivan Tsarevich suddenly jumped out.

"Well, for a long time," he said, "I've been waiting for you, and finally you've come. It is death for you," he said, "you are no longer to be on this fair earth, Ivan Tsarevich."

And in his turn he said, "Of course not. Or is it you or I who won't be on earth? You've lived enough; you've done much harm to many people."

He took the egg out of his pocket and shuffled it from hand to hand. As he was shuffling it from hand to hand, that Koshchei the Deathless was thrown from one corner to another.

"So you're a villain, Ivan Tsarevich, you got hold of my death." And then Koshchei the Deathless understood. And he tossed that egg from hand to hand.

"I'll torture you, wizard. As you tortured people, now I'll torture you, and then I'll commit you to death. Well all right, that's enough playing about with this," he said. And he took and aimed the egg directly at his forehead, and he fell, and it means that Koshchei the Deathless died.

Maria Tsarevna rushed to embrace him. "Well, you saved me from the wizard; now we've got to get away from here."

So then he and Maria Tsarevna left that house, and he said to her, "We have to burn down this palace so that it is no more—for Koshchei the Deathless the same as for this castle."

She said, "We have to do it, we have to burn it down."

They left the house, and they burned up that house and Koshchei the Deathless. They burned up that Mukhomor. The island was deserted, nothing remained on the island, and there was no way to get to the other side.

"Well, what now, Maria Tsarevna?" he said. "How will we get to the other side?"

"Well, that isn't your affair, Ivan Tsarevich," she said. "That's my affair.

She drew out of her pocket a magic ring of the wizard Mukhomor and she put it on his finger. Just then up came two youths.

"What do you wish, Maria Tsarevna and Ivan Tsarevich?"

"We would wish for you to carry us to the other side."

And before you could count to two, a boat appeared at the shore. And there were two lads in the boat, and they rowed them to the other side. Ivan Tsarevich told Maria Tsarevna how he had journeyed during her absence, how he had been forced to wander.

"Now then," she said, "now Ivan Tsarevich my tsardom is freed. As the wizard has been killed, that Koshchei the Deathless, let us go to my tsardom. Now you won't be ruling in your father's tsardom."

"That is fine," he said, "living in your tsardom or in my father's, but how will we get there?"

"Fine, we'll be there in a moment."

She again took the ring and tossed the ring from hand to hand, and just then the two lads reappeared. "What do you wish, Maria Tsarevna and Ivan Tsarevich?"

"We need a flying carpet to carry me to what was formerly my enchanted tsardom."

So they sat down on the flying carpet and momentarily they had traveled to Maria Tsarevna's tsardom. They came to that tsardom, and there the people were living as they had of old, all like ants in an anthill, and all the streets were busy, everything had come alive. So Maria Tsarevna went into her palace together with Ivan Tsarevich, and they were greeted as guests. Then they summoned the tsar, Ivan Tsarevich's father, and his brothers, and they put on a feast for the whole world. I was there, I drank wine, it flowed over my moustaches but none got into my mouth.

And they lived into deep old age.

(SUS 400A + 402 +544)

11

(THE REJUVENATING APPLES)

P. Ia. Nikonov

Now then, in a certain tsardom, in a certain country, there was a tsar, Brebius. And he had three sons: Vasilii, Grigorii, and Ivan, who was the very youngest. At first the children were small, but then the children began to grow, and the old man began to get old. His health got bad, he was losing his eyesight; it was weak. And so once he summoned his children.

"Well, my children," he said, "I am assigning you a task, to go beyond the thrice-nine seas, beyond the thrice-nine lands, to the thrice-nine tsardom, and fetch for me the living water, the rejuvenating apples, and the fire bird."

So then the oldest son said, "I'll go, Papa. I'll make the journey."

So then one fine day the oldest son saddled a horse, took supplies for the trip, and got ready for the journey and road. Whether he rode for a long time or a short time, I don't know where, but he came to a crossroads, and at the crossroads there stood a pillar. And there was some writing written on the pillar, something for all the roads: "By the first go, and you will be fed, but your horse will be hungry. Go by the second, and you will be killed. But by the third go, and you will be married." So then he thought and thought: "I'll go where I'll be married." So he went off there. He rode for a long time or a short time, and he came to where there stood a palace, a castle. And then from out of that palace a young girl came running.

"Well then, lad," she said. "Feed your horse, but not until he's full. And let him drink, but not until he's sated. And then hurry in to sleep with me, a maiden."

So he tied his horse to a sharpened stake with a golden ring, and he set off. He sat down at a table, and she did, too. She said, "Drink but not until you're drunk, eat but not until you're full." She gave him a warning: "Don't drink too much, then there'll be time to sleep with me."

So. Then he came in and there stood a little bed. "Well now," she said, "lie down here on the bed, you toward the wall and I on the edge."

He said, "No, you toward the wall."

Well anyway, she wouldn't go down toward the wall, so he set off there. He had no sooner lain down on the bed than he flew off into the cellar. So they had tricked him.

Well all right. Some time passed there, and the tsar was waiting for his son, but his son didn't come. So he got the second one ready. The second one rode off. Whether he rode for a long time or a short time, he again came up to that crossroads where the pillar stood. He read the inscription and he thought, "Well then, I'll go along this road that leads to marriage, and maybe there I'll also get some living water and the rejuvenating apples for Father."

He rode up to that very same castle. And that maiden came out again, with the same warnings she had given the other one. He also tied up his horse to that sharpened stake with the golden ring and set off into a hall. He came into a hall, she gave him the same warnings that she had given the first one. And the same thing happened to him as with the first one, with the same result. Well, again the tsar waited and waited, but there was no son.

The youngest spoke: "I'll go."

"Where will you go? The older ones went and didn't return, and you are my only comfort."

But now then, the son nonetheless paid no attention to his father. He began insisting. "Well then, I'll go," he said.

So he up and went. Then this Ivan Tsarevich rode there for a long or a short way, and he also came up to the crossroad. So he came up to it, and he read the inscription on the pillar. "So then," he said. "I'll go where I'll be killed. I'm still young to be married," he said.

So he was riding there near or far along this road. Suddenly he rode up in the open steppe, where there stood a hut on cock's legs, on needle-thin heels; it stood and went round. He said, "Hut, little hut, stay in your place. Let me, a young lad, go in and come out."

So then the little hut stood still and he went into the little hut, and a baba-yaga was sitting in that hut—she of the bony leg, firing up her stove, sewing a silk carpet with her hands. Her nose was poking into the grating, and she was sweeping up the floor with her tongue. And she said to herself, "Foo, foo, foo, I've never been to Rus', never taken on that Russian smell, but now that Russian smell has come right into my hut." She struck herself on one cheek, then righted it with another. "Oh, I am a fool," she said. "I'm just questioning a hungry guest. You have to feed, give a drink to, and send him off to sleep, and then ask him the news."

So she fed him and gave him something to drink, and sent him to sleep. And then she sat down at his head, and finally began asking him: "Where are you going, young lad? Where is your journey taking you?"

He said, "Well, Granny, I am the son of such and such a

tsar. Our papa has gotten really old, and he wanted to get young again, so he sent me for the living water and for the rejuvenating apples."

And she said to him, "Now then, my dearest, living water and rejuvenating apples—many have there been searchers, but few have returned. There are forty stakes there, and there's a head on every stake but one, and your head will be there too."

"Well never mind," he said. "I'm not afraid of that, Granny. Let there be forty stakes and thirty-nine heads, but maybe mine won't be left there. But if it is left there, then just a head is no misfortune. But if it is one, then it's just one."

So he tumbled off to sleep. He slept through the night, and he got up in the morning and said to her, "Well then, Granny, could you not help me?"

"I can help you."

So first she gave him a comb. "If it should happen that there's a chase after you, throw down this comb and say, 'Arise from the earth, thick forest, up to the sky so that no one can enter or ride through.'" And then she said, "And here's a flint stone, a little rock, and a second chase there'll be: 'Rise up, high mountains, so that no one can enter or ride through, nor even think in thought.'" And more too: "And here's a kerchief. If there's a third chase after you, wave this kerchief and say, 'Become a fiery river from one end to another, so that no one can enter or ride through, nor even think in thought.' And now I'm giving you my winged horse, and this winged horse will carry you to the place where you'll take the living water and the rejuvenating apples. And further on there," she said, "this horse will tell you what to do from then on."

So he took the horse, saddled it, and left his own there with the granny. So then he set off on this horse. He rode either near or far, for soon a tale is told but not so soon is a deed done. He arrived. There stood a castle, and around this castle had been built a stone wall, and the entire yard was behind stone walls. So then the horse spoke:

> So, Ivan Tsarevich, behind this castle walls there stands a vast palace, and in this palace there lives a maiden, a spirit of the fields, with her own army, and she has three regiments of maidens. They have just now come from a war, and all are asleep unconscious. You go into the first room, and there the first regiment sleeps. They sleep all disheveled, but don't you move even one. Then pass through into the second room, and in the second room it will be just the same. And in that same disorder that second regiment is sleeping. Then, well, you will pass through the third, and in that third it will be the same, they will be found in the same disorder. Well you be quiet and pass through all three rooms, of all these maidens.

"Then in the fourth," he said, "and there will be sleeping the ataman herself, that's the very field spirit. She is also sleeping all disheveled, and don't you touch her. And beneath her right side is the living water and beneath the left are the rejuvenating apples, sewn up in little bags. You cut off these sacks from her, take them and leave her just so, and if you don't, you will stay there if you touch her."

So then he set off there, just as the horse had told him to. He got there. True, they weren't sleeping in any order. He passed through the first room, then the second room, where they were also sleeping—they'd worn themselves out fighting, you see. He passed through the third room, and it was the same, and he came to the fourth. And just as the horse had told him, so it was: She was sleeping all disheveled. He took everything as the horse had said, cut it out, collected everything together, and went right away from her. He went off a little ways, passed through just these rooms, and fell to thinking: "And why in fact, I was there, did nothing. I have to do something—I'll go back." So then he went back there, committed his crime, and went away from them. He went out of the rooms, came to the walls, but the horse was on that other side, standing there in a garden.

"Oh, Ivan Tsarevich, you did something wrong," he said. "We will both perish here. There in that bush is a well. Go and wash yourself, change your underclothes, shake yourself all over, and then get on me, and we'll ride!"

So then he did everything that the horse commanded of him: He washed all over, dried himself, got on the horse, and began to drive him through the town, through that castle, in order to leap over the walls. And in the castle they were sleeping as if dead, no one heard a thing. He drove his horse, drove it on, and then he leapt over the wall. The horse jumped, but he put a hind foot in the wall. He struck it with a hoof, and the strings began singing, the bells tolled, the alarm had been raised with them. Then these maiden warriors all leapt to their places.

"Who was here, what has happened, what took place here with us?"

Well, she was herself the manager, she had a book of black magic, and from this book she knew who would be with her, who would come, and what he would do. "Well, the criminal, the son of some tsar has come here, watered his horse, and didn't close over the well. So, all right," she said.

So she sent out a party to pursue him, to catch up to him no matter what. So he was riding along for a certain time, when suddenly his horse said, "Look, Ivan Tsarevich, isn't there someone chasing after us?"

He looked back and saw a cloud of dust had risen up. "There is, good horse, and the chase isn't far behind."

"Well," he said, "throw down what that granny gave you."

So then he threw down that comb. "Rise up, thick forest, so no one can pass through or ride through, nor even think in thought."

So then the forests were there, as had been said—from the earth to the sky—and no one could pass through or ride through, nor even think in thought. They came to a stop and then returned back to her.

"Go, second regiment," she said. "Take shovels and dig out the stumps and roots such that it won't be there anymore. Clear the way." So they right away rode up and dug for a little while. And momentarily they had dug through, and they set out after them.

Well, again the horse spoke: "Look back, Ivan Tsarevich, isn't there a pursuit after us?"

He looked, and again a pillar of dust had risen up.

"Now isn't there something else that granny gave for our salvation?"

He took and pulled out the flint, and he threw it. "Rise up, high mountains, from the earth to the sky, so no one can pass through or ride through."

And so they stayed there beyond the mountains, and Ivan Tsarevich rode on further. And at the same time, they turned back, came, told her, and so on and on.

"Saddle up my seven-verst mare." The mare was for seven versts: She twitched her tail, and every step she took was seven versts. "I'll go myself." She mounted her horse, that same one, and then she rode off. She mounted that horse, that same one, and she cleared the path.

Well, on that mare it wasn't long before she caught up to his horse. She began drawing near. And his horse said, "Look, Ivan Tsarevich, isn't there a chase behind us? What do you have from that granny? Throw down all the rest."

So he pulled out that kerchief. "Rise up, fiery river, from end to end, so that no one can pass or ride through, or think with a thought."

So she stopped at that river there and shouted out after him: "You villain, just you wait for me, I'll come to you in seven years."

And he thought: "Well, all right, come then, but this time I've gotten away. I haven't perished at all."

So then he was riding along to that granny, and he got there. The granny said to him, "Did you do everything as you were supposed to?"

"All is in order."

He took his horse, gave her back hers, and thanked the granny. So then he set off. He rode up again to that crossroads. He rode up to that pillar, and he read the inscription. "Well now I'll go where you get married. What the hell, I won't go home without that."

So he took that road and set off. He came to that same castle, tied his horse to the sharpened stake with the golden ring. Out a maiden came running and said, "Feed your horse until it's not full. Water it until it's not drunk its fill."

So he went into that room, and on the tables was all that a soul could require, all was laid out. He sat down at the table, and she served him.

"Eat," she said, "but not until you're full, drink but not until you're drunk. And then come to sleep with me, a maiden."

He said, "All right, wait. I haven't eaten for a long time. I want to eat, and drink also," he said.

So he ate and drank. "Now then," he said. "Now I can sleep."

So he came to this bed. She said to him, "Lie down on the bed," she said.

"No," he said, "it can't be that a man should be among you women."

He saw that something wasn't quite right, that they were playing him for the fool. But he didn't talk with her; he grabbed her by the hips and tossed her on the bed. When he had done so, she fell right into that cellar. He thought, "Aren't my brothers there?"

And they: "Who, who, who is it? She's flown down herself. Trample her down there, so that she never rises out of there again and will never do it again."

And then he added, "I'll come. Somewhere there's an entrance to her secret cellar." So he went out and found the door, opened the locks, found that cellar, and out of there came those people who had gone there to get married. The grooms came out—so many you couldn't count them—kings, knights, bogatyrs, and then at the end his brothers. After all of these, she came out.

"Well, you've lived long enough destroying folk," he said. He took off her head and tossed it. Then he said to his brothers, "Now let's go home to Father. You have no horses, so we'll all three have to ride on one."

So they came again to that pillar. He tore off two inscriptions. "These roads have been cleared now, anyone can ride them as he likes." He said to his brothers, "Let's go along this road where you can have plenty, but your horse will be killed."

Well, his brothers weren't immediately so keen. But then, even if there was no desire, they'd have to go. Their brother was riding there, just so. So again they set off along that road, the third. So they rode there, and there stood a huge courtyard, and that yard was full of livestock—bulls. So then he said to his brothers, "Well, we'll kill the bulls."

So right away they killed the bulls, cooked them, and ate their fill of the meat. In the morning they got up and set off hunting. They left the oldest one to cook. So they went off hunting, and they found a hunter-bogatyr wandering through the forest. Whether he was lost or just what, no one knows.

"Take me along," he said, "we'll be like four brothers—you are three."

"Come along with us," one said. "No matter, you won't hold us back."

So then they took him. "We'll hunt a bit, and then we'll go to where we had our quarters." But in their absence, that other brother had cooked and cooked, but only managed to make soup.

"Well," he said, "this soup is really fatty and the meat is good."

Suddenly there came the one the size of a thumbnail, with a beard an arm's length. "Foo," he said, "some ignoramus has taken it upon himself to kill my cattle. Who told you to live here and kill my cattle?" "I'll make you pay for this," he said. And without a word, he grabbed that lad and began roughing him up. So he roughed and struck him, and roughed him some more, and then he lifted up a flagstone and descended into the underworld.

The brothers came back, and the soup wasn't ready, and he was lying there unconscious.

"What's the matter with you?"

"I got poisoned by fumes."

So then the brothers killed a bull, made some soup, fed him, and the next morning they said, "Stay and cook."

So now then, the brothers rode off, and they were three, as the fourth had been left to make the soup. And so, once more he butchered a bull. He cooked the soup, made it, and the soup was good. "Well I'll feed them with soup, today there are no fumes. It's good."

And just then, there came the one the size of a thumbnail with a beard an arm's length. "Foo, ignoramus," he said. "You've come to live in my yard and kill my cattle. Get out of here. I'll deal with you; I'll make quick work of you." So he started roughing him up again, he knocked and bashed him from corner to corner. He took the soup and drank it all, cleaned the kettle, and again went back to where he had come from.

He lay there, he lay there until his brothers came. And then, not long before his brothers came, he came to somehow and began preparing a soup. His brothers came.

"Well, is the soup ready?" they asked.

"No, it's still not ready. There was such a smell of fumes that I couldn't move."

"Well, good," they said.

They took and slaughtered a bull, once more made the soup, and they fed him. The brothers slept through the night, but in the morning the youngest brother said, "You go out hunting. I'll do the cooking myself."

They still hadn't left the guest to cook. So afterwards he took and killed a bull, was cooking it, stirring it, when suddenly the door opened and in the door came that same one the size of thumbnail, his beard an arm's length.

"Foo. An ignoramus has made his way to live in my house, to kill my cattle. Get out, I'll deal with you. I'll make quick work of you."

"Oh," he said, "it's not my brothers you're dealing with, but with me!"

He grabbed him by his big beard and began roughing him up. He shook and shook and shook him, and the soup boiled. He roughed him up some more, then grabbed him by his beard, spread out a canvas, clapped the beard in the canvas, and let him hang there. And then he began to stir the soup again so it wouldn't spill over. He kept on stirring the soup.

"Oh," he said, "this soup will be good today."

But he kept twisting and twisting, and somehow his beard was torn loose from him, and he fell down as a result and leapt away, with the other after him.

"Oh you, curse your grandmother!"

So now then, he went out into the yard, raised up that flagstone, and down he went beneath the flagstone!

"So here's where he lives," he said, "in an underworld tsardom. Well fine, all right. I'll have to go down there."

He came and finished cooking the soup, and it was really good. His brothers came from the hunt. Their brother was walking about, healthy. The brothers said, "Well now then, today there were no fumes?"

"Now I know your fumes. Sit down and eat, then we'll do our deed."

So then they ate their fill, they devoured the soup. They said, "Well, all right, we'll lie down and sleep a bit. The deed can be tomorrow."

In the morning they got up from their sleep. So when they were up, they cooked a bull—just one they cooked. "Well, now we have to kill bulls and make straps and go where I saw him go," he said. So they started slaughtering the bulls, one bull after another. They packed the meat in tubs and cut the skins into straps. When they had killed sufficient bulls and cut sufficient straps, and the meat—well some they ate and some they salted, in the tubs. So then, when they had killed enough bulls and cut enough straps, they made a trunk something like a cradle. And in this cradle they descended and descended, but not quite to the bottom.

"It's not enough," they said. "We have to kill more bulls."

Finally they had killed all the bulls, cut all the straps and descended, and the trunk went down to the very bottom. "Well now," he said, "you go, Eldest Brother, go there into the underworld."

"No, why me!" he said. "I won't go, I don't dare."

"Well, Next Brother," he said. "Then you go," he said. "You've lived longer on earth, you know more, so off you go."

"No," he said, "I don't dare, I won't go, whatever needs to be done, there's nothing for me to do there."

Well, what's to be done!

"Then I'll go."

But they wouldn't send that other one—he was a foreigner, you see.

"So," he said, "only on that condition that when I come back, you'll pull me up and won't leave me under the ground. I'll give you a time limit of three full days. You wait, and if I don't come in three days, it means that I am not among the living."

So he sat down in the cradle, and they pushed him off. So they lowered him, they lowered him down for a long time or a short time. Soon they had lowered him down there to the bottom. When they had lowered him to the bottom, he got out, left the cradle there. From that pit there was a path, a trail. So then he set off along that trail, along that way. A copper house was standing there, and in that house sat beneath a window a maiden weaving, weaving—and then still weaving at the loom, when a horse and soldier leapt up.

"What are you doing, Maiden?" he said.

"I'm weaving a trap for Koshchei the Deathless."

"Don't weave traps for Koshchei the Deathless. I'll take you to marry my oldest brother."

She had been kidnapped by Koshchei the Deathless and carried away to the underworld. So she took and cut the straps to the loom, and nothing more happened. He went on farther. He came to where a silver house stood, and again a maid was weaving at a loom.

"What are you doing?" he said.

"I am weaving a trap for Koshchei the Deathless for Ivan Tsarevich," she said.

"Don't weave it," he said. "I'll marry you to my middle brother."

So she took and cut the loom and nothing happened. Everything ended, she finished her work. He went on farther, and this time there stood a gold house, and in this house a maid was doing just what the others had been doing—she was also weaving a trap for Koshchei the Deathless.

"Don't weave that trap," he said, "and I'll marry you."

"Here's the situation, Ivan Tsarevich, I won't weave any trap, and you come with Koshchei the Deathless, and he's at home, wrapped around it three times, with his toes in his mouth. He was so small, but now what he's become! So." She said: "He will fight with you; you will fight with him. He will drop you, but don't let him beat you up. Say: 'Let me say farewell to the wide world—I won't go anywhere.' He will let you go to say farewell to the wide world. There are two wells on your right hand, and in one well is living water and in the water dead water," she said. "On the right side is the living and on the left is the dead. You drink so much of the living water that you can carry that well from place to place, and where the living was put the dead, and where the dead was put the living. Change the places of these wells. Only then are you to come and fight him, and you will touch him and strike him only one time," she said. "And he will shout 'let's fight again.' But don't you repeat this a second time, for one time is sufficient for him. And he will beg. He'll say, 'Let me go to say farewell to the wide world.' And you let him go, and he will drink some of that water, and you will cut off his head," she said.

So after that, he set out, and he came on to that place and that Koshchei the Deathless. And there stood a gold house. And he had wrapped himself around that house three times, and his toes were in his mouth.

"Ah, Ivan Tsarevich, I've been waiting for you for a long time. Have you come to me? Well now you won't get away from me. You and I will fight."

"Well, come out," he said.

Koshchei the Deathless let himself go around that house, and he became like Ivan Tsarevich. So they began fighting, but they didn't fight for long. He floored Ivan Tsarevich like an oat stook. It seemed easy for him, that devil, just so.

"Well, Koshchei the Deathless, don't hit me," he said, "let me say farewell to the wide world."

"Go," he said. "You won't go off anywhere."

So he went there to those wells, drank that water. He drank and drank, but he couldn't move the well, and he didn't want to drink anymore. "I'll go and fight," he said.

That Koshchei the Deathless knocked him down again. "Don't kill me, Koshchei the Deathless," he said. "Let me go and say farewell to the wide world."

So that Koshchei the Deathless: "Well go. It's all the same, Ivan Tsarevich, you will never get away from me. You've got yourself here, and you'll be here!"

He went off again and drank his fill of the water from that barrel there. But he still couldn't move it from place to place. Again they started fighting. And Koshchei the Deathless again knocked him down.

"Well, don't kill me," he said. "Let me once more say farewell to the wide world."

"Well, go," he said. "You won't get away."

He went there once more. He drank and drank that water, and those barrels he moved from place to place. Where the living water had been he placed the dead, and in place of the dead the living. So then he went, and he and Koshchei the Deathless started fighting. And he knocked Koshchei the Deathless down. "Go to the devil's mother," he said.

So then Koshchei the Deathless saw that Ivan Tsarevich had outfought him.

"Well, Ivan Tsarevich," he said, "don't kill me. Let me say farewell to the wide world."

"No," he thought, "if I release him, then the devil knows that in fact he'll run off and drink his fill of that water. No, it'll be better to kill him, damn him." He drew his saber right then and cut off his head, and he shouted, "Beat me a second time."

"No," he said, "Among us we beat only once, that's enough."

Not wasting any time, he took and dragged him to the house and burned him up together with the house. So he burned up Koshchei completely, such that his spirit wouldn't anymore reek on earth, so that he wouldn't live any longer in that underworld. When all was settled, he came to that girl, and she was already ready.

"I've been ready for a long time, Ivan Tsarevich," she said. "What did you do with him?"

"I burned him up," he said. "Completely, in the fire."

"So you burned him up," she said. " All the better. Now there won't be any more danger."

She got ready, and they set off.

"But you know what, Ivan Tsarevich? I didn't take the house with me—we have to take the house."

He said, "But how will we take the house with us? It's not some sort of toy; you can't put it in your pocket."

She took out a little egg, went and rolled it around the house, and the house went into the little egg. And he placed it in his pocket. "There's your house for you!" he said.

Well then, they went on farther to the second maid. The second was also ready. She said to her, "Take and roll this little egg. We won't leave this house here. Koshchei is no more; let's not have these houses anymore, either."

From the second they went to the third. So they came to the third, and she also put her house in the little egg. She rolled it around and again into the pocket. So then they came to that place where the brothers were waiting, and the brothers had waited until the very last moment. They thought he was no longer alive, for three full days had passed.

"Well, sit down, the one for the eldest," he said. "Sit in front in this cradle, and they'll raise you up there to the top."

So they shook the straps, they moved, and then they pulled it up to the top. They pulled and raised her up to the top, and they looked: "Who's that in the cradle there?"

"Oh, why there's a maid there," they said. "Well, Maid, come on up to the top," they said. "But if it's our brother, then we'll let him down to the bottom. He dealt with Koshchei the Deathless, but there's nothing there for us."

The brothers were afraid. So then they put the second one in there, and they raised her, for the second brother. And then they lowered the cradle again. They asked her, "Who is there?"

"Your brother," she said, "and then there is one more maid."

"Well, all right, we'll raise her up," they said.

They raised up the second one and lowered it down for the third. They lowered down the cradle, and the cradle arrived. He said to her, "Get in the cradle, they'll raise you up."

"No Ivan Tsarevich," she said. "They'll raise me up, but they won't raise up you, as you will remember. You won't be able to get out of here."

"No," he said, "my brothers wouldn't do that to me. I saved them; they'll raise me up."

They finally agreed about it, and she nonetheless took her leave.

"Well, you'll remain here. They'll raise me up, but not you," she said.

But nonetheless she agreed, she went up toward the top, and he remained.

"Once more," they said, "who's there, is just our brother remaining?"

But they didn't want to lower the cradle. But then they lowered the cradle, he sat down, and they raised it toward the top. They dragged it up to the top and saw their brother, so they sliced the straps with a knife, and their brother went back down into the pit again. He fell and lay there for some length of time, how long isn't known. Then they said to those girls,

"We'll go home. Don't you tell our father that we left our brother here. We'll all live together, and the one that was his, we'll give to this bogatyr, our adopted brother." After that the maids agreed.

This Ivan Tsarevich lay there for some time, came to, and set off along the road to where the houses had stood. When he got there, all was deserted. There was nothing anywhere. There was nothing where the houses had been, but the houses were in his pocket! Well, what use are the houses when there was nothing else? He went up to the well, and in the well all was mixed up, all was messed up. There was a trail from these wells off to one side, and he set off along the trail. He was there for a long time or a short time, and then he saw a house standing there. And in this house a blind old woman walked about, feeling her way about with her hands.

Then the old woman spoke: "Foo, foo, foo, I was never in Rus', never sensed a Russian soul, but now a Russian soul has come to me, into my house. Well, whoever are you and where have you come from? How did you get here?" she said.

He said, "I am the son of such and such a tsar. I was sent for the living water and the rejuvenating apples. And so, Granny, I went along this road and was at Koshchei the Deathless's. I saved three maidens." He said, "But then my brothers wouldn't raise me up to the top. They took them, but they didn't take me, and now I remain here."

"Well," she said, "don't grieve, my dear." "I will get you home," she said.

"Do me that favor, and I, Granny, will make you young, and you will be young. And as one ought, I'll restore your life to you."

So afterward, he fetched some of that living water, rubbed it on the old woman's eyes, and she could see! Now then, he took and fetched the rejuvenating apples, rejuvenated her, and what a woman she became!

"Well, Ivan Tsarevich, you will be there, I'll get you there. Wherever you need to be, I'll send you on to earth."

So then that woman fed him and put him to sleep. He slept a bogatyr's sleep, and he slept without waking up.

So then this woman said, "Now then, Ivan Tsarevich, kill lots of birds and beasts, and salt the meat. You need to fill up these three barrels. Only then will you end up on that earth, on the ground out of this underworld."

This old woman went out onto the porch, she went out and whistled, and all the birds came flying up. She, this old woman, was the commander of all the birds. Well, so all the birds began gathering around her. Only one was missing. "Why isn't she here? Where has she gone? Where has she got to?"

And then that bird came flying in, the one they needed, the very largest. "So, where have you been to, you were gone so long. And I've been waiting for you, and now you answer."

"Forgive me, Granny," she said. " I was in such and such a place, in some tsardom, and such and such a girl was giving birth to two boys. And I," she said, "helped carry water to her and prepared everything for their residing on the ship, all the produce. She was equipping the ship, and she wanted to go after giving birth, to sail. She would go to some tsardom or other, to journey for some time to some tsar. There was some sort of tsar's son, and he left her with these boys, and she was going there to him," she said.

"How long will it be before she is there with him?"

"No sooner than in seven years. She promised him in seven years, you see. And I was there when she gave birth."

"Aha, she didn't managed to put all the heads on the stakes, but she got tied up herself."

But Ivan Tsarevich thought, "Very well, let them go. After much time I'll get somewhere. She's on one road, and I'm on another."

So then that old woman said to this bird, "Now you've got to take this man to such and such a place."

"Granny," said the bird, "that is far away. We'll need three barrels of meat for the road for our nourishment (that's how far they would fly." "Well, and that meat will have to be prepared for me," she said.

And then the old woman said, "Ivan Tsarevich, prepare the meat."

And so, after that he began going out hunting. He started hunting and started killing animals. He killed a lot of meat, and in a long time or short time there, he had killed three barrels of meat. The bird afterward came flying back again.

"All right then, I am ready, and I'll carry you," she said. "Now you get on, Ivan Tsarevich."

They placed the three barrels of meat on the bird. Ivan Tsarevich got on himself and set off. He flew with that bird. The bird flew and then began looking around, and he would toss her a piece of meat from these barrels. And when she looked around, then he'd toss it. One barrel was emptied, he started the second, then the third was emptied, and he asked her, "Well, is it lighter for you now?"

"Noticeably lighter," she said.

"And have we flown far?"

"We have flown far, but we haven't flow half way yet."

There remained just one barrel. And the old woman said, "Ivan Tsarevich, if she gets you to that place, write. You won't bring me any notes, so I'll settle up with you (this was to the bird). Write whether this bird gets you there healthy and whole or with some sort of damage."

So then she kept on looking around. And he would toss some meat, and the barrel soon emptied.

"Is it far to fly still?"

"Yes," she answered him. "It's not so far to fly, but not that little—a decent amount."

But there wasn't any more meat. He tossed the last barrel away. She again looked back at him, she wanted to eat, but he had nothing to throw. She went down, down over the water, for she was flying over the sea. So then he saw her looking back, and there was nothing else to do: He took and cut his calf out. Well, then he threw it to her, she ate it up, and he held the knife in his hands. He asked, "Is it farther to fly yet?"

"Yes, it's still somewhat more to fly."

Well so he took and aimed his knife; he'd have to cut out the other calf. She looked back, and he threw her the second calf.

"Is it still far to fly?

"You still don't see the ground," she said to him. "Well, that's where the place is."

So he once more aimed his hand and cut out a muscle, and he threw it to her. "Well now then," he said, "is it far to fly?"

She said, "Now we are flying up to the place. Now I'll carry you onto the shore."

So then she carried him onto the shore. He went and wrote to the old woman that this and that, that he'd cut out his calves and muscle, and been left to fickle fate. And so he sat there for a long time or short time on that shore; he had to sit there because he couldn't move anywhere. And he sent the letter off to the old woman. The bird flew for a long or short time and flew to the old woman, handed the letter over to the old woman, and the old woman read it through and said, "You, bitch, you ate his calf muscles and the muscles of his arms. You go and vomit up those calves and muscles for him. He's sitting on the shore there, dying."

So then that bird got ready and flew back there to him, spat up his calves and then afterwards spat up his arm muscles. She took and rubbed him with the living water, and he got well. And he set off to get where he was going, to journey. He set off to get from that shore to his own tsardom, to his father. And so he walked and went along, and got lost, and whether a long time passed or little, I don't know. Well anyway, time passed, and his brothers had also arrived, they had just arrived home. But he kept getting lost, yet he finally made his way to his own tsardom. He thought it over.

"What am I to do now, go to Father? They will arrive all three of them and maybe they have already arrived. Father won't believe that I am his son. So much time has passed now and I have changed. I've become so manly. He'll say, 'I don't need that, I have a son.'"

He came up to his tsardom, and he was walking along when there stood there this old shack. And in that shack there lived just an old man. "Grandfather, let me in to live with you. It must be boring to live alone. Let me be your comrade," he said.

The old man invited him in. He reached in his pocket, then went to his horse and came back, then gave the old man some money, and said, "Go and fetch some wine and various other good things!"

So the old man went to the city for it all.

"Well, what's going on that's good in the city?"

"The tsar's sons have come, and there'll be a holiday, a marriage at the tsar's. The sons have come with brides; they'll be married."

"Well, Grandfather," he said, "now, do you know what? There'll be some work for you."

"And what kind of work will that be?"

"You take a caulking gun and caulk around your house. And those tsareviches will come to rent houses from you—they'll need three."

So the old man went, he went around the house, caulking, and those grooms rode up.

"We need to get married," they said, "but the brides won't get married! 'We don't have wedding clothes. Fetch some like the ones we had there. And let it all be as it was there within three days,' they said."

So the grooms went back and forth there. They sought craftsmen who knew what kind of clothes they had had, what kind of clothing they needed to make, but there was no one. No one knew. And they themselves didn't know, the grooms. They went about the city, they went out of the city, and then an old man came out onto the street. Ivan Tsarevich said, "Go and stitch up your kaftan," he said, "they will hire you."

"Grandfather, don't you know how to work as a tailor? Can't you make up three dresses just like our brides had there?" But what kind they themselves didn't know. The color or the style they didn't give him.

The old man: "Let me," he said. "I'll do it; I'll make them up."

"Well, old man, make them up. How much will your work cost?"

"For three dresses, three hundred rubles each," the old man said.

"Then, Grandfather, work so that they will be ready by tomorrow. Whatever it takes, and if they aren't ready, then it's your head from your shoulders!"

Then the little old man went into the hut in tears. So well, this and that, he himself didn't know what he'd taken on. Then Ivan Tsarevich ran out.

"Why are you crying, Grandfather?"

"Well, you see, it's just this and that."

"Stop feeling sorry," he said. "We'll do everything, only you took it on too cheaply for three hundred rubles a dress. Perhaps that is the cost; you don't give them for less than three thousand, and we'll do it. Don't feel sad," he said. "Lie down to sleep; morning is wiser than evening. You'll get up in the morning, and all will be ready. We'll do it."

So the old man went off to sleep, and Ivan Tsarevich got up in the night. From the eggs he opened up the houses, went there, and carried out their dresses, did up the pins, and sent them off to the old man before dawn. Well, the old man got up from his sleep, took the packages for the brides. And then there came three men from the tsareviches.

"Well, Grandfather, are the dresses ready?"

"Yes, they're ready," he said.

"Which have you done for whom?"

"There they are," he said, "they'll take a look and find which is for which one."

So then they took the dresses, handed over the money to the old man. The old man took a thousand rubles for each dress from them. They took and handed over the dresses to them. They examined them, did the girls—the dresses.

"Oh," they said, "he's here. Well, now we need slippers, which we had there."

Well, Ivan Tsarevich once more spoke to that old man: "You stitch something together somehow, some boots. They are demanding slippers."

The old man at one time stitched wonderfully. Well, they went about the shops, bought some, and did they perchance know then what kind they needed.

"Let's go to that old man," they said. "Maybe that old man can make them again."

The old man was mending his worn-out shoes and sitting outside.

"Grandfather, do you know how to make shoes?"

"Yes, I know how. I can make any kind of slippers you desire, and I can make anything else you desire."

"Make us the kind that our brides had there, Grandfather; we need wedding slippers."

"All right, I'll take that on."

"Well, you make them, however much they cost. We'll be there with the money—only make them. But make them by morning. Let them be ready by tomorrow. And if you don't make them, your head from your shoulders," they again spoke to the old man.

The little old man fell deep into thought again and set off for home in tears. Ivan Tsarevich: "Don't cry, Grandfather," he said. "Get up in the morning; all will be ready. Now here's what: go into town and buy something to eat, whatever is needed, bring in some wine. But don't cry, be happy. They may cry," he said, "but we will be happy."

The old man brought all those supplies from the town, and Ivan Tsarevich got the old man drunk. When the old man had gotten drunk, he tumbled off to sleep. Ivan Tsarevich went and opened up the houses, fetched the slippers out of them, their tassels, then tied up their ties in their kerchiefs, and handed them over to the old man.

"So, Grandfather, hand these over to them. They will ask which is for whom, and you say they will themselves figure it out."

So then they came. "Well now, Grandfather," they said, "is everything ready?"

"It's ready," he said.

"Whose are which slippers?"

"They themselves will sort that out, each will find hers."

So then, the grooms carried the slippers to them, and the girls examined them. "Yes, these are the slippers. He is somewhere here, but only how can we find out?"

Well then the grooms said, "Now we've got your wedding dresses, we've got your slippers. So now you can marry us, you can be ours."

They said, "No, we can't be yours yet. Build us houses just like the ones we had there."

There's a fine kettle of fish! And they don't know, once everything has been fetched, then houses. He must be somewhere, but it's difficult to find him.

Meanwhile, time passed. A ship sailed the sea, it also neared. So now then, soon to say, they had also passed so much time, searching, but no one could take it upon himself to make these houses. Who knows what sort of houses these had been!

"Well, let's go to the old man," they said. "Maybe the old man can make them." They thought then that, well, perhaps since the old man could make all the dresses, all the tassels for the slippers, that he could make their houses—what was that to him?

"Well, Grandfather, couldn't you make some houses for us? Three houses in one night, and all just like the others were."

"Yes, why not, I'll make them," the old man replied.

"How much will you charge for a house?"

"A hundred thousand each," he said.

Ivan Tsarevich had told him: "Take a hundred thousand each."

"That's expensive," they said. "It's a lot you're asking."

"Expensive for a house, but for cheaper do the work yourselves," the old man replied to them.

"Well, all right," they said. "We'll give it to you, Grandfather, only work so that by morning everything is ready. And if you don't do it, then your head from your shoulders."

The old man was once more aggrieved. He went home. Ivan Tsarevich said, "Stop grieving, Grandfather. Go to bed, and in the morning when you get up, all will be ready."

So the little old man tumbled off to bed and slept, but Ivan Tsarevich went in the night to the tsar's place, and took and revealed all the houses. "Go," he said, "pound on the houses, whichever one you like, but don't hand over the houses to anyone except the masters. The masters will come, and you'll get your money from them."

The tsar slept and slept, and in the morning he got up. He looked, and out of the window it was as if a fire was burning. What houses were these? "These were, probably, the houses of my sons." And the old man was walking around there, pounding on them. The tsar afterwards came up to the old man and said, "What are you doing here, Grandfather?"

"Well, I'm making these for your sons, for the brides of your sons."

"And how much will they cost?" he said.

"Each house is for a hundred thousand."

"Well, even if that's expensive," he said, "they are worth that money. Here's the money, now leave the houses."

"No, I won't leave the houses until I hand them over to whoever needs them," the old man said.

The tsar went away, came back, and handed over the money, but the old man wouldn't leave the houses. He gave them to the sons, and the sons gave him still more money.

So then in the morning the girls woke up from their sleep. "Our houses are here, and Ivan Tsarevich is here!" So they started readying the wedding, but the girls wouldn't get married. They were still fussing with this and with that. Well fine, but in the end they began agreeing, and that one who was for Ivan Tsarevich, she still wouldn't marry that son. Finally in the end, she also agreed to marry him.

So they began playing out the wedding. The weddings had only just begun, they were at their height, when suddenly a ship came. So then this ship came, and suddenly from the ship they spread out this cloth to the tsar's palace itself. So they tossed out this cloth and shouted, "Hand over the guilty one, Tsar, or we'll burn down your entire city. We'll take it apart log by log—don't mind that there are those maidens there, and over there the grooms."

So then there was nothing for the tsar to do. He said to his eldest son, "Well, you were out wandering about for a long time, why didn't you get married there? Go onto the ship—are you not the guilty one?"

Well, he got dressed and ever so quietly set off. He didn't dare walk on the cloth, he walked along side it. And on the cloth two boys ran about and shouted, "Mama, Papa is coming over there."

And she answered, "No, that isn't Papa, that's your uncle. Your papa saved him from death, and he laughed at him. Well, we'll have to receive him and treat your uncle as is appropriate."

He went on board the ship. He had no sooner set foot than they tackled him and began beating him on the butt. They gave him a thrashing, and then they said, "Go away, you aren't the guilty one." They began shouting, "Tsar, hand over the guilty one."

Well, then the tsar said to the second one, "Well then, you go. Aren't you the guilty one? You were also gone for a long time."

And that one also went off quietly, immediately, but he also didn't dare walk in the middle of the cloth, he went along the edge. And the little boys ran: "Mama, it's Papa coming."

"No, that's not Papa, that's your second uncle. He also made fun of your papa. We'll have to receive him and treat him as is proper." Well she also received him on board the ship, tied him to the windlass, and they flogged him. They received him well.

Then afterwards he went home. He said to his father, "I'm not the guilty one."

Just then Ivan Tsarevich went to the tsar's stables, took a horse, and the stable hands shouted, "Some sort of thief has been here!"

But now then, I forgot: There was this third son, the adopted one, and he simply ran away from the tsar. He didn't dare go on board the ship for his reception.

But Ivan Tsarevich, when he had taken the horse from the stables, mounted the horse, and rode onto the cloth and began winding it up. He ripped off some for someone's trousers, for others a jacket, for others a vest. "Now then," he said, "drunkards, get drunk, but don't think ill of Ivan Tsarevich!" (He wasn't afraid.)

So then all the sons came running up. "Mama, Papa's horse is coming!"

"Now that is your papa riding it," she said. "We must receive him and treat him as is proper."

He rode his horse right onto the ship. The children immediately unsaddled the horse and took their father into the guest cabin. The ship moved away from the wharf, he raised the sails and set off; only the rejuvenating apples and the living water had he obtained.

Well, so the ship sailed off into the sea, and it departed to that tsardom where the beautiful lady came from. They sailed in there into that tsardom of hers, and they had the wedding, and they put on a feast for the whole world. That's all the tale, and he remained there living in that tsardom.

(SUS 301A + 301B + 400*B + 551)

12

ABOUT A WIFE SVETLANA

M. O. Dmitriev

In no uncertain tsardom, in no uncertain country, but namely in the one in which we live (for example, like here in Avdeevo), there lived and dwelt a tsar, and this tsar had three sons: Nikolai, Fedor, and Ivan. So they lived on and on, and the sons grew up to be big, the tsaritsa died, and the tsar himself became old. But he didn't know to which son he should leave his inheritance. He thought and thought about it and decided: "I'll give them each an arrow, and they'll marry the one where their arrows land."

So he gave them each an arrow. Nikolai shot his arrow, and it hit a general's house. The second son, Fedor, shot and hit a captain's, and the third, Ivanushka, shot, and his arrow went goodness only knows where. So, since it was unknown where the arrow had flown to, he had to go looking for it. So Ivan said to his father, "So, Father, whether you give me your blessing or you don't, I'll go looking for that arrow."

Then the tsar said, "What will it be without my blessing— better with a blessing. The Lord bless you. Go, my child."

He set off. He walked and he walked and he walked. Wherever he went, there was nothing but the open steppe; gaze and you saw nothing else anywhere. He walked and walked, and then he saw standing there a little hut on a cock's leg, on wooden tongs, turning around. He went up to the hut and said, " Little hut, little hut, stand still. I have no time to waste, I need but to spend the night."

The little hut stopped. He entered it, and in the hut sat an old woman without a tooth in her mouth or an eye in her head.

"Come in, come on in! Come in, come on in, Ivan Tsarevich. Have you come far and long is your journey?"

"Yes," he said. "You see, Granny, I set off to look for my bride. My father gave me an arrow to shoot, and the arrow flew off I don't know where, so I've set off to look for my bride."

"Yes, my child. I am your bride. I have your arrow."

"Say, woman, you are joking. Stop these jokes!"

"No, Ivan Tsarevich. These aren't jokes—I'm serious."

"Oh, the devil take you and your arrow. I can just go away without the arrow."

"No you can't. You can't go away."

He set off to go, he intended to go, but he couldn't get out. Everywhere there was mud and such a sticky swamp that he couldn't take a single step. He walked about, but he couldn't get out of the hut, and night was falling. He would have to spend the night there. He tried again on the second day, but it was the same, and on the third day it was the same. "All right, old woman, you're some joker!"

"No, Vaniusha, no way am I a joker! I'm your wife!"

So then she told him a secret: "I have to live as this aged old crone for three years. Koshchei the Deathless has cursed me. He wanted to marry me, but I hid from him. So he cursed me to be this monster. And I have to live like this for three years, and after three years I'll be alive and well."

When the third night came she said to him, "So Ivan Tsarevich, I am not going to lie down and sleep with you, but you can look at me and see me as I really am."

So he'd take a look. Once the sun had gone down, she took the ring off her finger. Then he looked at her, and she was such a beauty, so attractive, that he would have been happy to take her at once, embrace, and kiss her. But she wouldn't permit it. So they spent the night. On the third day he took her by the hand and led her home.

"So, Papa," he said, "I've found my bride."

And the bride, without a tooth in her mouth and without an eye in her head, really wasn't very beautiful.

His brothers and sisters-in-law (his brothers had gotten married while he had been away) all laughed and mocked him. So what! His father put them in separate houses (the tsar had quite enough houses).

The father lived until deep old, age and he needed to entrust someone with his inheritance. But he just couldn't decide to whom this inheritance should be entrusted. So he said, "My children, I am going to give you a task, and whoever fulfills this task let the Lord bless as tsar in this tsardom. But keep in mind that you will have to fulfill three tasks."

"All right, Papa, now then, speak and tell us."

"So my children," he said, "here is some material. Let your wives sew me a carpet. Whichever one of your wives sews the best carpet will be the tsar in this tsardom."

One of them said, "But my wife doesn't know how to sew a carpet. She's a general's daughter."

"I'm giving you three full days."

The second said, "My wife is a captain's daughter. But she knows how to sew."

Ivanushka stood up and said, "I don't know whether my little old woman can do anything, or whether she can't."

Ivanushka came back unhappy. His head was hanging lower than his mighty shoulders. The old woman said to him, "What is it, Vaniusha, that you're unhappy, that your wild head is hanging lower than your mighty shoulders. What is it? Did your father insult you?"

"Of course not! He didn't insult me. He gave me a task. Here is some material, and he says we have to sew a carpet for him. He said the same to all of us. And whichever one of us sews the best carpet will be blessed as tsar over the entire tsardom."

"Oh," she said, "that's not a very big task. Pray to God and go to sleep; the morning is wiser than the evening."

She took the material, she took a stool, an axe, and she chopped and hacked it all up, and then she opened the window and shouted, "Blow, wild winds, carry all this silk into the open steppe."

The winds swept it up—and carried it off! The other brides sent their servants: "Go find out how the old woman is going to begin." They looked through the windows, and then they chopped up their material, opened the window and said, "Blow, wild winds, carry all this silk away into the open steppe." The wind carried away the silk.

In the morning the old woman got up early and opened the window: "Servants, servants, my trustworthy servants, bring me a carpet such that my husband could take out on parade." The carpet came flying as was to be expected.

And the servants observed the other brides. They opened theirs up but they weren't worth a damn, they were nothing at all. They ran about trying to buy up something, they hurried, sewing away and all.

The time came to go with the carpets. (If you do something carelessly, what will come of it?) They came to their father with the carpets. "So now then, Nikolai, show me your carpet." Nikolai showed him his carpet. He looked and looked at it. "This carpet is fit for a peasant's hut.

No one else would spread it out. And you, Fedor?" Fedor showed him his carpet. He looked and looked at it. "This one is somewhat cleaner. This carpet, when the owner sweeps up the manure in the yard, could be spread out and then shaken a second time but not clean up the yard. That's what it would be good for. And you, Ivan?" Ivan offered his carpet and the tsar unrolled it, and looked and looked. "Yes," he said, "I have ruled for many years, but probably I've never been worthy of such a carpet. This is some carpet!"

So then they all had tea; he provided hospitality for his children. "And now take up the second task."

"And what will be the second task, Papa?"

"Each of you is to sew me a suit of clothes in which I could go out on parade. Whichever one of you makes the best parade costume will be tsar in the tsardom."

One said, "My general's daughter can sew everything, so she'll certainly sew it."

The second said, "But my captain's daughter can also sew one."

But Ivanushka just stood there. "I don't know whether my old lady can do it or not." He went home, again unhappy.

He came home, and the old woman said, "Well then, Ivanushka, you're unhappy, and your wild head you've hung lower than your mighty shoulders. Why?"

"Well Wife," he said, "my father has given us another task."

"And what is it?"

"He's ordered us to make him a parade uniform. Whoever makes the best will be tsar in the tsardom."

"Oh, Ivanushka, that's no big task. Pray to God and go to sleep, for the morning is wiser than the evening." Then she took an axe, chopped up everything, and opened a window: "Blow you wild winds, and carry off these silks into the steppe."

The winds blew and carried everything away. There the servants took a look, and then they came back and told her everything. They cut it out and sent it back to the steppe. In the morning the old woman got up, opened the window, and shouted: "Blow, you wild winds! Bring the uniform in which our little father could go out on parade." The uniform came flying up. But the others commanded and commanded, but nothing was brought. Again, they had to run about, buy up materials, sew, and so on, but they couldn't sew it together as was required. The time came, and they all went to the tsar with the tasks fulfilled. They came to him.

"Well, Nikolaiushko, show me your uniform, what your wife has made." He looked and looked at it. "This uniform is not only not for me, a tsar, but would not be worn by a simple soldier. And you, Fedor?"

Fedor handed his over. He looked and looked at it. "Even a shepherd would be ashamed to wear this, let alone me, a tsar. And you, Ivanushka?"

Ivan gave him the uniform. He looked and looked at it. "Yes," he said, "in such a uniform I myself don't yet have the right to go out on parade. It wouldn't be quite right."

The tsar was amazed. He provided hospitality for his children. He fed them and gave them drinks. "Now then," he said, "take up your third and last task. Here is a sack of flour for each of you." (In olden days we had poods, and so in poods a sack was sixteen kilograms of white flour.) "Let them bake bread. Whichever one bakes the best bread will be the tsar in the tsardom. That is the last task."

Well, since it was the last task, one of them said, "Mine knows how to do that."

The second said, "And mine knows how to also."

But Ivanushka said, "I don't know what my old woman can do (whether she knows how to or not.)"

He came home, carrying the little bag. His wife asked him, "Well, Ivan Tsarevich? Why are you going about unhappy, why have you hung your wild head?"

"You see, Father gave us each a pood of flour and ordered to bake a bread. It's the last task. Whichever bride bakes the best, her husband will be tsar in the tsardom."

"If that's all," she said, "pray to God and go to sleep. The morning is wiser than the evening."

She poured some ice water into the yeasty starter, shook all the flour in, threw it in the oven, stirred it a little, threw it into the oven, and bustled about. The oven hadn't been heated, but it didn't matter: A fine white loaf with good crumble would soon be baked. The servants noted it and came and reported it. Those other brides did the same: They fetched some ice water, mixed it, and put it in the oven. In the morning the old woman got up, opened the oven, and began taking out the loaf. The bread had baked, as it ought to. But you can't tell in a tale or describe with a pen how it turned out!

But everything flowed all out everywhere for the other brides. The ice melted, and the dough flowed out through all the cracks and crevices. They tried cleaning it up and washing everything, then buying flour and starting the whole thing again. But the starter was fresh and no good. They baked it up and brought it to the tsar.

The tsar looked at a loaf. He looked and looked at it and then he himself spoke: "Even soldiers wouldn't eat this loaf, and it certainly isn't fit to bring to a tsar or to some guest or other. How is yours, Fedor?"

Fedor handed his over. He looked and looked at it. "Horses wouldn't eat this loaf, let alone a human being. And yours, Ivanushka?"

Ivanushka gave him his loaf. The tsar looked and looked at it, and then he nodded his head: "I have lived a long, long time, but I've never eaten such bread! This is real bread!" (He was praising it.) Then he said, "Now children," (he offered them food and drink, obviously, he did everything), "in three days come to a ball and I shall bless Ivanushka with the tsardom, because he has fulfilled all the tasks better than you other two. But you must certainly come with your wives."

The three days passed. Ivanushka watched as Nikolai came with his wife and Fedor arrived with his wife. Then he said, "All right, my wife, Svetlana, let's go. My father has commanded that I come with you."

"But how can I come and be laughed at by people?"

"No, Father has commanded it. Because of you he has blessed me to be tsar in the tsardom. I can't go without you."

"All right, Ivanushka. But in any case you should go alone, and I'll quietly make my own way."

"Look here, stop these games and come."

"I'll come, I'll come. Trust me." Ivanushka got ready to set off. Then she said, "Only tell your father not to be afraid of me, not to be frightened."

All right, so good. Ivanushka went alone, and his father complained to him: "What are you doing? I told you to come with your wives, as you can see my other sons have done. But you . . ."

"Papa, Papa, my wife is coming. But she has asked me to tell you not to be afraid of her."

"What? Why should I be afraid!"

When everything was ready, the tables, everything had been prepared, all the foods had been prepared, suddenly there was a troika of horses and golden carriages. All around were guards, everything. Some foreign tsar had arrived to pay a visit. But he sat there and said, "Papa, don't be afraid. It's probably just my old woman arriving."

They ran out to greet them, and in fact the old woman drove up. They had the feasts, the eating and drinking. They caroused and drank as was proper. Then they all went their own separate ways.

Ivanushka came and lay down to sleep with his wife. She always had this ring in her mouth. When she took the ring off at night, into her mouth—she kept it in her mouth. And then, you see she had probably had a little too much to drink and was soundly asleep. She opened her mouth, and out popped the little ring. She had only three more weeks to stay an old woman. He took the ring, went out, and threw it into the sea.

She slept and slept, and when morning came, she sensed the time, she got up and groped for the ring—but the ring wasn't there! She looked here and there, and there and here, but nowhere could she find the ring.

"Ivan Tsarevich, where is my ring?"

"On the bottom of the sea."

"So on the bottom of the sea! Well, goodbye, goodbye forever!"

He didn't see or hear anything, where she went, but she was gone. He had lost her. He no longer had any desire to sleep or to rest. He paced, wept, walked with but rare steps through the rooms. That's what he did! He was just waiting until that hour when his father would get up. His father got up, he went to him and reported, "Well, Papa, I've lost my wife."

"So, you've lost her! Since you've lost her, you are unworthy of my lands until you find her. When you have found her, you will receive the tsardom."

So now what? He would have to go searching for her. They baked him a backpack of hardtack and collected everything he would need for the trip and journey. He set off. He walked and walked and walked. He saw standing there a little hut on a cock's leg, on wooden tongs, on a cat's tail, twirling around. He went up to the little hut and said, "Little hut, little hut, stand still. Let me in, O Lord, and let me out. I've no time to wait, I need only to sleep the one night."

The little hut stopped and he entered it. There sat an old woman in a golden chair, sharpening a golden tow (some sort of ball of string, narrator)[1] "Greetings, Ivan Tsarevich. Far have you come, and will your path take you far?"

He popped the old woman on the ear. "Oh, you old crone! You ought first hasten to feed me and offer drink, and then question, but I see you don't know how to begin."

The old woman got out of her chair, farted and knocked over the table. She farted again and burned the cabbage soup. She dug at the oven door with her nose, got a chunk of bread, and set the table. "Eat, Ivan Tsarevich!"

---

1. The narrator seems to be confused. (trans.)

Well, he ate.

"So now then, have you come far and will your path take you far?"

Then he told her: "I've lost my wife and have set out to search for her."

"Oho," she said, "I am the oldest auntie. She comes visiting me once every three years. But then, if that's how it is, so be it. People help people—and I ought to help you a little. Here's my ball and thread. Wherever this ball rolls, you follow. The little ball will roll up to a hut, and you enter that hut, just as you did here. There my middle sister lives alone. Perhaps she can help you somehow. But I can't help you with anything else."

So then he set off. The ball rolled and he walked. He came to a little hut. The hut was identical, so he went in the hut. There sat an old woman, also in a gold armchair, winding up thread into a ball.

"Come in, come in, Ivan Tsarevich Have you come far and far is your path?"

He popped the old woman on the ear. "Oh, you old crone! You ought first hasten to feed me and offer drink, and then question."

The same thing happened. She farted and knocked over the table. She farted again and burned the cabbage soup. She dug at the oven door with her nose, got a chunk of bread, and set the table. "Eat".

Well then, he ate.

"Now then," he said, "I was sent here to you by your sister."

"All right. So be it. People help one another—and I'll help you. She is my guest every three months. But you go to my youngest sister; she visits there more often."

So he set off. She gave him a little ball, with the same sort of string. "Now then," she said, "wherever this little ball rolls, you follow it."

He set off. He walked and walked. The little ball rolled, and he went. He came to another such little hut. He went into the hut and there sat an old woman doing exactly the same thing. "Come in, come right on in, Ivan Tsarevich. Far have you come, and will your path take you far?"

He popped the old woman on the ear. "Oh, you old crone. You ought to have learned to feed me and give drink, and then ask, but first you are asking."

She also farted and knocked over the table, farted again and burned the cabbage soup. She dug at the oven door with her nose, got a chunk of bread, and set the table. "Eat!"

He ate and spoke: "So now then, your middle sister sent me to you."

"So my sister sent you. And a sister probably sent you to that sister, didn't she?"

"Yes."

"Well, once my sisters help, I'll have to help too. She," she said, "will be visiting me tomorrow. You will find her here. But the whole business depends on you. I'll hide you, and when she is already sleeping, I'll bring you in. Then you take her by the throat (she'll wake up), and with all your strength squeeze and choke. Choke her," she said, "until she gives you a promise. When she has given you the promise, then you can let her loose. But until she gives you the promise, choke her to her death, just choke."

"All right," he said, "let's do it."

So she hid him there. Her niece came flying in to her. The woman, this auntie, fed her and gave her something to drink, and then put her down to sleep on a bed. She put her down on the bed, and she lay down. And she lay there a while and fell into a deep sleep. She went to sleep. Then the woman went and brought Ivan Tsarevich in. As she was leading him in, she added, "Well, Ivan Tsarevich, don't let go, choke her with all your strength."

He came in and looked at her. She was such a beauty, so attractive, that instead of choking, her he decided just to take her by the end of one finger. The moment he touched her, she jumped up: "Be thrice cursed you, Auntie, by me!"

She disappeared. Then that auntie began scolding him: "Oh, you villain, you villain! Now you're deprived of her forever, and you've deprived me of a niece." (And that's how he became a "Fool".) So now the woman was bitter, ever so bitter, but she got over it. "Well, here's my last help for you. I'm giving you this ball of string, so go now. Wherever the ball rolls, you follow it. You will come to a little hut just like this one. But there," she said, "you'll find sitting not an old woman but an old man. Make no mistake—don't strike him in the ear as you did me, who's just a silly old woman. If he decides to help you, maybe something will come of it. But if he decides not to help you, nothing will come of it, and you won't see her again. It would be best if I wrote him a note. This is our older brother," she said. What she wrote in this note no one knows. "So," she said, "don't look at the note, and if he asks 'Where are you going, is your journey long?' just give him this note."

So he set off, he departed. He walked and walked, and he walked and walked, and then he came to that little hut. He entered the little hut. And there in fact sat an old man.

"Greetings, greetings, Ivan Tsarevich! Have you come far, and is your journey long?"

He took out the note and handed it over. The old man glanced at the note: "Be cursed that man who has to do with baba yagas! Well, what's to be done once your sister asks it—a brother must help out. Here's what, my friend," he said, "you go back home now. Go back home and make for yourself three copper hats. While you are going to your bride, let them be pierced by the rains. Make three pairs of copper boots, and wear them while you're walking. And here's a little book and some advice. Look in the book and at the advice, and what the advice advises, you fulfill it strictly, ever so strictly. Perhaps," he said, "something will come of it."

So good. He had spent some time getting to that old man, but he was home in just three hours. He got home and looked in the book, he looked at the advice. The advice advised him to prepare meat for three years; or rather, to get everything ready for three years so that he would have double what he needed—water, supplies, meat, and so on. So that there would be enough for three years and then to set off on a journey with a caravan. Prepare some carts, prepare the meat, and everything. So they got everything ready and departed on the journey. They rode and went on, they walked and went on. After a long or short time a hat wore out, but the boots held up. Then he saw a herd of elephants rumbling along, and no one could resist it. He looked in the book, he looked at the advice, and the advice advised him to feed and water the elephants. He ordered: "From those carts dig out some hunks of meat so that the elephants can eat." But the elephants didn't touch the meat, they refused to eat meat.

"Open a barrel of water, we need to water the elephants." They started opening the barrels. The elephants drank and drank until they had drunk their fill. Then they ran off, trumpeting in their own voices.

So they continued on their journey further. They rode and rode, and then they saw a flock of geese, and no one could resist it. Again he looked in his book, he looked at the advice. The advice advised: "Feed the geese and water the geese." He ordered: "Scatter some wheat grain, and feed the geese until they are full. And open some barrels of water and water them."

They watered and fed the geese, the geese ate, and flew off, honking.

They rode on further. They rode on and on. They rode up to a smithy. This Ivan Tsarevich ran into the smithy. He had just entered the smithy, when the smith hit his hand with his hammer, and the blood was flying. Ivan Tsarevich unwrapped his scarf from his neck and bound up the smith's hand. The smith looked at him and thanked him: "So, Ivan Tsarevich, you have done a good thing for me, perhaps I will be of use to you in your life."

They continued riding on. And then they rode up to the tsardom where Koshchai the Deathless lived with his wife. They arrived. But Koshchai had gone off to work. Ivan Tsarevich went up to his wife. "Oh," she said,

"Ivan Tsarevich, you have not come for me, you do not wish to see me. You have come for Koshchai the Deathless."

"Oh," he said, and he hung his head.

Koshchai returned from work and came in. And there was Ivan Tsarevich. "So, I have a guest," he said.

"Yes, a guest. You stole my wife from me," he said, "and I have come for her."

He said, "You can have your wife if you can fulfill three of my commandments."

"And what are these commandments?"

"Do you see that lake? By morning, by the daylight, it must be dry. Even if you go wading in your shirt, your shirt must not get wet. Then you will get back your bride, your wife."

He thought and thought about it. How could he dry up the lake in one day? "Well, all right," he said, "let's try it."

Night fell. When it was dark, so many elephants came running up out of nowhere and began sucking up the water with their trunks. They sucked and sucked. By morning, by daybreak, they had sucked up everything, absolutely everything, so that your shirt wouldn't get wet! He came to Koshchai: "Well, Koshchai, I have fulfilled your commandment. You can give me my wife."

"No, I told you that you had to fulfill three commandments."

"And what is the second?"

"By morning in this very place where the lake was you must put up a golden-roofed tower in no way worse than the one in which I live."

"All right, fine. I'll try, and perhaps something will come of it."

It was getting toward evening. It had just begun to get dark. Then out of nowhere: smiths, carpenters! Such a racket began. He couldn't get any peace. By morning, by daylight, all was ready. The tower was a hundred times better than Koshchai's. When Koshchai got up, he went to him: "So," he said, "accept your tower, Koshchai, but give me back my wife."

Koshchai came and looked and looked at it. "No," he said, "you haven't fulfilled the third task. When you fulfill the third one, I'll give you back your wife."

"Well, what is the third task?"

He led him to a shed. In the shed to the very top, to the ceiling, it was filled with all sorts of grains. If you'd been there, you'd have seen it! "Now then," he said, "you are to sort this shed by grain types such that every seed is separate from all other kinds. If you manage this by morning, you'll get your wife back."

"All right, let's try!"

But how could he sort them out? Sacks of various mixed grains—you wouldn't soon sort them, and here was a whole shed full. It was getting toward evening. It had just begun to get dark. Suddenly out of nowhere, such a mass of geese and swans appeared that they carried off every grain in the shed separately. All the seeds were placed in various little piles.

But Koshchai had no time to sleep. When the birds appeared, he looked and saw the shed being taken apart, so many birds had come flying over. He himself flew off, carrying his wife with him, heaven knows where.

Morning came. Ivan Tsarevich stirred. Neither Koshchai nor his wife was there—they had flown off.

So now then. He looked in his book, he looked for advice. The advice: Everything that had been left, all the supplies, belongings, leave everything there. Then either head home with those accompanying him, or he was to take to the road alone.

But Koshchai had flown off to the mountains, and around the mountains he erected three barriers. The first barrier was where six serpents slept; they were well fed. The second barrier was where twelve slept, and twelve were well fed. And the third barrier was where there were twenty-four sleeping and twenty-four well fed.

He selected the strongest horse, the best one, got on it, and rode off. He rode and rode, whether for a long or short distance, whether near or high up, and then he saw: Two devils were quarreling, and one of them had an oak and the other a pine with its many roots, and they were struggling against each other, hitting each other. He rode up and said, "What are you doing, you two silly devils?"

"You see, we are beating each other," they said.

"And why are you beating each other?"

"Well," they said, "we walked and walked, and we found three things, and we can't divide them. There are two of us and three things. One could go to two of us, but we won't give the other one to the other of us."

"What are these things?"

"Well, there's this hat that makes you invisible, and an elm club."

"Oh, you silly devils. I'll soon divide them for you."

"And how will you do it?"

"It's very simple. Each of you bring me a good stick. I'll throw one to one side and the other to the other side, and whoever brings it to me first will get all three things."

"That's right," they said. "Oh, we are such old fools. We've been battering each other for three days and nights now."

So they each brought him a good stick. He picked them up. (This lad, he could throw a long way!) "Don't you run until I shout 'Go!'" He tossed one stick to one side and the other to the other side. Then he got on his horse. "Go!" One devil went one way and the other, the other. He put the invisible hat on his head and set off ahead with all the things.

The devils came running back—to no man, no hats, there were no things at all, just nothing. And so they bowed low: "We thank you humbly for indisputably judging us. We are such fools that we would have gone on fighting for goodness knows how long."

All right. Ivanushka rode on ahead and approached that barrier where six serpents were sleeping and six were feeding. As he was riding up, all the serpents raised their heads and hissed enough to make your ears hurt.

And he said, "All right, Elm-club, go and amuse those serpents for an hour or so." The Elm-club began beating them, and soon had beaten them all up. The barrier was passed.

He was riding up to the second, which was even more terrifying. He said the same thing: "Now then, Elm-club, amuse those serpents for an hour or so!"

The Elm-club did the same thing. Not a half hour passed before all had been trampled into fluff and dust. And he rode past that barrier.

He rode up to the third barrier. It was even more frightening there. "Elm-club, amuse those serpents for an hour or so!"

The Elm-club began beating them. Not an hour had passed before all of them were dead. He rode on.

He let his horse go in the open steppe and went off to the tsar, to Koshchai the Deathless. Of course, Koshchai wasn't at home, he was out hunting. But his wife caught sight of him: "Oh, Ivan Tsarevich, what for? No way are you going to see me for long. Wherever you carry me off to, he'll find us. When he sees you in a minute, he'll kill you."

"Never mind. He won't kill me," he said. He called her his wife, Svetlana. "So now, my wife Svetlana, we have to find out how he is to meet his death. That's the most important thing about him."

He looked in his little book, he consulted his advisory. The advisory advised him to find where lay Koshchai's death. Then he said, "Find out at any cost. Learn where he is to meet his death."

When Koshchai went off to work, he would live there with them. When Koshchai was at home, he would put on the invisible hat and sit down somewhere in a corner. No one could see him there. Svetlana became more cheerful. Whenever Koshchai would come from work, she had just been embracing Ivan Tsarevich, so she was cheerful.

"So, Wife Svetlana, you always talked and were so despondent, but anyway you've started to get accustomed to things. You'll have a life here with me! Am I hunchbacked? Is my nose crooked? It would be so wonderful to live with me!"

"Here's the problem, Koshchai," she said, "I'll go on living in any case, but you are soon to die."

"What! No one can find out how I am to die."

"No, Koshchai. These days I'm afraid of your death."

"So what? Since you're afraid of my death, I'll tell you once and for all where my death lies. In the sea, in the ocean, on the island of Buian there stands an oak, and beneath the oak is a stone, and in that stone is a trunk, and in that trunk is a hare, in the hare a duck, and in the duck an egg. That's where my death is!"

And having said this, the next day he rode off to work, to hunt.

But this Ivan Tsarevich had been Svetlana's guest for a time. He collected all the necessary little things, and then he set off to find Koshchai's death. He rode off, but he forgot the self-providing hospitality tablecloth. He rode on and on. He would eat a little of what he had put in his backpack at Svetlana's, but he began running out of supplies. There was nothing more to eat. Suddenly he saw an eagle perched on a pine tree. "Oh," he said, "let me kill that eagle. I'll roast it. Even though it will be unsalted meat, it's meat. I won't die from hunger."

With rifle in hand he took aim. It pleaded with him in a human voice: "Ivan Tsarevich, don't kill me; perhaps I'll be of use to you."

"What the devil! Whoever heard of an eagle talking in human language. But there it is, human language. I guess I won't kill it. I won't die of hunger."

So then he rode on further. When he had ridden by that eagle, he saw a dog running along. "Well, let me shoot the dog."

But the dog pleaded with him: "Ivan Tsarevich, don't kill me, perhaps I'll be of use to you."

"The devil take it! Now that dog has started talking like a human." He didn't kill it, he left it.

So then he rode out to the sea. He rode up to the sea, the ocean. He looked, and somebody had placed a weir next to the bank, and in the weir was a huge pike. "Oh," he said, "so much the better! Even if you shouldn't take somebody else's catch . . . Frying a pike—why, the flesh isn't bad!"

He pulled the pike out of the weir and got ready to clean it. But the pike pleaded with him in a human voice: "Ivan Tsarevich, let me go! Don't butcher me, and maybe I'll be of use to you."

He thought and thought. "Maybe I'll let it go; all these things are speaking in human voices."

He stared and stared. His eyes barely could see out to sea. Wherever the island was, his eyes couldn't see that far, and he had to get to that island. He looked in his little book, he consulted his little advisor, and that advisor said to him: "Wave your club three times over the water and the way will open for you." So he waved three times with his club, and suddenly there was a road, straight to the island.

So he rode for a long way or a short way, and then he got to that island, Buian. He came onto the island, and there was this single pine. He came up to it. It was enormous. How could he fell such a tree? Again he looked in his little book, he consulted his little advisor, and the advisor advised: "Get your Elm-club to amuse itself with the roots for an hour or so."

He looked back at the pine. "Elm-club, amuse yourself with the roots for an hour or so." The elm-club began whacking at the roots, thwack-thwack, a wind roared, and it felled the pine.

How to break the stone beneath the pine the mind couldn't fathom. Once again he said, "Elm-club, amuse yourself with this stone for an hour or so." The elm-club hammered and hammered and soon turned the stone into sand. There was the trunk, all bound up and impenetrable. "Now then, Elm-club, amuse yourself with this trunk for an hour or so."

The elm-club began banging at the trunk. It struck it once. It broke open the trunk, and out jumped the hare and started running. Everything was lost! Suddenly out of nowhere the dog appeared and whined and whined, and it brought him the hare. What could be better!

But let's get it right now. However correctly they were cutting open the hare, the duck popped out and flew off. The duck flew away and carried off everything. Out of nowhere the eagle. He flapped and flapped his wings. He attacked the duck and brought it back and handed it over. So fine. He gutted the duck, and yes, in fact there was an egg in the duck. The egg seemed to him a little dirty, so he went down to the sea to rinse it off. He started rinsing it, but the egg rolled away down into the sea and to its bottom.

"Now," he said, "there'll be no way to find that egg as it's rolled to the bottom of the sea."

But then out of nowhere the pike appeared. It splashed and flipped the egg up onto the dry land with its tail. He was overjoyed. He stuck the egg in his pocket, waved the elm-club three times over the sea, and again a road appeared to the far shore. So he rode back. Koshchai wasn't there.

He ate and drank. Then he sat down in his corner. Koshchai came, his wife was so cheerful because his death had been brought back in the tsarevich's hands. He shouted: "So, Wife, why are you so cheerful? Why are you so pink-cheeked? It must be so wonderful to live with me!"

But Ivan Tsarevich stood up there in the corner: "Wonderful or not so wonderful, you are soon to die!"

Ivan Tsarevich spoke. He removed the invisible hat. Koshchai was about to attack him, to choke him, but Ivan Tsarevich threw the egg on the floor. And thus Koshchai met his end.

"Now," he said, "my wife, Svetlana, for now and forever we will be together." He decided not to go back to his father or his brothers. He remained there ruling in that tsardom, managing things. He visited those aunts and that uncle.

I was there, I drank mead-beer. The beer was warm. It flowed over my lips, but nothing got into my mouth.

(SUS 402 + 400_1 + 518 +302_1)

13

BUR-KHREBER

M. O. Dmitriev

In a certain tsardom, in a certain land, namely in the one in which we live (for example, like here at the depot), there lived and dwelt a tsar. And this tsar issued an edict: Whoever after three years had no children—married folk that is—would be buried in the ground up to the knee. So they lived and lived some more, and they lived through those three years, and the tsar had not a child born. And he had issued the order, but he had to go to be buried up to the knee himself. He collected a bag full of things and set off. He walked high or low, far or near; soon a tale is told, but not so soon is a deed done. He walked and walked, and he met an old man.

"Greetings, my good man!"

"Greetings, greetings, Tsar and free man. Have you walked far, is your way far? Why, people help people, and perhaps I can in some way help you?"

"But how can you help me? You see," he said, "according to my own order, I lived for three years and there were no children. So I set out to bury myself up to my knee."

"Oh, Tsar and free man, and you don't want to tell an old man. But I will in this something help you. You go on, and ahead there is this Kuben Lake[1]. Walk up to it, and right there in that Kuben Lake there will be some fishermen fishing. You go up; they will be pulling in their haul of fish. Right at the moment of your approach, they'll be hauling in their catch. There'll be one perch in the catch, and it will be one-eyed. You buy that perch from them, but don't take it for nothing. But if for some reason they won't take money from the tsar, then you go to the village and put some money in the church. And then go home. Your wife will eat this perch—and there'll be a child."

1. Kuben Lake is a large lake located north of Vologda.

Well, the tsar was overjoyed, he ran off at the double. He went up to Kuben Lake and he had just gone up to the fishermen, and they were hauling in their catch. And in fact, in that catch was a solitary perch, and it was one-eyed. Well he said, "Fishermen, sell me that perch."

"Why, Your Royal Highness, what now? Have we never seen money? Could we take money from you?"

"No, take the money. I must only take it for money."

But no way would the fishermen take any. So since they wouldn't take any money, he went off to the village, and there he found the village elder. "Let's go to the church." They came to the church, he put down the money for the perch, and then went off home. He came, they cleaned the perch, cooked a fresh fish soup, his wife ate the perch—and became pregnant. The servant girl sipped the soup—and became pregnant. They ate up the soup, tossed the leftovers into the yard, a dog licked the liquid, and also became pregnant.

So now then, all at once, it means, they all conceived, so to say, they all got in the family way, they all "calved." And so they all gave birth. The tsar's they called Ivan Tsarevich, the servant's, Ivan the servant's son, and the dog's Bur-Khreber. Now Bur-Khreber, he was also a human. And so they began to grow, to grow up, and to run about and play. Bur-Khreber, as he ran about the village, about his town, whomever he yanked by the arm, the arm came off. If he brought down his arm on someone's head, that one became a hunchbacked kid. The tsar was inundated with complaints, noise, roaring. They ordered Bur-Khreber taken in. They put him in a dungeon, and he said, "Oh, Tsar and free man, you have put me in a dungeon, but I am not angry with you. Buy me a squiffer, an accordion. When I'm bored, I can play my squiffer, and it will be happier for me."

Now then, what's a squiffer for a tsar? It's not worth quibbling about. He bought the squiffer and gave it to him in the dungeon. And he, when morning had passed, took up his squiffer, sat down on a hill, and began to play his squiffer. And he played so pitifully, so painfully. Why, whoever was going out to work, they didn't manage to get to work. They listened tearfully to it all. Well, so things went on in the dungeon. You can sit there. They feed you well, and give you enough to drink. Time went on, and well, they survived until his brothers, Ivan Tsarevich and Ivan the servant's son, thought of getting married. So then they asked their father's blessing. This is what their father said: "Well now then, lads," he said, "since you've lived up to this, I'll bless you to get married. Wherever you find her, whomever you want, you take her."

So fine. The brothers mounted their horses—they took them from the tsar—they mounted their horses and rode off. And they rode by the dungeon. They turned up next to Bur-Khrebe. The dungeon was open a little, and he was playing. They rode up to him. "Hello brothers, and have you ridden far?"

"Of course we have, Brother, we're setting out to get married."

"Take me with you!"

"But how should we take you, Bur-Khreber? We would take you with pleasure, but you would once again misbehave. You would end up in trouble again."

"Well, all right, all right, don't take me—but you won't go far away."

The brothers rode off. They rode and rode, far or near, high or low, for soon a tale is told, but by its results is a deed done. They rode up, three roads and three inscriptions. On one, go to one side and you'll be happy, your horse unhappy. Go on the other road, and your horse will be happy but you unhappy. Or take the third road, and your horse will be unhappy and you'll be unhappy. They stood there and stood there, they thought and they thought: Which road should they take? They didn't dare move in any direction.

"Here's what, brothers, we'll have to return and take Bur-Khreber. Otherwise, without him we'll fail."

So fine, they returned.

"Well now then, Brother, let's go."

"But wait, ask for some sort of little horse from the tsar."

They came there and Ivan Tsarevich: "Well, Papa," he said, "give us a horse for Bur-Khreber."

"Well, let him go to the yard, and let him take the one he wants."

He went to the yard and crippled half the horses. If he laid a hand on a head, the head bent to the ground, and it wouldn't ever bend back up. If he threw a hand on the back, the back broke. If he grabbed one by the tail, he would tear off the tail. And so he crippled half the horses, and he came up: "Well, brothers, go on," he said. "Perhaps he has some better little horse? If not, I'll go on foot." He came: "Papa, is there some horse that's a little better? Give it to Bur-Khreber. There's no horse there on which he could ride."

"What? How did he become so strong? Well, if he can handle it, there in the open steppe is an oak tree, and beneath that oak is a horse, the old but powerful horse of my grandfather. So if he can control it, let him take it."

The brothers came and told him. He went to the oak. He bowed down to the oak, the oak opened up, and out from under the oak galloped this old but powerful horse, wanting to break him up with his hooves. He struck him alongside the cheek, the horse flipped over three times, and became quieter than water! He got on and rode off. So they came to that crossroads, thought a little, and then they set off to where the horse was unhappy and they were unhappy. They rode and they rode, and then they came up to this: Suddenly there was a river of fire, and over the river was Kalin Bridge. So the brothers didn't dare to ride onto that bridge. He said, "Brothers, we could ride over it, but we won't. We have to find out who rides over this bridge."

They went down to where there was a hill not far from the bridge, and they unfurled their tent, ate and drank, then lay down to sleep. They lay down to sleep, but as soon as his brothers had fallen asleep, Bur-Khreber came and sat down under the bridge. Then as this business approached midnight, he heard the clatter of a horse's hooves. A wind began bending the forest to the ground. A three-headed serpent came riding up on a horse, and the horse stumbled. The serpent kicked it with its feet on its plump ribs, on its ears. "Oh, you wolf bait, you mash bag, I don't fear any tsar's son, any king's sons. I'm only afraid of Bur-Khreber, and if he even turned up here, I would put him on one palm and with the other I'd squash him—and nothing but a flat pancake would remain."

He couldn't tolerate such words, and he leapt out from under the bridge: "Get out of here, you cursed monster, let's fight!"

Well, as soon as a woman could bake a pancake, as they say, he dealt with it. He sliced off one head, tossed all the heads on the hill, and the corpse he threw into the river. He went back to his brothers there, and he lay down. He lay down in the tent as if he hadn't been anywhere. A whole day passed, and on the second the same thing. And whom were they guarding against? No one knew anything except Bur-Khreber. So the next day they again ate and drank, and in the evening they lay down to sleep. As soon as his brothers were asleep, Bur-Khreber was again under the bridge. He rode up under the bridge. The business started up again as midnight approached. Again the forest shook, but this time even more fiercely. A horse was stamping its feet even stronger. It stumbled. A six-headed serpent was coming. It struck it on its plump ribs, on its ears. "Oh, you wolf bait, you mash bag, why are you stumbling? I don't fear any tsar's son, any king's son—only Bur-Khreber, but he isn't here." "And if he were," he said, "I'd put him in my hand and squash him with the other and just a pancake would remain of him."

He leapt out from beneath the bridge: "Get out of here, you cursed monster, let's fight!"

Well, he dealt with this one very quickly. He cut off all six heads, the heads on the hill, and he tossed the corpse into the river. He came back and again lay down and slept. He slept, and in the morning they got up, again ate and drank, a day passed, in the evening again with sleep approaching they ate and drank, and again lay down to sleep. And he said, "Brothers, today I'll go stand watch."

He placed three glasses of water on the table. He placed three matches, and he put up three candles. "So," he said, "don't be asleep at twelve o'clock. If at twelve o'clock the matches turn black, the candles are lighted, and in the glasses there turns out to be blood instead of water, get on your horses as quickly as possible: I won't be alive."

"Well, all right, Brother, go!"

So he set off. He set off, and again he sat down beneath the bridge and he sat there. Suddenly a nine-headed serpent came riding up. And again the forest shook. The forest shook, and an intolerable storm broke out. The horse stumbled. The serpent beat the horse on its plump ribs, on its ears. "Oh, you wolf bait, you mash bag, why are you stumbling? I'm not afraid of any tsar's sons or king's sons; I am only afraid of Bur-Khreber, and he's not here. If he were, I would put him in one hand, smash him with the other, and there'd remain only ash. I'd blow, and the ash would be scattered over the steppe."

Well, he couldn't tolerate that. He leapt out from underneath the bridge. "Get out of here, you cursed monster. Let's fight!"

And so they came at each other. They came at each other, and for a long, long time they struggled. The serpent pulled him into the water up to his chest. But he sensed that his brothers were asleep, that they'd be no help. He had to save them. The serpent would kill them, just as it would kill him. He shook his foot, and a boot flew right into the tent. The boot hit one of them in the arm, the other in a foot. They jumped up. The candles were burning, in the glasses blood had appeared instead of water, and they were distraught: Their brother had perished. And they hadn't made a move.

But the old but powerful horse had been observing this battle, and he saw that his rider had been pulled into the water up to his chest. He ran and let that serpent have it with his hooves, he bit him with his teeth, he struck him with his hooves and dragged it out onto the dry land. When he had dragged it out, it started struggling against him. Then Bur-Khreber struck it, and then little by little a head flew off, then a second, a third, and then gradually all nine heads. He separated all nine heads from it. Again he left the heads there and tossed away the corpse. He came back. His brothers were groaning. One had a sore arm, the other a sore leg.

"Well, you fools, I ordered you not to sleep, but then you slept, so say 'thank you' for letting you know."

Well, the morning passed, they ate and drank.

"Now, brothers," he said, "we can ride off."

They got on their horses and rode up, and they saw the heads by the bridge, and then they knew what Bur-Khreber had been fighting with. They rode up and had just managed to cross over the bridge, when the bridge caught fire, and the bridge burned up. So then they rode on further. They rode far or near, high or low, for soon a tale is told, but a deed is measured by its results. And then two more crossroads. That is to say, that by the straight road it was five hundred kilometers, and by the roundabout road, five thousand.

"Well," he said, "you brothers go by the straight road, and I'll take the roundabout one. But if you arrive before me, wait for me a little, I'll soon be along—there won't be much difference," he said.

They set off for the five hundred kilometers, and he for the five thousand. He rode and got on, and then he saw a tsardom. He sent his horse off into the steppe, and he himself went into the tsardom. He turned himself into a gadfly and flew into a room and sat down behind a shelf. He sat down, and then the matron ran in, an old maid.

"Mama, Mama! They say that Bur-Khreber is passing by here. What would I be like for him? He killed my husband, so what would I be for him?"

"And just what, my child, would you be?"

"I", she said, "will go out into the open steppe. I'll be a mirage, and I'll turn into a little golden well with silver water. When they drink of this water, it will tear all of them apart."

"Oh, do it, do it, my child."

She went away, and another came running up. "Mama, Mama! They say that Bur-Khreber is passing by here. What would I be like for him? He killed my husband."

"And with what can you do that to him."

"I'll be a heat wave. I'll go out into the open steppe and turn into an orchard, the apples will be beautiful enough to knock your eyes out. From the heat they'll try an apple. They'll eat an apple, and it will tear them apart."

"Well, let it be so, let it be so, my child."

The second went away and the third bride came running up: "Mama, Mama, they say that Bur-Khreber is passing by here. What would I be like for him? He killed my husband."

"And what will you be for him?"

"I," she said, "the sun will bake. There'll be a huge heat wave. I'll go out into the open steppe and turn myself into a plank bed, with a down cover, but the moment he lies down, it will tear him apart."

"Well, let it be so, let it be so, my child."

He flew off and started making a racket. "Oh," she said, "the villain; he's figured it all out. He heard it all, that's it!"

And they guessed that he was there. He once more went out into the steppe, got on his horse, and rode off. He came, his brothers were at the crossroads, and he rode up, he managed it. They rode off, a heat wave, drowsiness fell upon them, as never before—and suddenly there was a well.

"Well, Brother, we need to drink some water. Otherwise, we will all doze off. We'll soon fall from our horses."

"Drink, we must drink. But just wait a little. I'll drink first, and then I'll let you."

He went up to it, and with his lash he whipped a crisscross: "The husband fell, let the wife fall—and the next generation be gone!" Only blood flowed.

"Oh, you ride off with such a brother, and you'll see no good!"

"Never mind, never mind, brothers, this was necessary."

Well, they didn't even manage to set off—an orchard, and such a one! And apples such as simply to knock your eyes out!

"Well, Brother, if only we could eat some apples!"

"Good, good, we'll eat some, brothers. But," he said, "I'll eat and then I'll let you, and this being the case, don't you move before I do."

He jumped down from his horse and crisscross on the limbs with his lash: "The husband fell, let the wife fall—and the next generation be gone!" Only blood was formed, and more than that there was nothing left anywhere.

"Well, here there's nothing to say to you, nothing at all. You would have eaten, and afterwards whatever you please, you would have done it."

"But it was necessary!"

They rode off, they dozed. Suddenly here's what, if you please: a plank bed with a down cover.

"Well, Brother, we have to rest. We've already ridden so far without rest."

"We'll rest, we'll rest. I'll try it and then you."

So it was. He got off his horse, whacked it crisscross with his lash: "The husband fell, let the wife fall—and the next generation be gone!" In place of the bed, blood flowed. That was all.

"So now then, brothers, ride as fast as you can—faster, drive on faster."

And they rode off. They rode and they rode, and they saw a tsardom. They rode up to the tsardom. They rode up to the tsar, but they had on—like a tsarevich—all uniforms, and everything they had taken. So the tsar invited them there, received them well, and he had this daughter. The daughter was beautiful. But, that is to say, they had to marry off Ivan Tsarevich. Well, they began courting Ivan Tsarevich, and if you please, all were agreed, they were delighted. They summoned the whole world to the feast, and for twelve days. They drank and they caroused, they put on this wedding, then they led the young couple off to sleep. And Bur-Khreber said to Ivan Tsarevich, "Ivan Tsarevich, my brother, leave me as the head doorman at the doors. The tsar," he said, "won't permit anybody but me, and don't you let anybody but me. Well, he won't quarrel very strongly against your will. Just in case something bad happens to you, then you say that perhaps you be allowed to go to the toilet. Then come to me, and we'll talk it over."

So they led the young couple off to sleep. Apparently the tsar didn't oppose putting Bur-Khreber there. "We have only two matchmakers, and we'll place them there as doormen," he said.

"Never mind," he said, "He'll stand there."

So they left Bur-Khreber there. They lay down to sleep. Ivan Tsarevich had just lain down when she threw an arm on him so that he could scarcely breathe. Then she threw a leg on him so that he thought that in just a minute he would die.

"Maria Tsarevna, couldn't I just go to the toilet?"

"Go, scoundrel, you'll not get away. Nonetheless, you'll be mine." (A fine wedding!)

So then he opened the door, and Bur-Khreber: "Well, how are things?"

"Well, Brother, it's like this: When I asked to go to the toilet, she sent me off: 'Go, scoundrel, you'll not get away.' Like that."

"Let's exchange clothes."

So they changed clothes. Ivanushka stayed there, and Bur-Khreber went in to her. So then he lay down, and she, apparently because it was dark, couldn't distinguish them, who had lain down next to her. She threw her arm, she threw a leg, and then she herself went on top, to strangle him right away. He got her around her braids and threw her off. And he had these rods with him, the ones with which he had harried the serpent, and he began beating her with these rods. He beat her so much that he mixed up her body with her nightgown. Then they lay down. They lay there, and she began embracing and kissing him properly.

"Maria Tsarevna, something is making me ill. Your water, apparently, doesn't agree with my stomach, so I'll have to go out to the toilet."

"Vaniusha, my dearest, go, go. Perhaps I should go with you?"

"That isn't necessary. Somehow I'll manage it."

He went out.

"Well, all right, Ivan Tsarevich, you go now."

Again they changed clothing and everything. Well, he lay down. She embraced, kissed—everything.

"Vaniusha, I won't permit myself any coarseness anymore. We'll just go on living." She stated all the conditions. Well, fine. (But usually after the first night, they played out their love affair there, after the first night. I don't know how it is with you, but with us for the young couple they specially heat up the bathhouse and they are led into the bathhouse.)

So they went into the bathhouse. Vaniusha undressed, but she didn't undress. "Maria Tsarevna, why are you so shy? Why don't you undress?"

"Well, you treated me very well in the night, so that I can't get my shirt off my body!"

He stupidly went and said, "Good." He said, "No heart for another's hands."

And she: "Oh, witch! It wasn't he. Well, fine, nevertheless I'll catch you."

So then they finished up not quite bathing. But they'd lost respect.

Again there was drinking and carousing. They went through the whole wedding; they partied long. This Maria Tsarevna gave them the keys to all the rooms—please, go wherever you like. And so Bur-Khreber went through all the rooms, and he had just entered one room . . . the bridge collapsed, the bridge somersaulted, and he was beneath the bridge, and his legs were cut off at the knee, like nothing before. And then with those matchmakers, with Ivan the servant's son, and even with Ivan Tsarevich. She made Ivan Tsarevich a herder, and she made Ivan the servant's son a double-bladed mill. The mill turned the millstones with his hands and ground flour with his feet. And without his legs Bur-Khreber became powerless. Well, all right. But when Bur-Khreber fell into that underworld, well his legs were sawed off, just like that. He crawled about without any legs.

Then suddenly a person: "What don't you have?"

"I don't have any hands."

He felt another. "What don't you have?"

"I have no eyes."

"Well, brothers, we are living, nonetheless," said Bur-Khreber.

Then in the night he went and lifted a corner. "Now then, you swim out, you the blind and you the armless."

The blind one and the armless one swam out. He was there. Either they gave him something, or he himself put something under it so that the corner didn't fall, and he himself swam out. A cart stood there, and he sat down in that cart.

He said, "You, armless one, lead the blind one, and blind man, pull me along."

So they set off. The armless one took the blind one by the hand, and they dragged Bur-Khreber. They dragged Bur-Khreber for a time. Far or near they road and came out onto the Post Road. When they had ridden out onto the Post Road, the blind one and the armless one left the cart. One ran to one side, the other to the other. But nonetheless robbers fell on them. Well, and where would he, legless, go? So he stuffed his legs into his pocket and dragged them along with himself.

Forcefully he rolled out into a ditch, into some bushes. The robbers rode by; they didn't see him. Then suddenly up rode Baba Yaga. Up rode Baba Yaga. "Here's a cart, so that means that Bur-Khreber is around here somewhere. I need him. I'll teach him, that strongman! He's without legs, so he can't do anything to me."

He heard how she was deliberating, so he got himself out of there. "Well, Yaga," he said, "go on, go wherever you can. Otherwise, deal with me!"

"Oh-ho, you're here!"

The moment she ran out, he grabbed her. He pummeled and pummeled her and then climbed onto her shoulders.

"So, Baba Yaga," he said, "carry me until you've carried me to the living and the dead waters. Otherwise, you'll certainly perish in my hands. Never mind that I'm without legs. You'll perish in my hands."

She lugged him along until she'd lugged him to a well. "Here's the living water," she said.

"Now then," he said, "break off a bough—there, that bough, a dry bough."

She broke it off and gave it to him. But he didn't climb down from her shoulders. He threw it into the well, and the bough caught fire. He let her have it about the head. "Oh, you witch, deceiving me? Nevertheless, until you carry me to the living water, I won't let you go."

She lugged him along further. She lugged and lugged him. Again there was a well. "Here's the living water."

"Now then, break off that bough."

She broke off the bough and handed it to him. He threw it into the well—the bough immediately burst into flower. "Aha, so from now on you're free. But don't you ever meet up with me again. Not only don't search for me, don't meet up with me. If you do, that will be your death. I'll strangle you anyway."

He sat down in the well and held his legs to the stumps. And he really began pouring water on them, rubbing them. His legs began growing together. They grew together. He rubbed first the one and then he rubbed the other. He felt himself strong on his feet. Well, fine. He set off.

He walked and walked and walked. Far or near, high or low. But soon a tale is told, but in fact a deed is measured by its success. He walked up to the sea. He walked along the sea. He walked and walked. Suddenly there was a hut, a shack on the shore.

In that tsardom, water serpents had begun going to the tsardom and eating people. Well one would grab five or six people, carry them off, and eat them. And they presented these conditions to the tsar: "If you wish, then send us a single person by your free will."

So the tsar then fixed a lottery: when and who should go. Well, he sent there, he sent people, one each twenty-four hours. And the turn came to his own daughters. There were three daughters. So the turn came to his daughters. And so they led up the eldest daughter for the serpent to devour.

And as he was walking about the sea, he entered a shack, and he saw a girl sitting there. He sat down and started talking: "Why are you so sad, Maiden?"

"But how am I to be cheerful," she said, "when I have been carried here for devouring? Soon out of that sea a serpent will arise and eat me."

"Well, perhaps he'll eat two," he said.

"Yes, but he'll eat even five."

Well, they talked and yakked for a while—everything honestly—and he said, "Search about my head, Miss."

Well, she sat down to search about his head. And he hung a forty-pood sledgehammer over his head.

"In case I fall asleep, then you swing this sledgehammer. It will fall on my head, and I'll wake up, if you can't wake me."

So she searched and searched, and he fell asleep. He fell asleep and she saw the serpent had arisen and then she remembered that sledgehammer. So she let it swing and it swung. And then the sledgehammer—bop—hit him on the noggin. He jumped up.

"What is it?" he said.

"Look there, you see, that serpent is coming, and he'll eat me right away."

And it was approaching. It came up to the window. And it sat down next to the window. (Just like I'm keeping watch here by the window right now.)

"Ho!" it said, "earlier on it was difficult to wait for the one person, but here are two together."

Bur-Khreber came out. "Yes, yes, there are two. Please, come here and eat me first."

"It's all the same to me."

They struggled, but he in an instant cut off its heads. (That serpent was a three-headed one.) He carried the heads out beyond the shack and tossed them away; and the corpse he carried off and tossed it into the sea.

Then he and the maiden lay down to sleep, and did they ever embrace!

They sat there a whole day, and the next day they led in the second sister. When they had carried in the second sister, the first said: "Oh, the second one is alive." And he ordered her to hide him. She turned him into a needle and stuck him in the wall, and the servant didn't notice.

"Oh," she said, "no one has been here the entire night."

"Well, that's good luck for you, it seems."

The servants rode away back. And they talked, and they talked it over: "What? Shall we take her back, or not take her back? It will be more cheerful with the two of them. Let them spend the night together." So they were left.

They had just ridden away when that girl turned him back from being a needle. One sister said to the other: "Here is my rescuer."

So well, now three, and still more cheerful. So then evening came. And he said: "Well, search around my head. Dig in!"

She sat down, began digging, and scratching, and again he placed that sledgehammer over his head. He said: "In case I don't get up, swing that sledgehammer, the two of you, swing it. It will strike me on the head, and then I'll wake up."

Things went on until midnight. A six-headed serpent came out, rose up. "Oho, earlier it was difficult to wait for just the one, but here we have three all at once. That's great!"

They tried to wake him. They tried and they tried, they tried and they tried, but no way could they. And they had completely forgotten about the sledgehammer. And that girl, the first one, so sincerely cried that a tear fell on his face and burned like fire. He leapt up.

"What was that?" he said.

"Look, the six-headed serpent is coming."

He went outside. "Well, let's have at it."

And he dealt as quickly with the six-headed one as with the three-headed one. The heads behind the shack, and the corpse he carried off and threw into the sea. They lived on for three more days. On the third day they brought the third sister. They brought the third sister—and these others were alive!

"So how's this?" they said. "Who was here?"

"No one. No one was here."

"Oh, then obviously the serpent has decided not to come any more at all. Now that's good."

So the grooms had brought these maidens, their brides. Everything had already been arranged for marriage. They'd just to arrange the order. If they were still alive, that means the grooms were ready. Well, so good. Again they stuck that young man into the wall as a needle. And so they brought the third one. Well then, to be taken or not to be taken?

So then, let them be. Once the serpents have determined not to come, then let the three spend the night. So they left all three. That groom rode off, and they turned him back from being a needle. And again there were four of them; it was more cheerful that way. The day passed. Evening came. Again he said, "Well, once more search my head."

"All right, but if you once more fall asleep?"

"Well, whatever," he said, "nothing will happen to me. Once upon a time my legs were sawed off, and they then grew back. And my head, if it's cut off, nonetheless it will grow back."

You see, when he had set off from that well, he had poured himself a bottle of the living water.

She sat down to search, to rummage about on his head, and he fell soundly asleep. And then the nine-headed serpent again came crawling out.

"Oh," it said, "earlier it was difficult to get hold of just one, but here are four at a time."

They began trying to wake him up. They tried and they tried, they tried and they tried. And they could not wake him. So then they let fly swinging the sledgehammer. They swung it, and the sledgehammer fell on his head. He jumped up. He jumped up, and the serpent leapt out to meet him, and they began struggling. They struggled and struggled. Little by little, little by little that serpent dragged him to the shore and then into the water, into the sea. And those sisters, all with a cry, pitying their rescuer. What, so to say, afterwards he'll devour us anyway. And so they all came running out after him, and the serpent said: "Who are you?"

"These are my bogatyr-sisters, coming to my defense."

"Oh, this dog has saved them!"

And so the serpents severed his head.

So then they rode back with their victory. It was time to put on the wedding. They put on one wedding, then the second. But that girl wouldn't submit . . . They were having the wedding, but she went to this booth and cried.

"All the same," she said, "he has perished, and I'll perish with him. They'll bury us in the same place. I will not be parted from him."

Well then afterward, when they had cut off all the heads, their dresses were all bloodied. She brought a change of clothing. She began changing his, and in his pocket she felt the little bottle. "Aha, once he told me that at one time his legs had been cut off. Perhaps I might be able to bring him to life with this little bottle?"

With sadness she rolled the head to the body. She placed it were it should be and began sprinkling it from this little bottle, and rubbing it in. He shuddered, shuddered again, and stood up. He jumped up: "Oh, how long I've slept."

"Yes," she said, "If you hadn't told about your legs, you would have slept forever, and I would have fallen asleep with you. So then your story and the bottle helped."

"Well good, let's lie down and rest."

So they slept. And over there the others wondered: Where is that bride? They needed to play out the third wedding. So then they came. They put on the wedding, they drank and caroused.

So then, we destroyed all those serpents. No longer will our country have to experience that, they boasted.

And then that other pair came. The girl said, "Well, Papa, that other one isn't my groom, the one who is sitting at the table with you. This is my groom and my rescuer."

So they all jumped up from the tables. "What is that that you are saying?"

And he said, "Never mind, never mind. Your Royal Highness, in order for me to prove who is the rescuer and who is the false one, we'll have to go," he said. "We'll have to gather by the sea. Let's ride down there."

So then either by car or on foot they went there. They came to the sea, and he said, "Well, if you could rescue them, then come here. Come on, come on."

And there was a whole pile of those serpent heads. "Well, try now. Can any one of you carry away those heads to the seashore?"

So they took the heads, but no way could they lift them to that place. Where they were, they could scarcely move them, just wiggle them. But he went up to any head, stuck out his leg, and kicked it high. You could scarcely see the head. "Your Royal Highness, watch out that you aren't killed by one of these heads."

Well, then the tsar bowed to him from his waist. "Well, my good man, do whatever you wish to these villains, these sons-in-law."

"I won't do anything with them. They married your daughters, so let them be your sons-in-law. But you, my friend, won't marry this daughter. I'll marry her."

Well, they had the wedding. They put on the wedding. When they had signed the papers: "Well, now what, brothers-in-law? What punishment for you, then?" "You, villain," he said, "go quietly. I haven't touched you yet. But what shall be the punishment given you others?"

And they didn't know how to answer. One of them, he pulled out all his hair from front to back. From then on they went around bald. Before then there were no bald ones. And he placed his hand on the head of the other—he became a hunchback. Up until then there had been no hunchbacks, but since then there have been hunchbacks going about.

Well fine. They put on the wedding. Everything was fixed.

"So now," he said, "my young wife, we'll have to get on my horse, as I have to go tell my brothers. How's it with my brothers? How are they getting on?"

So they set off. They rode and they rode. They heard a mill working away. The millstone was turning. They rode up, and they entered the mill.

"Well now," he said, "this is a mill? It's time to get up. You've done enough of this pounding and grinding."

"I'll try. For however many minutes you stand there, you'll get that many lashes."

"Let's finish this. I'm telling you, let's finish this pounding. You're not going to pound away here anymore."

"If only our brother were here . . . You talk a lot of nonsense, and I'm to receive the lashes. No, you won't fool me."

"I am your brother, Bur-Khreber."

"If Bur-Khreber were alive, he wouldn't permit this. The poor guy, he perished somewhere without any legs."

"No, no," he said.

And since they had been born from one and the same perch, they all had the same mark on their chest. And well, their birthmarks or just plain marks remained.

"So then, show me your chest, and I'll show mine to you. You'll see I'm really your brother Bur-Khreber."

So he looked, and truly it was so! That whole burden was thrown off him.

"Well, Brother, somehow lead me home."

"No, Brother, we still won't be home for a long time. We still have to find Ivan Tsarevich. Let's go."

So he got him ready, and they rode off. They rode and they rode, and then suddenly they heard a shepherd blowing his horn. The shepherd sounded the horn, and they rode right there. They rode up to the shepherd: "Greetings, greetings!"

"Well, how are things? And what's going on?"

"What? Don't speak of it," he said. "If you'd come a minute later, forty female bogatyrs would be handing out forty lashes. Just a minute earlier, I drove over here—I even came late—and forty female bogatyrs were handing out forty lashes. Scarcely alive, I rushed about."

"Well, stop doing this work if you don't like it."

"Stop it?! They would take off my head."

"They won't take off your head! I say to you, stop it."

"But certainly not. That would be if Bur-Khreber were here, then I would, I'd stop this work. But he, poor guy, perished just like we're going to die right now."

"But I'm that Bur-Khreber."

Then Ivan the servant's son said, "So then, Brother, don't you even recognize me?"

They showed their chests, they showed their marks. He was convinced. "Well, thank God that you're alive."

Then he and Bur-Khreber exchanged clothes. This one set off as the chairman with the other's wife. And Bur-Khreber drove up before the house. And there on the balcony sat these forty female bogatyrs, and he was driving the cattle home at noon. When he pulled on one's tail, off fell the tail. If he pulled on a hind leg, the leg came out of its socket, and that one didn't work any more. If he threw a hand on a horn, it couldn't get its head out of the ground, it just couldn't. So he crippled half the herd while he was driving them. And when they looked at him from there, they saw it. "Oh, that scoundrel, and that's all!"

And so those forty bogatyrs all ran at him. The first only just managed to run up to him, and he grabbed her. Wherever he waved an arm, five or six of them at least would fly and be half-dead, and all forty he crippled. He rode up to the tsarevna herself. And she was still sitting there on the balcony. And he ran up to the balcony, leapt up and grabbed hold of the balcony, and the balcony came tumbling down. And he right away tore off her head.

They chose a fine girl and married off that Ivan Tsarevich right there. And they made him tsar. And they married Ivan the servant's son off to another girl, and they made him the substitute for the tsar. And on the death of the tsar, his father-in-law, he received the tsardom.

And they go visiting each other even now. I was with them not long ago. And they are living well. Such a feasting there was! And that's all of this little tale. (I heard this little tale from my father. Everything that I know, it's all from my father.)

(SUS 303 + 300A + 519 + 300_1)

14

YOUR FRIEND LIUBODEI

M. O. Dmitriev

There lived this peasant, and he had three sons: Peter, Fedor, and Ivan. Everybody called Ivanushka "the Fool," Vania the Fool, and that's all. They lived there, and the sons all grew up. They sowed the spring crop, and the wheat grew well. But somebody in the night started beating, breaking, and trampling it, and they couldn't figure who was playing such dirty tricks.

Their father said, "Well, my sons, we will have to hire a watchman in order to keep our harvest."

The brothers said, "Why should we hire a watchman? We can stand watch by the night, or four nights, or two of us for eight. And during that time we'll manage to catch the hooligan."

So they began standing watch. The first night fell to Peter, the second to Fedor, and the third to Ivanushka. Peter got ready to stand watch, to guard the wheat. He dressed well, took a loaf of bread, and went away from the fence probably about a half-kilometer. Then he lay down beneath a fir, chewed on his bread, and went to sleep. He slept through the night, and the wheat was all smashed, so he left the fence and went the devil knows where—far away. When the night had passed, he came back and shouted, "Brothers, open the door!"

His brothers jumped up on their feet and opened the doors for their brother. "Did you see anything?"

"I shivered through the whole night there, but I didn't see anybody."

The second night Fedor got ready to go. Fedor got dressed even more warmly, took a larger hunk of bread and went even farther away from the fence. He lay down beneath a fir tree and also slept soundly. He slept through the night. What could he see there? Nothing. In the morning he came back: "Brothers, open the door!"

His brothers jumped up on their feet and opened the doors for their brother. "Well, Brother, did you see anyone?"

"I shivered through the whole night there, but I didn't see anybody."

Well, on the third night it was Ivan the Fool's turn to go. Ivan the Fool set off in an old ripped kaftan. He took a little chunk of bread, and he set off. He lay down next to the fence, and he just lay there and watched. It was nearly midnight. Suddenly from the east there appeared a pink glow. And then from there, three horses came running. One had a golden hide. A second was silver. Out of their nostrils sparks flew. Behind them stood a pillar of fire. The horses came running up, went into the field, and didn't so much eat as they did trample the wheat with their feet. He sneaked up to the horses, but the horses jumped up and ran away. They ran away, and he looked about and suddenly saw a man standing on the edge of the field. He stealthily crept up and caught the man. He caught the man and then marched home with the man. He too shouted, "Brothers, open the doors!"

His brothers leapt to their feet and opened the doors. "Well, Brother, did you see anybody?"

"Here's our criminal!" he said.

They began feeding this man and giving him drinks, and they loudly questioned him. But the man didn't answer anything to anyone. No one knew who this man was, nor did they know where he came from or what people he belonged to. Rumor got about that in this particular place such and such a man had caught a thief who wouldn't speak any language or answer any questions. The affair came to the attention of the tsar. The tsar heard of it and came to visit the peasant. He arrived. "Well, my good man, you have an unknown person?"

"Yes, there's one here."

"Show him to me. I can speak twelve languages. Perhaps he'll answer me in one of them." They tried all the languages but he didn't answer in any of them. "Well, peasant, sell him to me. I'll summon a man from every country that I know on the whole earth. Maybe someone will know which language he'll answer in. We'll find out who he is."

The peasant replied, "Well, My Lord, I'll sell him to you, but you can't believe how much of my wheat he has eaten. We'll put him on the floor, and you pour gold on him so that his head will be covered in gold. You can have the man, and I'll have the gold."

The tsar agreed. They delivered the gold and started pouring it out. Then the tsar took the man and left the gold for the peasant. He brought him home and put him in prison. He placed guards over him, sentries, to watch so that no one let him out of the dungeon. They fed and gave him drink as was needed. And then he demanded people from all countries that he knew. When that was done, time passed.

Soon a tale is told, but in fact not so soon is the deed done. The tsar had a son, and this son liked shooting with a bow and arrow. He once shot an arrow, and it suddenly went through a window and into the dungeon. He went up to the window: "Is there a kind man in that dungeon? Give me my arrow!"

"Such a man there is, and the arrow is in my hands. But I'll hand it over only with the condition that you let me out."

"And how can I let you out when there are so many watchmen, so many sentries? Would they let me into the dungeon, up to the gates?"

"They'll let you. Go home and watch in what room and on what nail they hang the key. Then take the key. If the sentries or the watchmen won't let you pass, then just show them the key and say that your papa entrusted this key to you and that you won't let me out. They'll let you in. Then I'll give you the arrow and you will let me out."

So that's what they did. Just as this man had said, he went and got the key, but the sentry and the watchman wouldn't let him pass, so he said, "What do you mean? My papa entrusted this key to me, and you won't let me pass!" They let him in. He let the man out, and the man gave him his arrow.

"Well, farewell," he said. "Perhaps I'll someday be of use to you."

And so it's unknown where and when, but he didn't see that man any more. He set off somewhere, got himself lost and just melted away. The boy closed the dungeon and left. Just then, the people invited from all countries arrived. The tsar greeted and treated them.

"Now then, my lords," he said. "I have this man here, and although he wasn't caught by me, he lives here, and he speaks no language. I myself know how to talk in twelve languages. No matter whom I have invited, whoever knows languages, he will not answer any questions to anybody about anything. I am interested to find out whether anyone recognizes him, or which language he will answer someone in."

"So let's try. Some of us speak five, some six, some ten. From various directions we are all specialists."

So they went to the dungeon. When they got there, there was no one in the dungeon. "How can this be?" He walked about among the guards and sentries. "How did you lose this man?"

"Your Highness! We didn't lose him—your son let him out. You entrusted him with the keys, and therefore we didn't have the right to turn away your son. Your son let him out!"

He called out, "Vaniushka, was it you who let that man out?"

"Yes, I let him out."

"And why did you let him out?"

"I shot with my bow, and the arrow flew through the window. He gave me back my arrow, and for that I let him out."

"Oh, you fool! You will not inherit my tsardom until you find that man and bring him to me." Then he entertained the people and they departed. The tsar put together an entire royal uniform and gave it to his son. He gave him documents, he gave him everything to prove that he was in fact a tsar's son. And he gave him a soldier. "Now go and find that man. And don't come back home until you do find him."

So they rode off. They rode off, and the day was hot and humid through the steppe. There wasn't a drop of water anywhere for even a swallow. They rode on and on, and then suddenly they came upon a well. So they encountered a well and decided to have a drink. They rode up to the well. The water was pure and good but awfully deep down. How could they get any? There was nothing there—not a bucket, nothing except a mug or cup.

"Well," he said, "let's have a drink anyway. Let's rip up that oak sapling and weave a rope, and then one of us can go down on the rope, drink his fill, and the other will haul water back up for the other one."

And so that's what they did. They ripped up the oak sapling and wove a rope. "All right, soldier, you go down!"

"What do you mean? Could you possibly pull me out? You go down, and I'll put you out." And so the boy in all stupidity lowered himself down. He drank. He filled the mug for the other.

"All right, pull me up now, soldier!"

"No, I won't pull you up until you give me an oath: You must be my servant."

Now it's not particularly pleasant to perish in a well, so he gave his oath. He crawled out and changed his clothes. The soldier was on the horse; Ivan Tsarevich slogged along on foot. He went on foot. And so they went far or near, or high or low, for soon a tale is told, but a deed is done by good efforts. They arrived in another tsardom. They stopped. They went right to the tsar. They stopped at the tsar's and began talking with him.

The tsar: "Yes, yes, yes! I know your tsardom very well, and your tsar, too. Of course, I don't know you, but I know your father well."

The tsar had a daughter. Ivan Tsarevich of course ought to have ridden on further. But the soldier had time on his hands. Moreover, there was this tsar's daughter here still. And he was in the royal uniform. In that royal uniform, you see. Now then. He proposed a courtship to the tsar. And the tsar said, "No, my good man. There can be no wedding. She won't be married for three years. She's young. If you like, you can live here. But if you wish to depart, then depart. But any conversation on this theme must wait until three years have passed."

Ivan Tsarevich ordered them to go away home or to some happy place—just to get away from there. But this "uncle" wouldn't let the soldier go home; he was to go somewhere else. "Let's wait," he said. "It won't be long. We'll wait here."

So they began living there. They just started in living there. Three years . . . And Ivan Tsarevich was put to work delivering wood to the various rooms. The tsar's daughter paid no attention to the tsarevich who was courting her, she just trailed along after Ivanushka. She noted that in the uniform and the behavior and everything, something didn't quite add up. Then she went to her father and said, "Papa, we have this one lad who's courting me. Couldn't we find some better work for him than to deliver wood to the various rooms?"

"Why, you can change the work if that's how you feel. Let's make him our senior groom. Let the younger ones herd, and he can be the leader, like the lieutenant over the regiment. That will be better," he said.

So they made him the senior groom. He became the senior groom. And tomorrow he would have to drive the horses out to pasture. When they opened the stables, all the horses lifted their tails and ran away into the forest, into the open steppe—no one knew where. The grooms could give a bigger damn; they could only stagger around from their drunkenness. "Hey, good man! Let us go to a tavern to straighten out our heads! Otherwise, you'll get nothing from us."

"All right, you guys go and straighten out your heads! But don't be gone long. Not long so that everything will be in order. Don't get drunk as you did last evening."

"Could we possibly let that happen? Get on with you!"

"Go then!"

The herders went to the tavern "to straighten out their heads." And he set off down the road. He walked and walked. Suddenly the road split into two. Between the roads was a huge boulder. He sat down on it, sadness came over him, and he started to cry. "If only I could live and be happy," he said. "Here I have to herd horses. And where they go and where they graze, only the devil knows, and when will I drive them home."

He had just been thinking all this, when suddenly behind him: "Greetings, Ivan Tsarevich!"

He turned and said, "Hi!"

"Come be our guest."

"Who sent you?"

"Your friend Liubodei."

He thought and thought about it, and then said, "Let's go."

So he set off visiting. He went visiting. He got there. It was a palace better than his father's. He entered the palace and saw the man whom he had let out of his father's dungeon. And they gave him so many presents. They gave him so much hospitality that even a tsar in his dreams could not dream of such privileges. He was feted! Time passed for the herder. He kept on watching it. Somehow he had to go look for the horses. But this Liubodei had three daughters. So then the oldest daughter came running up to him: "Ivan Tsarevich, here is my scarf for you!"

And Liubodei said, "Oh, Ivan Tsarevich! Don't look on a maiden's favors. I'll give you presents no worse than that. Here's my bread and salt tablecloth. Wherever you go, just spread out this cloth and say 'Raven's Village,' and you will have plenty of everything."

He accepted that gift and another, and then he set off. He sat down on the boulder. The maid hadn't told him how to use the scarf. So he sat down on the boulder and thought, "Everything turned out fine, but how am I to drive in the horses?" He was overcome by sadness. He remembered that scarf, the girl's gift. He shook it as if it were covered in dust or something. Suddenly out leapt twelve young lads.

"Greetings, Ivan Tsarevich! What do you order us to do?"

"This is what I order you to do: Six of you men are to round up the horses and put them in the stables, and arrange it so that all is in order there. And six are to go to the tavern and drive those scoundrel herders home. Whip them, but lightly."

It didn't take those lads long. The horses ran, and the herders ran. No one saw anything: who was driving them, who was flogging them. The lad just worked as they were all supposed to.

Well, on the second day he set off more boldly. With such a gift it was possible to be saved. He set off into the forest, released the horses, and the horses ran off in the same manner. And as for the herders: "Well, good man, let us go to the tavern and tie one on. Yesterday we encountered such villains, though we didn't see a thing, but they whipped us, they beat us with whips until our skins burst. They hit us so that we can barely move now."

"Oh, you good for nothing villains. Go on then, but stay away from these villains. Beware! Next time these villains will beat you up even more," he said.

So now then. He came and sat down on the boulder and started thinking about all this unpleasantness. "I'm still just a herder. There's still nothing to live for. I'm just a herder."

Again from behind him a man: "Greetings, Ivan Tsarevich!"

"Hi! Hello! Who sent you here?"

"Your friend Liubodei. You are invited to be his guest."

He went on the second day, only somewhat more bravely. He got there. The same treatment, many gifts . . . Time passed and he had to go. He started getting ready, when the middle daughter came running up: "Ivan Tsarevich, here's for you from me—a little belt from my very heart. When you are in trouble, just snap this belt, and you'll never be unhappy."

But Liubodei said, "Ivan Tsarevich, don't look on a maiden's favors. I'll give you gifts no worse than hers. Here, take my purse that's never empty."

"Why, thank you."

He took that gift and one other and set off. He came to the boulder. There were no horses and no herders. Time had run out. He shook the scarf, and out leapt twelve young men. He snapped the belt, and out leapt twelve young men.

"What do you order us to do?"

"This is what I order you to do: Twelve young men are to find the horses, round them up, and drive them into the stables. And the other twelve young men are to go into the bar, find the herders, and drive them home. Whip them as is necessary."

So the lads were ready in an instant. They began working. They did everything. They drove in the herders, they drove back the horses, and all was in order.

So then on the third day he had to go back into the forest. They went into the forest, the horses all ran away, and the herders pleaded with him again: "Well, good man, yesterday we were beaten even more fiercely. We didn't see anybody, but they struck us and whipped us so that we can hardly move. If you don't let us go, it'll be all the same. We still won't be any good as workers to you."

"Oh, you villains. Go, but don't meet up with those villains, for they'll straighten you out, they'll make you behave as you ought to."

So off they went to the tavern, and he came and sat on the boulder. Behind him the same man came up: "Greetings, Ivan Tsarevich!"

"Greetings! Who sent you?"

"Your friend Liubodei."

So they set off. They came, and the repasts were offered, as was necessary. Time ran out for the herder, of course. He began getting ready to go home. When he was ready, the youngest daughter came running up to him: "Ivan Tsarevich, take off your leggings, and show me your right thigh!"

So he lowered his leggings. With a pencil she wrote something on his thigh. What she wrote no one could see, and no one knew. And her father said, "Ivan Tsarevich, don't look on a maiden's favors. I'll give you a gift no worse than hers. Here," he said, "is my golden bridle. If you're in some bad situation, just wave this bridle, and three golden-maned horses will leap out. From any bad luck you need to escape, it will get you out of it."

So he took the gifts and went away. He left. He came, sat down on the boulder, and thought: "Life has gotten so much better. I can herd, but I'm still no tsar—just a herder."

The time ran out, and he waved the scarf. Out leapt the twelve young men: "What do you order us to do?"

"I order twelve young men to round up the horses, drive them into the stables, give them their fodder, so that everything is in order. Then twelve young men are to go to the tavern, find those villains, those herders, and beat and thrash them until their skins crack."

Well, the lads did all this in a hurry. For soon a tale is told, but a deed is done by accomplishments, and while all this was being demonstrated, the three years passed. The soldier began courting her. But the tsar's wife had died. The tsar said, "No, my good man, there can be no wedding just now. First you have to marry me off, and then I will give you one of my daughters. Since the three years have passed, I will not deceive you."

"But where shall I find you a bride?"

"My bride is beyond the thrice nine lands, in the thrice- ten tsardom, and she is a fierce sorceress. Whoever goes there to make a marriage will never return. But see that you bring her back to me. I will get married to her, and then I will give you my daughter."

"Only you must give me my servant, Ivanushka," he said.

"Your Ivanushka is always at your command, please."

"Provide us with a boat."

Well, the tsar provided them with a boat. There was no fuel, nothing on the boat—not a man, nothing at all. The soldier took himself there, lower in the hold where it was more comfortable to sleep when the boat was sailing or when it wasn't. Since that was the business at hand, Ivanushka waved the scarf, and out jumped twelve young lads. He snapped the belt, and out jumped twelve more young lads. "What do you order to be done?"

"I order you to heat up the stove in the boat so that the boat might immediately go there, to the thrice-ten kingdom."

Everything whirred, everything hissed, and the little boat set off. It went and it went, did the little boat. Suddenly they looked, and there was a man running through the water. He ran up and hopped right onto the little boat. "Who sent you here?" he asked.

"Your friend Liubodei."

"And who are you, anyway?"

"I am Frost," he said.

"Get in the boat and let's go."

They had only just taken that one on when another came running. He leapt onto the boat. "Greetings, Ivan Tsarevich!"

"Hi! Who sent you here?"

"Your friend Liubodei."

"And who are you?"

"I'm Fius."

"Get in the boat, and let's go."

The next person came running and jumped onto the little boat. "Greetings, Ivan Tsarevich!"

"Greetings! Who sent you?"

"Your friend Liubodei."

"And what are you good for?"

"I'm Insatiable."

"Get in the boat; let's go!"

They went on, and then the next man came running: "Greetings, Ivan Tsarevich!"

"Hi! Who set you?"

"Your friend Liubodei."

"And what are you good for?"

"I'm Unquenchable."

"Get in the boat, and let's go!"

They set off again, and the next man came running. "Greetings, Ivan Tsarevich!"

"Hi! Who sent you?"

"Your friend Liubodei."

"And what are you good for?"

"I can leap up to the heavens, count the stars, and throw out any extras!"

"Get in the boat and let's go."

The next man came running. "Greetings, Ivan Tsarevich!"

"Hi! Who sent you?"

"Your friend Liubodei."

"And what are you good for?"

"I can leap about in the sea, count the pike, and toss out the extras!"

"Get in the boat, and let's go."

The next man came running. He jumped into the boat. "Hi, Ivan Tsarevich!"

"Hi! Who sent you?"

"Your friend Liubodei."

"And what are you good for?"

"I can leap along the sea, count the sands, and throw out any extras."

"Get in the boat and let's go"

So, while he was receiving all of these friends, they arrived. All around this tsardom where the bride lived, a palisade had been erected, all around her tsardom. And on each and every stake was a tsar's head. That was how many suitors had come to her. Just on one stake there was no head. And then the laborer said, "My friend, your head should be on that stake."

"All right," he said, "they'll hang my head in its proper place!"

They came and made their report. She invited them in. And the courting negotiations began. Of course, it wasn't for himself, but rather, as he said, for some other tsar. He was the responsible person, so to speak.

"Yes," she said. "The age is most suitable. I have nothing against it, nothing against marriage, but you have had a long journey. You are all covered in dust and smoke. Wouldn't you like to pay a visit to my bathhouse?"

"Yes, perhaps that wouldn't be bad, not bad at all."

She had known that these matchmakers were coming. Her bathhouse was three arshins square, and the walls were two meters thick. The walls were made of copper and heated up to the point that sparks flew when anyone entered, and all were burned up.

"All right, bride to be, give us each a switch." She gave them each a switch and they entered the passageway. "Who will go in first?"

Frost: "I will."

Fius: "I will."

And so they went. Frost encircled all the sparks in the bathhouse and put them in the corners. While they were entering the bathhouse, snow froze them in the corners. There was nothing left. They came in.

"Well, my dear guests, how is it?"

"What is this that the bride has snow in the corners, that frost sparkles, and that we are what—supposed to freeze?"

She ran over there, and in fact that was the case. A cold sweat broke out from her head to her heels. All right. (Let's get back to the courtship.)

"All right, matchmakers, every wedding party is made beautiful by its hospitality. If in a day I could make some bread and vodka for you, would you drink it?"

"On our trip there was neither bread nor vodka. We would drink it with pleasure!"

"Please!"

"In three days everything will be ready."

"Very good! If it's three days, it's three."

In three days she had brought in so much, baked so much, and there were barrels of wine and beer. With all these, the town was overflowing, the whole tsardom was. You couldn't pass anywhere.

"Now then, please come and taste everything!"

The man went back into the passageway. "Well lads, who can eat and drink the most?"

"I can," said Insatiable.

"I can," said Unquenchable.

They went along, and no one stopped anywhere. Everywhere everything just disappeared. They went about the city, and nowhere was anything left—not a gram nor a milligram, not a crumb nor a spoonful. Nothing remained; everything disappeared. They came and said, "So now, bride! What is this, joking with us? There's no point to joking with us, with the groom's party! Now it's time to get ready to travel."

So then. She ran about and checked things out. There wasn't a thing left anywhere. "And there wasn't enough to eat or drink for two of our lads."

They got ready and set off. Some went into the hold. (Ivan Tsarevich, you know, Ivan the tsar's son, but now he's a servant; at this very time he's still a servant.) These twenty-four young men from the scarf and from the belt, and those three or four men he invited along went below.

"Now," he said, "prepare some good tongs, forge some heavy copper rods, and heat them all up until they're red hot."

The bride got ready, boarded the little boat, and they all set sail back. They went and they went. Suddenly the bride disappeared. "Oh lads! We've lost the bride. We've lost her, and how shall we get her back?"

One of them said, "Wait! Wait! She flew away to the heavens as a star. I'll fetch her right back from there."

The one who could leap to heaven and count the stars flew off and was back. He sat her down. He said, "Listen, Maria Tsarevna, come along peaceably, or it will be too bad for you."

"I give you my solemn oath to God that nothing further will happen."

They set off again. Suddenly out of nowhere the bride disappeared. The bride was lost. "Well, lads, we've lost the bride again.

One of them said, "Wait, wait and I'll listen for her." He fell down with his ear to the ground. "She's down there carrying on like a pike. I'll go find her." And he set off looking. He chased and chased after her, and then he caught her and pulled her back into the boat. "Maria Tsarevna, come along peaceably, or we will punish you. There's no way you can get away from us."

"By the true God and the cross, that's it, nothing more will happen."

So they set off. They hadn't gone far when the bride went missing. She disappeared again. One of them said, "Well, lads, we've lost the bride, but wait and I'll listen. Aha, she's lying there on a bank, there in the sand."

He was let down there. One, two, and he had her, and by that time the tongs had been tempered, and they grabbed her with them. The rods were heated red-hot. They grabbed her with the tongs and started beating her with the rods. They beat her and beat her and beat her, and she made her oaths, she promised everything.

"So now there'll be a little order."

They got there. They started leaving the ship. The friends all went their own ways. The twenty-four young men also took themselves off. No one was left at all. They all left the shift by the gangplank. That soldier pushed Ivan Tsarevich into the sea. He pushed him into the sea and took the bride by the hand. And he also sent a radiogram so that he would find out how to meet up with the bride of his father-in-law. If, he said to himself, they met him coolly, he would turn the whole tsardom on its head, destroy it. But then the tsar rang the bell himself, and he fired blanks from his cannon, while all about were guards. Everything was set up. So the soldier brought her in, and the wedding was put on. They had the wedding, and the soldier said, "Your Royal Highness, may we not have our wedding now?"

"Well, please. I'll report this to my daughter, and we'll begin. We'll set the day for the wedding and all that."

And he said, "Let's begin tomorrow, and that will be that."

So the tsar went to his daughter: "Well, Daughter, it's time for marriage. You've entered your marriageable years, and your groom has been waiting for you for more than three years. There's no need to talk about it any more. Tomorrow we'll start the wedding."

"No, Father, there'll be no wedding tomorrow. He has waited for me for three years; I'm just asking him to wait for three more weeks."

For those three weeks she went about. She kept going about the ship. Somewhere, something ought to remain of him. She wasn't searching for that groom there—the one being readied for her—but for Ivanushka, the real tsarevich. And she went about, she walked and walked. And then on the very last day of the three weeks, she came and suddenly chanced upon a pea coat. She grabbed the pea coat and was overjoyed.

"Well," she said, "at least here's his pea coat as a memento. I'll put it on and it will be just as if I were going about with him, in his pea coat." She stuck her hand in a pocket. And there were that scarf and belt. But she just kept walking. And she kept on crying. She pulled out the scarf, and there was something about it that she didn't like. She gave it a shake, and suddenly out jumped the twelve young men.

"What do you order us to do, Maria Tsarevna?"

"I order you to find your master. Where is your master? First of all, find your master. Where is your master?"

So they went here and there. They ran here and there. But they couldn't find anything anywhere. Then they remembered how they had dived into the water, and they found him in the water and brought him back. Then she gave another command: "Now prepare a crystal coffin for two."

Once that had been done, you see, he would lie in the coffin with her. So they made the coffin and everything. They lay him in it, and she lay down, and everything was proper and correct. And then suddenly it occurred to her: "I'm a fool not to pity my life because of him. But I'm sorry that I put him in here when he's all wet. He's completely wet. I'll have to change him."

And suddenly they undressed him. And when they had undressed him, there on his right thigh was that signature, and she saw it. She bent over and read it. "Now then, lads. In such and such a place there are the living and the dead waters. Bring them here."

And they went there in a flash and brought back the living water and the dead. They brought it and started wiping him, wiping him all over. They wiped and wiped. Suddenly he shuddered and then shuddered again. Then he jumped up: "Oh, how long I've slept!"

She said, "Yes, Ivan Tsarevich, you slept a long time, and if it hadn't been for me, you would have slept forever on the bottom of the sea." Then she said, "I'll go home now, and you stay here."

"No, you stay here, too, if that's the case."

"That's how it is. It's time to start the wedding. They've been waiting for me for a long time."

"Never mind; let them wait. Everything will be all right now."

He spread out his bread and salt tablecloth, Raven's Village, and there was plenty of everything. Eat and drink!

"Now," he said, "eat and drink!" And they did. "Then we'll lie down and rest."

They lay down to sleep and rested for a while. He took the scarf and out leapt the twelve young men: "What do you command us to do?"

Then he waved the bridle and three horses appeared. "One of you twelve is to sit on a horse and ride to the tsar." He wrote out the following denunciation: "Your Royal Highness, I ask you to greet your son-in-law and daughter not like you greeted that villain. The one sitting in the dungeon is not your son-in-law. Your son-in-law is the one sleeping with your daughter on the bank. If I have a poor reception, I'll turn your tsardom on its head. When you meet that villain of a son-in-law who is in the dungeon, sit on the balcony and see how a real son-in-law arrives."

Well now, the tsar was out of his mind. The tsar didn't know what to do. "Where did this other son-in-law come from? And on what horse did he come here?" But he arranged a reception. There they rested a little and slept. Once more he shook the bridle and out leapt three horses. "All right now," he said, "Maria Tsarevich, mount this horse, and I'll get on another, and one of you twelve young men get on the third, and you ride on ahead of us. Grab that villain on the balcony by the foot and ride into the open steppe, drag him until he flies apart: his arms in one place, his feet in another, and his boasting head in still another. Let him exist no longer!"

And that's what they did. Then he came himself, and the tsar greeted him well and they had the wedding. They began living and prospering. And thus Ivan Tsarevich didn't return to his father.

That's all of my little tale.

(SUS 502 + 513A)

15

ABOUT A MIGHTY WARRIOR, TSAR PEREGAR, WHO REEKED OF DRINK

O. I. Dmitriev

Once he was strolling about the city, throwing a sword up next to the eaves and kicking a ball so that it flew up to the clouds, and he said to himself: "Oh, I can go out with the mighty warriors into the open steppe. I can fight with those mighty warriors, try my strength."

So he had just passed along an open road, when the tsar's daughter caught sight of him. She was sitting in her chambers. "Oh," she said, "if only that young man would marry me, I would accept him with all my soul."

From that very thought she became pregnant, she got pregnant, and the royal servants began saying that "Your royal daughter is with child."

His majesty examined her and exiled her from his tsardom. "Get out of here, you witch, go where you will."

So then she was walking along the postal road, and then she saw a little path going into the woods. She walked along it for a while, and the path got better and better. And the path led her to a house in the woods. She entered the house but found nothing in it. She got on top of the stove, sat down on a sheepskin jacket, and thought, "Someone will come!"

Suddenly the earth shook, and she saw the mighty warrior coming into the hut. "Foo-foo! Never has it been heard that a Russian soul came here, but here is a Russian soul. If it's an old man, then it's my grandfather; if a middle-aged man, then my father; if it's an old woman, then it's my grandmother; if a middle-aged woman, then my mother; but if it's a beautiful maiden, let her be my wife, my beloved. Show yourself! If you don't show yourself, I'll take this house apart stone by stone and find you." She showed herself. "Come down here!"

"Oh, brave kind young man, I would come down, but I'm completely naked."

He handed her some clothing, ordered her to come down, and began questioning her: "Tell me, my darling, from what land, from what horde, from which father, which mother, are you?"

"I am the daughter of a tsar, and once I happened to see a man digging a sword next to the eaves and tossing a ball. It flew up to the clouds, and I thought in my mind, "If only this young man would ask me to marry him, I would agree with all my soul, and in just such a summer time as this."

"Oh, my darling, I myself was the one who was there, and here I am now. You shall be my wife, and I shall be your husband."

So when the time had passed, his wife produced a son, and they gave him the name "Tsarevich Dum." He grew not by the years, but by the hours, and when he was six years old he began going everywhere and helping out. Once his father was going out to war to try his strength against a great army and with a bogatyr, and he came up to his loving son, and his son was asleep. "Oh, Wife," he said, "I don't know whether I'll be alive, so I must say farewell to my son. But I dare not wake him; he is still so very young, and he might injure himself."

But his son heard everything. He wasn't sleep, but he said nothing and pretended to be sleeping.

So Tsar Peregar went out, and when he came back, he released his horses and sat down to take his tea. "Oh, Wife, I've only got three more days to live because my strength and that bogatyr's are equal. I can lift a boulder only to my knees, and he can lift it only to his knees. I really ought not fight with him as he just got married, but the oath has been taken, and we must decide who will kill whom." He was to leave the following day. He came up to his son, but he didn't dare awaken him. "It would ruin his youth to no purpose." "Well, Wife, God bless him to walk in my footsteps, as I have done."

So then he rode off, but the next day Tsar Peregar returned alive and well.

On the third day he said, "Today something will be decisive. I'll either be alive or I'll be killed." Their son heard this oath. When evening came, he heard that his father was already snoring. "What kind of bogatyr is he? I'll just get on his good horse and go out into the open steppe and take a good look at him."

His father was already asleep so he got on his good horse and rode off into the open steppe. He listened hard, and then he rode up to that boulder that they were supposed to lift up to their knees. He picked it up in one hand and tossed it fifty versts off to the side. "Oh," he said, "It was nothing at all for me to lift that boulder. Now I'll ride over to where these warriors' armor is lying, such that they can't act, can't move in this armor, these warriors." Tsarevich Dum put on the armor. "Oh," he said, "This armor is cheap. It's lighter than a dressing gown." He kicked the armor and trampled it on the damp earth, and it all fell apart. "Now I'll just find out where this bogatyr lives who's supposed to fight with my father."

So once more he rode into the open steppe, and there was the bogatyr. "So, a wee, little boy, you're too young to be riding out here. But then it's your life to determine."

Then Dum Tsarevich spoke: "Let's ride in combat, and we'll test our strength, you and I." So then Dum Tsarevich tossed him off like a buttered blin—that's how long he struggled with that bogatyr. Then he got on his good horse and rode back to his father. And he tied up the horse as always, and he went into the dining room and lay down to sleep, as if he hadn't been anywhere.

So then on the third day Tsar Peregar rode off into the open steppe to fight with this bogatyr. "Well, Wife, don't wake up our son. He might harm himself in his tender years." So then Tsar Peregar mounted up and rode down onto the open steppe. And he rode to that boulder where he had tested his strength, but the boulder was nowhere near. "Oh, it's obvious he's become really strong and mighty, and he'll destroy my strength."

Again he got up onto his good horse and was off to the armor. He came up to the armor, but the armor had all been scattered. He looked at it and rode out into the open steppe, and there in the open steppe laid the brazen head of that bogatyr. "Obviously, the lord has brought his servant, and he defeated my enemy," he said.

Tsar Peregar and his son and his mother sat down to drink tea, and he began telling his son how the lord had given him his servant, how he had defeated his enemy. "Oh, Father, wasn't it perhaps I who was there? Wasn't it I who defeated him?"

Then the father almost fainted from the horror. "Oh, such a son has been born that even if I don't say it, he'll kill me. Oh, you my young son, Dum Tsarevich, go and take for yourself Olena Sorokoumovna. I struggled and fought for her, I wanted to marry her, but since I have already gotten married, the Lord bless you with her as a bride. And here, my son, is my horse as a gift," he said.

So the father saw his son sitting there, but in the steppe the dust got up such that he didn't see where the good lad had ridden to. So then he rode far or near, and high or low. Soon a tale is told, but in its success is a deed measured. He came to a really old, old woman in this hovel. And he entered into the dining rooms, and the old woman yelled at the top of her lungs, "Oh, you villain, you thief, why did you enter my home without my asking?"

"Oh, you old devil, you would better feed me rather than shout!"

And he struck the old woman on the forehead such that he knocked her block off, and she went flying out onto the road and ran off. "Well, Dum Tsarevich, you brought Granny a fine gift. You can take my granddaughter Olena Sorokoumovna as your bride."

So he ate and drank, and he spent the night there. In the morning he set off. The old granny instructed him: "You go to my other sister. She's stronger than I am, so you give her an even stronger 'gift' so that she'll feel it and hear you."

So he got on his good horse and set off into the open steppe. And he came to that second granny, and he didn't ask or report to her, he just entered her house.

The woman jumped up and shouted at the top of her lungs: "Why did you come into my house without my asking?"

He whopped the old woman on the ear such that she flew outside, and then she came running back in. "Well, Dum Tsarevich, you've brought a fine gift for an old woman. You can take my granddaughter Olena Sorokoumovna as your bride." And then she started feeding him and giving him something to drink, and she questioned him. "Tomorrow you will ride to our third sister and then, God willing, give her an even more powerful gift, for she is stronger than we are."

So he got on his good horse and let fly into the open steppe. And he rode to that granny, and he didn't ask her anything. He just went into her chambers.

And she started shouting in a strange voice: "Oh, you villain, you robber, who ordered you to enter this house without my asking?" The old woman was about to whop him when he whopped her and she went flying away outside. She came running in from outside, fed him and gave him something to drink, and then she spoke these words: "Well, Dum Tsarevich, you have brought fine gifts to a woman. You can take Olena

Sorokoumovna, our granddaughter, as your bride. But, good lad, Dum Tsarevich, you must ride for three years, and I will accompany you for three days. Eat, drink, and eat some more, and then go to sleep with God."

So he drank and ate and tumbled off to sleep. In the morning he got up. The granny went out onto the street and shouted like a bogatyr: "Mogul-Bird, fly over here!"

There was an answer: "Mogul-Bird isn't at home! She flew off over the deep blue sea."

She shouted again: "Who ordered her to fly off there without my saying so?"

After three hours Mogul-Bird came flying up.

"Well, Mogul-Bird," she said, "take Dum Tsarevich to Olena Sorokoumovna."

"Oh, Granny, give me three days' rest. I have flown far; I can't fly any farther," Mogul-Bird answered her.

She stamped her feet. "I won't give you that," she said. "Not only three days, but only three hours will you rest."

Mogul-Bird answered her, "Salt me forty barrels of meat so that I'll have something to eat flying over the sea, and fill forty barrels of blood."

So then the granny came to Dum Tsarevich and she said, "Oh, you, Dum Tsarevich, go now to the fenced yard and take my very best oxen, and salt forty barrels of meat and fill forty barrels of blood." She reckoned that that would take Dum Tsarevich about three full days, and thus Mogul-Bird could get a little rest in that time.

He went out into that fenced yard and started slaughtering the oxen. Whichever one would approach, he would grab in his hands and tear apart—and into a barrel. And in three hours he had salted forty barrels of meat and filled forty barrels of blood.

Then he mounted Mogul-Bird and was off! They rode out with about half a cartload, and then there was less than half the meat and blood. And she said to Dum Tsarevich, "I shall myself drown and drown you, too, because there's nothing left to eat."

Dum Tsarevich thought about it for a moment, and then cut the muscles from his legs and threw them to her. And these muscles had the equivalent of forty barrels. When they caught sight of the city, Mogul-Bird could fly on no farther.

"Dum Tsarevich, feed me; otherwise, I shall drown and drown you, too.

He thought about it for a moment and then cut the muscles from his arms. Thus she flew on to where she had to go.

"Get off," she said, "get off, young lad, from Mogul-Bird."

"Oh, Mogul-Bird," he said. "No only can't I get down—I can't even move."

"What did you feed me with, what did you give me to drink during those last parts of our flight, my good lad? Go off onto the damp earth."

So he went off onto the damp earth, and he sat down on a little bush. And Mogul-Bird replied to him, "Oh, you good lad, sit for a while and wait for me. I'll go and fetch you some magic things. We'll rub them and your muscles will be as before, and you will have the strength you had before," she said.

She flew off over the deep blue sea and brought the magic things and she made him as he was before. The good lad took his leave of her and set off for the royal tsardom.

When she was flying off, he set off and he saw a herder watching over a herd of cows. "Greetings, young herder," he said. "Do you have a long task here?"

"Three hundred days."

"And how much do you get for it?"

"Three hundred rubles."

"You don't know, young man, by what reason-wit one could find Olena Sorokoumovna?"

"You'll not find such a person by reason-wit as she is, nor can you find an ill word from her ever."

"What's your name, herder?"

"My name is Jasinka."

"Jasinka," he said, "let's exchange clothing, and I'll give you three hundred rubles and you go home with God while I herd your cows."

Jasinka thought about it with all his brain: "I've already done half of it, but he'll still give three hundred rubles and fine clothing."

So Jasinka got the money and took himself off, while Dum Tsarevich began herding. He drove the animals about for the morning half of a day, to twelve o'clock. Olena Sorokoumovna came out and said: "Oh, Jasinka, why have you driven the animals in so early?"

"My stomach hurt, it wanted to go home. I couldn't go on any farther."

So on the second day he got up and shouted, drove the animals outside. But Olena Sorokoumovna said, "Jasinka, you always blew your horn and played. But now why aren't you playing?"

"I'm not blowing the horn because my head aches."

He drove the cows into the open steppe, spread out a white tent, and lay down to rest. And at that time the first woman sent him a gift: She sent him a pig with golden bristles. Then the pig ran to the tsar's palace, scratched herself, and left a lot of gold. The tsar had eight sons-in-law and then he summoned his sons-in-law: "So, sons-in-law, there was this pig with the golden bristles, and it left a lot of gold. Whoever catches it will have a lot of gold, and you'll mount the throne as tsar."

They went out into the open steppe and saw this tent that had been spread out there. And this good lad was sleeping there, while his horse and the pig with the golden bristles were eating wheat. So then they walked around, they strolled about, but they didn't dare go up close. When the good lad woke up, they saw him: "Greetings, young lad, whose son are you and where are you from?"

"I am a merchant from beyond the seas."

"Sell us your piggy with the golden bristles. Whatever you require we'll give to you."

"I don't want a thing. I'll just give it to you. There are eight of you young lads, so cut off eight fingers, and I'll give her to you for that."

So they stopped to think about it. "We have good doctors; they'll manage to heal our hands." So each of them went and cut off a finger for him, eight in all.

Then the second granny sent him the golden-horned deer as a present for him. The deer came, scratched itself against the tsar's palace, knocked it off its place, and ran away. Once more he demanded of his sons-in-law: "Sons-in-law, find that golden-horned deer, and God will bless you with the tsardom."

They set off, they caught sight of the tent. The young lad was sleeping there, and the deer was there, and the pig was there, and the good horse stood there. Until he awoke they walked about. When he had awakened, they said, "Greetings, good lad, whose son are you and where are you from?

"I am a merchant from beyond the seas."

"Sell us the deer," they said. "Whatever you need, just take it."

"I don't need anything. There are eight of you young lads; cut off a toe from your feet. That will be enough for me."

So they stopped to think about it. "We have good doctors. They'll manage to fix our feet, and then one of us will be on the throne, and the others will be big royal servants." So they each cut a toe from a foot. So he sent off the deer and drove the cattle home, so that by twelve o'clock they were there.

"Jasinka, why did you drive the cattle in so early?"

"My stomach aches, and my head aches."

So he came home, lay down to sleep, and he slept for three full days, without raising his head. Then Olena Sorokoumovna came to find out whether he was alive or not, because he hadn't been going out with the cattle. She opened the door and stood in the doorway. She could scarcely stand in the door from the bogatyr's breathing. She went back to her father. "Father, let me marry Jasinka."

Well, her father answered her, "Olena Sorokoumovna, would you marry a herder? Why, once before you predicted that when your husband was born, the water and sand would become mixed, an eagle would screech. But now you would marry a herder." But no way could her father dissuade her, and so he married her off to Jasinka.

When he was married, he set off with the cattle, and the third granny sent him a mare with a golden forehead as a present. The mare with the golden forehead came running up, scratched herself such that the royal palace shook even more than before. The tsar called his sons-in-law: "Find," he said, "and bring here that mare with the golden forehead. When you have brought her in, then the one who brings her in will mount the throne as tsar, and I'll make the others big royal servants.

So Jasinka set off with the cattle into the forest. He hadn't been with the cattle even until midday when he returned them all back.

"Jasinka, why have you brought the cattle in so early?"

"Oh, Olena Sorokoumovna," he said, "I want to search with my brothers, with the sons-in-law, for the mare with the golden forehead. They say they're going to make someone a big royal servant."

So then Jasinka asked, "My lord and little father, will you give me a horse to ride into the open steppe to search for the mare with the golden forehead?"

"Go, servants, and give him a horse that has been ridden for six years already. Jasinka will ride it, and that horse can kill him off. Then my Olena Sorokoumovna won't be married to a herder." So six men led in the horse, and they could hardly hold it. "Jasinka, get on, ride!"

But Jasinka was a lad with experience. He got on that good horse, but with his face to its tail. And they all thought: He doesn't even know how to mount. Now comes his certain death."

He slapped the horse with his hand and said "Giddup," and then he slapped him with the other and said, "Shoo." And the horse hardly carried him out of the royal courtyard before he fell, and that was the end of him. He shouted for his magic horse: "Good horse, come here!" The magic horse came running up.

"Oh, good horse, can we find the mare with the golden forehead today?"

> The mare with the golden forehead is my very own mother, and when I was still very young, I bit off her right teat. For that reason, Dum Tsarevich, go back and fetch three bronze, three iron, and three lead rods to whip the mare with the golden forehead. Go back and make a stuffed animal that looks just like a horse. When I run up to her, she will rush at me with all her might, but you sit in a fir tree and then when I run up to the fir, I'll run around it and you throw the stuffed animal and she'll think that it's me. And she'll rear up and stamp her feet, and at that moment you get on her and hold tightly and whip her with these rods until she is pacified.

So then the good horse took off running, and she ran up under that fir tree. And then at the right moment, he sat on her and began whipping her. And Dum Tsarevich whipped her until such time as she pleaded with him, "Oh, whenever you think of me, I'll be there."

So then Dum Tsarevich got on and rode off. Those other lads, his brothers-in-law, met up with him.

"So then, good lad, where are you from?"

"I'm a merchant's son from abroad."

"Sell that mare with the golden forehead to us. Whatever you want for her we'll give you."

"I don't need any gold or any of your silver. Just cut off the ring finger from each of your hands and a strip from each of your backs. That will be enough for me."

They mounted up and thought, "There are good doctors who will heal our backs." They cut off the ring finger from each of their hands, and he handed over the mare with the golden forehead.

"Oh brave and good lad, merchant from overseas, you are invited to our feast, to a great ball."

"Yes, I will come to you, but don't forget me," he said.

They had just led the horse away, when she jerked up—and they saw her no more.

So then the overseas merchant went to their feast, to their great ball. "Father, seat him in the chief place," the tsar's sons-in-law said. So then they poured out a goblet of green wine and offered it to their great guest. But their guest didn't drink the wine; he poured it out the window. The tsar didn't like that at all.

"He ought not have poured it out. You have to drink the royal vodka!"

So they poured him a second goblet, but again out the window he poured it out. And he didn't like that at all, that his Olena Sorokoumovna was seated at the lowest place. And therefore he kept on pouring out the wine.

He poured him a third and it went out the window too. His majesty certainly didn't like this, and his sons-in-law bowed low to him: "Your Royal Highness, perhaps they have that custom that they pour out even the fifth and sixth, and then they start drinking."

So they poured out a fourth. He drank it and bowed. "I humbly thank you, but now give me some rest."

"Go into that bedroom, the bedroom in which Jasinka slept. Our Jasinka is lost, and no one knows whether he is alive or dead."

So he made his way into that room and lay down to sleep. When the feasts had finished, and the great balls, then Jasinka's wife came to sleep.

"Oh," he said, "Olena Sorokoumovna, couldn't you and I do something?"

"Here's what, brave and good lad: If you want to sleep, then sleep. Otherwise, we'll hand you over for execution if you talk like that."

So once more he didn't say anything. He lay there and lay there, and then he said, "Now then, Olena Sorokoumovna, wouldn't it be possible—just a little of this and that?"

"Oh, you villain!"

She jumped up and ran to the bell, but he persuaded her that he wouldn't do it any more.

So on the next day they had a great feast. They invited their guest to this honorable feast. When he came, they sat him down at the best place, but Olena Sorokoumovna was seated at the farthest point. And they poured out a goblet of green wine, not a very large goblet—just half a bucket full, with a weight of a pood and a half. He took it and downed it in a single gulp. Then the lad drew out a woman's kerchief that Sorokoumovna had given Jasinka, and he put Jasinka's ring on his hand. And then Olena Sorokoumovna leapt up and kissed him on the lips.

"I told you, Father, that when the sun rises, it begins to shine."

Then they received the lad not as before. They began feeding him and giving him drink in better style. So then the lad, when he had taken a drink, said, "Oh, my brothers and brothers-in-law, why do you ride and drink and eat wearing gloves?" He drew something out of his pocket. "Aren't these your ring fingers?" he said. "Let's go into the open steppe and we'll shout to see whom these animals will obey: the little deer, the pig, and the mare with the golden forehead."

The brothers and brothers-in-law went out and began shouting, but the deer didn't appear. So they said, "Now you shout, good lad!"

He shouted, and the deer, the pig, and the mare with the golden forehead came running.

His majesty got on his knees before him: "Well, Son-in-law, do whatever you think is best with them."

He clobbered one of them on the head, and all his hair flew off. He hit the second one lightly, and he became a hunchback. The others he dealt with more severely, and they became hunchbacks with a hump in back and another hump in front. And then they all knew that the good lad was Dum Tsarevich.

"Well, Dum Tsarevich, now you will live as a gentleman and become the tsar. So then rule as long as you live."

(SUS 530A)

16

ABOUT AN ENCHANTED MILL

F. F. Kabrenov

In a certain tsardom, in a certain country, and in fact in the one in which we live, on a flat place, like on a harrow, about two hundred versts to one side . . . This is no tale; it's the pre-tale. The tale will be on Saturday after dinner when we eat soft bread and sip sour borsch. Then I'll tell you the tale.

In a certain place there lived an old man with his old woman. They were rich, but they had no children. They kept a mare, a cow, and a sheep. Once, after they had been thinking it over, the old man said to the old woman: "Yes, Old Woman, now we have become old. We'll die, and all our wealth will be worthless, there's no one to leave it to. And so that people don't just cart it away, we ought to build ourselves a mill—and one that has an entrance but no exit."

Well, the old woman agreed to this. He got up in the morning quite early, washed himself quite well, prayed to God, and equipped himself for the way, the road. Whether he walked near or far, low or high, soon a tale is told but a deed is measured by its success. He met a peasant quite by chance. They exchanged greetings, and the peasant asked the old man, "Where are you going, Grandfather, where does your path take you?"

"Well, I've set off to find a craftsman, I have to build a mill that has an entrance but no exit."

"Now then, I'll build it. Only give me for the work that which you don't know you have at home."

So the old man answered: "I know everything. If the mare give birth to a colt, I'll give you the colt; if the cow calves, I'll give you the calf; if the bitch has pups, I'll give you a pup."

"So then, you're agreed to give me what you don't know you have at home?"

"I agree."

So they wrote out a contract. They cut one of the old man's fingers, and with his own blood he wrote, "I shall give for the work on the mill that which I don't know I have at home."

So then the peasant said to him: "Now, Grandfather, go home. In what place are you thinking of building the mill, and shall I build you a big one? Measure it out, and pound in stakes at the corners."

They bid each other farewell, and the old man went home. And at that time while the old man was out, the old woman got pregnant and gave birth to a little boy and a little girl. She called the boy Ivan and the little girl Maria. So as the old man was approaching the house, the old woman caught sight of him out the window, still in the field, she saw the old man coming, and she was overjoyed and went out to meet him with the little boy and little girl. When she went up to the old man, he asked her, "And whose children are these? Where did you get them?" The old woman told him that after his leaving she had given birth to two children. The old man quickly guessed it!

"Why, it wasn't just any simple person, likely, whom I engaged to build the mill. It was not for nothing that he asked for what I didn't know I had at home. I didn't know about these children, so I've given them to the devil for his work."

But he didn't say anything to the old woman. He came home, measured out the place, and pounded in the stakes at the corners. When night came, then the work began. They hauled the logs, they built the mill. In the morning there was nobody there. But the mill was half-built in one night. When Vania and Mania were sleeping behind the partition, the old man said to the old woman, "You don't know what, do you?"

"No."

"Why, for building that mill I gave our children to no one other than the devil."

And the old woman replied, "Well, if they've been given over, there's nothing to be done."

They both cried a bit, and then they went off to sleep. Meanwhile, Vania was sleeping, but Mania didn't sleep. She heard everything that her father and mother had said. In the morning, when the parents went off to work, Mania said to Vania: "Vania, didn't you hear anything?"

"No."

"Well, you and I have been given to the devil for the building of that mill. Vania, let's run away from Father and from Mother."

"Let's!"

So in the morning when their parents had left, Mania took a little comb, a piece of flint, and a piece of cloth with her, and they set off on the way and road. They walked for a long time, and finally Mania said to Vania, "Vania, lie down flat on your chest and listen with your ear. What's beneath us, what's above us, what's in front, and what's behind."

Vania fell to the ground on his chest, listened with his ear, and said, "Beneath us is the earth, above us the sky, in front of us the road, and behind us the pursuit. The devil is catching up to us, and he'll soon be here."

Once they had gone, the devil finished building the mill and began asking the old man for the reckoning. But the old man replied, "My children have gone away, and I don't know where."

"Well, maybe they got away from you, but they won't get away from me!"

And he set off to catch up to Mania and Vania. Mania took the comb, threw it, and said, "Where I threw this comb, let there be dense thickets, impassable swamps from the east to the west so that no one on foot can pass, nor a horse, nor a bird fly through, nor a beast find passage."

And so there sprang up dense thickets, impassable swamps. And the devil was beyond the thicket, and he shouted, "No matter, you scoundrel, you won't get away from me!" He began cutting the woods and building bridges, and meanwhile Mania and Vania ran on further.

A second time Mania said to Vania, "Vania, lie down flat on your chest, listen with your ear. What's beneath us, what's above us, what's in front, and what's behind?"

Vania fell to the ground on his chest, listened with his ear, and said, "Beneath us is the earth, above us the sky, in front of us the road, and behind us the chase. The devil is catching up to us, and he'll soon be here."

Mania threw the piece of flint and said, "Wherever that piece of flint fell, let flint mountains rise up from the east to the west, and henceforth and forever, so that no one on foot can pass, nor a horse, nor a bird fly through, nor a beast find passage."

The flint mountains sprang up. But beyond the mountain the devil shouted, "No matter, you scoundrel, you won't get away from me!" He began hacking at the mountains to make a passageway for himself, but meanwhile Vania and Mania continued on their way.

Mania said to Vania, "Vania, lie down flat on your chest, listen with your ear. What's beneath us, what's above us, what's in front, and what's behind?"

Vania fell to the ground on his chest, listened with his ear, and said to his sister, "The devil is chasing us, and he'll soon be here."

Mania waved the piece of cloth and said, "When I wave this piece of cloth, let a fiery river start burning from the east and to the west from now on and forever, so that no one on foot can pass, nor a horse, nor a bird fly through, nor a beast find passage." And the river burst into flame.

"Oh, you scoundrel, you knew what to do!" The devil stayed beyond the river. So then Mania and Vania rested on the bank and then set off further down the road and path. They walked for a long time or short, low or high, for soon a tale is told but a deed is measured by its success. They came into a forest and saw a house. They went into the house and it was all empty there; there was no one there. Then Mania said to Vania, "Vania, let's hide beneath the stove and wait until evening. Perhaps someone will come in the evening."

And that's what they did: They hid. The time passed until evening, and then a little old man came into the hut. "Foo, foo, it smells of a Russian soul! Someone's in this house!" And he began to call out, "Who's in this house? If it's an old, little old man, let him be my grandfather. If he's of my age, let him be my blood brother. If it's little children, let them be my godchildren. But come out, whoever's in the house. I won't do anything."

So Mania and Vania came out from beneath the stove. The little old man and his godchildren greeted each other, and they began living there and residing. The old man went out hunting, and Mania and Vania lived at home. Once the old man said to Mania and Vania: "Now, my godchildren, tomorrow I'm going out for my last bloody battle with the devil. Here's a glass of water for you, and if by nightfall I haven't come home, don't you sleep all night. You watch, and if the water turns to blood, you will know that I am no longer among the living. And you, Vania, run to the stables, and there two oxen will be standing. You untie them and say, 'Where there were two oxen, now let there be two dogs. Serve me as you have served my godfather.'"

So the time passed, and evening came. Vania and Mania sat down at the table and began looking at the glass. They looked, and the water became murky and turned to blood. Then Vania ran to the stables, untied the two oxen and said to them everything that his godfather had told him to. They immediately turned into two dogs. They licked Ivan, they rubbed up against him. Vania went into the hut, and the dogs went from one side to the other. So then Vania and Mania lived there as a pair, and Vania went out to obtain food. Time passed, whether a long time or a short time, and

Mania decided to go to that river where the devil had stayed. He came up to that river and saw there, not the devil, but a handsome lad walking about with an accordion in his hands. And he said to Masha, "Miss, take me across the river, and we'll fall in love!"

She already liked this admirer! "But how will I ferry you across? Why, the river is on fire, and I have neither a raft nor a boat."

"Go home. You have on the table there a piece of cloth. Wave it across the river and say, 'Let Kalin Bridge rise over the river!' Then I'll come across."

Mania ran home right away, took the cloth, tossed it over the river, and Kalin Bridge appeared—and the lad walked across the river. They kissed and caressed and went into the house. Much time had passed since Mania and Vania had lived there, and she forgot: Instead of a cavalier, she had brought across the devil.

Evening came, and then her brother came from hunting, and the devil turned into a needle and stuffed himself into a crack.

The dogs leapt into the hut, smelled the scent of the devil, and began jumping at the walls, searching for the devil. And Vania didn't know what had happened. His sister said nothing to him, and he could scarcely quiet his dogs. In the morning he got up and went off to work, and the devil came out of a crack and said to Masha, "Here's what, Masha, destroy your brother. You see, there's no life for me here!"

"And how am I to kill him?"

"Well, when your brother comes in from work, you fall ill and tell him that beyond the thrice-nine land, in the thrice-nine tsardom, in the thrice-nine country, in the sea-ocean, on the island of Buian there is this she-bear. And he must kill this bear, drain out her blood, and bring it to you to pour on yourself, and you will be well. And he loves you and will go. But no matter who has gone there, no one has ever come back."

And the devil filled Mania with its spirit, so that she no longer loved her brother. When Vania came from hunting, Mania told him everything that the devil had told her to. Vania loved his sister and said to her, "Little Sister, don't grieve, bake me some biscuits, and in the morning I'll set off on the path and road."

So in the morning he got up early, washed himself well, prayed to God, and set off on the path and road. He walked near or far, low or high; now soon a tale is told, but a deed is measured by its success. He came to the sea and ocean, but he didn't know how to get to the island Buian. Then his dogs spoke to him, “Here’s how, Vania, we’ll swim along side you, and you sit on one of us. If that one gets tired, you sit on the other.”

And so they swam across the sea and ocean. When they came out on dry land, Vania looked: There came the sow bear. He took his rifle in his hands and wanted to shoot, but the bear spoke in a human voice: “Don’t shoot me, Ivan, don’t destroy my soul in vain. Whatever you need, I’ll fulfill everything for you.”

“But I have to kill you, drain out your blood, carry it to my sister, and smear it on my sister so that she will be well.”

“Well, for such trifles you don’t have to kill me. I’ll give you some blood anyway.” And she went and cut a paw, drained out a vial of blood, gave it to Vania, and said, “Here you are, Vania. Here’s the blood and for you the gift of my little cub, my son, for your youthful glory and for the saving of your life.”

He said goodbye to the bear and set off on the way back. When he came up to the sea and ocean, the bear cub said to Ivan, “Get on me, Master, I’ll carry you over the sea and ocean alone.” When they had swum across the sea and ocean and come out on dry land, the dogs went along side him, and the bear cub came behind. Thus Vania was protected on three sides. They came home again, and the devil squeezed himself into the crack again. With difficulty he dissuaded his band of protectors.

In the morning he got up and again went away into the forest, and the devil came out of the crack and said to Mania, “However you wish, but it is necessary for you to kill your brother. Otherwise, you see, there’s absolutely no life for me.”

“And how am I to do it?”

“Well, toward evening fall ill, when your brother comes in from hunting, and say to him, ‘There is in such and such a place a nightingale-robber. You ought to kill this nightingale, bring me the blood of this nightingale, and then I would smear myself with its blood and I would be well . . .’”

In the evening her brother came in from hunting and she told him everything as the devil had instructed her. But no sooner is a tale told, and this time too he set out to search for the nightingale-robber. He approached it and looked: The nightingale was perched on seven oaks, and that nightingale was just preparing to whistle when Ivan took up his rifle and then immediately the nightingale began speaking in a human voice: “Don’t shoot me, Vania, don’t destroy my soul in vain. Whatever you need, I’ll do it!”

"But I have to kill you, to drain out your blood and carry it home, to smear it on my sister so that she will get well."

"Oh, for such trifles you don't have to kill me!"

He went and pecked his foot and filled a vial of blood. "Here's my blood for you, and here's my nightingale son for your young glory and for saving your life."

So now the nightingale flew in front, the dogs ran along the sides, and the bear in the rear, so that Ivan was protected from all four sides. He came home, and the devil squeezed himself into the crack as a needle, such that Vania's little band scarcely caught the scent of the devil. The nightingale flew about, pecking the walls, the dogs rushed about, and the bear scratched the crack with his claws. It was such that Vania could scarcely dissuade his band, and he didn't know what was going on.

He spent the night, and in the morning he again went out hunting, and the devil came out of his crack and said to Mania, "In any way possible you have to kill your brother. There's no life for me here with him."

"And how am I to kill him?"

"Once again fall ill this evening, when your brother comes back from hunting, and tell him that in such and such a place there is a mill, and he ought to go to this mill, bring back some chaff for you to chew and make you well."

So then a lot of time had passed, and Mania and Vania had forgotten about that mill. When Vania came from hunting, his sister told him everything as the devil had instructed her. So sooner is a tale told, and this time, too, Vania set out on the path and road. He came to that mill, but the bear and a dog said, "Here's what, Vania, you and the nightingale stay here, and we'll go in and get the chaff."

When they had jumped through the twelve doors, these doors shut with twelve locks. Then Vania remembered about that mill, that it was that very mill that had an entryway but no exit. Vania and the nightingale cried, the bear and dogs howled, but there was nothing to do—Vania and the nightingale went back alone.

He came home. But this time the devil wasn't afraid. He saw that Vania had only the nightingale, and he said to Vania, "Now I'm going to eat you up!"

"And why should you eat me? My body has been baked by the sun and dried out by the wind. My sister would better heat up the bath, I would go and wash up and give myself, my warm, soft body over to the devil for his devouring."

And his sister answered, "And I thought a long time ago to heat it up for you! If you want a bath, then go and heat it, there is time for it!"

When Vania saw that all his sister's feeling for him, her brother, had gone away, he grieved, but there was nothing to be done. He went to heat up the bathhouse himself. He heated it for a day, then he heated it a second, and he started heating it a third when the nightingale said to Ivan, "Vania, I'll fly to that mill, and find out whether our band is alive." He flew there, perched on the mill, and whistled, and the band howled and shouted out, "Is our master alive?"

"The master's alive and he's heating the bathhouse!"

"Let him heat it three more days. We've gnawed through three doors, and we'll gnaw through six more, and the three with iron hinges we'll rip off. And then we'll come out."

The nightingale flew to the bathhouse to the master and told him everything that the little band had told him. He heated it for two more days and began carrying up the water. And the nightingale flew to find out whether the band was still alive. He flew there, whistled, the band howled for a long time and asked, "Is our master still alive?"

"He's alive. He's carrying water to the bathhouse!"

"Let him carry it still longer. We've gnawed through six doors—three more to gnaw through, and the three with iron hinges we'll rip off. Then we'll in any case come out to our freedom!"

The nightingale flew and told everything to the master. So Vania carried water a day, he carried it a second, and a third, and then he went to wash. He washed for a day, he washed for a second, and he began washing a third. And the nightingale flew to the mill to find out whether the band was alive. He flew to the mill, whistled, and the band howled: "Is our master alive?"

"The master is alive. He's in the bathhouse washing."

Then they rushed forward and ripped down the three doors with iron hinges, and the nightingale began showing them the way. They ran to the bathhouse, saw that the master was living, and the bear said to the nightingale, "Fly to the devil, Nightingale, and tell him that the master is ready, that he doesn't want to go to the house but rather wants to offer his body for your eating in the bathhouse. And you, dogs, stand in front on the sides. When the devil comes to the bathhouse, you forcibly pull him into the bathhouse, and I'll stand here, grab him and throw him into the fireplace. Let him burn up there." So, you see, the fireplace was heated red-hot.

The nightingale came flying and told the devil what the bear had instructed him, and the devil set off for the bathhouse to eat Ivan. He had just got up to the entrance when the dogs grabbed him and pushed him into the bathhouse, and the bear grabbed him in his arms and pitched him into the fireplace. And so the devil burned up.

Ivan came out of the bathhouse, put up a pillar in the middle of the yard, raised a barrel of pitch on it, and a second barrel nearby. Then he raised his sister up and said to her, "This is for you, Sister, because you delivered me to the devil to be eaten. I won't forgive you until you've drunk this barrel of pitch and until you've filled the other barrel with tears."

And he set off journeying. The nightingale flew in front, the dogs went at his sides, and the bear brought up the rear.

Well, sooner a tale is told, they came to a certain city, and Ivan saw that everyone in the city was in mourning. He came up to one old granny on the edge of town. "Granny, why is it that all of you in the city are in mourning?"

"Well, here's why: Earlier on, this three-headed serpent came out and devoured the people. It ate whoever happened to be there, but now they've started handing over for its eating by lot. And the lot has fallen on the tsar's daughter. Since she's her father's only daughter, that's why everyone is in mourning. She's already been taken off to the sea. There's a guard hut there, and a single lame groom with a regiment has ridden off to save her life, because he bragged that he could save the tsar's daughter in order to marry her."

"Here's what, Granny, do you have a shed?"

"Yes, I have."

"I'll put my band of friends in it, and I myself will go off somewhere. And if my band should start to howl, then you, Granny, let them out."

And he went away. He locked up his band. He came to that sea, to the guard hut, and he saw sitting there this young lady. Then she said to him, "Why did you come here, young man? The three-headed serpent will come out of the sea, devour me, and he won't leave you!"

"If he eats me, he'll choke! It would be better for you to search about my head!"

So the young lady began searching about his head, and he fell asleep. The sea began rocking and out swam the three-headed serpent, and he shouted, "Oh, today the tsar is rich; he's given two heads at once!"

Then the young lady began trying to arouse Ivan, since the serpent was already near the hut. She started crying, and a tear burned Ivan's cheek.

Ivan woke up, caught sight of the serpent, leapt out of the hut, and sliced off its three heads at once. The corpse he threw into the sea, the heads he put under a stone, and then he himself went back into the hut and from such heavy work he fell asleep. Now the lame groom saw everything—how this man had come out of and gone back into the hut—so he didn't stand long in the forest. He rode up to the hut and saw that the man was asleep. He took his sword and chopped off his head. He chopped for three days, three hours, three minutes, and three seconds. He took the tsarevna and carried her back to the tsar, ordering her to say that he had saved her. The tsar joyfully wanted to put on the wedding, but the tsarevna put off the wedding for three days.

The band of animals began howling at the granny's, and the granny let them go free. The band immediately ran to the sea. It ran up, and the animals saw that the master was dead. The nightingale immediately fetched some living water and some dead, and they brought the master back to life. They came to the granny in her yard, and Ivan said to his band, "Now then, you dogs and bear, go to the tsar as guests. See whether he'll receive you."

So the two dogs and the bear ran to the tsar. The tsar was astonished: Where had these animals come from? Nor had they questioned anything of the gatemen at the gates or the doormen at the doors. They ran right by into the dining room and sat down at the table. The tsarevna came out and guessed that these were no ordinary dogs and bear. She ordered that they be given the very best food. She fed the bear and the dogs, and she tied on each a red necktie. She had just finished tying on the last one, when they leapt up from the table and ran away. They ran to Ivan, and Ivan said, "So the tsarevna has not forgotten. She received the dogs and the bear, and that means that she'll receive even me. I'll go now myself."

The nightingale flew ahead, the dogs ran along side, and the bear set off behind. They came up to the tsar's palace, and out the window the tsarevna caught sight of her neckties on the dogs and bear. She ordered her servants to receive Ivan. When Ivan had been ushered into the chambers, she threw herself around his neck and began kissing him. Then she said, "Now here's what, Papa. This man saved me from the servant and not that lame groom. The lame groom killed him and held a knife up to me so that I would say that he had killed the serpent." They brought over the lame groom and questioned him as to how he had killed the serpent. And Ivan said, "If you killed the serpent, then go and show the tsar where the serpent's heads lie."

So they all rode over to the sea, and the lame groom walked about and said, "The corpse was thrown into the sea, and the heads are beneath this stone!"

And Ivan said, "Then take them out and show them to the tsar!"

But the lame groom couldn't get even a puff of air beneath the stone. Ivan walked up to the stone, lifted it up with one hand, and with the other he got the heads, showed them to the tsar, put them back under the stone, and said to the groom, "Now show us again!" When the tsar saw that nothing was going to come of the lame groom, he ordered him executed, and he immediately wanted to marry Ivan to his daughter.

"Here's what, My Lord, I have of family only this one sister, and I need to fetch her for the wedding."

"Tell me where she is, and I'll send my fancy carriages and grooms, and we'll get your sister right away."

"As you wish, My Lord, but I have to go myself and fetch my sister."

And he set out after his sister. He came to his sister, let her down from the pillar, and he let down the barrel, too, and saw that not a spoonful of pitch had been drunk and not a teardrop spilt, because she was still filled with the devil's spirit. Then he said to her, "Well, Sister, I've undertaken to get married. I forgive you; now let's go to the wedding!"

"Yes, Brother, I've been baked by the sun and dried out by the wind. I'd like to heat up the bathhouse to wash; I would like to go to the wedding cleaner."

"All right, heat it up!"

So she went off to heat it up, but she thought to herself: "Hasn't a single bone from that devil been left here?" She went into the bathhouse and began digging around in the ashes of the fireplace, and suddenly came upon a tooth of that devil. She took it, came to her brother, and said, "I've decided not to heat up the bathhouse because it would take too long. Let's go just as we are, and perhaps I can wash myself there."

So they came to the lord. Immediately there was an honorable feast and afterwards the wedding. The young folk went to church to pray, but the sister remained behind to prepare the bed for the young couple. While she was preparing it, she sewed the devil's tooth up in the pillow. The young ones came from church, drank, ate, and then went off to sleep. They had just opened the room, when the dogs and bear burst into the room. They tore apart the pillow and let loose down throughout the room. Ivan led the dogs and bear out of the room, and his sister went to collect up the down. But she really wasn't collecting the down so much as she was looking for the devil's tooth. She found it, and again she sewed it into a pillow. So no sooner is a tale told, the dogs and the bear again tore apart the pillows and let loose down a second time, and a second time the sister sewed the tooth in a pillow.

Then Ivan locked up his band of animals in a shed and came in and fell down to sleep. The tooth jumped out of the pillow and right into Ivan's forehead—it killed Ivan. Then his sister went and spoke to the tsar: "Oh, Your Royal Highness, if you don't get my brother out of your city and don't kill his band, it will be evil for you."

The tsar didn't have long. They immediately made a coffin, laid Ivan in it, and placed iron bands on the coffin. And they carried that coffin with Ivan to the sea to an island, and the order was given to shoot Ivan's band in three days. One nanny was placed to look after the band. She brought them food and said, "My dear animals, I'm so sorry for you. Tomorrow they're going to shoot you."

The animals began to snuggle up to her, and she began to pity the band. She went and left the edge of the doors open. The animals leapt out, and on the trail where the coffin had been taken they ran, searching for their master. They ran up to the sea, but then there was no more trace. The nightingale flew onto the island and found out that the master was lying there in a coffin. It then flew back and told the dogs and the bear. They rushed into the sea and swam over the sea to the island. They ran to the coffin, but no way could they get their master out of the coffin. They saw that it was fastened with three cast iron bars. Then the bear spoke: "Here's what, lads, when I was walking overland to the island, I saw a large herd of goats, and in that herd was an enormous billy goat with really enormous horns. Perhaps he might help us in some way?"

The bear went up to the herd of goats, took that goat and brought him to the coffin. He placed him there and said, "So here's your task, goat: Break these three hoops."

The goat bleated in anger, ran back from the coffin, bleated again, ran at the coffin, stuck his horns into a hoop—and broke the hoop. Well sooner is a tale told: then the second and the third. And the bear carried the goat back to its former place. He put it in the middle of the herd, and the herder's eyes bugged out. What sort of miracle was this: A bear had carried off a goat and then brought it back!

The bear came, opened the coffin, took the master out of it, and he saw the tooth in Ivan's forehead. So then the nightingale went and pecked at the tooth. It pecked it and tried to break it. And the tooth popped out and killed the nightingale. A dog started licking the nightingale and the tooth jumped out of the nightingale and killed the dog, and thus it killed the other one, and there remained but the bear. He was determined to claw that tooth out of the dog. He scratched the tooth such that it began to shake as if in jelly. He dragged the dog up to a large pine and with a twig he began moving the tooth. The tooth popped out, struck the pine, broke up, and flew off no one knows where. The bear roared, and all the beasts came running. He gave them the task of fetching the living water and the dead.

Then the beasts pointed to a single hare, and it quickly brought the living water and the dead. When it had brought the water, the bear began bringing them back to life. He brought one dog to life and then the other, he revived the nightingale, and then he revived the master. The master got on the bear, they swam across the sea, and they came to the tsar. Ivan said to the tsar, "Do you have any ungelded colts, Your Royal Highness?"

"We have some."

"Give me them, four of them."

He tied his sister to the four ungelded colts, led them into the open steppe, and let them loose in various directions. And so these colts tore Ivan's sister apart as they ran off in various directions, and are even now running about.

And our Ivan began living with Maria Tsarevna and they lived until deep old age.

(SUS 313A + 315 + 315A + 300_1)

17

IVAN TSAREVICH AND KOSHCHEI THE DEATHLESS

F. F. Kabrenov

In a certain tsardom, in a certain country—indeed in the one in which we live—on a flat place like on a harrow, about two hundred versts away, there lived and dwelt a tsar. This tsar had three daughters and a son, Ivan. So then the eldest daughter grew up and took it into her head to go out walking in the open steppe to see people and to show herself.

So they went out into the open steppe to walk, a fierce storm arose, seized our maiden, and carried her off no one knows where. All the nannies, the servant girls, became really frightened, recollected the great force, went to the tsar, and told him about their journey. Of course, the tsar was saddened. He and the tsaritsa grieved, but there was nothing to be done.

So a long or short time passed, and the middle daughter grew up and took it into her head, and decided by herself to go out into the open steppe to walk. For a long time her parents tried to dissuade her, but there was no way to dissuade her, and so they had to let this daughter go out walking. So she got ready with her nannies, her servant girls, and went out into the open steppe. The same thing happened with this one as with the first. A storm came up and carried her off no one knows where.

Thus did the nannies return to the tsar and told him about what had happened. The tsar was saddened, so saddened, but there was nothing to be done.

So then the youngest daughter grew up and took it into her head to decide to go out walking in the open steppe. Her father was much aggrieved and no way would he let her go walking in the garden. The tsar said, "I've lost two daughters, and to let you go would be to lose you. Never will I agree." But with great pleading the daughter begged to go walking in the open steppe. Then he gave her nannies this order: "If you lose my last daughter, don't come back home!"

So then they went out into the open steppe for a walk, and then, on account of their sins, there arose a strong wind. There arose a storm and carried the tsarevna away no one knows where. The nannies and the servant girls came together, grieved, were saddened, and they didn't dare appear before the tsar, so they departed in different ways.

Well, so then the tsar had lost three daughters, but he still had a son, Ivan, still small, who personally didn't know his sisters. When he grew up, he was finally twelve years old. Often his father told him about the sisters, his daughters, who had got lost somewhere—and no one knows where. And so this went on until he was sixteen years old. And when Ivan was sixteen years old, then he said to his father, "Let me go into the open steppe for a walk, to see people, to show myself off, to measure my strength with bogatyrs, and to search for my sisters."

When his father heard such words from his son, he was deeply saddened, and he said to his son Ivan, "What do you mean, our dear son, Ivan! We have lost three daughters, your sisters, and are we to let you go, to lose you? Then there would be no one to look at and drive away the sorrow and sadness."

But no matter how his father and mother tried to dissuade their son, Ivan, they could not talk him out of it. Finally son Ivan spoke up: "Papa, permit me and I'll go. And don't permit me, I'll still go looking for my sisters."

So his mother baked him some supplies for the road, he put it all in a sack, took his sisters' photographs, and in the morning he got up early, washed himself thoroughly, prayed to God, and set out down the road and path. Whether he walked near or far, for soon a tale is told, but by success is a deed judged. He walked, and he saw a house standing in the open steppe. He entered this house, and there was just a woman there. He took out a picture from his belt, looked at the picture, then at the woman, and it turned out that it was his eldest sister.

"Greetings, Sister!"

"Greetings, Brother. Why have you come here? Soon Raven Ravenson will come flying in. Talon Talonson—brass nose, lead tail—and he'll rip you apart. And it won't be good for me."

Then Ivan said to his sister, "But, Sister, people help people, can it be that you won't help me?"

So she gave him something to drink, fed him, and hid him behind the stove. Suddenly there arose a whirlwind. In flew Raven Ravenson, Talon Talonson, brass nose, lead tail, he fell against the floor—and became a young man! "Foo, foo, foo! The scent of a Russian!"

"But you have flown over the Russian land and you have taken on that Russian scent. You smell of it yourself, and you have brought it to me!"

Then his wife brought him the soup from the stove, fed and gave her husband something to drink, put him to bed, and she herself began searching his head and telling him that her brother had come, her relative had come. Then he said, "Well then, lead him out, wherever he is."

So she led out her brother Ivan.

"Greetings, Brother-in-law," he said.

"Greetings, Brother-in-law!"

"Now then, Sister, bring us about a half bucket of vodka so that my brother-in-law and I can get acquainted."

When they had sat down at the table, they began drinking, and one brother-in-law began questioning the other: "Tell me, Brother-in-law, where have you been and where is your journey to take you?"

And the other answered, "I set out for the thrice-nine land, for the thrice-nine tsardom, the thrice-nine country, to court Maria Tsarevna."

And his brother-in-law answered, "Well, Brother-in-law, you've thought up a big task. It's not such a sly trick to marry Maria Tsarevna; she has this servant girl who hates all foreign men on earth. Twenty-nine lads have gone there, and all those Ivanov Tsareviches (truly all Ivanovs) never came back. So thus you'll go as the thirtieth, and probably you won't come back either. Well, Sister, give something to Ivan for the road!"

Then his sister brought him a welcoming tablecloth and said, "Well, Brother, this will be useful for you along the way and path. When you feel like eating, just spread out this tablecloth, and everything will be on it that you could possibly want."

His brother-in-law threw himself on the floor—and became a raven. He plucked out a feather from beneath his right wing and said to his brother-in-law, "And here's a gift from me. Tuck this feather behind your belt. If this feather begins to quiver, my heart will quake. I will know that my brother-in-law is not alive, he's dead."

So Brother-in-law remained a guest at his brother-in-law's, arose in the morning, said farewell to his brother-in-law and sister, and set off down the way and path. He walked near or far, low or high, for soon is a tale told, by its success is a deed judged. And so he came up to a second house. He entered the house, and again he saw this woman in the house. He took out a photograph, looked at the portrait, looked at the woman, and found out that this was his second sister.

"Greetings, Sister!"

"Greetings, Brother! Why have you come here, Brother? Soon Raven Ravenson, Talon Talonson, brass nose, cast iron tail, will come flying in. He'll rip you apart, and it won't be good for me"

"Oh, Sister, people help people. Can it be that you won't help me?"

Then his sister fed and gave a drink to her brother, and hid him beneath the stove. She had just managed to tidy up everything, when in flew Raven Ravenson, Talon Talonson. He fell on the floor and became a young man. "Foo, foo, foo! The Russian scent. Who's in this house? Speak!"

Then his wife answered, "You have flown over that Russian land, you have taken on that Russian scent, you have breathed it, and brought it to me."

She fed and gave him something to drink, put him to sleep, and sat down to search his head. And she told him how her brother had come, her relative had come. Then he got up and said, "Well, come out, wherever you are!"

When his wife had led out her brother, then his brother-in-law said, "Greetings, Brother-in-law!"

And Ivan said, "Greetings, Brother-in-law."

"Now then, Wife, bring us a bucket of vodka so that my brother-in-law and I can get acquainted."

They sat down at the table and began drinking, and the one brother-in-law began asking the other, "Where are you going? Where is your path taking you?"

And the other answered, "I'm going beyond the thrice-nine lands, to the thrice-nine tsardom, in the thrice-nine country, to court Maria Tsarevna."

Then his brother-in-law spoke: "Oh Brother-in-law. You've thought up a big task. Maria Tsarevna isn't hard to marry, but she has this servant girl who doesn't like anyone strange. Twenty-nine lads have come here—all of the Ivan Tsareviches, but whoever has gone there, not one has come back. And you'll be going as the thirtieth." And he said to his wife, "Now then, Wife, give something to your brother!"

So then his wife brought out the self-playing gusli. "So, Little Brother, perhaps this gift will be useful to you on your journey. Whenever you are sad about something, take out the self-playing gusli, that will cheer you up!"

Then Raven Ravenson fell on the floor, became a raven, plucked out a feather from under his right wing and gave it to his brother-in-law. "So, Brother-in-law, tuck this feather behind your belt. If this feather begins to quiver, my heart will quake. I will know that my brother-in-law is not alive, he's dead."

In the morning he got up rather early, said farewell to his brother-in-law, and set off down the way and path. He went near or far, low or high, for soon a tale is told, but by its success is a deed judged. He came into the open steppe and saw a house standing there in the steppe. He went into this house and saw a woman there. He took out a photograph, looked at the portrait, looked at the woman, and recognized his third sister. He greeted his sister.

And the woman greeted her brother and said to her brother,

"Why have you come here, Brother? Soon Raven Ravenson, Talon Talonson, the golden nose and steel tail, will come flying in and he'll tear you to pieces, and it will not be good for me."

And her brother said, "Oh Sister, people help people. Can it be that you won't help me?"

Then she fed and gave her brother something to drink, hid him behind the stove. Suddenly in flew Raven Ravenson, fell behind the stove—and became a young man. "Foo, foo, phoo. It smells of a Russian scent. Tell me, Wife, who is in the house?"

And she answered, "You have flown about Rus, taken on the Russian scent, breathed it out yourself, and brought it to me."

So then his wife fed and gave him something to drink, put him to bed, began herself to search his head, and began telling him that her brother had come, her relative had come.

"Well, then, lead him out, wherever he is."

So then the sister led out her brother. The brothers-in-law greeted each other, and then the husband said to his wife, "Now then, bring out a bucket and a half of vodka so that there's something for us to treat him with."

They sat down at the table and began entertaining him. His brother-in-law began questioning Ivan: "Where are you going? Where is your path taking you?"

And his brother-in-law answered, "I am going beyond the thrice-nine lands, to the thrice-nine tsardom, to court Maria Tsarevna!"

"Oh, Brother-in-law, you've thought up a big task. Twenty-nine lads have gone there—and they were all Ivan Tsareviches. But whoever went there, not a one came back. It's not such a sly thing to marry Maria Tsarevna, but she has this servant and she doesn't like strangers. You'll be the thirtieth to go there, but likely you won't come back."

And then he said to his wife, "Now then, Wife, bring out and give something to your brother!"

So then his sister brought out a flying carpet. "So now then, Brother, why go on foot? Sit on this flying carpet, and it will carry you. You'll soon be at Maria Tsarevna's."

Then Raven Ravenson fell against the floor, became a raven, plucked a feather from under his right wing, and gave it to his brother-in-law. "So, Brother-in-law, tuck this feather behind your belt. If the feather begins to quiver, my heart will quake. I will know that you are not alive, but dead!"

And so they caroused throughout the night until dawn, and in the morning Ivan took his leave of his brother-in-law and set out on the way and path. He sat down on his flying carpet and flew over the thrice-nine lands to the thrice-nine tsardom to the thrice-nine country. And he landed in the garden of Maria Tsarevna. But that servant girl saw a strange person in the garden. She grabbed him under his arms and threw him into a dungeon. But Ivan Tsarevich knew that twenty-nine lads had come there—all Ivan Tsareviches. He knew that all were sitting in the dungeon, so he began greeting and speaking to his comrades: "Greetings, lads, how are you getting along?"

They answered, "We live well at Maria Tsarevna's. We don't overeat moldy bread or drink too much swamp water."

And he answered, "Well, I'm not going to eat any of that."

And they responded, "We'll see what you eat!"

Then Ivan Tsarevich got out his welcoming tablecloth, and when he had spread it out, there appeared every sort of tidbit and expensive imported wines. And he said, "Let's sit down at the table, lads, and take advantage of all this."

So they all sat down at the welcoming tablecloth, began drinking and eating, treating themselves. They all drank too much, ate too much, and then began singing songs. And so they burst out, and all thirty lads knocked down the bricks of the dungeon.

Then Maria Tsarevna guessed it and said to her servant girl, "Well then, servant girl, go and ask that newcomer whether he hasn't something new, since for a long time those twenty-nine lads have sat quietly in the prison, and now in a single day that newcomer has created all this."

So the servant girl went into the prison and asked the newcomer, "Well, new one, don't you have something new, something for sale?"

And he responded, "There is this flying carpet, but it isn't for sale. There's a condition, and one that I'm conscience-stricken even to say it."

And the servant girl asked, "What is that condition?"

And Ivan answered, "My secret dream is to spend the night with Maria Tsarevna!"

Then the servant girl came to Maria Tsarevna and said, "That newcomer has a flying carpet, only it's not for sale. There's a condition, and it's even a matter of conscience for him to speak of it."

And Maria Tsarevna said, "Speak, whatever is it?"

"Well yes, there is this flying carpet—only this is the condition: to sleep the night with you."

"Oh then, is that all there is to it," answered Maria Tsarevna. "When he comes here to sleep, we shall prepare some little bites to eat and some drinks. And when he has been well entertained, we shall pour some sleeping herbs in, and then he'll lie senselessly until dawn. And after dawn you will do everything that you have to."

That's how it was, and that's how it was done. When evening came, the servant girl came into the dungeon and said to the newcomer, "Now then, newcomer, come with your promise to sleep with Maria Tsarevna."

So when he came to Maria Tsarevna's, he sat down at the table, and they began treating him. He ate until he was sated; he drank wine until he was half-drunk. Then in the last glass they poured some sleeping herbs. When Ivan had drunk that last glass, he fell senselessly from his chair, and the servant girl put him unconscious to bed with Maria Tsarevna. In the morning the servant girl came, took Ivan Tsarevich under the arms, and carried him to the dungeon. (She was a strong one!) But our Ivan Tsarevich didn't grieve one bit in the dungeon. Again he spread his welcoming tablecloth, invited his comrades, and they began to entertain themselves. They sang songs such that the bricks from the prison tumbled down.

Again Maria Tsarevna said to the servant girl, "So now, ask that newcomer whether he hasn't something new."

So the servant girl came to the dungeon and asked, "Well then, newcomer, don't you have something new?"

"There is," he replied.

"And what is it?"

"It's a self-playing gusli, but it's not for sale. There's a condition."

And the servant girl asked, "What is the condition?"

And Ivan Tsarevich answered, "To sleep a night with Maria Tsarevna!"

So she ran once more to Maria Tsarevna and told her that the newcomer has some self-playing gusli, and that his condition is to sleep a night with Maria Tsarevna!

"All right," she answered.

Again, until evening, and then they received him to sleep once more. This went on until evening, then the servant girl came to the dungeon and said, "Well then, newcomer, take your self-playing gusli, and let's go to Maria Tsarevna."

He came. Our Ivan Tsarevich sat down at the table and began to be entertained. He ate until he was full, he drank until he was drunk, and then they poured some sleeping drops into the last glass. When our Ivan Tsarevich had drunk the herbs, he became unconscious. Then the servant girl carried him to Maria Tsarevna's bed to sleep. The time passed until morning, it began to get light. The servant girl came, grabbed Ivan Tsarevich, and tossed him in the prison.

And again he was not saddened. He greeted his comrades and said, "And how are you getting along, lads?"

And they answered, "You can't eat too much of Maria Tsarevna's moldy bread or drink too much of her swamp water!"

Then for a third time he unfolded his welcoming tablecloth and sat his comrades down at the cloth, and they began to treat themselves. They ate until they were full, drank until they were drunk, and then they started singing songs until the roof nearly flew off. Well, this time they celebrated the whole day, drinking, rejoicing.

Well, Maria Tsarevna knew this time, too, that the newcomer had something hidden. She whiled away the time until evening and said to her servant girl, "Now then, servant girl, go to the dungeon. Ask the newcomer what he has there that's hidden. If there is such an object, drag him here at once to sleep with me. Now we know how to deal with him."

So the servant girl went to the dungeon and asked, "Don't you have something for sale?"

But he answered, "There is, but it's not for sale. There's a condition."

"And what do you have?"

"A welcoming tablecloth. And my objective is to sleep a night with Maria Tsarevna."

So then the servant girl took Ivan under his arms and carried him to Maria Tsarevna's room. And Maria Tsarevna had already prepared all the foods, and she had prepared the sleeping herbs. (Now they only dropped them in by the drop.) But this time our Ivan didn't make the mistake. He began eating until he was full, but with the drinking he resorted to trickery. He looked around: Neither the servant girl nor Maria Tsarevna paid any attention to him as he was drinking the vodka. But he poured the vodka over his collar, over the back of his shirt. When they gave him the glass with the herbs, he poured it over his shoulder, and pretended to be drunk, staggered, and fell from his chair. Then the servant girl grabbed him and carried him to Maria Tsarevna's bed. Then she went away and hooked the door this time.

Then Ivan Tsarevich said to Maria Tsarevich, "So now then, Maria Tsarevna, twice you have deceived me, but this time you have erred."

They began to embrace and slept through the whole night. In the morning the servant girl came, opened the door, and looked: Maria Tsarevna was in the embrace of Ivan Tsarevich. She woke Maria Tsarevna up, who said to her, "Here's what, servant girl, this Ivan Tsarevich will be my husband, and I his wife. We'll have to hand over the keys to all the storerooms, houses, and factories, and let him rule over our land."

When they had handed over all the keys to him, the servant girl instructed him: "Now then, Ivan Tsarevich, go throughout all the storerooms and all the houses, but this little key to this lock—you'll find it—don't enter this chamber. This chamber is completely empty, and in it you'll find nothing good."

When Ivan Tsarevich had taken the keys, he immediately went and opened the dungeon and said to his comrades, "Well, lads, come out of the prison now, and go wherever you want."

But they answered, "We have already spent long years and don't want to go anywhere. If we can stay with you, we will live with you and work at anything you order us to do." And so the entire bunch remained to live forever with Ivan Tsarevich.

And thus Ivan Tsarevich took the keys and went round all the storerooms and cellars. He examined all the treasures, and he took it upon himself to enter the forbidden house, which the servant girl had forbidden him to enter. He opened the room and saw the room was completely empty, except that in one corner a candle was burning a couple of inches from the floor. It would burn to the floor, something would knock, and the candle would jump another inch or so from the floor—and it would burn. Ivan Tsarevich only wanted to get out of the room, when something spoke up in the corner with a human voice: "Free me, Ivan Tsarevich, I will save you from two deaths."

So Ivan Tsarevich spoke: "How can I save you?"

Then the voice from the corner answered, "Look! In that wall there is a button. You press on the button, and I'll come out free."

Then Ivan Tsarevich went up to the button, and he had barely pressed on it with his finger when out of there leapt Koshchei the Deathless and said, "Now, Ivan Tsarevich, you have been saved from your first death."

He went and killed the servant girl and carried Maria Tsarevna off to his own tsardom. Then Ivan Tsarevich guessed, he understood, why it had been forbidden to go into that room, and he understood from what deaths he had been saved. When Ivan Tsarevich had been left without Maria Tsarevna and the servant girl, he gathered his twenty-nine lads and said to them, "Lads, help me take Maria Tsarevna away from Koshchei the Deathless!"

And they answered, "We're happy to serve you, Ivan Tsarevich. You freed us from death, from eternal slavery."

So they all got ready, and they set off for Koshchei the Deathless's tsardom. They walked near or far, low or high, for soon a tale is told, but by its success is a deed judged. They hadn't gone fifty versts from his tsardom, and he left his twenty-nine lads in an ambush, and went on alone to Koshchei the Deathless. He came up to his house and saw that Maria Tsarevna was alone in the house, that Koshchei the Deathless wasn't there. But Maria Tsarevna somehow, probably, wouldn't have recognized him, if he hadn't been given an engagement ring. She rejoiced at his coming, and with joy agreed to go back with him.

They had gone more than half the way when Koshchei the Deathless came home and saw that Maria Tsarevna wasn't there—and set out to give chase. Not having gone ten kilometers from the ambush, Koshchei the Deathless caught up to Ivan Tsarevich and Maria Tsarevna and said, "So, Ivan Tsarevich, you will now be saved from your second death."

He took Maria Tsarevna away and carried her off back home. Then Ivan Tsarevich brought all his twenty-nine comrades out of the ambush, led them off about twenty kilometers, left them, and he himself went to Koshchei the Deathless alone. But he wasn't at home. For a second time he took Maria Tsarevna and went right up to the ambush. This time Koshchei the Deathless caught up to them, killed all thirty Ivan Tsareviches, and took Maria Tsarevna home.

So now then our Ivan Tsarevich lay in the open steppe. The birds had already begun to peck at his eyes, and the feathers began to quiver and the hearts began to quake. Then his brothers-in-law flew together and agreed to go in search of their brother-in-law. They flew for a long time over the towns and villages, over the sleepy thickets, over the steaming swamps, and they flew out over the open steppe and saw in the open steppe a bird pecking a man's eyes. They landed on the ground and saw their brother-in-law. Then the oldest brother-in-law said, "You sit here a little while, brothers-in-law, and I'll fly to this certain country where I know that this certain tsar has the living and the dead waters."

So the brothers-in-law agreed to sit and stand guard over their dead brother-in-law, and Raven Ravenson, Talon Talonson, golden nose, steel tail, flew off for the living and the dead waters. When he had brought the living water and the dead, he splashed the body of Ivan Tsarevich with the dead water, and those wounds which the birds had pecked open quickly grew together. He splashed him with the living water. Ivan Tsarevich woke up and said, "Oh, how long I've slept! I woke up just at the right time."

And his brothers-in-law answered:

> If it weren't for us, you would have slept forever in the steppe. You managed to get Maria Tsarevna, but you didn't manage to live with her. But now if you want to get Maria Tsarevna, to take her away from Koshchei the Deathless, then go beyond the thrice-nine lands, to the thrice-nine country, where Koshchei's mother lives, and take it on to herd for three days her twelve golden-faced mares together, and she'll give you whatever you desire. She'll accept nothing in Christ's name for her labors: She's afraid of Christ. And don't you take gold or silver. She will propose that you take her very best mare—but don't even take that. But look: In the stables, next to the manger, completely covered in dung so it's scarcely to be seen, there will be lying a colt, and you take that colt then. For in the very hoof of that colt is to be found Koshchei's death. If she doesn't want to give it to you, you say to her that you won't take anything else. And if she won't give the colt to you, then let "my labors be for Christ's sake." Then she'll agree to hand it over to you. And when you take the colt, that colt will help you get Maria Tsarevna back.

So they said farewell to their brother-in-law and flew to their own houses, and our Ivan Tsarevich set off down the road and path, beyond the thrice-nine lands, beyond the thrice-nine seas, to the thrice-nine tsardom, to the thrice-nine country to Koshchei's mother. He went through a forest, a strong storm came down upon him, it started to rain hard, and he was forced to spend the night beneath a tree. When he had flopped down beneath the tree, he found there was a nest in the tree and a single little bird had been tossed out by the storm. And it was completely naked, without any down at all. Then our Ivan took this little bird, climbed up into the tree and looked: In the nest were two more baby birds. He placed the baby bird back in the nest, took off his jacket, and with it he protected the nest from the storm, and then he climbed back down to the ground and fell asleep. Just at that time the storm quieted down, the mother raven came flying back and shouted out in a human voice, thinking that her nest had been destroyed. She said, "Unlucky will be the one who destroyed my nest and kidnapped my children."

But one little chick answered, also in a human voice, "Be still, Mama, be still. There's someone sleeping out beneath this tree, and don't you awaken him. When we grow up to be big, we shall perform two great services for him. If it weren't for him, we would all have frozen. He saved us from the cold."

Then the mother raven took his jacket, descended down to the ground, and covered Ivan with this jacket, where he slept until morning. But he heard everything that the little ravens had told their mother. In the morning he got up and set off further. As he walked, he had to walk beside a sea, and just at that time during a terrible storm it tossed up onto dry land a multitude of lobsters, such that there was no place for Ivan to step. No matter how carefully Ivan walked in order not to crush a single lobster, he accidentally kicked a lobster into the sea. And that lobster shouted out from there, "I'll pay you back for this, Ivan!"

Ivan was saddened by this and began kicking the lobsters back into the sea. And whichever lobster fell into the water would shout out, "Thank you, Ivan, I'll pay you back for this."

Ivan was so infuriated by these words—he didn't understand what was going on. He walked a whole day and night about the sea, and he just kept kicking the lobsters. And then he spent a day in his malice, saying, "Why don't I see a single lobster?"

And then he set off for Koshchei's mother's. When he arrived at Koshchei's mother's, his mother immediately guessed what it was all about. She knew it was Ivan Tsarevich, and she said to him, "So now then, Ivan Tsarevich, take it upon yourself to herd for me for three days twelve white-faced mares, and if you herd them for three days, then for your work I'll give you whatever you desire. But if you don't herd them, then your head will be on a stake." With her hand she showed him human heads on stakes. She thought, "And he knows that there is this colt, and the colt has my son's death in his hoof. But nonetheless, that colt won't go to anyone, because no one can herd my white-faced mares." And then she said, "Go into the dining room now, and eat and drink whatever you wish. And sleep until morning, and in the morning come to the gates and count the white-faced mares and drive them out into the cemetery."

So our Ivan did just that. He went into the dining room, ate, drank, and tumbled off to rest until morning. And Koshchei's mother ordered her blacksmiths to heat up iron rods in their forge and thrash those white-faced mares until morning. In the morning when Ivan Tsarevich came to the gates, he just managed to count the white-faced mares, but he didn't see where they ran off about the open steppe. Only by their hoof prints did he go to the forest. He sat the whole day on a stone and wept, and he thought, "Where am I to search for those white-faced mares when not a single one is here?"

So then it began to become evening, and all the mares came running from the forest right to Ivan, and on each of them sat two or three little ravens, pecking their backs. When the twelve white-faced mares were all gathered together, the little ravens said in a human voice, "Now then, Ivan, for you one task has been performed."

Just then Ivan understood what was going on when that night he had saved the little ravens, and they had said, "We will perform two tasks for you." And he drove the mares to Koshchei's mother. And those mares were so pecked by the little ravens that they feared to jump to either side. When he had driven them into the yard, Koshchei's mother counted and took the white-faced mares, and she ordered Ivan to go rest. And that night she gave the very strictest order to her smiths to thrash the white-faced mares with iron rods. The time passed until morning, and Ivan Tsarevich came to the gates, and he just managed to count the white-faced mares. But this time Ivan Tsarevich didn't give it a thought. He went into the forest and sat down in his former place. When time passed until evening, the little ravens drove the white-faced mares this time, too, and then they said, "Now then, Ivan, a second task has been performed. Expect nothing more from us."

He drove the white-faced mares to Koshchei's mother, and she counted them, and took them, and ordered Ivan to go rest until morning. But she didn't believe the smiths; she stood next to the forge, heated up the rods, and thrashed the mares until morning. In the morning Ivan Tsarevich got up, went to the gates, but he didn't manage to count the white-faced mares even, as they had all run away somewhere. Only by their hoof marks did he go up to the sea into which he had tossed the lobsters. And in that sea he just barely saw a single white-faced mare. He sat down on the seashore and fell into thought because he didn't know what to do. "How will I fetch those mares now? I've nothing to ride on. There's no boat, no raft."

And thus he sat until very evening on the shore of the sea. It was getting to be evening, and the mares began swimming closer and closer to the shore. Whichever one came out on the shore had lobsters hanging on its legs. But the mares could scarcely stand on their legs, since the lobsters had so drilled into them with their claws. And then Ivan caught on to what the lobsters had said. And he drove the white-faced mares to Koshchei's mother. When he had driven the white-faced mares to Koshchei's mother, she counted them and said, "Well, all right, Ivan Tsarevich, go and rest, and tomorrow come for our reckoning."

In the morning Ivan came, and Koshchei's mother opened a chest of silver and said, "Take as much as you need, Ivan."

Ivan said, "I don't need it."

Then she led him to the stables and said, "Take my very best mare."

But Ivan said, "I don't need it."

He himself looked for what his brothers-in-law had said, and he spied that colt, which was barely visible beneath the dung. He let him out of there and then he said to Koshchei's mother, "Give me this colt for my work."

But Koshchei's mother said, "What do you mean, Ivan. For such ardent work one wouldn't know what of value to reward you with. But this colt—what would you do with it? He'll perish tomorrow, and all your work will perish with him."

And he answered, "Well, if you won't give me the colt, then let my work all be 'for Christ's sake.'"

Then Koshchei's mother said, "No, alms for Christ's sake I don't need for your work. I must give you for your work whatever you wish."

So then he took the colt and led it out by its rope. He led it into the open steppe, and the colt spoke in a human voice: "Here's what, Ivan Tsarevich. Take off the rope, let me go free, and you yourself lie down and rest. Don't worry: I won't leave you. Give me three waterings to roam, and on the third morning let me go and suckle my mother's milk. Then I'll come back to you."

So then our Ivan removed the tow from the colt and let him go free. And he himself flopped down to rest, and he fell into an unwakeable sleep. Three mornings passed since the colt ran away, and three mornings passed before the colt came running back and saw that his master was asleep. He awakened him and said, "Get up, Ivan, you can't shorten the road by sleeping, but by paying attention. Now mount up and hold on to me. Everything you need I'll fulfill for you."

Then Ivan said, "I need to get to Koshchei the Deathless and take Maria Tsarevna away from Koshchei the Deathless."

Then the colt reared up beneath Ivan Tsarevich, he soared up higher than the standing forest, lower than the moving clouds, and he flew to Koshchei the Deathless in his castle. But once again Koshchei the Deathless wasn't at home. That instant Maria Tsarevna recognized Ivan Tsarevich by his ring and believed that this man was Ivan Tsarevich. They embraced, they kissed, and they went out of the yard to the colt. He was about to mount up on his colt when the colt spoke in a human voice, "You can't get on me right now; you are too heavy. Go on ahead with Maria Tsarevna and I'll follow you."

So they set off along the path and way. They walked off a little distance, a few versts from the castle of Koshchei the Deathless. Koshchei the Deathless flew home and saw that Maria Tsarevna wasn't there, and he set off in pursuit. He caught up to Ivan Tsarevich and began taunting him: "Your labors have all been in vain, Ivan Tsarevich, even though you herded my mother's twelve white-faced mares. But you took the wrong colt; the right colt was in another manger."

And he began circling around the colt from its head, because the colt had his death in a rear hoof. No matter how he tried to catch him, no matter how he twisted about, the colt outwitted him, leapt up, and struck Koshchei with his hind foot so that Koshchei the Deathless fell down dead, and he said to Ivan Tsarevich, "So now then, Ivan, lay a bonfire, and burn Koshchei the Deathless, and scatter the ashes in the open steppe."

And that's what Ivan Tsarevich did. He burnt Koshchei the Deathless and scattered the ashes in the open steppe, and he and Maria Tsarevna and the colt came to Maria Tsarevna's tsardom and lived there until old age. And with that our tale is finished.

(SUS 552A)

Commentaries to Tales

1. Nechaev, 12. SUS 301A + 301B. This type, "Three Underworld Tsardoms," is one of the most popular in the East Slavic tradition, and it is widely reported from Europe as a whole.

2. Nechaev, 7. SUS 302_1 + 402. The combination is rare in East Slavic, and SUS does not list it.

3. Nechaev, 19. SUS 518 + 560. The first sujet is common throughout the East Slavic territory, as is the second. The combination is not listed in SUS.

4. Nechaev, 11. SUS 301B. By repeating sequences, Korguev made a very long tale out of a very common sujet. He was fond of tales where one of the parents was non-human. See Haney, Jack V., *An Anthology of Russian Folktales*, pp. 302–21, where the hero kills his father, a bear.

5. Nechaev 3, SUS 516**. This uncommon sujet was repeated over and over to make this tale.

6. Nechaev 13. SUS 300*B +303 + 513A. Magic, and therefore an unnatural parent, gives this unusual combination of types charm beyond that of the typical long tale.

7. Nechaev 5. SUS 575. Korguev enjoyed substituting the "modern" airplane for the traditional eagle.

8. Nechaev 4. SUS 502. The attempt to make this tale of the tsarevich into a tale with a peasant hero is not entirely satisfactory, but this is an interesting variation on a theme that is not all that common in the Russian folk tradition.

9. Nechaev 15. SUS 725 +518 + (507). The motif of a hero's involvement in regicide is most unusual, but that is not all that is rare in this combination of tale types.

10. Pomor'e 34. SUS 402 + 400A +302. Nikonov's tales are among the best told among the Pomors. The combination of tale types is not otherwise attested among the East Slavs.

11. Pomor'e 35. SUS 301A + 301B + 400* + 551. Although this tale was given no title in its original form, it is clearly of the "Rejuvenating Apples" type. Nikonov claimed to have learned his tales from his father. This complex tale is a fine example of his art.

12. Pudozh 2. SUS 402 + 400_1 + 518 +302_1. This tale was recorded in 1975 from a narrator, M. O. Dmitriev, who may have been the last recorded in the Karelian area. According to Dmitriev, he had learned the tale from his father. The combination of types is unique to the Pudozh tradition.

13. Pudozh 1. SUS 303 + 300A + 519 + 300_1. M. O. Dmitriev shows considerable skill in weaving these four types into one wondertale. The hero's name, and its local variants, are unknown except in the Pudozh tradition.

14. Pudozh 3. SUS 502 + 513A. Also recorded by T. Sen'kina and Z. Tarasova in 1975. This is a very unusual combination of tale types. Other recordings of this tale are considerably shorter.

15. Pudozh 10. SUS 530A. This tale was told by O. I. Dmitriev to the folklorist V. Dmitrichenko in 1938. According to the editors of the Pudozh tales, this is a most rare tale, and even in the Pudozh tradition only its second part has ever been recorded. The editors of SUS do, however, list a number of versions of this tale type. It is not known beyond the East Slavic territory. The elements taken from the bylina tradition are particularly strong in the early part of the tale.

16. Pudozh 24. SUS 313A + 315 + 315A +300_1. This tale is widely known from the Russian north, but not in this particular combination of tale types. It was recorded in 1948 by F. Belovanova in Pudozh when Kabrenov was 52 years old.

17. Pudozh 27. SUS 552A. Kabrenov told this tale to Belovanova in 1946. The mixing of traditional and contemporary elements in the tale is striking. Note especially the interesting fact that the three brothers-in-law who are animals have but one name and yet three different physical appearances.

*Bibliography**

Aarne, Antti, *Verzeichnis der Märchen mit Hilfe von Fachgenossen*, Helsinki, 1910.

Barag, L., I. P. Berezovskii, K. P. Kabashnikov, N. V. Novikov, compilers, *Sravnitel'nyi ukazatel' siuzhetov. Vostochnoslavianskaia skazka*, Leningrad, 1979. (SUS)

Belomorskie skazki. Rasskazannye M. M. Korguevym, Ed. A. N. Nechaev, Leningrad, 1938.

Chistov, K. V., *Russkie skaziteli Karelii*, Petrozavodsk, 1980.

Gottschall, Jonathan, *Literature, Science, and a New Humanities*, New York, 2008.

Haney, Jack V., *An Anthology of Russian Folktales*, Armonk, NY, and London, 2009.

Haney, Jack V., *The Complete Russian Folktale*, vols. I-VII, Armonk, NY, and London, 1999–2006. (CRF)

Kiuru, E. S., and A. P. Razumova, *Fol'kloristika Karelii*, Petrozavodsk, 1978. (FK)

Kurets, T. S., *Nositeli fol'klornykh traditsii: Pudozhskii raion Karelii*, Petrozavodsk, 2003.

Prishvin, M., *V kraiu nepuganykh ptits*, Petrozavodsk, 1957.

Propp, V., *Morphology of the Folktale*, 2nd edition, revised and edited with a preface by Louis A. Wagner, Austin, 1990.

Razumova, A. P., and T. I. Sen'kina, compilers, *Russkie narodnye skazki Karel'skogo pomor'ia*, Petrozavodsk, 1974. (Pomor'e)

Razumova, A. P., and T. I. Sen'kina, compilers, *Russkie narodnye skazki Pudozhskogo kraia*, Petrozavodsk, 1982. (Pudozh)

Sen'kina, T. I., *Russkaia skazka Karelii*, Petrozavodsk, 1988. (Karelia)

Sen'kina, T. I., "Skazochnik M. M. Korguev. (O dvukh osobennostiakh ispol'nitel'skoi manery)," *Problemy literatury Karelii I Finliandii*, Alto, E. L., E. I. Markova, and E. G. Karkhu, eds., Petrozavodsk, 1988. (PLKF)

Sen'kina, T. I., *Russkaia skazka Karelii*, Petrozavodsk, 1988. (Karelia)

Skazki M. M. Korgueva, Edited and introduction by A. N. Nechaev, Petrozavodsk, 1939. (Nechaev)

Thompson, Stith, *The Types of the Folktale*, Bloomington, IN, 1961. (A-T)

Uther, Hans-Jörg, *The Types of International Folktales: A Classification and Bibliography, Based on the System of Antti Aarne and Stith Thompson*, Helsinki, 2004.

*Abbreviations in parentheses refer to bibliographic citations throughout this work.

A-T-U / SUS NUMBERS

www.ingramcontent.com/pod-product-compliance
Lightning Source LLC
Chambersburg PA
CBHW060809310726
48980CB00002B/285
9781617037306